The Nyarlathotep Cycle

Tales about the God of a Thousand Forms

Chaosium Mythos Fiction

Robert Bloch's Mysteries of the Worm
Cthulhu's Heirs
The Shub-Niggurath Cycle
The Azathoth Cycle
The Book of Iod
Made in Goatswood
The Dunwich Cycle
The Disciples of Cthulhu 2nd revised edition
The Cthulhu Cycle
The Necronomicon
The Xothic Legend Cycle
The Hastur Cycle 2nd revised edition

Call of Cthulhu® Fiction

The Nyarlathotep Cycle
The God of a Thousand Forms

H. P. Lovecraft
Robert Bloch
Lin Carter
John Cockroft
Robert C. Culp
August Derleth
Lord Dunsany
Robert E. Howard
Gary Myers
Philip J. & Glenn A. Rahman
Ann K. Schwader
Richard Tierney
J. G. Wagner
William Butler Yeats

Selected and Edited by Robert M. Price
Cover art by H. E. Fassl
Interior art by Dave Carson

A Chaosium Book
1997

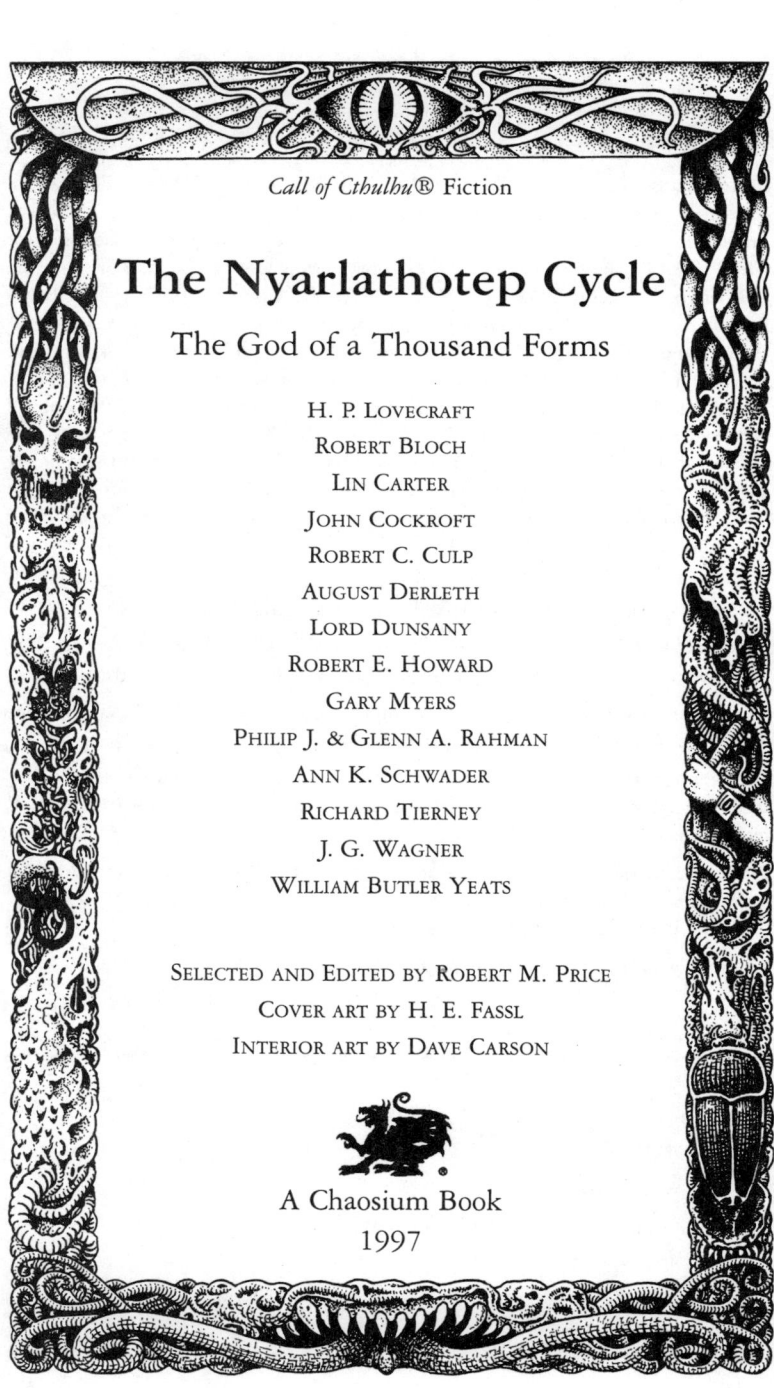

The Nyarlathotep Cycle is published by Chaosium, Inc.

This book is copyrighted as a whole by Chaosium, Inc., ©1997; all rights reserved.

"Silence Falls on Mecca's Walls" ©1989 by Alla Ray Morris for Robert E. Howard, *Shadows of Dreams*; appears by permission of Barbara Baum for Robert E. Howard Properties. "The Dweller in Darkness" ©1944 by Popular Fiction Company for *Weird Tales* November 1944; reprinted by permission of the author's agents, JABberwocky Literary Agency. "The Titan in the Crypt" ©1963 by Ziff-Davis Publishing Company for *Fantastic Stories of Imagination* vol. 12, #2, February 1963. "Fane of the Black Pharaoh" ©1937 by Popular Fiction Publishing Company. "Curse of the Black Pharaoh" ©1989 by Cryptic Publications; appears by permission of Robert M. Price, literary executor for the estate of Lin Carter. "The Temple of Nephren-Ka" ©1977 for *Fantasy Crossroads* #10/11, March 1977; appears by permission of the authors. "The Papyrus of Nephren-Ka" appears by permission of the author. "The Snout in the Alcove" ©1977 by DAW Books, Inc. for *Year's Best Fantasy Stories: 3*; this new version appers by permission of the author. "The Contemplative Sphinx" ©1994 by Cryptic Publications. "Ech-Pi-El's Ægypt" ©1993 by Ann K. Schwader.

We invite any authors whom we have been unable to trace to contact us.

Cover art by H. E. Fassl. Interior art by Dave Carson. "The Papyrus of Nephren-Ka" illustration by Robert C. Culp. All artwork is copyright by the respective artists.

Cover layout by Eric Vogt. Editing and interior layout by Janice Sellers. Editor-in-chief Lynn Willis. Proofreading by James Naureckas and Tod Briggs.

The reproduction of material from within this book for the purposes of personal or corporate profit, by photographic, digital, or other methods of electronic storage and retrieval, is prohibited.

Please address questions and comments concerning this book, as well as requests for free notices of Chaosium publications, by mail to Chaosium, Inc., 950 56th St., Oakland, CA 94608-3136, U.S.A. Also visit our web page at:

http://www.sirius.com/~chaosium/chaosium/html

FIRST EDITION

1 2 3 4 5 6 7 8 9 10

Chaosium Publication 6019. Published in May 1997.

ISBN 1-56882-092-5

Printed in Canada.

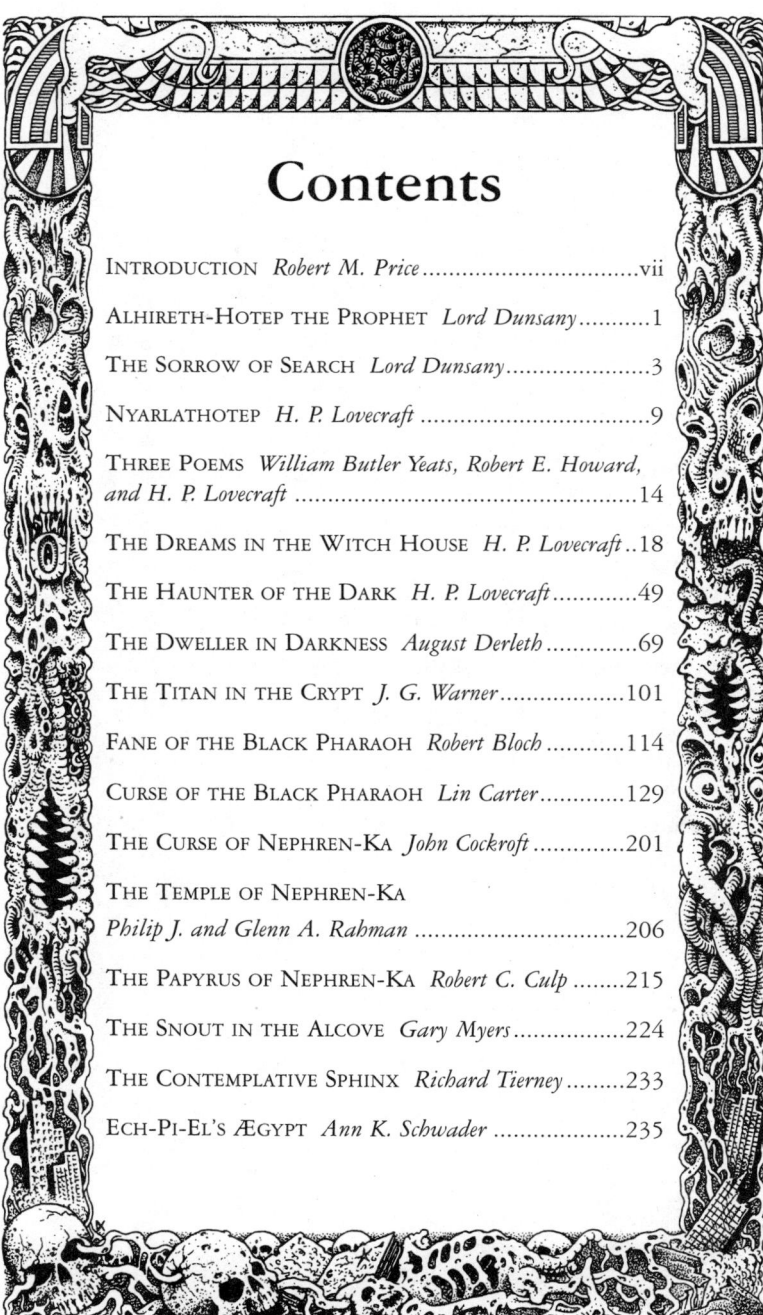

Contents

INTRODUCTION *Robert M. Price* vii

ALHIRETH-HOTEP THE PROPHET *Lord Dunsany* 1

THE SORROW OF SEARCH *Lord Dunsany* 3

NYARLATHOTEP *H. P. Lovecraft* 9

THREE POEMS *William Butler Yeats, Robert E. Howard, and H. P. Lovecraft* 14

THE DREAMS IN THE WITCH HOUSE *H. P. Lovecraft* ..18

THE HAUNTER OF THE DARK *H. P. Lovecraft* 49

THE DWELLER IN DARKNESS *August Derleth* 69

THE TITAN IN THE CRYPT *J. G. Warner* 101

FANE OF THE BLACK PHARAOH *Robert Bloch* 114

CURSE OF THE BLACK PHARAOH *Lin Carter* 129

THE CURSE OF NEPHREN-KA *John Cockroft* 201

THE TEMPLE OF NEPHREN-KA
Philip J. and Glenn A. Rahman 206

THE PAPYRUS OF NEPHREN-KA *Robert C. Culp* 215

THE SNOUT IN THE ALCOVE *Gary Myers* 224

THE CONTEMPLATIVE SPHINX *Richard Tierney* 233

ECH-PI-EL'S ÆGYPT *Ann K. Schwader* 235

Dedicated to my friend
John Skilkin,
the real Henry Armitage

Introduction:
The Theology of Nyarlathotep

Of all of H.P. Lovecraft's invented deities, Nyarlathotep is perhaps the most teasing and enigmatic. In *The Dream-Quest of Unknown Kadath* Nyarlathotep is said to assume a thousand forms, and the variegated use of the character throughout Lovecraft's fiction bears this out. The image of Nyarlathotep appears as if refracted into a number of clashing partial images, something like a Cubist painting: Precisely because one's eye can construe no single image, one somehow feels he is seeing more truly the multifaceted reality of the thing. Despite and yet because of the shattered refraction, one senses an underlying unity throughout the many depictions of the god Nyarlathotep. He is thus something of a microcosm of the Cthulhu Mythos as a whole, which Lovecraft "designed" to appear as if not designed—fragmentary and contradictory, just like the confused remnants of actual ancient myth cycles. When he makes Nyarlathotep an entity one thousandfold in form, he is utilizing a genuine mytheme which occurs, among other places, in early Christian mythology. In the Apocryphal Acts of the Apostles, Christ appears to his disciples, both before and after his resurrection, in several apparently physical forms simultaneously so that, e.g., when James and John see Jesus summoning them to leave their nets and follow him, John beholds him as a beardless youth, while James sees a balding, bearded elder. No sooner do they compare notes than Christ's image changes yet again. This element of polymorphousness implies that such a deity has no true form at all, that all its forms, and ultimately all forms of all beings, are merely illusions. The true reality, as Buddhism says, is beyond *Namarupa*, beyond Name-and-Form. So it is with Nyarlathotep, who is both the "soul and messenger" of the "blind, voiceless, tenebrous, and mindless Other Gods" on the one hand and "their Crawling Chaos" on the other. With this bizarre collection of epithets Lovecraft provides us the clues we need to penetrate into the hidden arcana, the Deep Things of Nyarlathotep.

Lovecraft had a way of misleading his readers and correspondents with half-truths when it came to explaining the origins of the various words and names he had coined. As Will Murray has established, HPL may have said plainly that Arkham was based on Salem, Kingsport on Marblehead, Dunwich on the Wilbraham-Monson-Hampden region of Massachusetts, and Innsmouth on Newburyport, but a closer scrutiny both of the stories and of the map reveals that Arkham was in fact based on Oakham and New Salem, Kingsport on Rockport, Dunwich on Greenwich, and Innsmouth on Gloucester. Similarly, though Lovecraft said he had coined names like Nug and Yeb to suggest a "Thibetan or Tatar ring", Murray showed that Nug and Yeb seem far more likely to have been Lovecraft's version of the pair of analogous Egyptian gods Nut and Geb. Nyarlathotep was no conscious invention of HPL at all, since it came to him in a dream and was probably a creative unconscious fusion of two names from Lord Dunsany, the prophet Alhireth-Hotep and the deity Mynarthitep. Nonetheless, the name certainly possesses an Egyptian ring, derived from Dunsany, who no doubt was consciously using the Egyptian suffix "-hotep" (meaning "[So-&-so] is satisfied"), an honorific appendage to a name.

From this Egyptian connection stem the various Egyptian associations Lovecraft made with Nyarlathotep. I believe, however, that Nyarlathotep provides us with a case just the opposite of that of Nug and Yeb in that, whereas Lovecraft said he meant these "evil twins" to recall Tibetan mysteries and disguised their Egyptian origins, with Nyarlathotep he has concealed an essentially Hindu/Buddhist conception behind the trappings of Egyptian lore. In short, I want to persuade you that Nyarlathotep is the Hindu god Nath, or Siva.

How can Nyarlathotep at once fill three seemingly disparate roles as the soul, messenger, and "crawling chaos" of the Other Gods/Great Old Ones? The paradigm that would seem to accommodate all the evidence most economically and naturally (see Thomas S. Kuhn, *The Structure of Scientific Revolutions*, if you haven't already!) would seem to be Saiva Advaita Vedanta, or the monistic mystical philosophy of Siva-worship championed by Gaudapada and Sankara. For Nyarlathotep to be the "soul" of the Other Gods would mean that "he" is their common essence, that root divinity of which the Other Gods are themselves half-real personifications on a lower level of (human) perception which Sankara called "lower knowledge" or *avidya*, ignorance—that is, a knowledge that correctly apprehends a penultimate level of reality. One may have clear knowledge of what is going on in a vivid dream, but the dream experience is less real than waking life; thus, while one is in the dream state and takes it seriously one's knowledge is at the same time ignorance of the higher level of reality. For Nondualism, even waking reality is penultimate to the higher knowledge of *Atman/Brahman*. On our level of worldly existence and perception the personal gods of Saivism (Siva, Kali, Ganesa, etc.) are as real as we ourselves as individual egos are, but transcending this conventional "reality" is a more real level of Being surpassing even the gods. This is the Godhead itself which is, again, beyond all name and form. All things are temporary, and thus illusory, manifestations of it. Nyarlathotep, as the "soul" of the Other Gods, is the undifferentiated Godhead, *Brahman* (a neutral, because impersonal or superpersonal, term).

Likewise, for Nyarlathotep to be "chaos" refers to the state of Pure Being, before the first moment of its illusory refraction into seeming differentiation. It is this state of *Tathata* ("suchness") or *Sunyata* ("emptiness", "void") that the mystic seeks to penetrate—some by simple meditation upon the Oneness; others by fantastic and, in the case of Saivite-Buddhist Tantra, grotesque techniques, such as sex-mysticism or the gustatory transgressions of the corpse-eating cult of Leng.

In this Hindu-Buddhist understanding of the Mythos, Azathoth (the blind idiot creator god familiar from Gnosticism) would represent a lower personification of the Suchness, the Chaos, as a demiurge creator. For him to "mould the world in play" is, as Hindu cosmogony has it, for the *Brahman* to play a game of illusions with itself, the canonical metaphor for explaining how the delusory world of appearance (*maya*) can have come about in the beginning if really there is but the One. As *laya* ("play") it is not real diversity, only pretend. Azathoth, then, represents creation from the standpoint of lower knowledge. The "Other" Gods, the hinted Reality behind the discrete gods of conventional myth (Ganesa, Kali, Siva), remain unknown until mystic revelation breaks through, as in the *Upanishads* and the Vedanta *Sutras*, upon which the Advaita Vedanta system is based. In the Saivite *Tantras*, it is Siva who reveals the truth, transcending his own apparent existence. In the Vaisnavite

Bhagavad Gita it is Visnu/Krisna who takes illusory avatar form to reveal to Arjuna that the true Reality behind appearances (including that who now speaks this very revelation!) is the *Brahman*.

Nyarlathotep, especially as portrayed in *The Dream-Quest of Unknown Kadath*, is like the Tantric Siva or Krisna in the *Gita*. He bears the name and form of a discrete god, but this appearance is mere seeming, a figment of perception assumed for the sake of communication with yet-unenlightened souls. The appearance of Nyarlathotep in any of his forms is a taking on of the *Nirmankhya*, the transformation body of the Buddhas on the plane of *maya*. Many early Christians believed, as we have seen, that the "incarnation" of Jesus was an adoption of the semblance of flesh for the sake of communication with mortals. Mahayana Buddhists say the same of Prince Siddhartha, while the Alawi sect (to which Hafez Assad of Syria belongs) predicates it of Ali, the heir of Muhammad. As the great Theosophist scholar G. R. S. Mead observed in his book *Simon Magus*, to say that the revealer takes on illusory flesh to communicate with the human race is implicitly to say that human flesh and the material order of which it is a part are equally illusory. The assuming of the *Nirmankhya*, the illusory body, is not an alternative to incarnation, as Christian theologians maintain. The whole point is that it is the very nature of incarnation, whether the god's or our own. That is what the revelation is all about.

Lovecraft, in "The Haunter of the Dark", calls the steeple-confined entity "an avatar of Nyarlathotep", a term borrowed directly, of course, from Hindu theology. An *avatar* ("descent") is the coming of a god in a physical body to perform some mission of salvation in the world of *Samsara* (the realm of *maya* and mortality). Usually it is Visnu who is pictured as appearing in a number of avatars including Krisna, the divine hero Ram, and many others. Siva is on occasion said to have appeared as an avatar as well, such as Gorakhnath, founder of the Kanphata sect of yogis.

Siva is assigned the role of the Destroyer. He rings down the curtain on each cycle of world history. As Lord of the Dance he maintains the cosmos by his never-tiring dance, but when he decides to sit one out, the world ends for the time being, passing into a long night of rest until it springs forth again for another cosmic cycle. In this role, too, Nyarlathotep obviously resembles Siva. He is the soul of the mindless, tenebrous gargoyles who dance. His prophesied coming at the end of the age seems to happen on schedule. His arrival is no invasion, no transgression. He will terminate this world because the cycle is complete, though it is implied there are, and will be, others, since we read in the *Fungi from Yuggoth* that the demiurge Azathoth persists in assigning "each cosmos its eternal law."

It is precisely at this point that the Satanic image of Nyarlathotep enters the picture. In *The Dream-Quest* Lovecraft describes the personified Nyarlathotep as having the dark features of a "fallen archangel", a Miltonic Lucifer, while in "The Dreams in the Witch House", Nyarlathotep takes the role of the medieval Black Man of the witches' sabbaths, the Satanic whoremaster and initiator of witches. Siva is not Satan. What he does is divine providence, the way of all the universe. In the eyes of those whose petty, worldly preoccupations clash with that plan, the eschatological agent, the ender of the age, must appear as the Antichrist. "I suggest that the mechanism of reversal has been at the root of the idea that the 'Antichrist' must be something 'evil.' What if this turns out not to be the case at all?" (Mary Daly, *Beyond*

God the Father: Toward a Philosophy of Women's Liberation, 1996). That is what Nietzsche and Crowley saw. Self-proclaimed Antichrists, they were not heralds of evil in their own eyes, but knew they would be so regarded by others for their "transvaluation of values."

Lovecraft's protagonists, as is well known, fight a rearguard battle against the recognition that their world view of placid scientific rationalism has been exposed as mere "lower knowledge" by an unsuspected "higher knowledge" that relativizes the former and indeed nullifies it. They are trying pathetically to fend off the truth which only seems evil because it is inimical to their petty self-serving view of the world. In Lovecraft's stories Wilmarth, Armitage, Peaslee, Thurston and the rest are all fleeing from the deadly revelations of science into a new dark age of superstition. Wilmarth admits that it is greater scientific knowledge at which he flinches: "I started with loathing when told of the monstrous nuclear chaos beyond angled space which the *Necronomicon* had mercifully cloaked under the name of Azathoth." It's not a revelation of the reality of the supernatural that makes poor Wilmarth quail; it is the scientific truth that Einstein could not brook either: that God should play dice with the universe.

We can find the same thing in Arthur Machen, who was in many ways Lovecraft's mentor. In "The Great God Pan" (see *The Dunwich Cycle* in this series), what is the horror which myth had mercifully cloaked under the name of Pan? Though presented with all the poisoning loathsomeness of Akeley's revelations, the secret of Helen Vaughan was that of the subtle ground of all being. It is, in Aristotelian terms, the prime matter, matter not yet distinguished by any particular form. Machen's understanding, seen equally in "The Novel of the Black Seal" (in *The Hastur Cycle*) and "The White People" (in *The Dunwich Cycle*), is neo-Platonic: The ordered world is good, but the primordial Chaos of raw matter underlying it is/was evil precisely by token of being without form and void. (This is why Plotinus rejected Gnosticism: Gnostics thought the material world was evil even in its ordered form.) Machen (or at least his narrator in "The White People") judged the "real sin" to be that Promethean hubris whereby mere mortals seek to overpass the barrier wisely set between them and the inchoate Fountains of the Deep, because in that case the sinner ventures to dissolve the once-firm ground beneath his own feet. Wilmarth and the others have committed "real sin", but haven't the courage to follow through. They have summoned the revealing angel, but their numinous terror is so great when he arrives that they curse him as Satan and retreat into blissful ignorance.

In terms of Advaita Vedanta and Mahayana Buddhism, what we are hearing here is the nervous fear of the intimidated ego which knows it must perish if we turn instead to follow the path into Being itself. Our stubborn "self-blinded, earth-gazing" ego-selves cringe from that revelation like the demons did when Jesus approached: "Have you come to destroy us before the time? Do not torment us!" Think of C. S. Lewis's *The Great Divorce*, the scene in which the angel offers to free the damned soul of its damnation if it will but allow the angel to hack away the soul's damning sin, which appears as a red demon rooted to its shoulder. The sinful soul desires release, but the monkey on his back puts up a fight. We will not leave hell for heaven if it means parting with the reality we have known, no matter how oppressive, no matter how wretched, since it seems to be our nature to cling pathetically to the familiar. Though it may be obvious we ought rather to enter life maimed than to be thrown whole into the Gehenna of fire, we will refrain from cutting off the offending hand, eye, or foot and take our chances. As it says in the *Bardo Thödöl* (the Tibetan *Book of the Dead*), we are seeing the emergence of the Truth (Suchness), but due to our *avidya* it appears refracted into the form of discrete entities, the Peaceful Deities. Even that is too much for our ill-prepared worldly perspective, so the Truth is further distorted through our own *upadhis*, our bad karma, into the frightful images of the Wrathful Deities, whose fangs bristle and drip with gore. Thus does Siva come to appear as Satan, i.e., to the unregenerate.

It is from the conventional standpoint of Walter Gilman, which he shares to a greater degree with his superstitious Polish neighbors than he imagines, that the Black Man appears to be the medieval Satan. He is actually the jet-skinned revealer Krisna, who offers Gilman a supernatural eye to scan the vistas of the Realm Beyond. Arjuna had supplicated him: "I desire to see Thy form as God, O Supreme Spirit! If Thou thinkest it can be seen by me, O Lord, Prince of mystic power, then do Thou to me reveal Thine immortal Self." Recalling Nyarlathotep's revelation to Randolph Carter of "my thousand other forms", Krisna replies, "Behold My forms, son of Prtha, by hundreds and by thousands, of various sorts, marvelous, of various colors and shapes. ... But thou canst not see Me with this same eye of thine own; I give thee a supernal eye: Behold My mystic power as God!" (*Gita*, XI).

Lovecraft provides a single example of a seeker after "forbidden" truth (i.e., forbidden by Mara, Lord of the Samsaric plane, just as he forbade Prince Siddhartha to learn the higher knowledge of Nirvana). This character is Robert Olmstead, protagonist of "The Shadow over Innsmouth." (Though in this particular case, the name Nyarlathotep does not appear, this is hardly material since the Truth is beyond Name-and-Form anyway.) Here is the man who starts out a denizen of Plato's allegorical cave of *avidya*, lower knowledge, and at length ascends to the bright sunlight of higher knowledge. At first, from the shadow-world perspective of conventional perception and belief, Olmstead glimpses the "horrors" of Innsmouth as if they formed the "Gate o' hell" and perceives his own ineluctable succumbing to those horrors as damnation, until the process is complete. Then what had appeared to be darkness is revealed as light. (Robert Blake got this far, too, but apparently no farther: Darkness had begun to become light, and light darkness, as he began to share the perspective of the revealing avatar of Nyarlathotep.) Then what Olmstead had once called Satanic ("Devil's Reef") was revealed to be the gate of heaven, wondrous Y'ha-nthlei, whose glories he could but hymn in the cadences of the 23rd Psalm, "And in that lair of the Deep Ones we shall dwell amidst wonder and glory forever." How has he seen what Lovecraft's other protagonists could not bear the sight of? Because Olmstead had the requisite "supernal eye": "[Y]e hev kind o' got them sharp-readin' eyes like Obed had."

Someone will say, isn't the reader supposed to take this finale as chilling evidence of the loss of the narrator to the horrors he had feared? Why, yes, if the reader is still himself unregenerate, a victim of lower knowledge—though even this hierarchical metaphor is reversed in the moment of enlightenment, since "higher" knowledge turns out to the knowledge of Deep Things among the Deep Ones. If the conventional religionists hear Gnostic revelations as the "deep things of Satan"

(Revelation 2:24), to the ears of the awakened Gnostic they are "the deep things of God" (1 Corinthians 2:10). By the random thrashings of Azathoth, a printer's error in Best Supernatural Stories of H.P. Lovecraft created a striking and felicitous parallel in the opening of "The Whisperer in Darkness": "Notwithstanding the deep things I saw and heard."

I believe that some such theology as I have sketched out here is necessary if we are to understand the basic presupposition of all Lovecraft's stories of Nyarlathotep: the existence of a cult worshiping Nyarlathotep. In view of this we must be able to envision some sort of understanding of Nyarlathotep that might be embraced as a holy mystery by its adherents, no matter how frightful it might seem to outsiders. It is such an insider's perspective I have sought to supply here. *Iä!* Nyarlathotep!

* * *

Let me thank James Ambuehl, Ben P. Indick, Thomas Cockcroft, Chris Powell, Steve Miller, Richard L. Tierney, Josh Bilmes, John Stanley, Marc Michaud, S. T. Joshi, Sam Moskowitz, Cele Lally, Mike Ashley, and Darrell Schweitzer for their invaluable assistance in rounding up stories and background information for this volume! They are among the Million Favored Ones!

Robert M. Price
Hierophant of the Crawling Chaos
Sealed Valley of Hadoth
Hour of the Unfurling of the Bands of Nephren-Ka
November 8, 1996

A LHIRETH-HOTEP is one of a chain of false prophets whose ill-omened exploits and exploitations are recounted in Lord Dunsany's droll scripture *The Gods of Pegana*. One and all sooner or later run afoul of Mung, a god who is not to be mocked. Obviously Alhireth-Hotep is one of the names which must subconsciously have inspired Lovecraft to create Nyarlathotep. Beyond the name itself, it is worth speculating whether perhaps Alhireth-Hotep's being a charlatan has left its mark upon HPL's portrayal of Nyalathotep as a mere showman, though of course there turns out to be more to him than meets the three-lobed burning eye!

"Alhireth-Hotep" first appeared in Lord Dunsany's collection *The Gods of Pegana* in 1905.

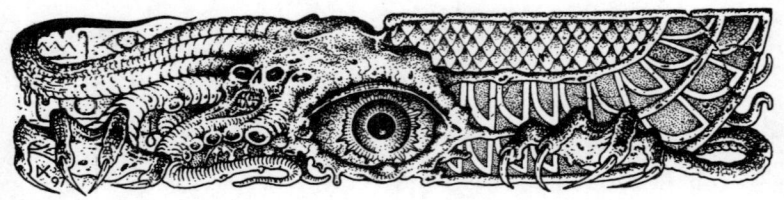

Alhireth-Hotep the Prophet

by Edward John Moreton Drax Plunkett,
Lord Dunsany

WHEN Yug was no more men said unto Alhireth-Hotep: "Be thou our prophet, and be as wise as Yug."

And Alhireth-Hotep said: "I am as wise as Yug." And men were very glad.

And Alhireth-Hotep said of Life and Death: "These be the affairs of Alhireth-Hotep." And men brought gifts to him.

One day Alhireth-Hotep wrote in a book: "Alhireth-Hotep knoweth All Things, for he hath spoken with Mung."

And Mung stepped from behind him, making the sign of Mung, saying: "Knowest thou All Things, then, Alhireth-Hotep?" And Alhireth-Hotep became among the Things that Were.

THIS tale (which appeared in Lin Carter's Ballantine Adult Fantasy collection of Lord Dunsany, *At the Edge of the World*, retitled "Of the Gods of Averon") is another likely source for the name "Nyarlathotep", but it also may have had a role in inspiring Lovecraft's "The Other Gods", in that both stories involve the motif of a prophet coming to discern the existence of mysterious gods greater than those on exhibit in the conventional pantheon. Both prophets' quests to find these gods end dismally. The larger frames of reference, however, are quite different.

In "The Other Gods", Barzai the Wise becomes, albeit unwillingly, a case of the classic type of the ascended apostle (see Geo Widengren, *The Ascension of the Apostle and the Heavenly Book*). This mytheme goes back at least as far as the claims of the king of Babylon to ascend each New Year to the throne of Marduk where the secrets of the Tablets of Destiny were vouchsafed, though it is already implicit in the journey of the shaman to the spirit plane. The frightful doom that awaits Barzai, recalling that of his prototype ben-Azai in the Jewish tale of the Four Who Entered Paradise, symbolizes the holy terror of the *Mysterium Tremendum* (Rudolf Otto, *The Idea of the Holy*).

The quest of Shaun in Dunsany's tale is that of the religious seeker who is "blown about by every wind of doctrine" (Ephesians 4:14) throughout what sociologists of religion call a "conversion career" (James T. Richardson, "Types of Conversion and 'Conversion Careers' in New Religious Movements", 1977), never seeming to realize that the new revelation may soon be as thoroughly undermined as the old one.

Dunsany, inspired here as so often by the felicitous marriage of Hebrew idiom with Elizabethan style in the King James version of the Bible, puts to good, though subversive, use a couple of biblical scenes. When the thunder rolls and the prophets come squawking that it was their god who spoke, we cannot but think of John 12:28-29. When the king, sick of priestcraft and mummery, dismisses his sages and diviners, seeking genuine revelation instead, we hear echoes of Pharaoh and Nebuchadnezzar doing the same, eventually seeking the aid of Joseph (Genesis 41:1-8) and Daniel (Daniel 2:1-16), respectively. In short, the parable teaches that the love of truth is the true worship, and that the truth may be like the North Star: We must navigate by it but can never hope to get to it. The story has much in common with another wise fable about religious faith, Fritz Leiber's "Lean Times in Lankhmar."

"The Sorrow of Search" first appeared in Dunsany's collection *The Gods of Pegana* (1905).

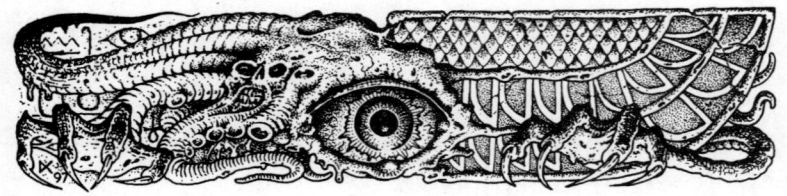

The Sorrow of Search

by Edward John Moreton Drax Plunkett,
Lord Dunsany

IT is also told of King Khanazar how he bowed very low unto the gods of Old. None bowed so low unto the gods of Old as did King Khanazar.

One day the King, returning from the worship of the gods of Old and from bowing before them in the temple of the gods, commanded their prophets to appear before him, saying:

"I would know somewhat concerning the gods."

Then came the prophets before King Khanazar, burdened with many books, to whom the King said:

"It is not in books."

Thereat the prophets departed, bearing away with them a thousand methods well devised in books whereby men may gain wisdom of the gods. One alone remained, a master prophet, who had forgotten books, to whom the King said:

"The gods of Old are mighty."

And answered the master prophet:

"Very mighty are the gods of Old."

Then said the King:

"There are no gods but the gods of Old."

And answered the prophet:

"There are none other."

And they two being alone within the palace the King said:

"Tell me aught concerning gods or men if aught of truth be known."

Then said the master prophet:

"Far and white and straight lieth the road to Knowing, and down it in the heat and dust go all wise people of the earth, but in the fields before they come to it the very wise lie down or pluck the flowers. By the side of the road to Knowing—O King, it is hard and hot—stand many temples, and in the doorway of every temple stand many priests, and they cry to the travellers that weary of the road, crying to them:

"'This is the End.'

"And in the temples are the sounds of music, and from each roof arises the savour of pleasant burning; and all that look at a cool temple, whichever temple they look at, or hear the hidden music, turn in to see whether it be indeed the End. And such as find that the temple is not indeed the End set forth again upon the dusty road, stopping at each temple as they pass for fear they miss the End, or striving onwards on the road, and see nothing in the dust, till they can walk no longer and are taken worn and weary of their journey into some other temple by a kindly priest who shall tell them that this also is the End. Neither on that road may a man gain any guiding from his fellows, for only one thing that they say is surely true, when they say:

"'Friend, we can see nothing for the dust.'

"And of the dust that hides the way much has been there since ever that road began, and some is stirred up by the feet of all that travel upon it, and more arises from the temple doors.

"And, O King, it were better for thee, travelling upon that road, to rest when thou hearest one calling: 'This is the End,' with the sounds of music behind him. And if in the dust and darkness thou pass by Lo and Mush and the pleasant Temple of Kynash, or Sheenath with his opal smile, or Sho with his eyes of agate, yet Shilo and Mynarthitep, Gazo and Amurund, and Slig are still before thee and the priests of their temples will not forget to call thee.

"And, O King, it is told that only one discerned the End and passed by three thousand temples, and the priests of the last were like the priests of the first, and all said that their temple was at the end of the road, and the dark of the dust lay over them all, and all were very pleasant and only the road was weary. And in some were many gods, and in a few only one, and in some the shrine was empty, and all had many priests, and in all the travellers were happy as they rested. And into some his fellow travellers tried to force him, and when he said:

"'I will travel further,' many said:

"'This man lies, for the road ends here.'

"And he that travelled to the End hath told that when the thunder was heard upon the road there arose the sound of the voices of all the priests as far as he could hear, crying:

"'Hearken to Shilo'—'Hear Mush'—'Lo! Kynash'—'The voice of Sho'—'Mynarthitep is angry'—'Hear the word of Slig!'

"And far away along the road one cried to the traveller that Sheenath stirred in his sleep.

"O King, this is very doleful. It is told that the traveller came at last to the utter End and there was a mighty gulf, and in the darkness at the bottom of the gulf one small god crept, no bigger than a hare, whose voice came crying in the cold:

"'I know not.'

"And beyond the gulf was naught, only the small god crying.

"And he that travelled to the End fled backwards for a great distance till he came to temples again, and entering one where a priest cried:

"'This is the End,' lay down and rested on a couch. There Yush sat silent, carved with an emerald tongue and two great eyes of sapphire, and there many rested and were happy. And an old priest, coming from comforting a child, came over to that traveller who had seen the End and said to him:

"'This is Yush and this is the End of wisdom.'

"And the traveller answered:

"'Yush is very peaceful and this is indeed the End.'

"O King, wouldst thou hear more?"

And the King said:

"I would hear all."

And the master prophet answered:

"There was also another prophet and his name was Shaun, who had such reverence for the gods of Old that he became able to discern their forms by starlight as they strode, unseen by others, among men. Each night did Shaun discern the forms of the gods and every day he taught concerning them, till men in Averon knew how the gods appeared all grey against the mountains, and how Rhoog was higher than Mount Scagadon, and how Skun was smaller, and how Asgool leaned forwards as he strode, and how Trodath peered about him with small eyes. But one night as Shaun watched the gods of Old by starlight, he faintly discerned some other gods that sat far up the slopes of the mountains in the stillness behind the gods of Old. And the next day he hurled his robe away that he wore as Averon's prophet and said to his people:

"'There be gods greater than the gods of Old, three gods seen faintly on the hills by starlight looking on Averon.'

"And Shaun set out and travelled many days and many people followed him. And every night he saw more clearly the shapes of the three new gods who sat silent when the gods of Old were striding among men. On the higher slopes of the mountain Shaun stopped with all his people, and there they built a city and worshipped the gods, whom only Shaun could see, seated above them on the mountain. And Shaun taught how the gods were like grey streaks of light seen before dawn, and how the god on the right pointed upwards towards the sky, and how the god on the left pointed downwards towards the ground, but the god in the middle slept.

"And in the city Shaun's followers built three temples. The one on the right was a temple for the young, and the one on the left a temple for the old, and the third was a temple with doors closed and barred—therein none ever entered. One night as Shaun watched before the three gods sitting like pale light against the mountain, he saw on the mountain's summit two gods that spake together and pointed, mocking the gods of the hill, only he heard no sound. The next day Shaun set out and a few followed him to climb to the mountain's summit in the cold, to find the gods who were so great that they mocked at the silent three. And near the two gods they halted and built for themselves huts. Also they built a temple wherein the Two were carved by the hand of Shaun with their heads turned towards each other, with mockery on Their faces and Their fingers pointing, and beneath Them were carved the three gods of the hill as actors making sport. None remembered now Asgool, Trodath, Skun, and Rhoog, the gods of Old.

"For many years Shaun and his few followers lived in their huts upon the mountain's summit worshipping gods that mocked, and every night Shaun saw the two gods by starlight as they laughed to one another in the silence. And Shaun grew old.

"One night as his eyes were turned towards the Two, he saw across the mountains in the distance a great god seated in the plain and looming enormous to the sky, who looked with angry eyes towards the Two as they sat and mocked. Then said Shaun to his people, the few that had followed him thither:

"'Alas that we may not rest, but beyond us in the plain sitteth the one true god and he is wrath with mocking. Let us therefore leave these two that sit and mock and let us find the truth in the worship of that greater god, who even though he kill shall yet not mock us.'

"But the people answered:

"'Thou hast taken us from many gods and taught us now to worship gods that mock, and if there is laughter on their faces as we die, lo! thou alone canst see it, and we would rest.'

"But three men who had grown old with following followed still.

"And down the steep mountain on the further side Shaun led them, saying:

"'Now we shall surely know.'

"And the three old men answered:

"'We shall know indeed, O, last of all the prophets.'

"That night the two gods mocking at their worshippers mocked not at Shaun nor his three followers, who coming to the plain still travelled on till they came at last to a place where the eyes of Shaun at night could closely see the vast form of their god. And beyond them as far as the sky there lay a marsh. There they rested, building such shelters as they could, and said to one another:

"'This is the End, for Shaun discerneth that there are no more gods, and before us lieth the marsh and old age hath come upon us.'

"And since they could not labour to build a temple, Shaun carved upon a rock all that he saw by starlight of the great god of the plain; so that if ever others forsook the gods of Old because they saw beyond them the Greater Three, and should thence come to knowledge of the Twain that mocked, and should yet persevere in wisdom till they saw by starlight him whom Shaun named the Ultimate god, they should still find there upon the rock what one had written concerning the end of search. For three years Shaun carved upon the rock, and rose one night from carving, saying:

"'Now is my labour done,' saw in the distance four greater gods beyond the Ultimate god. Proudly in the distance beyond the marsh these gods were tramping, taking no heed of the god upon the plain. Then said Shaun to his three followers:

"'Alas that we know not yet, for there be gods beyond the marsh.'

"None would follow Shaun, for they said that old age must end all quests, and that they would rather wait there in the plain for Death than that he should pursue them across the marsh.

"Then Shaun said farewell to his followers, saying:

"'You have followed me well since ever we forsook the gods of Old to worship greater gods. Farewell. It may be that your prayers at evening shall avail when you pray to the god of the plain, but I must go onwards, for there be gods beyond.'

"So Shaun went down into the marsh, and for three days struggled through it, and on the third night saw the four gods not very far away, yet could not discern Their faces. All the next day Shaun toiled on to see Their faces by starlight, but ere the night came up or one star shone, at set of sun, Shaun fell down before the feet of his four gods. The stars came out, and the faces of the four shone bright and clear, but Shaun saw them not, for the labour of toiling and seeing was over for Shaun; and lo! They were Asgool, Trodath, Skun, and Rhoog—the gods of Old."

Then said the King:

"Tell me this thing, O prophet. Who are the true gods?"

The master prophet answered:

"Let the King command."

T HIS prose poem, mostly a direct copying down of a dream, marks the first appearance of Nyarlathotep, perhaps the most important of Lovecraft's Old Ones, since his role as messenger of the blind, voiceless, tenebrous gods enables him to appear in many contexts and forms. He marks the place where the veil is thinnest between human perception and the Wholly Other character of the Old Ones. Here the *Mysterium Tremendum* that no man may utter becomes, for a terrible moment, intelligible.

It is no accident that Lovecraft makes the harbinger of the doom of humanity a figure of science, almost a smiling front man demonstrating the exciting advances that will bring us a bright new future in the world of tomorrow. Here is the supernova of blinding, scorching light of knowledge that will send us, screaming, back into the comforting darkness of a new medievalism.

Will Murray ("Behind the Mask of Nyarlathotep", *Lovecraft Studies* #25, Fall 1991) has advanced the hypothesis that Lovecraft's dream image of Nyarlathotep was influenced by reports of the public demonstrations of Nikola Tesla, whose inventions were astonishing enough, but whose wild claims surpassed them. He seemed a dubious, even sinister, figure to some at the time, with his electrical tricks and marvels, jocosely revealed with the legerdemain of a modern Simon Magus on public stages across the country. He even boasted of a device that could crack the very earth asunder.

I cannot help thinking of a similar scene described by maverick philosopher of science Paul Feyerabend from his grad student days in Germany. He tells of

> Felix Ehrenhaft who arrived in Vienna in 1947. ... We knew that he was an excellent experimenter and that his lectures were performances on a grand scale which his assistants had to prepare for hours in advance. ... We were also familiar with the persistent rumors that denounced him as a charlatan. ... Ehrenhaft was a mountain of a man, full of vitality and unusual ideas. ... [We] who had intended to expose him sat in silent astonishment at his performance. ... But he went further and criticized the foundations of classical physics as well. The first thing to be removed was the law of inertia: Undisturbed objects instead of going in a straight line were supposed to move in a helix. ... Then new and surprising properties of light were demonstrated. ... Every day ... participants went by in an attitude of wonder and left the building (if they were theoretical physicists, that is) as if they had seen something obscene. [*Against Method*, 2nd edition, pp. 275-276]

What makes such demonstrations as those predicated of Nyarlathotep, Tesla, and Ehrenhaft more than sideshows? More than mere stage magic? They are tangible proof, or seem to be, that the reigning scientific paradigm is not the only way to construe reality. These showman inventors, of which Thomas Ligotti's Dr. Francis Haxhausen ("Mad Night of Atonement") is another, have managed not merely to conceive a whole different set of laws, relations, and forces of nature, but also to find a way to catch them, get hold of them, make them momentarily visible, as when Dr. Armitage sprays the Whateley monster with the clinging powder of Ibn-Ghazi. The great convincement of scientific theory is its "empirical fit"; it yields reproducible results and thus seems to demonstrate that its theoretical map of reality truly corresponds to the way things are. You can figure out a self-consistent scheme for launching a rocket to the moon and, lo and behold, it works! What if you could devise ways of demonstrating other and opposite theories? Mainstream science might want to brand them "lying wonders", but that is how science advances, new paradigms eventually replacing old ones, explaining and predicting what the old ones explained and predicted, and then some things they couldn't.

Thomas S. Kuhn (*The Structure of Scientific Revolution*) had already explained this much, but Paul Feyerabend went further, coming pretty close, if I understand him, to seeing theoretical models as something like placebos that get their results simply because you *think* they will. Perhaps they are like the exorcistic bogeymen invoked by tribal shamans that really work in (psychosomatic) healings because they give sufferers something to hold onto to marshal and focus their energies (see Claude Levi-Strauss, "The Effectiveness of Symbols", in his *Structural Anthropology*). In this case, we would still be positing that the mental creations of scientific theorists externalize themselves into the external world, but we would no longer think our models *reflect* exterior reality so much as *carving out the shape* of it. That, it seems to me, is a Lovecraftian revelation, the revelation of the aimless waves whose chance combining gives each frail cosmos its eternal law.

"Nyarlathotep" first appeared in *The United Amateur* for November 1920.

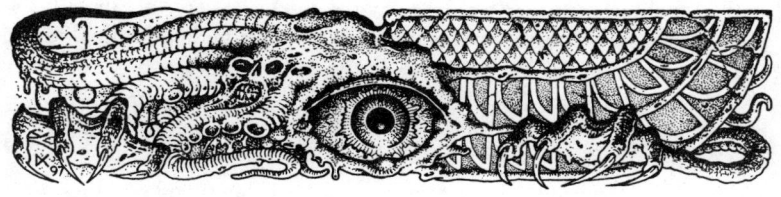

Nyarlathotep

by H. P. Lovecraft

NYARLATHOTEP ... the crawling chaos ... I am the last ... I will tell the audient void ....

I do not recall distinctly when it began, but it was months ago. The general tension was horrible. To a season of political and social upheaval was added a strange and brooding apprehension of hideous physical danger—a danger widespread and all-embracing, such a danger as may be imagined only in the most terrible phantasms of the night. I recall that the people went about with pale and worried faces, and whispered warnings and prophecies which no one dared consciously repeat or acknowledge to himself that he had heard. A sense of monstrous guilt was upon the land, and out of the abysses between the stars swept chill currents that made men shiver in dark and lonely places. There was a daemoniac alteration in the sequence of the seasons—the autumn heat lingered fearsomely, and everyone felt that the world and perhaps the universe had passed from the control of known gods or forces to that of gods or forces which were unknown.

And it was then that Nyarlathotep came out of Egypt. Who he was, none could tell, but he was of the old native blood and looked like a Pharaoh. The fellahin knelt when they saw him, yet could not say why. He said he had risen up out of the blackness of twenty-seven centuries, and that he had heard messages from places not on this planet. Into the lands of civilisation came Nyarlathotep, swarthy, slender, and sinister, always buying strange instruments of glass and metal and combining them into instruments yet stranger. He spoke much of the sciences—of electricity and psychology—and gave exhibitions of power which sent his spectators away speechless, yet which swelled his fame to exceeding magnitude. Men advised one another to see Nyarlathotep, and shuddered. And where Nyarlathotep went, rest vanished; for the small hours were rent with the screams of nightmare. Never before had the screams of nightmare been such a public problem; now the wise men almost wished they could forbid sleep in the small hours, that the shrieks of cities might less horribly disturb the pale, pitying moon as it glimmered on green waters gliding under bridges, and old steeples crumbling against a sickly sky.

I remember when Nyarlathotep came to my city—the great, the old, the terrible city of unnumbered crimes. My friend had told me of him, and of the impelling fascination and allurement of his revelations, and I burned with eagerness to explore his uttermost mysteries. My friend said they were horrible and impressive beyond my most fevered imaginings; that what was thrown on a screen in the darkened room prophesied things none but Nyarlathotep dared prophesy, and that in the sputter of his sparks there was taken from men that which had never been taken before yet which shewed only in the eyes. And I heard it hinted abroad that those who knew Nyarlathotep looked on sights which others saw not.

It was in the hot autumn that I went through the night with the restless crowds to see Nyarlathotep, through the stifling night and up the endless stairs into the choking room. And shadowed on a screen, I saw hooded forms amidst ruins, and yellow evil faces peering from behind fallen monuments. And I saw the world battling against blackness; against the waves of destruction from ultimate space; whirling, churning; struggling around the dimming, cooling sun. Then the sparks played amazingly around the heads of the spectators, and hair stood up on end whilst shadows more grotesque than I can tell came out and squatted on the heads. And when I, who was colder and more scientific than the rest, mumbled a trembling protest about "imposture" and "static electricity", Nyarlathotep drave us all out, down the dizzy stairs into the damp, hot, deserted midnight streets. I screamed aloud that I was *not* afraid, that I never could be afraid; and others screamed with me for solace. We sware to one another that the city *was* exactly the same, and still alive; and when the electric lights began to fade we cursed the company over and over again, and laughed at the queer faces we made.

I believe we felt something coming down from the greenish moon, for when we began to depend on its light we drifted into curious involuntary formations and seemed to know our destinations though we dared not think of them. Once we looked at the pavement and found the blocks loose and displaced by grass, with scarce a line of rusted metal to shew where the tramways had run. And again we saw a tram-car, lone, windowless, dilapidated, and almost on its side. When we gazed around the horizon, we could not find the third tower by the river, and noticed that the silhouette of the second tower was ragged at the top. Then we split up into narrow columns, each of which seemed drawn in a different direction. One disappeared in a narrow alley to the left, leaving only the echo of a shocking moan. Another filed down a weed-choked subway entrance, howling with a laughter that was mad. My own column was sucked toward the open country, and presently felt a chill which was not of the hot autumn; for as we stalked out on the dark moor, we beheld around us the hellish moon-glitter of evil snows. Trackless, inexplicable snows, swept asunder in one direction only, where lay a gulf all the blacker for its glittering walls. The column seemed very thin indeed as it plodded dreamily into the gulf. I lingered behind, for the black rift in the green-litten snow was frightful, and I thought I had heard the reverberations of a disquieting wail as my companions vanished; but my power to linger was slight. As if beckoned by those who had gone before, I half floated between the titanic snowdrifts, quivering and afraid, into the sightless vortex of the unimaginable.

Screamingly sentient, dumbly delirious, only the gods that were can tell. A sickened, sensitive shadow writhing in hands that are not hands, and whirled blindly past ghastly midnights of rotting creation, corpses of dead worlds with sores that were cities, charnel winds that brush the pallid stars and make them flicker low. Beyond the world vague ghosts of monstrous things; half-seen columns of unsanctified temples that rest on nameless rocks beneath space and reach up to dizzy vacua above the spheres of light and darkness. And through this revolving graveyard of the universe the muffled, maddening beat of drums, and thin, monotonous whine of blasphemous flutes from inconceivable, unlighted chambers beyond Time; the detestable pounding and piping whereunto dance slowly, awkwardly, and absurdly the gigantic, tenebrous ultimate gods—the blind, voiceless, mindless gargoyles whose soul is Nyarlathotep.

THESE three apocalyptic poems read almost as if their authors had collaborated in a round robin. In fact, that is just what they did, though none of them was aware of doing so. Together the poems tell a tale of the end of the world we know. Marco Frenschkowski ("W. B. Yeats' 'The Second Coming' und H. P. Lovecraft's 'Nyarlathotep': eine vergleichende Interpretation", *Das Schwarze Geheimnis* #1, 1994) shows how the first and third poems draw upon the images of the Antichrist legend (note the "beast" image in both) to herald the coming crisis of modern Western civilization. At first Lovecraft's apocalyptic scenario may seem to lack any dimension of social commentary or satire and to seem instead a statement of his cosmic futilitarianism pure and simple: The time for humanity is soon to be over, period. Remember how he populated his cults of the Old Ones with non-White, non-Western, Dionysian revelers threatening to supplant the Apollonian, rationalist, European establishment. His Mythos is pointedly not without its social dimension. Though Lovecraft disdained the prospect, he was otherwise a devotee of Nietzsche, who welcomed the Dionysian onslaught and proclaimed himself the Antichrist, as Aleister Crowley did, for heralding it.

Frenschkowski, a specialist in the ancient literature of dreams and visions (see his *Offenbarung und Epiphanie*, Tübingen, 1995), calls attention to the visionary nature of both poems. Yeats uses the language of the seer ("a vast image out of *Spiritus Mundi* troubles my sight. ... The darkness drops again") and Lovecraft receives the name Nyarlathotep, as well as his apocalyptic identity, in a dream, transcribed as the prose poem "Nyarlathotep."

Robert E. Howard's "Silence Falls on Mecca's Walls" fits perfectly between Yeats and Lovecraft. All three foretell the coming of the Antichrist, who emerges from the desert sands, whether of Egypt or Mecca. Here is the myth constituted by the three poems:

First, Yeats tells us that the time is fulfilled; the coming is at hand. The expectation is for the second coming of Christ, but as Crowley also saw, the truth is that the advent will be that of an entity to replace Christ as the Word of a new Aeon, even as Christ inaugurated the one now ending (for Howard's development of the mytheme whereby Christ had previously replaced the gods of the age before him, see his "The Gray God Passes"). Thus the second "coming of Christ" is a coming of a *second Christ*, who is thus, from the perspective of the old Aeon, the *Anti*christ, the Great Beast, the "rough beast." Its birth in "Bethlehem" signifies just this: another's turn to occupy the messianic manger.

Second, Howard uses the metaphor of the holy city of Mecca, where the Prophet Muhammad (= Mekmet) was born and where Islam began, to depict the distinctly non-virginal conception of Dejjal (the Islamic name for Antichrist) by Satan/Iblis in the very shadow of the Kaaba. The point is that, as the *Necronomicon* puts it, "Their habitation is even one with your guarded threshold." As a star announced the birth of the old messiah, strange stars, red and black, proclaim the nativity of the new one, who is yet older than the old: Ammon-Hoteph/Nyarlathotep.

Third, Lovecraft sketches the appearance of the Antichrist from Egypt in a blasphemous recapitulation of Matthew's midrashic interpretation of Hosea 11:1, "Out of Egypt have I called my son." For Matthew (2:15), this meant that, like the children of Israel, Jesus was God's son, called forth from Egypt in an exodus to the Promised Land. For Lovecraft, it is the Antichrist, someone else's son, as we saw in Howard's poem.

"By the word of two or three witnesses, let every matter be established."

Yeats' "The Second Coming" appeared, virtually simultaneously, in *The Nation* for November 6, 1920 and in *The Dial* for November 1920. "Silence Falls on Mecca's Walls" debuted long after Howard wrote it, in *Shadows of Dreams* (Donald M. Grant, 1989). The sonnet "Nyarlathotep" first appeared in *Weird Tales*, January 1931.

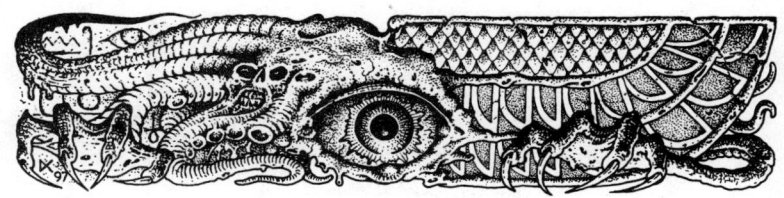

Three Poems

The Second Coming

by William Butler Yeats

Turning and turning in the widening gyre
The falcon cannot hear the falconer;
Things fall apart; the centre cannot hold;
Mere anarchy is loosed upon the world,
The blood-dimmed tide is loosed, and everywhere
The ceremony of innocence is drowned;
The best lack all conviction, while the worst
Are full of passionate intensity.
Surely some revelation is at hand;
Surely the Second Coming is at hand.
The Second Coming! Hardly are those words out
When a vast image out of *Spiritus Mundi*
Troubles my sight: somewhere in sands of the desert
A shape with lion body and the head of a man,
A gaze blank and pitiless as the sun,
Is moving its slow thighs, while all about it
Reel shadows of the indignant desert birds.
The darkness drops again; but now I know
That twenty centuries of stony sleep
Were vexed to nightmare by a rocking cradle,
And what rough beast, its hour come round at last,
Slouches towards Bethlehem to be born?

Silence Falls on Mecca's Walls

by Robert E. Howard

Silence falls on Mecca's walls
And true believers turn to stone;
A granite wind from out the East
Bears the rattle of bone on bone,
And to the harlot of the priest
Comes one no man has ever known.

The black stars fall on Mecca's walls
The red stars gem the pallid night;
The yellow stars are hinged in grey
But Ammon-Hoteph's stars are white.
Who weaves a web to hold at bay
The castled king of Mekmet's light?

Darkness falls on Mecca's walls.
The cressets glimmer in the gloom;
Along the cornices and groins
The scorpion weaves his trail of doom.
A woman bares her pulsing loins
To One within a shadowy room.

The star-dust falls on Mecca's walls,
The bat's wings flash in Mekmet's face;
The lonely fanes rise black and stark.
What brought what Shape from what strange place,
Across the gulf of utter dark,
To span the void of cosmic space?

Silence falls on Mecca's walls
Like mist from some fiend-haunted fen.
Stars, shuttles in a demon's looms,
Weave over Mecca, dooms of men.
A woman laughs—and laughs again.

Nyarlathotep

by H. P. Lovecraft

And at the last from inner Egypt came
The strange dark One to whom the fellahs bowed;
Silent and lean and cryptically proud,
And wrapped in fabrics red as sunset flame.
Throngs pressed around, frantic for his commands,
But leaving, could not tell what they had heard;
While through the nations spread the awestruck word
That wild beasts followed him and licked his hands.

Soon from the sea a noxious birth began;
Forgotten lands with weedy spires of gold;
The ground was cleft, and mad auroras rolled
Down on the quaking citadels of man.
Then, crushing what he chanced to mould in play,
The idiot Chaos blew Earth's dust away.

THOUGH the depiction of Nyarlathotep as a black man in "The Dreams in the Witch House" is by no means unparalleled in Lovecraft (occurring also in *The Dream-Quest of Unknown Kadath* and the sonnet "Nyarlathotep"), its presence here denotes the influence of Lovecraft's beloved and oft-cited *The Witch-Cult in Western Europe* by Margaret Murray. Not only do characters in "The Call of Cthulhu", "The Horror at Red Hook", and "The Whisperer in Darkness" possess and quote the book, but Robert Bloch's Norman Bates even winds up with a copy on his shelf!

"The Dreams in the Witch House" seems to have borrowed other details of witchcraft from Margaret Murray's *Witch-Cult*, too, including the witch-mark and even rodentine familiars like cuddly li'l Brown Jenkin.

As Robert H. Waugh ("Dr. Margaret Murray and H. P. Lovecraft: The Witch-Cult in New England", *Lovecraft Studies* 31, Fall 1994, pp. 2-10) shows, Lovecraft's picture of witchcraft was a synthesis of elements drawn from the fiction of Arthur Machen (e.g., "The Novel of the Black Seal", "The Shining Pyramid") and from Margaret Murray. From Machen HPL took the notion that witchcraft was the debased pagan legacy of an aboriginal dwarf race of Mongolian or Turanian hill people supplanted by the clean-limbed Aryans and Celts. He combined this with Murray's hypothesis that witchcraft was a suppressed pre-Christian fertility religion which received a secondary overlay of Christian diabolism at the hands of church inquisitors who misunderstood and persecuted it. (Lovecraft discussed these matters with fellow racialist Robert E. Howard, who rejoiced to use the same "Yellow Peril" version of the pre-Celtic Little People in several of his stories, e.g., "The Children of the Night").

Waugh points out a delicious irony. Murray thought she was vindicating the witches by relieving them of the onus of having been a kind of Satanist Ladies Auxiliary, showing them to represent the survival of an older, independent tradition instead. Lovecraft fictively reinterpreted this theory to make the pre-Christian witch cult the survival of something infinitely more hideous than Satanism! It is a development not particularly relished, I'll wager, by today's politically correct Wiccan witches, who have taken Murray's highly dubious theories as a license to grab a free ancient pedigree.

Here is an irony to match it: Who would have guessed that Lovecraft's own fictive Mythos would itself evolve into a branch of today's New Age neopagan occultism? Lovecraft always said he tried to use as much ingenuity and verisimilitude in writing his tales as a genuine hoax would require. It would appear he did his work too well!

Fritz Leiber was right: Lovecraft effected a Copernican revolution in horror by using the fearsome implications of modern science as the subtext for Gothic horror ("A Literary Copernicus" in S. T. Joshi (ed.), *H. P. Lovecraft: Four Decades of Criticism*). "The Dreams in the Witch House", as Leiber recognized (see his essay "Through Hyperspace with Brown Jenkin: Lovecraft's Contribution to Speculative Fiction" in *Four Decades*, pp. 140-152, or in *The Second Book of Fritz Leiber*, DAW, 1975, pp. 182-197), is a prime example. Keziah Mason is scary not because she is mixed up with Medieval superstition instead of humanistic, progressive science. Just the reverse! She is so frightening because she has out-Einsteined Einstein and breached the barriers of a world too overwhelming for us to know how to deal with.

"The Dreams in the Witch House" initially appeared in *Weird Tales*, July 1933.

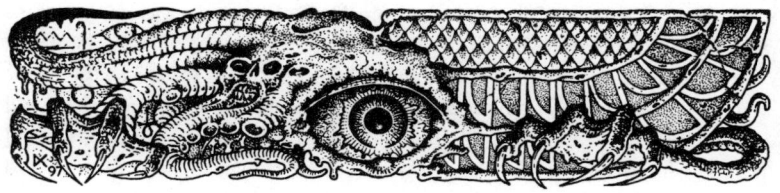

The Dreams in the Witch House

by H. P. Lovecraft

WHETHER the dreams brought on the fever or the fever brought on the dreams Walter Gilman did not know. Behind everything crouched the brooding, festering horror of the ancient town, and of the moldy, unhallowed garret gable where he wrote and studied and wrestled with figures and formulae when he was not tossing on the meager iron bed. His ears were growing sensitive to a preternatural and intolerable degree, and he had long ago stopped the cheap mantel clock whose ticking had come to seem like a thunder of artillery. At night the subtle stirring of the black city outside, the sinister scurrying of rats in the wormy partitions, and the creaking of hidden timbers in the centuried house were enough to give him a sense of strident pandemonium. The darkness always teemed with unexplained sound—and yet he sometimes shook with fear lest the noises he heard should subside and allow him to hear certain other fainter noises which he suspected were lurking behind them.

He was in the changeless, legend-haunted city of Arkham, with its clustering gambrel roofs that sway and sag over attics where witches hid from the King's men in the dark, olden days of the Province. Nor was any spot in that city more steeped in macabre memory than the gable room which harbored him—for it was this house and this room which had likewise harbored old Keziah Mason, whose flight from Salem Gaol at the last no one was ever able to explain. That was in 1692—the gaoler had gone mad and babbled of a small white-fanged furry thing which scuttled out of Keziah's cell, and not even Cotton Mather could explain the curves and angles smeared on the gray stone walls with some red, sticky fluid.

Possibly Gilman ought not to have studied so hard. Non-Euclidean calculus and quantum physics are enough to stretch any brain; and when one mixes them with folklore, and tries to trace a strange background of multi-dimensional reality behind the ghoulish hints of the Gothic tales and the wild whispers of the chimney-corner, one can hardly expect to be wholly free from mental tension. Gilman came from Haverhill, but it was only after he had entered college in Arkham that he began to connect his mathematics with the fantastic legends of elder magic. Something in the air of the hoary town worked obscurely on his imagination. The professors at Miskatonic had urged him to slacken up, and had voluntarily cut down his course at several points. Moreover, they had stopped him from consulting the dubious old books on forbidden secrets that were kept under lock and key in a vault at the university library. But all these precautions came late in the day, so that Gilman had some terrible hints from the dreaded *Necronomicon* of Abdul Alhazred, the fragmentary *Book of Eibon*, and the suppressed *Unaussprechlichen Kulten* of Von Junzt to correlate with his abstract formulae on the properties of space and the linkage of dimensions known and unknown.

He knew his room was in the old Witch House—that, indeed, was why he had taken it. There was much in the Essex County records about Keziah Mason's trial, and what she had admitted under pressure to the Court of Oyer and Terminer had fascinated Gilman beyond all reason. She had told Judge Hathorne of lines and curves that could be made to point out directions leading through the walls of space to other spaces beyond, and had implied that such lines and curves were frequently used at certain midnight meetings in the dark valley of the white stone beyond Meadow Hill and on the unpeopled island in the river. She had spoken also of the Black Man, of her oath, and of her new secret name of Nahab. Then she had drawn those devices on the walls of her cell and vanished.

Gilman believed strange things about Keziah, and had felt a queer thrill on learning that her dwelling was still standing after more than two hundred thirty-five years. When he heard the hushed Arkham whispers about Keziah's persistent presence in the old house and the narrow streets, about the irregular human tooth-marks left on certain sleepers in that and other houses, about the childish cries heard near May-Eve, and Hallowmass, about the stench often noted in the old house's attic just after those dreaded seasons, and about the small, furry, sharp-toothed thing which haunted the moldering structure and the town and nuzzled people curiously in the black hours before dawn, he resolved to live in the place at any cost. A room was easy to secure, for the house was unpopular, hard to rent, and long given over to cheap lodgings. Gilman could not have told what he expected to find there, but he knew he wanted to be in the building where some circumstance had more or less suddenly given a mediocre old woman of the seventeenth century an insight into mathematical depths perhaps beyond the utmost modern delvings of Planck, Heisenberg, Einstein, and de Sitter.

He studied the timber and plaster walls for traces of cryptic designs at every accessible spot where the paper had peeled, and within a week managed to get the eastern attic room where Keziah was held to have practised her spells. It had been vacant from the first—for no one had ever been willing to stay there long—but the Polish landlord had grown wary about renting it. Yet nothing whatever had happened to Gilman till about the time of the fever. No ghostly Keziah flitted through the somber halls and chambers, no small furry thing crept into his dismal eyrie to nuzzle him, and no record of the witch's incantations rewarded his constant search. Sometimes he would take walks through shadowy tangles of unpaved musty-smelling lanes where eldritch brown houses of unknown age leaned and tottered and leered mockingly through narrow, small-paned windows. Here he knew strange things had happened once, and there was a faint suggestion behind the surface that everything of that monstrous past might not—at least in the darkest, narrowest, and most intricately crooked alleys—have utterly perished. He also rowed out twice to the ill-regarded island in the river, and made a sketch of the singular angles described by the moss-grown rows of gray standing stones whose origin was so obscure and immemorial.

Gilman's room was of good size but queerly irregular shape, the north wall slanting perceptibly inward from the outer to the inner end, while the low ceiling slanted gently downward in the same direction. Aside from an obvious rat-hole and the signs of other stopped-up ones, there was no access—nor any appearance of a former avenue of access—to the space which must have existed between the slanting wall and the straight outer wall on the house's north side, though a view from the exterior showed where a window had been boarded up at a very remote date. The loft above the ceiling—which must have had a slanting floor—was likewise inaccessible. When Gilman climbed up a ladder to the cob-webbed level loft above the rest of the attic he found vestiges of a bygone aperture tightly and heavily covered with ancient planking and secured by the stout wooden pegs common in Colonial carpentry. No amount of persuasion, however, could induce the stolid landlord to let him investigate either of these two closed spaces.

As time wore along, his absorption in the irregular wall and ceiling of his room increased; for he began to read into the odd angles a mathematical significance which seemed to offer vague clues regarding their purpose. Old Keziah, he reflected, might have had excellent reasons for living in a room with peculiar angles, for was it not through certain angles that she claimed to have gone outside the boundaries of the world of space we know? His interest gradually veered away from the unplumbed voids beyond the slanting surfaces, since it now appeared that the purpose of those surfaces concerned the side he was on.

The touch of brain-fever and the dreams began early in February. For some time, apparently, the curious angles of Gilman's room had been having a strange, almost hypnotic effect on him; and as the bleak winter advanced he had found himself staring more and more intently at the corner where the down-slanting ceiling met the inward-slanting wall. About this period his inability to concentrate on his formal studies worried him considerably, his apprehensions about the mid-year examinations being very acute. But the exaggerated sense of hearing was scarcely less annoying. Life had become an insistent and almost unendurable cacophony, and there was that constant, terrifying impression of *other* sounds—perhaps from regions beyond life—trembling on the very brink of audibility. So far as concrete noises went, the rats in the ancient partitions were the worst. Sometimes their scratching seemed not only furtive but deliberate. When it came from beyond the slanting north wall it was mixed with a sort of dry rattling, and when it came from the century-closed loft above the slanting ceiling Gilman always braced himself as if expecting some horror which only bided its time before descending to engulf him utterly.

The dreams were wholly beyond the pale of sanity, and Gilman felt that they must be a result, jointly, of his studies in mathematics and in folklore. He had been thinking too much about the vague regions which his formulae told him must lie beyond the three dimensions we know, and about the possibility that old Keziah Mason—guided by some influence past all conjecture—had actually found the gate to those regions. The yellowed county records containing her testimony and that of her accusers were so damnably suggestive of things beyond human experience—and the descriptions of the darting little furry object which served as her familiar were so painfully realistic despite their incredible details.

That object—no larger than a good-sized rat and quaintly called by the townspeople "Brown Jenkin"—seemed to have been the fruit of a remarkable case of sympathetic herd-delusion, for in 1692 no less than eleven persons had testified to glimpsing it. There were recent rumors, too, with a baffling and disconcerting amount of agreement. Witnesses said it had long hair and the shape of a rat, but that its sharp-toothed, bearded face was evilly human while its paws were like tiny human hands. It took messages betwixt old Keziah and the devil, and was nursed on witch's blood, which it sucked like a vampire. Its voice was a kind of loathsome titter, and it could speak all languages. Of all the bizarre monstrosities in Gilman's dreams, nothing filled him with greater panic and nausea than this blasphemous and diminutive hybrid, whose image flitted across his vision in a form a thousandfold more hateful than anything his waking mind had deduced from the ancient records and the modern whispers.

Gilman's dreams consisted largely in plunges through limitless abysses of inexplicably colored twilight and bafflingly disordered sound; abysses whose material and gravitational properties, and whose relation to his own entity, he could not even begin to explain. He did not walk or climb, fly or swim, crawl or wriggle; yet always experienced a mode of motion partly voluntary and partly involuntary. Of his own condition he could not well judge, for sight of his arms, legs, and torso seemed always cut off by some odd disarrangement of perspective; but he felt that his physical organization and faculties were somehow marvelously transmuted and obliquely projected—though not without a certain grotesque relationship to his normal proportions and properties.

The abysses were by no means vacant, being crowded with indescribably angled masses of alien-hued substance, some of which appeared to be organic while others seemed inorganic. A few of the organic objects tended to awake vague memories in the back of his mind, though he could form no conscious idea of what they mockingly resembled or suggested. In the later dreams he began to distinguish separate categories into which organic objects appeared to be divided, and which seemed to involve in each case a radically different species of conduct pattern and basic motivation. Of these categories one seemed to him to include objects slightly less illogical and irrelevant in their motions than the members of the other categories.

All the objects—organic and inorganic alike—were totally beyond description or even comprehension. Gilman sometimes compared the inorganic matter to prisms, labyrinths, clusters of cubes and planes, and cyclopean buildings; and the organic things struck him variously as groups of bubbles, octopi, centipedes, living Hindoo idols, and intricate arabesques roused into a kind of ophidian animation. Everything he saw was unspeakably menacing and horrible, and whenever one of the organic entities appeared by its motions to be noticing him, he felt a stark, hideous fright which generally jolted him awake. Of how the organic entities moved, he could tell no more than of how he moved himself. In time he observed a further mystery—the tendency of certain entities to appear suddenly out of empty space, or to disappear totally with equal suddenness. The shrieking, roaring confusion of sound which permeated the abysses was past all analysis as to pitch, timbre or rhythm, but seemed to be synchronous with vague visual changes in all the indefinite objects, organic and inorganic alike. Gilman had a constant sense of dread that it might rise to some unbearable degree of intensity during one or another of its obscure, relentlessly inevitable fluctuations.

But it was not in these vortices of complete alienage that he saw Brown Jenkin. That shocking little horror was reserved for certain lighter, sharper dreams which assailed him just before he dropped into the fullest depths of sleep. He would be lying in the dark fighting to keep awake when a faint lambent glow would seem to shimmer around the centuried room, showing in a violet mist the convergence of angled planes which had seized his brain so insidiously. The horror would appear to pop out of the rat-hole in the corner and patter toward him over the sagging, wide-planked floor with evil expectancy in its tiny, bearded human face; but mercifully, this dream always melted away before the object got close enough to nuzzle him. It had hellishly long, sharp, canine teeth. Gilman tried to stop up the rat-hole every day, but each night the real tenants of the partitions would gnaw away the obstruction, whatever it might be. Once he had the landlord nail tin over it, but the next night the rats gnawed a fresh hole, in making which they pushed or dragged out into the room a curious little fragment of bone.

Gilman did not report his fever to the doctor, for he knew he could not pass the examinations if ordered to the college infirmary when every moment was needed for cramming. As it was, he failed in Calculus D and Advanced General Psychology, though not without hope of making up lost ground before the end of the term.

It was in March when the fresh element entered his lighter preliminary dreaming, and the nightmare shape of Brown Jenkin began to be companioned by the nebulous blur which grew more and more to resemble a bent old woman. This addition disturbed him more than he could account for, but finally he decided that it was like an ancient crone whom he had twice actually encountered in the dark tangle of lanes near the abandoned wharves. On those occasions the evil, sardonic, and seemingly unmotivated stare of the beldame had set him almost shivering—especially the first time, when an overgrown rat darting across the shadowed mouth of a neighboring alley had made him think irrationally of Brown Jenkin. Now, he reflected, those nervous fears were being mirrored in his disordered dreams.

That the influence of the old house was unwholesome he could not deny, but traces of his early morbid interest still held him there. He argued that the fever alone was responsible for his nightly fantasies, and that when the touch abated he would be free from the monstrous visions. Those visions, however, were of absorbing vividness and convincingness, and whenever he awaked he retained a vague sense of having undergone much more than he remembered. He was hideously sure than in unrecalled dreams he had talked with both Brown Jenkin and the old woman, and that they had been urging him to go somewhere with them and to meet a third being of greater potency.

Toward the end of March he began to pick up in his mathematics, though other studies bothered him increasingly. He was getting an intuitive knack for solving Riemannian equations, and astonished Professor Upham by his comprehension of fourth-dimensional and other problems which had floored all the rest of the class. One afternoon there was a discussion of possible freakish curvatures in space, and of theoretical points of approach or even contact between our part of the cosmos and various other regions as distant as the farthest stars or the transgalactic gulfs themselves—or even as fabulously remote as the tentatively conceivable cosmic units beyond the whole Einsteinian space-time continuum. Gilman's handling of this theme filled everyone with admiration, even though some of his hypothetical illustrations caused an increase in the always plentiful gossip about his nervous and solitary eccentricity. What made the students shake their heads was his sober theory that a man might—given mathematical knowledge admittedly beyond all likelihood of human acquirement—step deliberately from the earth to any other celestial body which might lie at one of an infinity of specific points in the cosmic pattern.

Such a step, he said, would require only two stages: first, a passage out of the three-dimensional sphere we know, and second, a passage back to the three-dimensional sphere at another point, perhaps one of infinite remoteness. That this could be accomplished without loss of life was in many cases conceivable. Any being from any part of three-dimensional space could probably survive in the fourth dimension, and its survival of the second stage would depend upon what alien part of three-dimensional space it might select for its re-entry. Denizens of some planets might be able to live on certain others—even planets belonging to other galaxies, or to similar dimensional phases of other space-time continua—though of course there must be vast numbers of mutually uninhabitable even though mathematically juxtaposed bodies or zones of space.

It was also possible that the inhabitants of a given dimensional realm could survive entry to many unknown and incomprehensible realms of additional or indefinitely multiplied dimensions—be they within or outside the given space-time continuum—and that the converse would be likewise true. This was a matter for speculation, though one could be fairly certain that the type of mutation involved in a passage from any given dimensional plane to the next higher plane would not be destructive of biological integrity as we understand it. Gilman could not be very clear about his reasons for this last assumption, but his haziness here was more than overbalanced by his clearness on other complex points. Professor Upham especially liked his demonstration of the kinship of higher mathematics to certain phases of magical lore transmitted down the ages from an ineffable antiquity—human or prehuman—whose knowledge of the cosmos and its laws was greater than ours.

Around the first of April Gilman worried considerably because his slow fever did not abate. He was also troubled by what some of his fellow lodgers said about his sleepwalking. It seemed that he was often absent from his bed, and that the creaking of his floor at certain hours of the night was remarked by the man in the room below. This fellow also spoke of hearing the tread of shod feet in the night; but Gilman was sure he must have been mistaken in this, since shoes as well as other apparel were always precisely in place in the morning. One could develop all sorts of aural delusions in this morbid old house—for did not Gilman himself, even in daylight, now feel certain that noises other than rat-scratching came from the black voids beyond the slanting wall and above the slanting ceiling? His pathologically sensitive ears began to listen for faint footfalls in the immemorially sealed loft overhead, and sometimes the illusion of such things was agonizingly realistic.

However, he knew that he had actually become a somnambulist; for twice at night his room had been found vacant, though with all his clothing in place. Of this he had been assured by Frank Elwood, the one fellow student whose poverty forced him to room in this squalid and unpopular house. Elwood had been studying in the small hours and had come up for help on a differential equation, only to find Gilman absent. It had been rather presumptuous of him to open the unlocked door after knocking had failed to rouse a response, but he had needed the help very badly and thought that his host would not mind a gentle prodding awake. On neither occasion, though, had Gilman been there; and when told of the matter he wondered where he could have been wandering, barefoot and with only his nightclothes on. He resolved to investigate the matter if reports of his sleepwalking continued, and thought of sprinkling flour on the floor of the corridor to see where his footsteps might lead. The door was the only conceivable egress, for there was no possible foothold outside the narrow window.

As April advanced, Gilman's fever-sharpened ears were disturbed by the whining prayers of a superstitious loom-fixer named Joe Mazurewicz, who had a room on the ground floor. Mazurewicz had told long, rambling stories about the ghost of old Keziah and the furry sharp-fanged, nuzzling thing, and had said he was so badly haunted at times that only his silver crucifix—given him for the purpose by Father Iwanicki of St. Stanislaus' Church—could bring him relief. Now he was praying because the Witches' Sabbath was drawing near. May Eve was Walpurgis Night, when hell's blackest evil roamed the earth and all the slaves of Satan gathered for nameless rites and deeds. It was always a very bad time in Arkham, even though the fine folk up in Miskatonic Avenue and High and Saltonstall Streets pretended to know nothing about it. There would be bad doings, and a child or two would probably be missing. Joe knew about such things, for his grandmother in the old country had heard tales from her grandmother. It was wise to pray and count one's beads at this season. For three months Keziah and Brown Jenkin had not been near Joe's room, nor near Paul Choynski's room, nor anywhere else—and it meant no good when they held off like that. They must be up to something.

Gilman dropped in at the doctor's office on the sixteenth of the month, and was surprised to find his temperature was not as high as he had feared. The physician questioned him sharply, and advised him to see a nerve specialist. On reflection, he was glad he had not consulted the still more inquisitive college doctor. Old Waldron, who had curtailed his activities before, would have made him take a rest—an impossible thing now that he was so close to great results in his equations. He was certainly near the boundary between the known universe and the fourth dimension, and who could say how much farther he might go?

But even as these thoughts came to him he wondered at the source of his strange confidence. Did all of this perilous sense of imminence come from the formulae on the sheets he covered day by day? The soft, stealthy, imaginary footsteps in the sealed loft above were unnerving. And now, too, there was a growing feeling that somebody was constantly persuading him to do something terrible which he could not do. How about the somnambulism? Where did he go sometimes in the night? And what was that faint suggestion of sound which once in a while seemed to trickle through the confusion of identifiable sounds even in broad daylight and full wakefulness? Its rhythm did not correspond to anything on earth, unless perhaps to the cadence of one or two unmentionable Sabbat-chants, and sometimes he feared it corresponded to certain attributes of the vague shrieking or roaring in those wholly alien abysses of dream.

The dreams were meanwhile getting to be atrocious. In the lighter preliminary phase the evil old woman was now of fiendish distinctness, and Gilman knew she was the one who had frightened him in the slums. Her bent back, long nose, and shrivelled chin were unmistakable, and her shapeless brown garments were like those he remembered. The expression on her face was one of hideous malevolence and exultation, and when he awaked he could recall a croaking voice that persuaded and threatened. He must meet the Black Man and go with them all to the throne of Azathoth at the center of ultimate chaos. That was what she said. He must sign the book of Azathoth in his own blood and take a new secret name now that his independent delvings had gone so far. What kept him from going with her and Brown Jenkin and the other to the throne of Chaos where the thin flutes pipe mindlessly was the fact that he had seen the name "Azathoth" in the *Necronomicon*, and knew it stood for a primal evil too horrible for description.

The old woman always appeared out of thin air near the corner where the downward slant met the inward slant. She seemed to crystallize at a point closer to the ceiling than to the floor, and every night she was a little nearer and more distinct before the dream shifted. Brown Jenkin, too, was always a little nearer at the last, and his yellowish-white fangs glistened shockingly in that unearthly violet phosphorescence. Its shrill loathsome tittering struck more and more in Gilman's head, and he could remember in the morning how it had pronounced the words "Azathoth" and "Nyarlathotep."

In the deeper dreams everything was likewise more distinct, and Gilman felt that the twilight abysses around him were those of the fourth dimension. Those organic entities whose motions seemed least flagrantly irrelevant and unmotivated were probably projections of life-forms from our own planet, including human beings. What the others were in their own dimensional sphere or spheres he dared not try to think. Two of the less irrelevantly moving things—a rather large congeries of iridescent, prolately spheroidal bubbles and a very much smaller polyhedron of unknown colours and rapidly shifting surface angles—seemed to take notice of him and follow him about or float ahead as he changed position among the titan prisms, labyrinths, cube-and-plane clusters and quasi-buildings; and all the while the vague shrieking and roaring waxed louder and louder, as if approaching some monstrous climax of utterly unendurable intensity.

During the night of April 19-20 the new development occurred. Gilman was half involuntarily moving about in the twilight abysses with the bubble-mass and the small polyhedron floating ahead, when he noticed the peculiarly regular angles formed by the edges of some gigantic neighboring prism-clusters. In another second he was out of the abyss and standing tremulously on a rocky hillside bathed in intense, diffused green light. He was barefooted and in his nightclothes, and when he tried to walk discovered that he could scarcely lift his feet. A swirling vapor hid everything but the immediate sloping terrain from sight, and he shrank from the thought of the sounds that might surge out of that vapor.

Then he saw the two shapes laboriously crawling toward him—the old woman and the little furry thing. The crone strained up to her knees and managed to cross her arms in a singular fashion, while Brown Jenkin pointed in a certain direction with a horribly anthropoid forepaw which it raised with evident difficulty. Spurred by an impulse he did not originate, Gilman dragged himself forward along a course determined by the angle of the old woman's arms and the direction of the small monstrosity's paw, and before he had shuffled three steps he was back in the twilight abysses. Geometrical shapes seethed around him, and he fell dizzily and interminably. At last he woke in his bed in the crazily angled garret of the eldritch old house.

He was good for nothing that morning, and stayed away from all his classes. Some unknown attraction was pulling his eyes in a seemingly irrelevant direction, for he could not help staring at a certain vacant spot on the floor. As the day advanced, the focus of his unseeing eyes changed position, and by noon he had conquered the impulse to stare at vacancy. About two o'clock he went out for lunch and as he threaded the narrow lanes of the city he found himself turning always to the southeast. Only an effort halted him at a cafeteria in Church Street, and after the meal he felt the unknown pull still more strongly.

He would have to consult a nerve specialist after all—perhaps there was a connection with his somnambulism—but meanwhile he might at least try to break the morbid spell himself. Undoubtedly he could still manage to walk away from the pull; so with great resolution he headed against it and dragged himself deliberately north along Garrison Street. By the time he had reached the bridge over the Miskatonic he was in a cold perspiration, and he clutched at the iron railing as he gazed upstream at the ill-regarded island whose regular lines of ancient standing stones brooded sullenly in the afternoon sunlight.

Then he gave a start. For there was a clearly visible living figure on that desolate island, and a second glance told him it was certainly the strange old woman whose sinister aspect had worked itself so disastrously into his dreams. The tall grass near her was moving, too, as if some other living thing were crawling close to the ground. When the old woman began to turn toward him he fled precipitately off the bridge and into the shelter of the town's labyrinthine waterfront alleys. Distant though the island was, he felt that a monstrous and invincible evil could flow from the sardonic stare of that bent, ancient figure in brown.

The southeastward pull still held, and only with tremendous resolution could Gilman drag himself into the old house and up the rickety stairs. For hours he sat silent and aimless, with his eyes shifting gradually westward. About six o'clock his sharpened ears caught the whining prayers of Joe Mazurewicz two floors below, and in desperation he seized his hat and walked out into the sunset-golden streets, letting the now directly southward pull carry him where it might. An hour later darkness found him in the open fields beyond Hangman's Brook, with the glimmering spring stars shining ahead. The urge to walk was gradually changing to an urge to leap mystically into space, and suddenly he realized just where the source of the pull lay.

It was in the sky. A definite point among the stars had a claim on him and was calling him. Apparently it was a point somewhere between Hydra and Argo Navis, and he knew that he had been urged toward it ever since he had awaked soon after dawn. In the morning it had been underfoot, and now it was roughly south but stealing toward the west. What was the meaning of this new thing? Was he going mad? How long would it last? Again mustering his resolution, Gilman turned and dragged himself back to the sinister old house.

Mazurewicz was waiting for him at the door, and seemed both anxious and reluctant to whisper some fresh bit of superstition. It was about the witch-light. Joe had been out celebrating the night before—it was Patriots' Day in Massachusetts—and had come home after midnight. Looking up at the house from outside, he had thought at first that Gilman's window was dark, but then he had seen the faint violet glow within. He wanted to warn the gentleman about that glow, for everybody in Arkham knew it was

Keziah's witch-light which played near Brown Jenkin and the ghost of the old crone herself. He had not mentioned this before, but now he must tell about it because it meant that Keziah and her long-toothed familiar were haunting the young gentleman. Sometimes he and Paul Choynski and Landlord Dombrowski thought they saw that light seeping out of cracks in the sealed loft above the young gentleman's room, but they had all agreed not to talk about that. However, it would be better for the young gentleman to take another room and get a crucifix from some good priest like Father Iwanicki.

As the man rambled on, Gilman felt a nameless panic clutch at his throat. He knew that Joe must have been half drunk when he came home the night before; yet the mention of a violet light in the garret window was of frightful import. It was a lambent glow of this sort which always played about the old woman and the small furry thing in those lighter, sharper dreams which prefaced his plunge into unknown abysses, and the thought that a wakeful second person could see the dream-luminance was utterly beyond sane harborage. Yet where had the fellow got such an odd notion? Had he himself talked as well as walked around the house in his sleep? No, Joe said, he had not—but he must check up on this. Perhaps Frank Elwood could tell him something, though he hated to ask.

Fever—wild dreams—somnambulism—illusions of sounds—a pull toward a point in the sky—and now a suspicion of insane sleep-talking! He must stop studying, see a nerve specialist, and take himself in hand. When he climbed to the second story he paused at Elwood's door but saw that the other youth was out. Reluctantly he continued up to his garret room and sat down in the dark. His gaze was still pulled to the southward, but he also found himself listening intently for some sound in the closed loft above, and half imagining that an evil violet light seeped down through an infinitesimal crack in the low, slanting ceiling.

That night as Gilman slept, the violet light broke upon him with heightened intensity, and the old witch and small furry thing, getting closer than ever before, mocked him with inhuman squeals and devilish gestures. He was glad to sink into the vaguely roaring twilight abysses, though the pursuit of that iridescent bubble-congeries and that kaleidoscopic little polyhedron was menacing and irritating. Then came the shift as vast converging planes of a slippery-looking substance loomed above and below him—a shift which ended in a flash of delirium and a blaze of unknown, alien light in which yellow, carmine, and indigo were madly and inextricably blended.

He was half lying on a high, fantastically balustraded terrace above a boundless jungle of outlandish, incredible peaks, balanced planes, domes, minarets, horizontal disks poised on pinnacles, and numberless forms of still greater wildness—some of stone and some of metal—which glittered gorgeously in the mixed, almost blistering glare from a polychromatic sky. Looking upward he saw three stupendous disks of flame, each of a different hue, and at a different height above an infinitely distant curving horizon of low mountains. Behind him tiers of higher terraces towered aloft as far as he could see. The city below stretched away to the limits of vision, and he hoped that no sound would well up from it.

The pavement from which he easily raised himself was a veined, polished stone beyond his power to identify, and the tiles were cut in bizarre-angled shapes which struck him less as asymmetrical than based on some unearthly symmetry whose laws he could not comprehend. The balustrade was chest-high, delicate, and fantastically wrought, while along the rail were ranged at short intervals little figures of grotesque design and exquisite workmanship. They, like the whole balustrade, seemed to be made of some sort of shining metal whose color could not be guessed in the chaos of mixed effulgences, and their nature utterly defied conjecture. They represented some ridged barrel-shaped object with vertical arms radiating spoke-like from a central ring and with vertical knobs or bulbs projecting from the head and base of the barrel. Each of these knobs was the hub of a system of five long, flat, triangularly tapering arms arranged around it like the arms of a starfish—nearly horizontal, but curving slightly away from the central barrel. The base of the bottom knob was fused to the long railing with so delicate a point of contact that several figures had been broken off and were missing. The figures were about four and a half inches in height, while the spiky arms gave them a maximum diameter of about two and a half inches.

When Gilman stood up, the tiles felt hot to his bare feet. He was wholly alone, and his first act was to walk to the balustrade and look dizzily down at the endless, cyclopean city almost two thousand feet below. As he listened he thought a rhythmic confusion of faint musical pipings covering a wide tonal range welled up from the narrow streets beneath, and he wished he might discern the denizens of the place. The sight turned him giddy after a while, so that he would have fallen to the pavement had he not clutched instinctively at the lustrous balustrade. His right hand fell on one of the projecting figures, the touch seeming to steady him slightly. It was too much, however, for the exotic delicacy of the metal-work, and the spiky figure snapped off under his grasp. Still half dazed, he continued to clutch it as his other hand seized a vacant space on the smooth railing.

But now his over-sensitive ears caught something behind him, and he looked back across the level terrace. Approaching him softly though without apparent furtiveness were five figures, two of which were the sinister old woman and the fanged, furry little animal. The other three were what sent him unconscious; for they were living entities about eight feet high, shaped precisely like the spiky images on the balustrade, and propelling themselves by a spider-like wriggling of their lower set of starfish-arms.

Gilman awaked in his bed, drenched by a cold perspiration and with a smarting sensation in his face, hands and feet. Springing to the floor, he washed and dressed in frantic haste, as if it were necessary for him to get out of the house as quickly as possible. He did not know where he wished to go, but felt that once more he would have to sacrifice his classes. The odd pull toward that spot in the sky between Hydra and Argo had abated, but another of even greater strength had taken its place. Now he felt that he must go north—infinitely north. He dreaded to cross the bridge that gave a view of the desolate island in the Miskatonic, so went over the Peabody Avenue bridge. Very often he stumbled, for his eyes and ears were chained to an extremely lofty point in the blank blue sky.

After about an hour he got himself under better control, and saw that he was far from the city. All around him stretched the bleak emptiness of salt marshes, while the narrow road ahead led to Innsmouth—that ancient, half-deserted town which Arkham people were so curiously unwilling to visit. Though the northward pull had not diminished, he resisted it as he had resisted the other pull, and finally found that he could almost balance the one against the other. Plodding back to town and getting some coffee at a soda fountain, he dragged himself into the public library and browsed aimlessly among the lighter magazines. Once he met some friends who remarked how oddly sunburned he looked, but he did not tell them of his walk. At three o'clock he took some lunch at a restaurant, noting meanwhile that the pull had either lessened or divided itself. After that he killed the time at a cheap cinema show, seeing the inane performance over and over again without paying any attention to it.

About nine at night he drifted homeward and shuffled into the ancient house. Joe Mazurewicz was whining unintelligible prayers, and Gilman hastened up to his own garret chamber without pausing to see if Elwood was in. It was when he turned on the feeble electric light that the shock came. At once he saw there was something on the table which did not belong there, and a second look left no room for doubt. Lying on its side—for it could not stand up alone—was the exotic spiky figure which in his monstrous dream he had broken off the fantastic balustrade. No detail was missing: the ridged, barrel-shaped center, the thin radiating arms, the knobs at each end, and the flat, slightly outward-curving starfish-arms spreading from those knobs—all were there. In the electric light the color seemed to be a kind of iridescent gray veined with green; and Gilman could see amidst his horror and bewilderment that one of the knobs ended in a jagged break, corresponding to its former point of attachment to the dream-railing.

Only his tendency toward a dazed stupor prevented him from screaming aloud. This fusion of dream and reality was too much to bear. Still dazed, he clutched at the spiky thing and staggered downstairs to Landlord Dombrowski's quarters. The whining prayers of the superstitious loom-fixer were still sounding through the moldy halls, but Gilman did not mind them now. The landlord was in, and greeted him pleasantly. No, he had not seen that thing before and did not know anything about it. But his wife had said she found a funny tin thing in one of the beds when she fixed the rooms at noon, and maybe that was it. Dombrowski called her, and she waddled in. Yes, that was the thing. She had found it in the young gentleman's bed—on the side next to the wall. It had looked very queer to her, but of course the young gentleman had lots of queer things in his room—books and curios and pictures and markings on paper. She certainly knew nothing about it.

So Gilman climbed upstairs again in mental turmoil, convinced that he was either dreaming or that his somnambulism had run to incredible extremes and led him to depredations in unknown places. Where had he got this outré thing? He did not recall seeing it in any museum in Arkham. It must have been somewhere, though; and the sight of it as he snatched it in his sleep must have caused the odd dream-picture of the balustraded terrace. Next day he would make some very guarded inquiries—and perhaps see the nerve specialist.

Meanwhile he would try to keep track of his somnambulism. As he went upstairs and across the garret hall he sprinkled about some flour which he had borrowed—with a frank admission as to its purpose—from the landlord. He had stopped at Elwood's door on the way, but had found all dark within. Entering his room, he placed the spiky thing on the table, and lay down in complete mental and physical exhaustion without pausing to undress. From the closed loft above the slanting ceiling he thought he heard a faint scratching and padding, but he was too disorganized even to mind it. That cryptical pull from the north was getting very strong again, though it seemed now to come from a lower place in the sky.

In the dazzling violet light of dream the old woman and the fanged, furry thing came again and with a greater distinctness than on any former occasion. This time they actually reached him, and he felt the crone's withered claws clutching at him. He was pulled out of bed and into empty space, and for a moment he heard a rhythmic roaring and saw the twilight amorphousness of the vague abysses seething around him. But that moment was very brief, for presently he was in a crude, windowless little space with rough beams and planks rising to a peak just above his head, and with a curious slanting floor underfoot. Propped level on that floor were low cases full of books of every degree of antiquity and disintegration, and in the center were a table and bench, both apparently fastened in place. Small objects of unknown shape and nature were ranged on the tops of the cases, and in the flaming violet light Gilman thought he saw a counterpart of the spiky image which had puzzled him so horribly. On the left the floor fell abruptly away, leaving a black triangular gulf out of which, after a second's dry rattling, there presently climbed the hateful little furry thing with the yellow fangs and bearded human face.

The evilly grinning beldame still clutched him, and beyond the table stood a figure he had never seen before—a tall, lean man of dead black coloration but without the slightest sign of Negroid features, wholly devoid of either hair or beard, and wearing as his only garment a shapeless robe of some heavy black fabric. His feet were indistinguishable because of the table and bench, but he must have been shod, since there was a clicking whenever he changed position. The man did not speak, and bore no trace of expression on his small, regular features. He merely pointed to a book of prodigious size which lay open on the table, while the beldame thrust a huge gray quill into Gilman's right hand. Over everything was a pall of intensely maddening fear, and the climax was reached when the furry thing ran up the dreamer's clothing to his shoulders and then down his left arm, finally biting him sharply in the wrist just below his cuff. As the blood spurted from this wound Gilman lapsed into a faint.

He awaked on the morning of the twenty-second with a pain in his left wrist, and saw that his cuff was brown with dried blood. His recollections were very confused, but the scene with the black man in the unknown space stood out vividly. The rats must have bitten him as he slept, giving rise to the climax of that frightful dream. Opening the door, he saw that the flour on the corridor floor was undisturbed except for the huge prints of the loutish fellow who roomed at the other end of the garret. So he had not been sleepwalking this time. But something would have to be done about those rats. He would speak to the landlord about them. Again he tried to stop up the hole at the base of the slanting wall, wedging in a candlestick which seemed of about the right size. His ears were ringing horribly, as if with the residual echoes of some horrible noise heard in dreams.

As he bathed and changed clothes he tried to recall what he had dreamed after the scene in the violet-litten space, but nothing definite would crystallize in his mind. That scene itself must have corresponded to the sealed loft overhead, which had begun to attack his imagination so violently, but later impressions were faint and hazy. There were suggestions of the vague, twilight abysses, and of still vaster, blacker abysses beyond them—abysses in which all fixed suggestions were absent. He had been taken there by the bubble-congeries and the little polyhedron which always dogged him; but they, like himself, had changed to wisps of mist in this farther void of ultimate blackness. Something else had gone on ahead—a larger wisp which now and then condensed into nameless approximations of form—and he thought that their progress had not been in a straight line, but rather along the alien curves and spirals of some ethereal vortex which obeyed laws unknown to the physics and mathematics of any conceivable cosmos. Eventually there had been a hint of vast, leaping shadows, of a monstrous, half-acoustic pulsing, and of the thin, monotonous piping of an unseen flute—but that was all. Gilman decided he had picked up that last conception from what he had read in the *Necronomicon* about the mindless entity Azathoth, which rules all time and space from a black throne at the center of Chaos.

When the blood was washed away the wrist wound proved very slight, and Gilman puzzled over the location of the two tiny punctures. It occurred to him that there was no blood on the bedspread where he had lain—which was very curious in view of the amount on his skin and cuff. Had he been sleepwalking within his room, and had the rat bitten him as he sat in some chair or paused in some less rational position? He looked in every corner for brownish drops or stains, but did not find any. He had better, he thought, sprinkle flour within the room as well as outside the door—though after all no further proof of his sleepwalking was needed. He knew he did walk—and the thing to do now was to stop it. He must ask Frank Elwood for help. This morning the strange pulls from space seemed lessened, though they were replaced by another sensation even more inexplicable. It was a vague, insistent impulse to fly away from his present situation, but held not a hint of the specific direction in which he wished to fly. As he picked up the strange spiky image on the table he thought the older northward pull grew a trifle stronger, but even so, it was wholly overruled by the newer and more bewildering urge.

He took the spiky image down to Elwood's room, steeling himself against the whines of the loom-fixer which welled up from the ground floor. Elwood was in, thank heaven, and appeared to be stirring about. There was time for a little conversation before leaving for breakfast and college; so Gilman hurriedly poured forth an account of his recent dreams and fears. His host was very sympathetic, and agreed that something ought to be done. He was shocked by his guest's drawn, haggard aspect, and noticed the queer, abnormal-looking sunburn which others had remarked during the past week. There was not much, though, that he could say. He had not seen Gilman on any sleepwalking expedition, and had no idea what the curious image could be. He had, though, heard the French-Canadian who lodged just under Gilman talking to Mazurewicz one evening. They were telling each other how badly they dreaded the coming of Walpurgis Night, now only a few days off; and were exchanging pitying comments about the poor, doomed young gentleman. Desrochers, the fellow under Gilman's room, had spoken of nocturnal footsteps shod and unshod, and of the violet light he saw one night when he had stolen fearfully up to peer through Gilman's keyhole. He had not dared to peer, he told Mazurewicz, after he had glimpsed that light through the cracks around the door. There had been soft talking, too—and as he began to describe it his voice had sunk to an inaudible whisper.

Elwood could not imagine what had set these superstitious creatures gossiping, but supposed their imaginations had been roused by Gilman's late hours and somnolent walking and talking on the one hand, and by the nearness of traditionally feared May Eve on the other hand. That Gilman talked in his sleep was plain, and it was obviously from Desrochers' keyhole-listenings that the delusive notion of the violet dream-light had got abroad. These simple people were quick to imagine they had seen any odd thing they had heard about. As for a plan of action—Gilman had better move down to Elwood's room and avoid sleeping alone. Elwood would, if awake, rouse him whenever he began to talk or rise in his sleep. Very soon, too, he must see the specialist. Meanwhile they would take the spiky image around to the various museums and to certain professors, seeking identification and stating that it had been found in a public rubbish-can. Also, Dombrowski must attend to the poisoning of those rats in the walls.

Braced up by Elwood's companionship, Gilman attended classes that day. Strange urges still tugged at him, but he could sidetrack them with considerable success. During a free period he showed the queer image to several professors, all of whom were intensely interested, though none of them could shed any light upon its nature or origin. That night he slept on a couch which Elwood had had the landlord bring to the second-story room, and for the first time in weeks was wholly free from disquieting dreams. But the feverishness still hung on, and the whines of the loom-fixer were an unnerving influence.

During the next few days Gilman enjoyed an almost perfect immunity from morbid manifestations. He had, Elwood said, showed no tendency to talk or rise in his sleep; and meanwhile the landlord was putting rat poison everywhere. The only disturbing element was the talk among the superstitious foreigners, whose imaginations had become highly excited. Mazurewicz was always trying to make him get a crucifix, and finally forced one upon him which he said had been blessed by the good Father Iwanicki. Desrochers, too, had something to say; in fact, he insisted that cautious steps had sounded in the now vacant room above him on the first and second nights of Gilman's absence from it. Paul Choynski thought he heard sounds in the halls and on the stairs at night, and claimed that his door had been softly tried, while Mrs. Dombrowski vowed she had seen Brown Jenkin for the first time since All-Hallows. But such naïve reports could mean very little, and Gilman let the cheap metal crucifix hang idly from a knob on his host's dresser.

For three days Gilman and Elwood canvassed the local museums in an effort to identify the strange spiky image, but always without success. In every quarter, however, interest was intense; for the utter alienage of the thing was a tremendous challenge to scientific curiosity. One of the small radiating arms was broken off and subjected to chemical analysis. Professor Ellery found platinum, iron and tellurium in the strange alloy; but mixed with these were at least three other apparent elements of high atomic weight which chemistry was absolutely powerless to classify. Not only did they fail to correspond with any known element, but they did not even fit the vacant places reserved for probable elements in the periodic system. The mystery remains unsolved to this day, though the image is on exhibition at the museum of Miskatonic University.

On the morning of April twenty-seventh a fresh rat-hole appeared in the room where Gilman was a guest, but Dombrowski tinned it up during the day. The poison was not having much effect, for scratchings and scurryings in the walls were virtually undiminished.

Elwood was out late that night, and Gilman waited up for him. He did not wish to go to sleep in a room alone—especially since he thought he had glimpsed in the evening twilight the repellent old woman whose image had become so horribly transferred to his dreams. He wondered who she was, and what had been near her rattling the tin can in a rubbish-heap at the mouth of a squalid courtyard. The crone had seemed to notice him and leer evilly at him—though perhaps this was merely his imagination.

The next day both youths felt very tired, and knew they would sleep like logs when night came. In the evening they drowsily discussed the mathematical studies which had so completely and perhaps harmfully engrossed Gilman, and speculated about the linkage with ancient magic and folklore which seemed so darkly probable. They spoke of old Keziah Mason, and Elwood agreed that Gilman had good scientific grounds for thinking she might have stumbled on strange and significant information. The hidden cults to which these witches belonged often guarded and handed down surprising secrets from elder, forgotten eons; and it was by no means impossible that Keziah had actually mastered the art of passing through dimensional gates. Tradition emphasizes the uselessness of material barriers in halting a witch's motions, and who can say what underlies the old tales of broomstick rides through the night?

Whether a modern student could ever gain similar powers from mathematical research alone was still to be seen. Success, Gilman added, might lead to dangerous and unthinkable situations; for who could foretell the conditions pervading an adjacent but normally inaccessible dimension? On the other hand, the picturesque possibilities were enormous. Time could not exist in certain belts of space, and by entering and remaining in such a belt one might preserve one's life and age indefinitely, never suffering organic metabolism or deterioration except for slight amounts incurred during visits to one's own or similar planets. One might, for example, pass into a timeless dimension and emerge at some remote period of the earth's history as young as before.

Whether anybody had ever managed to do this, one could hardly conjecture with any degree of authority. Old legends are hazy and ambiguous, and in historic times all attempts at crossing forbidden gaps seem complicated by strange and terrible alliances with beings and messengers from outside. There was the immemorial figure of the deputy or messenger of hidden and terrible powers—the "Black Man" of the witch-cult, and the "Nyarlathotep" of the *Necronomicon*. There was, too, the baffling problem of the lesser messengers or intermediaries—the quasi-animals and queer hybrids which legend depicts as witches' familiars. As Gilman and Elwood retired, too sleepy to argue further, they heard Joe Mazurewicz reel into the house half drunk, and shuddered at the desperate wildness of his whining prayers.

That night Gilman saw the violet light again. In his dreams he had heard a scratching and gnawing in the partitions, and thought that someone fumbled clumsily at the latch. Then he saw the old woman and the small furry thing advancing toward him over the carpeted floor. The beldame's face was alight with inhuman exultation, and the little yellow-toothed morbidity tittered mockingly as it pointed at the heavily sleeping form of Elwood on the other couch across the room. A paralysis of fear stifled all attempts to cry out. As once before, the hideous crone seized Gilman by the shoulders, yanking him out of bed and into empty space. Again the infinitude of the shrieking abysses flashed past him, but in another second he thought he was in a dark, muddy, unknown alley of foetid odors with the rotting walls of ancient houses towering up on every hand.

Ahead was the robed black man he had seen in the peaked space in the other dream, while from a lesser distance the old woman was beckoning and grimacing imperiously. Brown Jenkin was rubbing itself with a kind of affectionate playfulness around the ankles of the black man, which the deep mud largely concealed. There was a dark open doorway on the right, to which the black man silently pointed. Into this the grinning crone started, dragging Gilman after her by his pajama sleeves. There were evil-smelling staircases which creaked ominously, and on which the old woman seemed to radiate a faint violet light; and finally a door leading off a landing. The crone fumbled with the latch and pushed the door open, motioning to Gilman to wait, and disappearing inside the black aperture.

The youth's oversensitive ears caught a hideous strangled cry, and presently the beldame came out of the room bearing a small, senseless form which she thrust at the dreamer as if ordering him to carry it. The sight of this form, and the expression on its face, broke the spell. Still too dazed to cry out, he plunged recklessly down the noisome staircase and into the mud outside, halting only when seized and choked by the waiting black man. As consciousness departed he heard the faint, shrill tittering of the fanged, rat-like abnormality.

On the morning of the twenty-ninth Gilman awaked into a maelstrom of horror. The instant he opened his eyes he knew something was terribly wrong, for he was back in his old garret room with the slanting wall and ceiling, sprawled on the now unmade bed. His throat was aching inexplicably, and as he struggled to a sitting posture he saw with growing fright that his feet and pajama bottoms were brown with caked mud. For the moment his recollections were hopelessly hazy, but he knew at least that he must have been sleepwalking. Elwood had been lost too deeply in slumber to hear and stop him. On the floor were confused muddy prints, but oddly enough they did not extend all the way to the door. The more Gilman looked at them, the more peculiar they seemed; for in addition to those he could recognize as his there were some smaller, almost round markings—such as the legs of a chair or a table might make, except that most of them tended to be divided into halves. There were also some curious muddy rat-tracks leading out of a fresh hole and back into it again. Utter bewilderment and the fear of madness racked Gilman as he staggered to the door and saw that there were no muddy prints outside. The more he remembered of his hideous dream the more terrified he felt, and it added to his desperation to hear Joe Mazurewicz chanting mournfully two floors below.

Descending to Elwood's room he roused his still-sleeping host and began telling of how he had found himself, but Elwood could form no idea of what might really have happened. Where Gilman could have been, how he got back to his room without making tracks in the hall, and how the muddy, furniture-like prints came to be mixed with his in the garret chamber, were wholly beyond conjecture. Then there were those dark, livid marks on his throat, as if he had tried to strangle himself. He put his hands up to them, but found that they did not even approximately fit. While they were talking, Desrochers dropped in to say that he had heard a terrific clattering overhead in the dark small hours. No, there had been no one on the stairs after midnight, though just before midnight he had heard faint footfalls in the garret, and cautiously descending steps he did not like. It was, he added, a very bad time of year for Arkham. The young gentleman had better be sure to wear the crucifix Joe Mazurewicz had given him. Even the daytime was not safe, for after dawn there had been strange sounds in the house—especially a thin, childish wail hastily choked off.

Gilman mechanically attended classes that morning, but was wholly unable to fix his mind on his studies. A mood of hideous apprehension and expectancy had seized him, and he seemed to be awaiting the fall of some annihilating blow. At noon he lunched at the University Spa, picking up a paper from the next seat as he waited for dessert. But he never ate that dessert; for an item on the paper's first page left him limp, wild-eyed, and able only to pay his check and stagger back to Elwood's room.

There had been a strange kidnapping the night before in Orne's Gangway, and the two-year-old child of a clod-like laundry worker named Anastasia Wolejko had completely vanished from sight. The mother, it appeared, had feared the event for some time; but the reasons she assigned for her fear were so grotesque that no one took them seriously. She had, she said, seen Brown Jenkin about the place now and then ever since early in March, and knew from its grimaces and titterings that little Ladislas must be marked for sacrifice at the awful Sabbat on Walpurgis Night. She had asked her neighbor Mary Czanek to sleep in the room and try to protect the child, but Mary had not dared. She could not tell the police, for they never believed such things. Children had been taken that way every year since she could remember. And her friend Pete Stowacki would not help because he wanted the child out of the way anyhow.

But what threw Gilman into a cold perspiration was the report of a pair of revellers who had been walking past the mouth of the gangway just after midnight. They admitted they had been drunk, but both vowed they had seen a crazily dressed trio furtively entering the dark passageway. There had, they said, been a huge robed Negro, a little old woman in rags, and a young white man in his night-clothes. The old woman had been dragging the youth, while around the feet of the Negro a tame rat was rubbing and weaving in the brown mud.

Gilman sat in a daze all the afternoon, and Elwood—who had meanwhile seen the papers and formed terrible conjectures from them—found him thus when he came home. This time neither could doubt but that something hideously serious was closing in around them. Between the phantasms of nightmare and the realities of the objective world a monstrous and unthinkable relationship was crystallizing, and only stupendous vigilance could avert still more direful developments. Gilman must see a specialist sooner or later, but not just now, when all the papers were full of this kidnapping business.

Just what had really happened was maddeningly obscure, and for a moment both Gilman and Elwood exchanged whispered theories of the wildest kind. Had Gilman unconsciously succeeded better than he knew in his studies of space and its dimensions? Had he actually slipped outside our sphere to points unguessed and unimaginable? Where—if anywhere—had he been on those nights of daemoniac alienage? The roaring twilight abysses—the green hillside—the blistering terrace—the pulls from the stars—the ultimate black vortex—the black man—the muddy alley and the stairs—the old witch and the fanged, furry horror—the wrist-wound—the unexplained image—the muddy feet—the throat-marks—the tales and fears of the superstitious foreigners—what did all this mean? To what extent could the laws of sanity apply to such a case?

There was no sleep for either of them that night, but next day they both cut classes and drowsed. This was April thirtieth, and with the dusk would come the hellish Sabbat-time which all the foreigners and the superstitious old folk feared. Mazurewicz came home at six o'clock and said people at the mill were whispering that the Walpurgis-revels would be held in the dark ravine beyond Meadow Hill where the old white stone stands in a place queerly devoid of all plant life. Some of them had even told the police and advised them to look there for the missing Wolejko child, but they did not believe anything would be done. Joe insisted that the poor young gentleman wear his nickel-chained crucifix, and Gilman put it on and dropped it inside his shirt to humor the fellow.

Late at night the two youths sat drowsing in their chairs, lulled by the praying of the loom-fixer on the floor below. Gilman listened as he nodded, his preternaturally sharpened hearing seeming to strain for some subtle, dreaded murmur beyond the noises in the ancient house. Unwholesome recollections of things in the *Necronomicon* and the Black Book welled up, and he found himself swaying to infandous rhythms said to pertain to the blackest ceremonies of the Sabbat and to have an origin outside the time and space we comprehend.

Presently he realized what he was listening for—the hellish chant of the celebrants in the distant black valley. How did he know so much about what they expected? How did he know the time when Nahab and her acolyte were due to bear the brimming bowl which would follow the black cock and the black goat? He saw that Elwood had dropped asleep, and tried to call out and waken him. Something, however, closed his throat. He was not his own master. Had he signed the black man's book after all?

Then his fevered, abnormal hearing caught the distant, windborne notes. Over miles of hill and field and valley they came, but he recognized them none the less. The fires must be lit, and the dancers must be starting in. How could be keep himself from going? What was it that had enmeshed him? Mathematics—folklore—the house—old Keziah—Brown Jenkin ... and now he saw that there was a fresh rat-hole in the wall near his couch. Above the distant chanting and the nearer praying of Joe Mazurewicz came another sound—a stealthy, determined scratching in the partitions. He hoped the electric lights would not go out. Then he saw the fanged, bearded little face in the rat-hole—the accursed little face which he at last realized bore such a shocking, mocking resemblance to old Keziah's—and heard the faint fumbling at the door.

The screaming twilight abysses flashed before him, and he felt himself helpless in the formless grasp of the iridescent bubble-congeries. Ahead raced the small, kaleidoscopic polyhedron and all through the churning void there was a heightening and acceleration of the vague tonal pattern which seemed to foreshadow some unutterable and unendurable climax. He seemed to know what was coming—the monstrous burst of Walpurgis-rhythm in whose cosmic timbre would be concentrated all the primal, ultimate space-time seethings which lie behind the massed spheres of matter and sometimes break forth in measured reverberations that penetrate faintly to every layer of entity and give hideous significance throughout the worlds to certain dreaded periods.

But all this vanished in a second. He was again in the cramped, violet-litten peaked space with the slanting floor, the low case of ancient books, the bench and table, the queer objects, and the triangular gulf at one side. On the table lay a small white figure—an infant boy, unclothed and unconscious—while on the other side stood the monstrous, leering old woman with a gleaming, grotesque-hafted knife in her right hand, and a queerly proportioned pale metal bowl covered with curiously chased designs and having delicate lateral handles in her left. She was intoning some croaking ritual in a language which Gilman could not understand, but which seemed like something guardedly quoted in the *Necronomicon*.

As the scene grew clearer he saw the ancient crone bend forward and extend the empty bowl across the table—and unable to control his own emotions, he reached far forward and took it in both hands, noticing as he did so its comparative lightness. At the same moment the disgusting form of Brown Jenkin scrambled up over the brink of the triangular black gulf on his left. The crone now motioned him to hold the bowl in a certain position while she raised the huge, grotesque knife above the small white victim as high as her right hand could reach. The fanged, furry thing began tittering a continuation of the unknown ritual, while the witch croaked loathsome responses. Gilman felt a gnawing poignant abhorrence shoot through his mental and emotional paralysis, and the light metal bowl shook in his grasp. A second later the downward motion of the knife broke the spell completely, and he dropped the bowl with a resounding bell-like clangor while his hands darted out frantically to stop the monstrous deed.

In an instant he had edged up the slanting floor around the end of the table and wrenched the knife from the old woman's claws, sending it clattering over the brink of the narrow triangular gulf. In another instant, however, matters were reversed; for those murderous claws had locked themselves tightly around his own throat, while the wrinkled face was twisted with insane fury. He felt the chain of the cheap crucifix grinding into his neck, and in his peril wondered how the sight of the object itself would affect the evil creature. Her strength was altogether superhuman, but as she continued her choking he reached feebly in his shirt and drew out the metal symbol, snapping the chain and pulling it free.

At sight of the device the witch seemed struck with panic, and her grip relaxed long enough to give Gilman a chance to break it entirely. He pulled the steel-like claws from his neck, and would have dragged the beldame over the edge of the gulf had not the claws received a fresh access of strength and closed in again. This time he resolved to reply in kind, and his own hands reached out for the creature's throat. Before she saw what he was doing he had the chain of the crucifix twisted about her neck, and a moment later he had tightened it enough to cut off her breath. During her last struggle he felt something bite at his ankle, and saw that Brown Jenkin had come to her aid. With one savage kick he sent the morbidity over the edge of the gulf and heard it whimper on some level far below.

Whether he had killed the ancient crone he did not know, but he let her rest on the floor where she had fallen. Then, as he turned away, he saw on the table a sight which nearly snapped the last thread of his reason. Brown Jenkin, tough of sinew and with four tiny hands of daemoniac dexterity, had been busy while the witch was throttling him, and his efforts had been in vain. What he had prevented the knife from doing to the victim's chest, the yellow fangs of the furry blasphemy had done to a wrist—and the bowl so lately on the floor stood full beside the small lifeless body.

In his dream-delirium Gilman heard the hellish alien-rhythmed chant of the Sabbat coming from an infinite distance, and knew the black man must be there. Confused memories mixed themselves with his mathematics, and he believed his subconscious mind held the *angles* which he needed to guide him back to the normal world alone and unaided for the first time. He felt sure he was in the immemorially sealed loft above his own room, but whether he could ever escape through the slanting floor or the long-stooped egress he doubted greatly. Besides, would not an escape from a dream-loft bring him merely into a dream-house—an abnormal projection of the actual place he sought? He was wholly bewildered as to the relation betwixt dream and reality in all his experiences.

The passage through the vague abysses would be frightful, for the Walpurgis-rhythm would be vibrating, and at last he would have to hear the hitherto-veiled cosmic pulsing which he so mortally dreaded. Even now he could detect a low, monstrous shaking whose tempo he suspected all too well. At Sabbat-time it always mounted and reached through to worlds to summon the initiate to nameless rites. Half the chants of the Sabbat were patterned on this faintly overheard pulsing which no earthly ear could endure in its unveiled spatial fullness. Gilman wondered, too, whether he could trust his instincts to take him back to the right part of space. How could he be sure he would not land on that green-litten hillside of a far planet, on the tessellated terrace above the city of tentacled monsters somewhere beyond the galaxy or in the spiral black vortices of that ultimate void of Chaos where reigns the mindless demon-sultan Azathoth?

Just before he made the plunge the violet light went out and left him in utter blackness. The witch—old Keziah—Nahab—that must have meant her death. And mixed with the distant chant of the Sabbat and the whimpers of Brown Jenkin in the gulf below he thought he heard another and wilder whine from unknown depths. Joe Mazurewicz—the prayers against the Crawling Chaos now turning to an inexplicably triumphant shriek—words of sardonic actuality impinging on vortices of febrile dream—*Iä!* Shub-Niggurath! The Goat with a Thousand Young ....

They found Gilman on the floor of his queerly angled old garret room long before dawn, for the terrible cry had brought Desrochers and Choynski and Dombrowski and Mazurewicz at once, and had even wakened the soundly sleeping Elwood in his chair. He was alive, and with open, staring eyes, but seemed largely unconscious. On his throat were the marks of murderous hands, and on his left ankle was a distressing rat-bite. His clothing was badly rumpled, and Joe's crucifix was missing. Elwood trembled, afraid even to speculate what new form his friend's sleepwalking had taken. Mazurewicz seemed half dazed because of a "sign" he said he had had in response to his prayers, and he crossed himself frantically when the squealing and whimpering of a rat sounded from beyond the slanting partition.

When the dreamer was settled on his couch in Elwood's room they sent for Doctor Malkowski—a local practitioner who would repeat no tales where they might prove embarrassing—and he gave Gilman two hypodermic injections which caused him to relax in something like natural drowsiness. During the day the patient regained consciousness at times and whispered this newest dream disjointedly to Elwood. It was a painful process, and at its very start brought out a fresh and disconcerting fact.

Gilman—whose ears had so lately possessed an abnormal sensitiveness—was now stone-deaf. Doctor Malkowski, summoned again in haste, told Elwood that both eardrums were ruptured, as if by the impact of some stupendous sound intense beyond all human conception or endurance. How such a sound could have been heard in the last few hours without arousing all the Miskatonic Valley was more than the honest physician could say.

Elwood wrote his part of the colloquy on paper, so that a fairly easy communication was maintained. Neither knew what to make of the whole chaotic business, and decided it would be better if they thought as little as possible about it. Both, though, agreed that they must leave this ancient and accursed house as soon as it could be arranged. Evening papers spoke of a police raid on some curious revellers in a ravine beyond Meadow Hill just before dawn, and mentioned that the white stone there was an object of age-long superstitious regard. Nobody had been caught, but among the scattering fugitives had been glimpsed a huge Negro. In another column it was stated that no trace of the missing child Ladislas Wolejko had been found.

The crowning horror came that very night. Elwood will never forget it, and was forced to stay out of college the rest of the term because of the resulting nervous breakdown. He had thought he heard rats in the partition all the evening, but paid little attention to them. Then, long after both he and Gilman had retired, the atrocious shrieking began. Elwood jumped up, turned on the lights and rushed over to his guest's couch. The occupant was emitting sounds of veritably inhuman nature, as if racked by some torment beyond description. He was writhing under the bedclothes, and a great red stain was beginning to appear on the blankets.

Elwood scarcely dared to touch him, but gradually the screaming and writhing subsided. By this time Dombrowski, Choynski, Desrochers, Mazurewicz, and the top-floor lodger were all crowding into the doorway, and the landlord had sent his wife back to telephone for Doctor Malkowski. Everybody shrieked when a large rat-like form suddenly jumped out from beneath the ensanguined bedclothes and scuttled across the floor to a fresh, open hole close by. When the doctor arrived and began to pull down those frightful covers Walter Gilman was dead.

It would be barbarous to do more than suggest what had killed Gilman. There had been virtually a tunnel through his body—something had eaten his heart out. Dombrowski, frantic at the failure of his rat-poisoning efforts, cast aside all thought of his leases and within a week had moved with all his older lodgers to a dingy but less ancient house in Walnut Street. The worst thing for a while was keeping Joe Mazurewicz quiet, for the brooding loom-fixer would never stay sober, and was constantly whining and muttering about spectral and terrible things.

It seems that on that last hideous night Joe had stooped to look at the crimson rat-tracks which led from Gilman's couch to the near-by hole. On the carpet they were very indistinct, but a piece of open flooring intervened between the carpet's edge and the baseboard. There Mazurewicz had found something monstrous—or thought he had, for no one else could quite agree with him despite the undeniable queerness of the prints. The tracks on the flooring were certainly vastly unlike the average prints of a rat but even

Choynski and Desrochers would not admit that they were like the prints of four tiny human hands.

The house was never rented again. As soon as Dombrowski left it the pall of its final desolation began to descend, for people shunned it both on account of its old reputation and because of the new foetid odor. Perhaps the ex-landlord's rat poison had worked after all, for not long after his departure the place became a neighborhood nuisance. Health officials traced the smell to the closed spaces above and beside the eastern garret room, and agreed that the number of dead rats must be enormous. They decided, however, that it was not worth their while to hew open and disinfect the long-sealed spaces, for the foetor would soon be over, and the locality was not one which encouraged fastidious standards. Indeed, there were always vague local tales of unexplained stenches upstairs in the Witch House just after May-Eve and Hallowmass. The neighbors acquiesced in the inertia—but the foetor none the less formed an additional count against the place. Toward the last the house was condemned as a habitation by the building inspector.

Gilman's dreams and their attendant circumstances have never been explained. Elwood, whose thoughts on the entire episode are sometimes almost maddening, came back to college the next autumn and was graduated in the following June. He found the spectral gossip of the town much diminished, and it is indeed a fact that—notwithstanding certain reports of a ghostly tittering in the deserted house which lasted almost as long as that edifice itself—no fresh appearances either of Old Keziah or of Brown Jenkin have been muttered of since Gilman's death. It is rather fortunate that Elwood was not in Arkham in that later year when certain events abruptly renewed the local whisperers about elder horrors. Of course he heard about the matter afterward and suffered untold torments of black and bewildered speculation, but even that was not as bad as actual nearness and several possible sights would have been.

In March, 1931, a gale wrecked the roof and great chimney of the vacant Witch House, so that a chaos of crumbling bricks, blackened, moss-grown shingles, and rotting planks and timbers crashed down into the loft and broke through the floor beneath. The whole attic story was choked with debris from above, but no one took the trouble to touch the mess before the inevitable razing of the decrepit structure. The ultimate step came in the following December, and it was when Gilman's old room was cleared out by reluctant, apprehensive workmen that the gossip began.

Among the rubbish which had crashed through the ancient slanting ceiling were several things which made the workmen pause and call in the police. Later the police in turn called in the coroner and several professors from the university. There were bones—badly crushed and splintered, but clearly recognizable as human—whose manifestly modern date conflicted puzzlingly with the remote period at which their only possible lurking place, the low, slant-floored loft overhead, had supposedly been sealed from all human access. The coroner's physician decided that some belonged to a small child, while certain others—found mixed with shreds of rotten brownish cloth—belonged to a rather undersized, bent female of advanced years. Careful sifting of debris also disclosed many tiny bones of rats caught in the collapse, as well as older rat bones gnawed by small fangs in a fashion now and then highly productive of controversy and reflection.

Other objects found included the mangled fragments of many books and papers, together with a yellowish dust left from the total disintegration of still older books and papers. All, without exception, appeared to deal with black magic in its most advanced and horrible forms; and the evidently recent date of certain items is still a mystery as unsolved as that of the modern human bones. An even greater mystery is the absolute homogeneity of the crabbed, archaic writing found on a wide range of papers whose conditions and watermarks suggest age differences of at least one hundred fifty to two hundred years. To some, though, the greatest mystery of all is the variety of utterly inexplicable objects—objects whose shapes, materials, types of workmanship, and purposes baffle all conjecture—found scattered amidst the wreckage in evidently diverse states of injury. One of these things—which excited several Miskatonic professors profoundly—is a badly damaged monstrosity plainly resembling the strange image which Gilman gave to the college museum, save that it is large, wrought of some peculiar bluish stone instead of metal, and possessed of a singularly angled pedestal with undecipherable hieroglyphics.

Archaeologists and anthropologists are still trying to explain the bizarre designs chased on a crushed bowl of light metal whose inner side bore ominous brownish stains when found. Foreigners and credulous grandmothers are equally garrulous about the modern nickel crucifix with broken chain mixed in the rubbish and shiveringly identified by Joe Mazurewicz as that which he had given poor Gilman many years before. Some believe this crucifix was dragged up to the sealed loft by rats, while others think it must have been on the floor in some corner of Gilman's old room at the time. Still others, including Joe himself, have theories too wild and fantastic for sober credence.

When the slanting wall of Gilman's room was torn out, the once-sealed triangular space between that partition and the house's north wall was found to contain much less structural debris, even in proportion to its size, than the room itself, though it had a ghastly layer of older materials which paralyzed the wreckers with horror. In brief, the floor was a veritable ossuary of the bones of small children—some fairly modern, but others extending back in infinite gradations to a period so remote that crumbling was almost complete.

On this deep bony layer rested a knife of great size, obvious antiquity, and grotesque, ornate, and exotic design—above which the debris was piled.

In the midst of this debris, wedged between a fallen plank and a cluster of cemented bricks from the ruined chimney, was an object destined to cause more bafflement, veiled fright, and openly superstitious talk in Arkham than anything else discovered in the haunted and accursed building. This object was the partly crushed skeleton of a huge diseased rat, whose abnormalities of form are still a topic of debate and source of singular reticence among the members of Miskatonic's department of comparative anatomy. Very little concerning this skeleton has leaked out, but the workmen who found it whisper in shocked tones about the long, brownish hairs with which it was associated.

The bones of the tiny paws, it is rumored, imply prehensile characteristics more typical of a diminutive monkey than of a rat, while the small skull with its savage yellow fangs is of the utmost anomalousness, appearing from certain angles like a miniature, monstrously degraded parody of a human skull. The workmen crossed themselves in fright when they came upon this blasphemy, but later burned candles of gratitude in St. Stanislaus' Church because of the shrill, ghostly tittering they felt they would never hear again.

EVER read a story that did not live up to the hype of its title? This, I think, is because a title is an implicit story in its own right, one in competition with the longer, explicit one that follows it. Either one may win. Once I was telling Gahan Wilson about a story I wanted to get someone (the redoubtable Charles Hoffman, as it turned out) to write for *Shudder Stories*, "Plaything for the Chortling Fiend." Gahan quipped, "With a title like that, who needs a story?" Though Hoffman's story fully justified the title, Gahan was right.

Though "The Haunter of the Dark" is a powerful story in its own right, I believe it gains power from the fact that it is pregnant with several other titles it mentions, which are evocative implicit stories. There are two sets of these. First, we are told of five horror tales young Blake had composed before his obsession overtook him. They sound like parodies of Lovecraft's own story titles, but they are just as characteristic of the young Bloch's titles. In fact, three of them are based directly on Bloch's stories. "The Stairs in the Crypt" seems to be based on Bloch's "The Grinning Ghoul"; "The Feaster from the Stars" would be "The Shambler from the Stars"; and "The Burrower Beneath" reflects "The Blasphemy Beneath", a story Bloch had shown Lovecraft, but which was never published and does not survive as far as we know. The second set of titles is that of the rotting volumes Blake discovered on the shelves of the Starry Wisdom Church.

There is a third set, just anticipated. The veiled reference to the lost story "The Blasphemy Beneath" opens the door to a whole catalog of Blochian pseudobibliographic inventions that never escaped from the lab. Some of the stories Bloch had drafted and mailed to his mentor were "The Grave", "The Madness of Lucian Grey", "Nocturne Macabre", "Spawn of the Elder Pits", "The Fog", "The Touch of a Corpse", "The Merman", "The Fountain of Youth", and "Sons of the Serpent." Lovecraft also mentions a couple of grimoires Bloch had invented: Mazonides' *Black Spell of Saboth* and Petrus Averonius' *Compendium Daemonum*. Elsewhere in the Lovecraft-Bloch letters we learn that Lovecraft had suggested several possible titles for Bloch's story soon published as "The Feast in the Abbey." This was one of Lovecraft's coinages, but others were "Rimmon Abbey", "The Remnant", "Shadow Priory", and "The Abbey of Shadow." Shouldn't these be added to the list of titles, implicit stories, in the Robert Blake bibliography?

"The Haunter of the Dark" appeared originally in *Weird Tales* of December 1935.

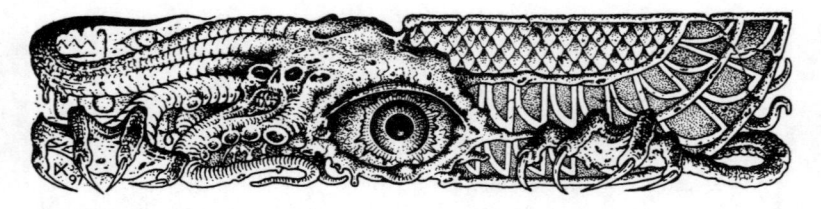

The Haunter of the Dark

by H. P. Lovecraft

(Dedicated to Robert Bloch)

> I have seen the dark universe yawning
> Where the dark planets roll without aim—
> Where they roll in their horror unheeded,
> Without knowledge or lustre or name.
>
> —Nemesis

CAUTIOUS investigators will hesitate to challenge the common belief that Robert Blake was killed by lightning, or by some profound nervous shock derived from an electrical discharge. It is true that the window he faced was unbroken, but nature has shown herself capable of many freakish performances. The expression on his face may easily have arisen from some obscure muscular source unrelated to anything he saw, while the entries in his diary are clearly the result of a fantastic imagination aroused by certain local superstitions and by certain old matters he had uncovered. As for the anomalous conditions at the deserted church of Federal Hill—the shrewd analyst is not slow in attributing them to some charlatanry, conscious or unconscious, with at least some of which Blake was secretly connected.

For after all, the victim was a writer and painter wholly devoted to the field of myth, dream, terror, and superstition, and avid in his quest for scenes and effects of a bizarre, spectral sort. His earlier stay in the city—a visit to a strange old man as deeply given to occult and forbidden lore as he—had ended amidst death and flame, and it must have been some morbid instinct which drew him back from his home in Milwaukee. He may have known of the old stories despite his statements to the contrary in the diary, and his death may have nipped in the bud some stupendous hoax destined to have a literary reflection.

Among those, however, who have examined and correlated all this evidence, there remain several who cling to less rational and commonplace theories. They are inclined to take much of Blake's diary at its face value, and point significantly to certain facts such as the undoubted genuineness of the old church record, the verified existence of the disliked and unorthodox Starry Wisdom sect prior to 1877, the recorded disappearance of an inquisitive reporter named Edwin M. Lillibridge in 1893, and—above all—the look of monstrous, transfiguring fear on the face of the young writer when he died. It was one of these believers who, moved to fanatical extremes, threw into the bay the curiously angled stone and its strangely adorned metal box found in the old church steeple—the black windowless steeple, and not the tower where Blake's diary said those things originally were. Though widely censured both officially and unofficially, this man—a reputable physician with a taste for odd folklore—averred that he had rid the earth of something too dangerous to rest upon it.

Between these two schools of opinion the reader must judge for himself. The papers have given the tangible details from a skeptical angle, leaving for others the drawing of the picture as Robert Blake saw it—or thought he saw it—or pretended to see it. Now, studying the diary closely, dispassionately, and at leisure, let us summarize the dark chain of events from the expressed point of view of their chief actor.

Young Blake returned to Providence in the winter of 1934-5, taking the upper floor of a venerable dwelling in a grassy court off College Street—on the crest of the great eastward hill near the Brown University campus and behind the marble John Hay Library. It was a cozy and fascinating place, in a little garden oasis of village-like antiquity where huge, friendly cats sunned themselves atop a convenient shed. The square Georgian house had a monitor roof, classic doorway with fan carving, small-paned windows, and all the other earmarks of early nineteenth-century workmanship. Inside were six-paneled doors, wide floorboards, a curving colonial staircase, white Aram-period mantels, and a rear set of rooms three steps below the general level.

Blake's study, a large southwest chamber, overlooked the front garden on one side, while its west windows—before one of which he had his desk—faced off from the brow of the hill and commanded a splendid view of the lower town's outspread roofs and of the mystical sunsets that flamed behind them. On the far horizon were the open countryside's purple slopes. Against these, some two miles away, rose the spectral hump of Federal Hill, bristling with huddled roofs and steeples whose remote outlines wavered mysteriously, taking fantastic forms as the smoke of the city swirled up and enmeshed them. Blake had a curious sense that he was looking upon some unknown, ethereal world which might or might not vanish in dream if ever he tried to seek it out and enter it in person.

Having sent home for most of his books, Blake bought some antique furniture suitable to his quarters and settled down to write and paint—living alone, and attending to the simple housework himself. His studio was in a north attic room, where the panes of the monitor roof furnished admirable lighting. During that first winter he produced five of his best-known short stories—"The Burrower Beneath", "The Stairs in the Crypt", "Shaggai", "In the Vale of Pnath", and "The Feaster from the Stars"—and painted seven canvases—studies of nameless, unhuman monsters, and profoundly alien, non-terrestrial landscapes.

At sunset he would often sit at his desk and gaze dreamily off at the outspread west—the dark towers of Memorial Hall just below, the Georgian courthouse belfry, the lofty pinnacles of the downtown section, and that shimmering, spire-crowned mound in the distance whose unknown streets and labyrinthine gables so potently provoked his fancy. From his few local acquaintances he learned that the far-off slope was a vast Italian quarter, though most of the houses were remnants of older Yankee and Irish days. Now and then he would train his field-glasses on that spectral, unreachable world beyond the curling smoke, picking out individual roofs and chimneys and steeples, and speculating upon the bizarre and curious mysteries they might house. Even with optical aid Federal Hill seemed somehow alien, half fabulous, and linked to the unreal, intangible marvels of Blake's own tales and pictures. The feeling would persist long after the hill had faded into the violet, lamp-starred twilight, and the courthouse floodlights and the red Industrial Trust beacon had blazed up to make the night grotesque.

Of all the distant objects on Federal Hill, a certain huge, dark church most fascinated Blake. It stood out with especial distinctness at certain hours of the day, and at sunset the great tower and tapering steeple loomed blackly against the flaming sky. It seemed to rest on especially high ground, for the grimy façade, and the obliquely seen north side with sloping roof and the tops of great pointed windows, rose boldly above the tangle of surrounding ridgepoles and chimney-pots. Peculiarly grim and austere, it appeared to be built of stone, stained and weathered with the smoke and storms of a century and more. The style, so far as the glass could show, was that earliest experimental form of Gothic revival which preceded the stately Upjohn period and held over some of the outlines and proportions of the Georgian age. Perhaps it was reared around 1810 or 1815.

As months passed, Blake watched the far-off, forbidding structure with an oddly mounting interest. Since the vast windows were never lighted, he knew that it must be vacant. The longer he watched, the more his imagination worked, till at length he began to fancy curious things. He believed that a vague, singular aura of desolation hovered over the place, so that even the pigeons and swallows shunned its smoky eaves. Around other towers and belfries his glass would reveal great flocks of birds, but here they never rested. At least, that is what he thought and set down in his diary. He pointed the place out to several friends, but none of them had even been on Federal Hill or possessed the faintest notion of what the church was or had been.

In the spring a deep restlessness gripped Blake. He had begun his long-planned novel—based on a supposed survival of the witch-cult in Maine—but was strangely unable to make progress with it. More and more he would sit at his westward window and gaze at the distant hill and the black, frowning steeple shunned by the birds. When the delicate leaves came out on the garden boughs the world was filled with a new beauty, but Blake's restlessness was merely increased. It was then that he first thought of crossing the city and climbing bodily up that fabulous slope into the smoke-wreathed world of dream.

Late in April, just before the eon-shadowed Walpurgis time, Blake made his first trip into the unknown. Plodding through the endless downtown streets and the bleak, decayed squares beyond, he came finally upon the ascending avenue of century-worn steps, sagging Doric porches, and blear-paneled cupolas which he felt must lead up to the long-known, unreachable world beyond the mists. There were dingy blue and white street signs which meant nothing to him, and presently he noted the strange, dark faces of the drifting crowds, and the foreign signs over curious shops in brown, decade-weathered buildings. Nowhere could he find any of the objects he had seen from afar; so that once more he half fancied that the Federal Hill of that distant view was a dream-world never to be trod by living human feet.

Now and then a battered church façade or crumbling spire came in sight, but never the blackened pile that he sought. When he asked a shopkeeper about a great stone church the man smiled and shook his head, though he spoke English freely. As Blake climbed higher, the region seemed stranger and stranger, with bewildering mazes of brooding brown alleys leading eternally off to the south. He crossed two or three broad avenues, and once thought he glimpsed a familiar tower. Again he asked a merchant about the massive church of stone, and this time he could have sworn that the plea of ignorance was feigned. The dark man's face had a look of fear which he tried to hide, and Blake saw him make a curious sign with his right hand.

Then suddenly a black spire stood out against the cloudy sky on his left, above the tiers of brown roofs lining the tangled southerly alleys. Blake knew at once what it was, and plunged toward it through the squalid, unpaved lanes that climbed from the avenue. Twice he lost his way, but he somehow dared not ask any of the patriarchs or housewives who sat on their doorsteps, or any of the children who shouted and played in the mud of the shadowy lanes.

At last he saw the tower plain against the southwest, and a huge stone bulk rose darkly at the end of an alley. Presently he stood in a windswept open square, quaintly cobblestoned, with a high bank wall on the farther side. This was the end of his quest, for upon the wide, iron-railed, weed-grown plateau which the wall supported—a separate, lesser world raised fully six feet above the surrounding streets—there stood a grim, titan bulk whose identity, despite Blake's new perspective, was beyond dispute.

The vacant church was in a state of great decrepitude. Some of the high stone buttresses had fallen, and several delicate finials lay half lost among the brown, neglected weeds and grasses. The sooty Gothic windows were largely unbroken, though many of the stone mullions were missing. Blake wondered how the obscurely painted panes could have survived so well, in view of the known habits of small boys the world over. The massive doors were intact and tightly closed. Around the top of the bank wall, fully enclosing the grounds, was a rusty iron fence whose gate—at the head of a flight of steps from the square—was visibly padlocked. The path from the gate to the building was completely overgrown. Desolation and decay hung like a pall above the place, and in the birdless eaves and black, ivyless walls Blake felt a touch of the dimly sinister beyond his power to define.

There were very few people in the square, but Blake saw a policeman at the northerly end and approached him with questions about the church. He was a great wholesome Irishman, and it seemed odd that he would do little more than make the sign of the cross and mutter that people never spoke of that building. When Blake pressed him he said very hurriedly that the Italian priests warned everybody against it, vowing that a monstrous evil had once dwelt there and left its mark. He himself had heard dark whispers of it from his father, who recalled certain sounds and rumors from his boyhood.

There had been a bad sect there in the old days—an outlaw sect that called up awful things from some unknown gulf of night. It had taken a good priest to exorcise what had come, though there had been those who said that merely the light could do it. If Father O'Malley were alive there would be many the thing he could tell. But now there was nothing to do but let it alone. It hurt nobody now, and those that owned it were dead or far away. They had run away like rats after the threatening talk in '77, when people began to mind the way folks vanished now and then in the neighborhood. Some day the city would step in and take the property for lack of heirs, but little good would come of anybody's touching it. Better it be left alone for the years to topple, lest things be stirred that ought to rest for ever in their black abyss.

After the policeman had gone Blake stood staring at the sullen steepled pile. It excited him to find that the structure seemed as sinister to others as to him, and he wondered what grain of truth might lie behind the old tales the bluecoat had repeated. Probably they were mere legends evoked by the evil look of the place, but even so, they were like a strange coming to life of one of his own stories.

The afternoon sun came out from behind dispersing clouds, but seemed unable to light up the stained, sooty walls of the old temple that towered on its high plateau. It was odd that the green of spring had not touched the brown, withered growths in the raised, iron-fenced yard. Blake found himself edging nearer the raised area and examining the bank wall and rusted fence for possible avenues of ingress. There was a terrible lure about the blackened fane which was not to be resisted. The fence had no opening near the steps, but around on the north side were some missing bars. He could go up the steps and walk around on the narrow coping outside the fence till he came to the gap. If the people feared the place so wildly, he would encounter no interference.

He was on the embankment and almost inside the fence before anyone noticed him. Then, looking down, he saw the few people in the square edging away and making the same sign with their right hands that the shopkeeper in the avenue had made. Several windows were slammed down, and a fat woman darted into the street and pulled some small children inside a rickety, unpainted house. The gap in the fence was very easy to pass through, and before long Blake found himself wading amidst the rotting, tangled growths of the deserted yard. Here and there the worn stump of a headstone told him that there had once been burials in this field, but that, he saw, must have been very long ago. The sheer bulk of the church was oppressive now that he was close to it, but he conquered his mood and approached to try the three great doors in the façade. All were securely locked, so he began a circuit of the Cyclopean building in quest of some minor and more penetrable opening. Even then he could not be sure that he wished to enter that haunt of desertion and shadow, yet the pull of its strangeness dragged him on automatically.

A yawning and unprotected cellar window in the rear furnished the needed aperture. Peering in, Blake saw a subterrene gulf of cobwebs and dust faintly litten by the western sun's filtered rays. Debris, old barrels, and ruined boxes and furniture of numerous sorts met his eye, though over everything lay a shroud of dust which softened all sharp outlines. The rusted remains of a hot-air furnace showed that the building had been used and kept in shape as late as mid-Victorian times.

Acting almost without conscious initiative, Blake crawled through the window and let himself down to the dust-carpeted and debris-strewn concrete floor. The vaulted cellar was a vast one, without partitions; and in a corner far to the right, amid dense shadows, he saw a black archway evidently leading upstairs. He felt a peculiar sense of oppression at being actually within the great spectral building, but kept it in check as he cautiously scouted about—finding a still-intact barrel amid the dust, and rolling it over to the open window to provide for his exit. Then, bracing himself, he crossed the wide, cobweb-festooned space toward the arch. Half choked with the omnipresent dust, and covered with ghostly gossamer fibers, he reached and began to climb the worn stone steps which rose into the darkness. He had no light, but groped carefully with his hands. After a sharp turn he felt a closed door ahead, and a little fumbling revealed its ancient latch. It opened inward, and beyond it he saw a dimly illumined corridor with worm-eaten paneling.

Once on the ground floor, Blake began exploring in a rapid fashion. All the inner doors were unlocked, so that he freely passed from room to room. The colossal nave was an almost eldritch place with its drifts and mountains of dust over box pews, altar, hourglass pulpit, and sounding board, and its titanic ropes of cobweb stretching among the pointed arches of the gallery and entwining the clustered Gothic columns. Over all this hushed desolation played a hideous leaden light as the declining afternoon sun sent its rays through the strange, half-blackened panes of the great apsidal windows.

The paintings on those windows were so obscured by soot that Blake could scarcely decipher what they had represented, but from the little he could make out he did not like them. The designs were largely conventional, and his knowledge of obscure symbolism told him much concerning some of the ancient patterns. The few saints depicted bore expressions distinctly open to criticism, while one of the windows seemed to show merely a dark space with spirals of curious luminosity scattered about in it. Turning away from the windows, Blake noticed that the cobwebbed cross above the altar was not of the ordinary kind, but resembled the primordial ankh or crux ansata of shadowy Egypt.

In a rear vestry room beside the apse Blake found a rotting desk and ceiling-high shelves of mildewed, disintegrating books. Here for the first time he received a positive shock of objective horror, for the titles of those books told him much. They were the black, forbidden things which most sane people have never even heard of, or have heard of only in furtive, timorous whispers; the banned and dreaded repositories of equivocal secrets and immemorial formulae which have trickled down the stream of time from the days of man's youth, and the dim, fabulous days before man was. He had himself read many of them—a Latin version of the abhorred *Necronomicon*, the sinister *Liber Ivonis*, the infamous *Cultes des Goules* of Comte d'Erlette, the *Unaussprechlichen Kulten* of von Junzt, and old Ludvig Prinn's hellish *De Vermis Mysteriis*. But there were others he had known merely by reputation or not at all—the *Pnakotic Manuscripts*, the *Book of Dzyan*, and a crumbling volume in wholly unidentifiable characters yet with certain symbols and diagrams shudderingly recognizable to the occult student. Clearly, the lingering local rumors had not lied. This place had once been the seat of an evil older than mankind and wider than the known universe.

In the ruined desk was a small leather-bound record-book filled with entries in some odd cryptographic medium. The manuscript writing consisted of the common traditional symbols used today in astronomy and anciently in alchemy, astrology, and other dubious arts—the devices of the sun, moon, planets, aspects, and zodiacal signs—here massed in solid pages of text, with divisions and paragraphings suggesting that each symbol answered to some alphabetical letter.

In the hope of later solving the cryptogram, Blake bore off this volume in his coat pocket. Many of the great tomes on the shelves fascinated him unutterably, and he felt tempted to borrow them at some later time. He wondered how they could have remained undisturbed so long. Was he the first to conquer the clutching, pervasive fear which had for nearly sixty years protected this deserted place from visitors?

Having now thoroughly explored the ground floor, Blake plowed again through the dust of the spectral nave to the front vestibule, where he had seen a door and staircase presumably leading up to the blackened tower and steeple—objects so long familiar to him at a distance. The ascent was a choking experience, for dust lay thick, while the spiders had done their worst in this constricted place. The staircase was a spiral with high, narrow wooden treads, and now and then Blake passed a clouded window looking dizzily out over the city. Though he had seen no ropes below, he expected to find a bell or peal of bells in the tower whose narrow, louver-boarded lancet windows his field-glass had studied so often. Here he was doomed to disappointment, for when he attained the top of the stairs he found the tower chamber vacant of chimes, and clearly devoted to vastly different purposes.

The room, about fifteen feet square, was faintly lighted by four lancet windows, one on each side, which were glazed within their screening of decayed louver-boards. These had been further fitted with tight, opaque screens, but the latter were now largely rotted away. In the center of the dust-laden floor rose a curiously angled stone pillar some four feet in height and two in average diameter, covered on each side with bizarre, crudely incised and wholly unrecognizable hieroglyphs. On this pillar rested a metal box of peculiarly asymmetrical form, its hinged lid thrown back, and its interior holding what looked beneath the decade-deep dust to be an egg-shaped or irregularly spherical object some four inches through. Around the pillar in a rough circle were seven high-backed Gothic chairs still largely intact, while behind them, ranging along the dark-paneled walls, were seven colossal images of crumbling, black-painted plaster, resembling more than anything else the cryptic carven megaliths of mysterious Easter Island. In one corner of the cobwebbed chamber a ladder was built into the wall, leading up to the closed trap door of the windowless steeple above.

As Blake grew accustomed to the feeble light he noticed odd bas-reliefs on the strange open box of yellowish metal. Approaching, he tried to clear the dust away with his hands and handkerchief, and saw that the figurings were of a monstrous and utterly alien kind, depicting entities which, though seemingly alive, resembled no known life-form ever evolved on this planet. The four-inch seeming sphere turned out to be a nearly black, red-striated polyhedron with many irregular flat surfaces—either a very remarkable crystal of some sort, or an artificial object of carved and highly polished mineral matter. It did not touch the bottom of the box, but was held suspended by means of a metal band around its center, with seven queerly designed supports extending horizontally to angles of the box's inner wall near the top. This stone, once exposed, exerted upon Blake an almost alarming fascination. He could scarcely tear his eyes from it, and as he looked at its glistening surfaces he almost fancied it was transparent, with half-formed worlds of wonder within. Into his mind floated pictures of alien orbs with great stone towers, and other orbs with titan mountains and no mark of life, and still remoter spaces where only a stirring in vague blackness told of the presence of consciousness and will.

When he did look away, it was to notice a somewhat singular mound of dust in the far corner near the ladder to the steeple. Just why it took his attention he could not tell, but something in its contours carried a message to his unconscious mind. Plowing toward it, and brushing aside the hanging cobwebs as he went, he began to discern something grim about it. Hand and handkerchief soon revealed the truth, and Blake gasped with a baffling mixture of emotions. It was a human skeleton, and it must have been there for a very long time. The clothing was in shreds, but some buttons and fragments of cloth bespoke the man's grey suit. There were other bits of evidence—shoes, metal clasps, huge buttons for round cuffs, a stickpin of bygone pattern, a reporter's badge with the name of the old *Providence Telegram*, and a crumbling leather pocket-book. Blake examined the latter with care, finding within it several bills of antiquated issue, a celluloid advertising calendar for 1893, some cards with the name "Edwin M. Lillibridge", and a paper covered with penciled memoranda.

This paper held much of a puzzling nature, and Blake read it carefully at the dim westward window. Its disjointed text included such phrases as the following:

"Prof. Enoch Bowen home from Egypt May 1844—buys old Free-Will Church in July—his archaeological work & studies in occult well known."

"Dr. Drowne of 4th Baptist warns against Starry Wisdom in sermon Dec. 29, 1844."

"Congregation 97 by end of '45."

"1846—3 disappearances—first mention of Shining Trapezohedron."

"7 disappearances 1848—stories of blood sacrifice begin."

"Investigation 1853 comes to nothing—stories of sounds."

"Fr. O'Malley tells of devil-worship with box found in great Egyptian ruins—says they call up something that can't exist in light. Flees a little light, and banished by strong light. Then has to be summoned again. Probably got this from deathbed confession of Francis X. Feeney, who had joined Starry Wisdom in '49. These people say the Shining Trapezohedron shows them heaven & other worlds, & that the Haunter of the Dark tells them secrets in some way."

"Story of Orrin B. Eddy 1857. They call it up by gazing at the crystal, & have a secret language of their own."

"200 or more in cong. 1863, exclusive of men at front."

"Irish boys mob church in 1869 after Patrick Regan's disappearance."

"Veiled article in J. March 14, '72, but people don't talk about it."

"6 disappearances 1876—secret committee calls on Mayor Doyle."

"Action promised Feb. 1877—church closes in April."

"Gang—Federal Hill Boys—threaten Dr. ——— and vestrymen in May."

"181 persons leave city before end of '77—mention no names."

"Ghost stories begin around 1880—try to ascertain truth of report that no human being has entered church since 1877."

"Ask Lanigan for photograph of place taken 1851." ...

Restoring the paper to the pocketbook and placing the latter in his coat, Blake turned to look down at the skeleton in the dust. The implications of the notes were clear, and there could be no doubt but that this man had come to the deserted edifice forty-two years before in quest of a newspaper sensation which no one else had been bold enough to attempt. Perhaps no one else had known of his plan—who could tell? But he had never returned to his paper. Had some bravely suppressed fear risen to overcome him and bring on sudden heart failure? Blake stooped over the gleaming bones and noted their peculiar state. Some of them were badly scattered, and a few seemed oddly *dissolved* at the ends. Others were strangely yellowed, with a vague suggestion of charring. This charring extended to some of the fragments of clothing. The skull was in a very peculiar state—stained yellow, and with a charred aperture in the top as if some powerful acid had eaten through the solid bone. What had happened to the skeleton during its four decades of silent entombment here Blake could not imagine.

Before he realized it, he was looking at the stone again, and letting its curious influence call up a nebulous pageantry in his mind. He saw processions of robed, hooded figures whose outlines were not human, and looked on endless leagues of desert lined with carved, sky-reaching monoliths. He saw towers and walls in nighted depths under the sea, and vortices of space where wisps of black mist floated before thin shimmerings of cold purple haze. And beyond all else he glimpsed an infinite gulf of darkness, where solid and semisolid forms were known only by their windy stirrings, and cloudy patterns of force seemed to superimpose order on chaos and hold forth a key to all the paradoxes and arcana of the worlds we know.

Then all at once the spell was broken by an access of gnawing, indeterminate panic fear. Blake choked and turned away from the stone, conscious of some formless alien presence close to him and watching him with horrible intentness. He felt entangled with something—something which was not in the stone, but which had looked through it at him—something which would ceaselessly follow him with a cognition that was not physical sight. Plainly, the place was getting on his nerves—as well it might in view of his gruesome find. The light was waning, too, and since he had no illuminant with him he knew he would have to be leaving soon.

It was then, in the gathering twilight, that he thought he saw a faint trace of luminosity in the crazily angled stone. He had tried to look away from it, but some obscure compulsion drew his eyes back. Was there a subtle phosphorescence of radio-activity about the thing? What was it that the dead man's notes had said concerning a *Shining Trapezohedron*? What, anyway, was this abandoned lair of cosmic evil? What had been done here, and what might still be lurking in the bird-shunned shadows? It seemed now as if an elusive touch of fetor had arisen somewhere close by, though its source was not apparent. Blake seized the cover of the long-open box and snapped it down. It moved easily on its alien hinges, and closed completely over the unmistakably glowing stone.

At the sharp click of that closing a soft stirring sound seemed to come from the steeple's eternal blackness overhead, beyond the trap-door. Rats, without question—the only living things to reveal their presence in this accursed pile since he had entered it. And yet that stirring in the steeple frightened him horribly, so that he plunged almost wildly down the spiral stairs, across the ghoulish nave, into the vaulted basement, out amidst the gathering dusk of the deserted square, and down through the teeming, fear-haunted alleys and avenues of Federal Hill toward the sane central streets and the home-like brick sidewalks of the college district.

During the days which followed, Blake told no one of his expedition. Instead, he read much in certain books, examined long years of newspaper files downtown, and worked feverishly at the cryptogram in that leather volume from the cobwebbed vestry room. The cipher, he soon saw, was no simple one, and after a long period of endeavor he felt sure that its language could not be English, Latin, Greek, French, Spanish, Italian, or

German. Evidently he would have to draw upon the deepest wells of his strange erudition.

Every evening the old impulse to gaze westward returned, and he saw the black steeple as of yore amongst the bristling roofs of a distant and half-fabulous world. But now it held a fresh note of terror for him. He knew the heritage of evil lore it masked, and with the knowledge his vision ran riot in queer new ways. The birds of spring were returning, and as he watched their sunset flights he fancied they avoided the gaunt, lone spire as never before. When a flock of them approached it, he thought, they would wheel and scatter in panic confusion—and he could guess at the wild twitterings which failed to reach him across the intervening miles.

It was in June that Blake's diary told of his victory over the cryptogram. The text was, he found, in the dark Aklo language used by certain cults of evil antiquity, and known to him in a halting way through previous researches. The diary is strangely reticent about what Blake deciphered, but he was patently awed and disconcerted by his results. There are references to a Haunter of the Dark awaked by gazing into the Shining Trapezohedron, and insane conjectures about the black gulfs of chaos from which it was called. The being is spoken of as holding all knowledge, and demanding monstrous sacrifices. Some of Blake's entries show fear lest the thing, which he seemed to regard as summoned, stalk abroad, though he adds that the streetlights form a bulwark which cannot be crossed.

Of the Shining Trapezohedron he speaks often, calling it a window on all time and space, and tracing its history from the days it was fashioned on dark Yuggoth, before ever the Old Ones brought it to Earth. It was treasured and placed in its curious box by the crinoid things of Antarctica, salvaged from their ruins by the serpent-men of Valusia, and peered at eons later in Lemuria by the first human beings. It crossed strange lands and stranger seas, and sank with Atlantis before a Minoan fisher meshed it in his net and sold it to swarthy merchants from nighted Khem. The Pharaoh Nephren-Ka built around it a temple with a windowless crypt, and did that which caused his name to be stricken from all monuments and records. Then it slept in the ruins of that evil fane which the priests and the new Pharaoh destroyed, till the delver's spade once more brought it forth to curse mankind.

Early in July the newspapers oddly supplement Blake's entries, though in so brief and casual a way that only the diary has called general attention to their contribution. It appears that a new fear had been growing on Federal Hill since a stranger had entered the dreaded church. The Italians whispered of unaccustomed stirrings and bumpings and scrapings in the dark windowless steeple, and called on their priests to banish an entity which haunted their dreams. Something, they said, was constantly watching at a door to see if it were dark enough to venture forth. Press items mentioned the long-standing local superstitions, but failed to shed much light on the earlier background of the horror. It was obvious that the young reporters of today are no antiquarians. In writing of these things in his diary, Blake expresses a curious kind of remorse, and talks of the duty of burying the Shining Trapezohedron and of banishing what he had evoked by letting daylight into the hideous jutting spire. At the same time, however, he displays the dangerous extent of his fascination, and admits a morbid longing—pervading even his dreams—to visit the accursed tower and gaze again into the cosmic secrets of the glowing stone.

Then something in the *Journal* on the morning of July 17 threw the diarist into a veritable fervor of horror. It was only a variant of the other half-humorous items about the Federal Hill restlessness, but to Blake it was somehow very terrible indeed. In the night a thunderstorm had put the city's lighting system out of commission for a full hour, and in that black interval the Italians had nearly gone mad with fright. Those living near the dreaded church had sworn that the thing in the steeple had taken advantage of the street lamps' absence and gone down into the body of the church, flopping and bumping around in a viscous, altogether dreadful way. Toward the last it had bumped up to the tower, where there were sounds of the shattering of glass. It could go wherever the darkness reached, but light would always send it fleeing.

When the current blazed on again there had been a shocking commotion in the tower, for even the feeble light trickling through the grime-blackened, louver-boarded windows was too much for the thing. It had bumped and slithered up into its tenebrous steeple just in time—for a long dose of light would have sent it back into the abyss whence the crazy stranger had called it. During the dark hour praying crowds had clustered round the church in the rain with lighted candles and lamps somehow shielded with folded paper and umbrellas—a guard of light to save the city from the nightmare that stalks in darkness. Once, those nearest the church declared, the outer door had rattled hideously.

But even this was not the worst. That evening in the *Bulletin* Blake read of what the reporters had found. Aroused at last to the whimsical news value of the scare, a pair of them had defied the frantic crowds of Italians and crawled into the church through the cellar window after trying the doors in vain. They found the dust of the vestibule and of the spectral nave plowed up in a singular way, with pits of rotted cushions and satin pew-linings scattered curiously around. There was a bad odor everywhere, and here and there were bits of yellow stain and patches of what looked like charring. Opening the door to the tower, and pausing a moment at the suspicion of a scraping sound above, they found the narrow spiral stairs wiped roughly clean.

In the tower itself a similarly half-swept condition existed. They spoke of the heptagonal stone pillar, the overturned Gothic chairs, and the bizarre plaster images, though strangely enough the metal box and the old mutilated skeleton were not mentioned. What disturbed Blake the most—except for the hints of stains and charring and bad odors—was the final detail that explained the crashing glass. Every one of the tower's lancet windows was broken, and two of them had been darkened in a crude and hurried way by the stuffing of satin pew-linings and cushion-horsehair into the spaces between the slanting exterior louver-boards. More satin fragments and bunches of horsehair lay scattered around the newly swept floor, as if someone had been interrupted in the act of restoring the tower to the absolute blackness of its tightly curtained days.

Yellowish stains and charred patches were found on the ladder to the windowless spire, but when a reporter climbed up, opened the horizontally sliding trapdoor and shot a feeble flashlight beam into the black and strangely fetid space, he saw nothing but darkness, and an heterogeneous litter of shapeless fragments near the aperture. The verdict, of course, was charlatanry. Somebody had played a joke on the superstitious hill-dwellers, or else some fanatic had striven to bolster up their fears for their own supposed good. Or perhaps some of the younger and more sophisticated dwellers had staged an elaborate hoax on the outside world. There was an amusing aftermath when the police sent an officer to verify the reports. Three men in succession found ways of evading the assignment, and the fourth went very reluctantly and returned very soon without adding to the account given by the reporters.

From this point onward Blake's diary shows a mounting tide of insidious horror and nervous apprehension. He upbraids himself for not doing something, and speculates wildly on the consequences of another electrical breakdown. It has been verified that on three occasions—during thunderstorms—he telephoned the electric light company in a frantic vein and asked that desperate precautions against a lapse of power be taken. Now and then his entries show concern over the failure of the reporters to find the metal box and stone, and the strangely marred old skeleton, when they explored the shadowy tower room. He assumed that these things had been removed—whither, and by whom or what, he could only guess. But his worst fears concerned himself, and the kind of unholy rapport he felt to exist between his mind and that lurking horror in the distant steeple—that monstrous thing of night which his rashness had called out of the ultimate black spaces. He seemed to feel a constant tugging at his will, and callers of that period remember how he would sit abstractedly at his desk and stare out of the west window at that far-off spire-bristling mound beyond the swirling smoke of the city. His entries dwell monotonously on certain terrible dreams, and of a strengthening of the unholy rapport in his sleep. There is mention of a night when he awakened to find himself fully dressed, outdoors, and headed automatically down College Hill toward the west. Again and again he dwells on the fact that the thing in the steeple knows where to find him.

The week following July 30 is recalled as the time of Blake's partial breakdown. He did not dress, and ordered all his food by telephone. Visitors remarked the cords he kept near his bed, and he said that sleepwalking had forced him to bind his ankles every night with knots which would probably hold or else waken him with the labor of untying.

In his diary he told of the hideous experience which had brought the collapse. After retiring on the night of the 30th he had suddenly found himself groping about in an almost black space. All he could see were short, faint, horizontal streaks of bluish light, but he could smell an overpowering fetor and hear a curious jumble of soft, furtive sounds above him. Whenever he moved he stumbled over something, and at each noise there would come a sort of answering sound from above—a vague stirring, mixed with the cautious sliding of wood on wood.

Once his groping hands encountered a pillar of stone with a vacant top, whilst later he found himself clutching the rungs of a ladder built into the wall, and fumbling his uncertain way upward toward some region of intenser stench where a hot, searing blast beat down against him. Before his eyes a kaleidoscopic range of fantasmal images played, all of them dissolving at intervals into the picture of a vast, unplumbed abyss of night wherein whirled suns and worlds of an even profounder blackness. He thought of the ancient legends of Ultimate Chaos, at whose center sprawls the blind idiot god Azathoth, Lord of All Things, encircled by his flopping horde of mindless and amorphous dancers, and lulled by the thin monotonous piping of a daemoniac flute held in nameless paws.

Then a sharp report from the outer world broke through his stupor and roused him to the unutterable horror of his position. What it was, he never knew—perhaps it was some belated peal from the fireworks heard all summer on Federal Hill as the dwellers hail their various patron saints, or the saints of their native villages in Italy. In any event he shrieked aloud, dropped frantically from the ladder, and stumbled blindly across the obstructed floor of the almost lightless chamber that encompassed him.

He knew instantly where he was, and plunged recklessly down the narrow spiral staircase, tripping and bruising himself at every turn. There was a nightmare flight through a vast cobwebbed nave whose ghostly arches reached up to realms of leering shadow, a sightless scramble through a littered basement, a climb to regions of air and street lights outside, and a mad racing down a spectral hill of gibbering gables, across a grim, silent city of tall black towers, and up the steep eastward precipice to his own ancient door.

On regaining consciousness in the morning he found himself lying on his study floor fully dressed. Dirt and cobwebs covered him, and every inch of his body seemed sore and bruised. When he faced the mirror he saw that his hair was badly scorched, while a trace of strange, evil odor seemed to cling to his upper outer clothing. It was then that his nerves broke down. Thereafter, lounging exhaustedly about in a dressing-gown, he did little but stare from his west window, shiver at the threat of thunder, and make wild entries in his diary.

The great storm broke just before midnight on August 8th. Lightning struck repeatedly in all parts of the city, and two remarkable fireballs were reported. The rain was torrential, while a constant fusillade of thunder brought sleeplessness to thousands. Blake was utterly frantic in his fear for the lighting system, and tried to telephone the company around 1 a.m., though by that time service had been temporarily cut off in the interest of safety. He recorded everything in his diary—the large, nervous, and often undecipherable hieroglyphs telling their own story of growing frenzy and despair, and of entries scrawled blindly in the dark.

He had to keep the house dark in order to see out the window, and it appears that most of his time was spent at his desk, peering anxiously through the rain across the glistening miles of downtown roofs at the constellation of distant lights marking Federal Hill. Now and then he would fumblingly make an entry in his diary, so that detached phrases such as "The lights must not go"; "It knows where I am"; "I must destroy it"; and "It is calling to me, but perhaps it means no injury this time" are found scattered down two of the pages.

Then the lights went out all over the city. It happened at 2:12 a.m. according to power-house records, but Blake's diary gives no indication of the time. The entry is merely, "Lights out—God help me." On Federal Hill there were watchers as anxious as he, and rain-soaked knots of men paraded the square and alleys around the evil church with umbrella-shaded candles, electric flashlights, oil lanterns, crucifixes, and obscure charms of the many sorts common to southern Italy. They blessed each flash of lightning, and made cryptical signs of fear with their right hands when a turn in the storm caused the flashes to lessen and finally to cease altogether. A rising wind blew out most of the candles, so that the scene grew threateningly dark. Someone roused Father Merluzzo of Spirito Santo Church, and he hastened to the dismal square to pronounce whatever helpful syllables he could. Of the restless and curious sounds in the blackened tower, there could be no doubt whatever.

For what happened at 2:35 we have the testimony of the priest, a young, intelligent, and well educated person; of Patrolman William J. Monahan of the Central Station, an officer of the highest reliability who had paused at that part of his beat to inspect the crowd; and of most of the seventy-eight men who had gathered around the church's high bank wall—especially those in the square where the eastward façade was visible. Of course there was nothing which can be proved as being outside the order of nature. The possible causes of such an event are many. No one can speak with certainty of the obscure chemical processes arising in a vast, ancient, ill-aired, and long-deserted building of heterogeneous contents. Mephitic vapors—spontaneous combustion—pressure of gases born of long decay—any one of numberless phenomena might be responsible. And then, of course, the factor of conscious charlatanry can by no means be excluded. The thing was really quite simple in itself, and covered less than three minutes of actual time. Father Merluzzo, always a precise man, looked at his watch repeatedly.

It started with a definite swelling of the dull fumbling sounds inside the black tower. There had for some time been a vague exhalation of strange, evil odors from the church, and this had now become emphatic and offensive. Then at last there was a sound of splintering wood, and a large, heavy object crashed down in the yard beneath the frowning easterly façade. The tower was invisible now that the candles would not burn, but as the object neared the ground the people knew that it was the smoke-grimed louver-boarding of that tower's east window.

Immediately afterward an utterly unbearable fetor welled forth from the unseen heights, choking and sickening the trembling watchers, and almost prostrating those in the square. At the same time the air trembled with a vibration as of flapping wings, and a sudden east-blowing wind more violent than any previous blast snatched off the hats and wrenched the dripping umbrellas of the crowd. Nothing definite could be seen in the candleless night, though some upward-looking spectators thought they glimpsed a great spreading blur of denser blackness against the inky sky—something like a formless cloud of smoke that shot with meteor-like speed toward the east.

That was all. The watchers were half numbed with fright, awe, and discomfort, and scarcely knew what to do, or whether to do anything at all. Not knowing what had happened, they did not relax their vigil; and a moment later they sent up a prayer as a sharp flash of belated lightning, followed by an earsplitting crash of sound, rent the flooded heavens. Half an hour later the rain stopped, and in fifteen minutes more the street lights sprang on again, sending the weary, bedraggled watchers relievedly back to their homes.

The next day's papers gave these matters minor mention in connection with the general storm reports. It seems that the great lightning flash and deafening explosion which followed the Federal Hill occurrence were even more tremendous farther east, where a burst of the singular fetor was likewise noticed. The phenomenon was most marked over College Hill, where the crash awaked all the sleeping inhabitants and led to a bewildered round of speculations. Of those who were already awake only a few saw the anomalous blaze of light near the top of the hill, or noticed the inexplicable upward rush of air which almost stripped the leaves from the trees and blasted the plants in the gardens. It was agreed that the lone, sudden lightning bolt must have struck somewhere in this neighborhood, though no trace of its striking could afterward be found. A youth in the Tau Omega fraternity house thought he saw a grotesque and hideous mass of smoke in the air just as the preliminary flash burst, but his observation has not been verified. All of the few observers, however, agree as to the violent gust from the west and the flood of intolerable stench which preceded the belated stroke, whilst evidence concerning the momentary burned odor after the stroke is equally general.

These points were discussed very carefully because of their probable connection with the death of Robert Blake. Students in the Psi Delta house, whose upper rear windows looked into Blake's study, noticed the blurred white face at the westward window on the morning of the ninth, and wondered what was wrong with the expression. When they saw the same face in the same position that evening, they felt worried, and watched for the lights to come up in his apartment. Later they rang the bell of the darkened flat, and finally had a policeman force the door.

The rigid body sat bolt upright at the desk by the window, and when the intruders saw the glassy, bulging eyes, and the marks of stark, convulsive fright on the twisted features, they turned away in sickened dismay. Shortly afterward the coroner's physician made an examination, and despite the unbroken window reported electrical shock, or nervous tension induced by electrical discharge, as the cause of death. The hideous expression he ignored altogether, deeming it a not improbable result of the profound shock as experienced by a person of such abnormal imagination and unbalanced emotions. He deduced these latter qualities from the blindly scrawled entries in the diary on the desk. Blake had prolonged his frenzied jottings to the last, and the broken-pointed pencil was found clutched in his spasmodically contracted right hand.

The entries after the failure of the lights were highly disjointed, and legible only in part. From them certain investigators have drawn conclusions differing greatly from the materialistic official verdict, but such speculations have little chance for belief among the conservative. The case of these imaginative theorists has not been helped by the action of superstitious Doctor Dexter, who threw the curious box and angled stone—an object certainly self-luminous as seen in the black windowless steeple where it was found—into the deepest channel of Narragansett Bay. Excessive imagination and neurotic imbalance on Blake's part, aggravated by knowledge of the evil bygone cult whose startling traces he had uncovered, form the dominant interpretation given those final frenzied jottings. These are the entries—or all that can be made of them.

"Lights still out—must be five minutes now. Everything depends on lightning. Yaddith grant it will keep up!...Some influence seems beating through it. ... Rain and thunder and wind deafen. ... The thing is taking hold of my mind. ...

"Trouble with memory. I see things I never knew before. Other worlds and other galaxies. ... dark .... The lightning seems dark and the darkness seems light. ...

"It cannot be the real hill and church that I see in the pitch-darkness. Must be retinal impression left by flashes. Heaven grant the Italians are out with their candles if the lightning stops!

"What am I afraid of? Is it not an avatar of Nyarlathotep, who in antique and shadowy Khem even took the form of man? I remember Yuggoth, and more distant Shaggai, and the ultimate void of the black planets. ...

"The long, winging flight through the void ... cannot cross the universe of light ... re-created by the thoughts caught in the Shining Trapezohedron ... send it through the horrible abysses of radiance ....

"My name is Blake—Robert Harrison Blake of 620 East Knapp Street, Milwaukee, Wisconsin. ... I am on this planet ....

"Azathoth have mercy!—the lightning no longer flashes—horrible—I can see everything with a monstrous sense that is not sight—light is dark and dark is light ... those people on the hill ... guard ... candles and charms ... their priests ....

"Sense of distance gone—far is near and near is far. No light—no glass—see that steeple—that tower—window—can hear—Roderick Usher—am mad or going mad—the thing is stirring and fumbling in the tower—I am it and it is I—I want to get out ... must get out and unify the forces. ... It knows where I am. ...

"I am Robert Blake, but I can see the tower in the dark. There is a monstrous odor ... senses transfigured ... boarding at that tower window cracking and giving way ... *Iä* ... *ngai* ... *ygg* ....

"I see it—coming here—hell-wind—titan blur—black wings—Yog-Sothoth save me—the three-lobed burning eye ...."

THIS tale, one of Derleth's finest, represents something of a "crossover" between two of his major fictional cycles, the Cthulhu Mythos and the Wisconsin Saga. This happy hybridizing is signaled at once by the opening lines, right out of "The Dunwich Horror", but applied to backwoods Wisconsin rather than New England. Derleth's command of regionalism is evident on every page, lending substance to what, in some other tales, comes off as tinny or trite. There is a sense of things happening in a rich, real world. The same is true of his characterization, at least of the two protagonists. The dialogue is in the main quite believable, curt and commonsensical where it needs to be, and sharp with Derleth's sense of underlying sarcasm. Several moments of the tale are not without a genuine sense of ominous menace.

No one will be surprised to hear that "The Dweller in Darkness" is Derleth's version of "The Whisperer in Darkness." The same basic motifs reappear here: the accidental discovery of Nyarlathotep as the grim reality behind local Indian legends, the inquiry of a local savant, the seizure and supplanting of a delver, etc. The major change wrung on the theme is that, this time around, it is the Wilmarth character, Professor Upton Gardner, who is the victim. This similarity to the Lovecraftian prototype need not disturb us. It is simply one more case of literary influence and intertextuality. "The Dweller in Darkness" goes no farther in this direction than some of Lovecraft's tales which are rather heavily dependent upon Machen.

"The Dweller in Darkness" is an important milestone in the development of the Cthulhu Mythos in that it marks the first appearance of Cthugha, the fire god. In fact, Derleth here has a character reproduce the very line of reasoning that led him to introduce the inhuman torch in the first place: If the Old Ones are elemental spirits in some sense, then where is the fire spirit? Francis T. Laney's Cthulhu Mythos glossary pointed out this lacuna in Derleth's system, and in this story he filled the gap. By the same token, Derleth expands his theme of intra-Old Ones conflicts, perhaps a more fruitful theme than the otherwise monotonous "Old Ones vs. Elder Gods" cliché, where the Devas and the Asuras slug it out again and yet again.

"The Dweller in Darkness" first appeared in *Weird Tales* for November 1944.

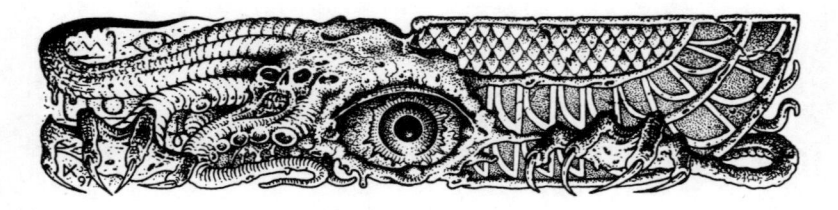

The Dweller in Darkness

by August Derleth

> Searchers after horror haunt strange, far places. For them are the catacombs of Ptolemais, and the carven mausolea of the nightmare countries. They climb to the moonlit towers of ruined Rhine castles, and falter down black cobwebbed steps beneath the scattered stones of forgotten cities in Asia. The haunted wood and the desolate mountain are their shrines and they linger around the sinister monoliths of uninhabited islands. But the true epicure in the terrible, to whom a new thrill of unutterable ghastliness is the chief end and justification of existence, esteems most of all the ancient, lonely farmhouses of backwoods regions; for there the dark elements of strength, solitude, grotesqueness and ignorance combine to form the perfection of the hideous.
> —H. P. Lovecraft

I

UNTIL recently, if a traveler in north central Wisconsin took the left fork at the junction of the Brule River highway and the Chequamegon pike on the way to Pashepaho, he would find himself in country so primitive that it would seem remote from all human contact. If he drove on along the little used road, he might in time pass a few tumble-down shacks where presumably people had once lived and which have long ago been taken back by the encroaching forest; it is not desolate country, but an area thick with growth, and over all its expanse there persists an intangible aura of the sinister, a kind of ominous oppression of the spirit quickly manifest to even the most casual traveler, for the road he has taken becomes ever more and more difficult to travel, and is eventually lost just short of a deserted lodge built on the edge of a clear blue lake around which century-old trees brood eternally, a country where the only sounds are the cries of the owls, the whippoorwills, and the eerie loons at night, and the wind's voice in the trees, and—but is it always the wind's voice in the trees? And who can say whether the snapped twig is the sign of an animal passing—or of something more, some other creature beyond man's ken?

For the forest surrounding the abandoned lodge at Rick's Lake had a curious reputation long before I myself knew it, a reputation which transcended similar stories about similar primeval places. There were odd rumors about something that dwelt in the depths of the forest's darkness—by no means the conventional wild whisperings of ghosts—of something half-animal, half-man, fearsomely spoken of by such natives as inhabited the edges of that region, and referred to only by stubborn head-shakings among the Indians who occasionally came out of that country and made their way south. The forest had an evil reputation; it was nothing short of that; and already, before the turn of the century, it had a history that gave pause even to the most intrepid adventurer.

The first record of it was left in the writings of a missionary on his way through that country to come to the aid of a tribe of Indians reported to the post of Chequamegon Bay in the north to be starving. Fr. Piregard vanished, but the Indians later brought in his effects: a sandal, his rosary, and a prayer-book in which he had written certain curious words which had been carefully preserved: "I have the conviction that some creature is following me. I thought at first it was a bear, but I am now compelled to believe that it is something incredibly more monstrous than anything of this earth. Darkness is falling, and I believe I have developed a slight delirium, for I persist in hearing strange music and other curious sounds which can surely not derive from any natural source. There is also a disturbing illusion as of great footsteps which actually shake the earth, and I have several times encountered a very large footprint which varies in shape."

The second record is far more sinister. When Big Bob Hiller, one of the most rapacious lumber barons of the entire Midwest, began to encroach upon the Rick's Lake country in the middle of the last century, he could not fail to be impressed by the stand of pine in the area near the lake, and, though he did not own it, he followed the usual custom of the lumber barons and sent his men in from an adjoining piece he did own, under the intended explanation that he did not know where his line ran. Thirteen men failed to return from that first day's work on the edge of the forest area surrounding Rick's Lake; two of their bodies were never recovered; four were found—inconceivably—in the lake, several miles from where they had been cutting timber; the others were discovered at various places in the forest. Hiller thought he had a lumber war on his hands, laid his men off to mislead his unknown opponent, and then suddenly ordered them back to work in the forbidden region. After he had lost five more men, Hiller pulled out, and no hand since his time touched the forest, save for one or two individuals who took up land there and moved into the area.

One and all, these individuals moved out within a short time, saying little, but hinting much. Yet the nature of their whispered hints was such that they were soon forced to abandon any explanation; so incredible were the tales they told, with overtones of something too horrible for description, of age-old evil which preceded anything dreamed of by even the most learned archaeologist. Only one of them vanished, and no trace of him was ever found. The others came back out of the forest and in the course of time were lost somewhere among other people in the United States—all save a half-breed known as Old Peter, who was obsessed with the idea that there were mineral deposits in the vicinity of the wood, and occasionally went to camp on its edge, being careful not to venture in.

It was inevitable that the Rick's Lake legends would ultimately reach the attention of Professor Upton Gardner of the State university; he had completed collections of Paul Bunyan, Whiskey Jack, and Hodag tales, and was engaged upon a compilation of place legends when he first encountered the curious half-forgotten tales that emanated from the region of Rick's Lake. I discovered later that his first reaction to them was one of casual interest; legends abound in out-of-the-way places, and there was nothing to indicate that these were of any more import than others. True, there was no similarity in the strictest sense of the word to the more familiar tales; for while the usual legends concerned themselves with ghostly appearances of men and animals, lost treasure, tribal beliefs, and the like, those of Rick's Lake were curiously unusual in their insistence upon utterly outré creatures—of "a" creature, since no one had ever reported seeing more than one even vaguely in the forest's darkness—half-man, half-beast, with always the hint that this description was inadequate in that it did injustice to the narrator's concept of what it was that lurked there in the vicinity of the lake. Nevertheless, Professor Gardner would in all probability have done little more than add the legends as he heard them to his collection, if it had not been for the reports—seemingly unconnected—of two curious facts, and the accidental discovery of a third.

The two facts were both newspaper accounts carried by Wisconsin papers within a week of each other. The first was a terse, half-comic report headed *Sea Serpent in Wisconsin Lake?*, and read:

> Pilot Joseph X. Castleton, on test flight over northern Wisconsin yesterday, reported seeing a large animal of some kind bathing by night in a forest lake in the vicinity of Chequamegon. Castleton was caught in a thundershower and was flying low at the time, when, in an effort to ascertain his whereabouts, he looked down when lightning flashed and saw what appeared to be a very large animal rising from the waters of a lake below

him, and vanish into the forest. The pilot added no details to his story, but asserts that the creature he saw was not the Loch Ness monster.

The second story was the utterly fantastic tale of the discovery of the body of Fr. Piregard, well preserved, in the hollow trunk of a tree along the Brule River. At first called a lost member of the Marquette-Joliet expedition, Fr. Piregard was quickly identified. To this report was appended a frigid statement by the President of the State Historical Society dismissing the discovery as a hoax.

The discovery Professor Gardner made was simply that an old friend was actually the owner of the abandoned lodge and most of the shore of Rick's Lake.

The sequence of events was thus clearly inevitable. Professor Gardner instantly associated both newspaper accounts with the Rick's Lake legends; this might not have been enough to stir him to drop his researches into the general mass of legends abounding in Wisconsin for specific research of quite another kind, but the occurrence of something even more astonishing sent him posthaste to the owner of the abandoned lodge for permission to take the place over in the interests of science. What spurred him to take this action was nothing less than a request from the curator of the state museum to visit his office late one night and view a new exhibit which had arrived. He went there in the company of Laird Dorgan, and it was Laird who came to me.

But that was after Professor Gardner vanished.

For he did vanish; after sporadic reports from Rick's Lake over a period of three months, all word from the lodge ceased entirely, and nothing further was heard of Professor Upton Gardner.

Laird came to my room at the University Club late one night in October; his frank blue eyes were clouded, his lips tense, his brow furrowed, and there was everything to show that he was in a state of moderate excitation which did not derive from liquor. I assumed that he was working too hard; the first period tests in his University of Wisconsin classes were just over, and Laird habitually took tests seriously—even as a student he had done so, and now as an instructor he was doubly conscientious.

But it was not that. Professor Gardner had been missing almost a month now, and it was this which preyed on his mind. He said as much in so many words, adding, "Jack, I've got to go up there and see what I can do."

"Man, if the sheriff and the posse haven't discovered anything, what can you do?" I asked.

"For one thing, I know more than they do."

"If so, why didn't you tell them?"

"Because it's not the sort of thing they'd pay any attention to."

"Legends?"

"No."

He was looking at me speculatively, as if wondering whether he could trust me. I was suddenly conscious of the conviction that he *did* know something which he, at least, regarded with the gravest concern; at the same time I had the most curious sensation of premonition and warning that I have ever experienced. In that instant the entire room seemed tense, the air electrified.

"If I go up there—do you think you could go along?"

"I guess I could manage."

"Good." He took a turn or two about the room, his eyes brooding, looking at me from time to time, still betraying uncertainty and an inability to make up his mind.

"Look, Laird—sit down and take it easy. That caged lion stuff isn't good for your nerves."

He took my advice; he sat down, covered his face with his hands, and shuddered. For a moment I was alarmed, but he snapped out of it in a few seconds, leaned back, and lit a cigarette.

"You know those legends about Rick's Lake, Jack?"

I assured him that I knew them and the history of the place from the beginning—as much as had been recorded.

"And those stories in the papers I mentioned to you ...?"

The stories, too. I remembered them since Laird had discussed with me their effect on his employer.

"That second one, about Fr. Piregard," he began, hesitated, stopped. Then, taking a deep breath, he began again. "You know, Gardner and I went over to the curator's office one night last spring."

"Yes, I was east at the time."

"Of course. Well, we went over there. The curator had something to show us. What do you think it was?"

"No idea. What was it?"

"That body in the tree!"

"No!"

"Gave us quite a jolt. There it was, hollow trunk and all, just the way it had been found. It had been shipped down to the museum for exhibition. But it was never exhibited, of course—for a very good reason. When Gardner saw it, he thought it was a waxwork. But it wasn't."

"You don't mean that it was the real thing?"

Laird nodded. "I know it's incredible."

"It's just not possible."

"Well, yes, I suppose it's impossible. But it was so. That's why it wasn't exhibited—just taken out and buried."

"I don't quite follow that."

He leaned forward and said very earnestly, "Because when it came in it had all the appearance of being completely preserved, as if by some natural embalming process. It wasn't. It was frozen. It began to thaw out that night. And there were certain things about it that indicated that Fr. Piregard hadn't been dead the three centuries history said he had. The body began to go to pieces in a dozen ways—but no crumbling into dust, nothing like that. Gardner estimated that he hadn't been dead over five years. Where had he been in the meantime?"

He was quite sincere. I would not at first have believed it. But there was a certain disquieting earnestness about Laird that forbade any levity on my part. If I had treated his story as a joke, as I had the impulse to do, he would have shut up like a clam, and walked out of my room to brood about this thing in secret, with Lord knows what harm to himself. For a little while I said absolutely nothing.

"You don't believe it."

"I haven't said so."

"I can feel it."

"No. It's hard to take. Let's say I believe in your sincerity."

"That's fair enough," he said grimly. "Do you believe in me sufficiently to go along up to the lodge and find out what may have happened there?"

"Yes, I do."

"But I think you'd better read these excerpts from Gardner's letters first." He put them down on my desk like a challenge. He had copied them off onto a single sheet of paper, and as I took this up he went on, talking rapidly, explaining that the letters had been those written by Gardner from the lodge. When he finished, I turned to the excerpts and read.

> I cannot deny that there is about the lodge, the lake, even the forest, an aura of evil, of impending danger—it is more than that, Laird, if I could explain it, but archaeology is my forte, and not fiction. For it would take fiction, I think, to do justice to this thing I feel. ... Yes, there are times when I have the distinct feeling that *someone* or *something* is watching me out of the forest or from the lake—there does not seem to be a distinction as I would like to understand it, and while it does not make me uneasy, nevertheless it is enough to give me pause. I managed the other day to make contact with Old Peter, the half-breed. He was at the moment a little worse for firewater, but when I mentioned the lodge and the forest to him, he drew into himself like a clam. But he did put words to it: he called it the Wendigo—you are familiar with this legend, which properly belongs to the French-Canadian country.

That was the first letter, written about a week after Gardner had reached the abandoned lodge on Rick's Lake. The second was extremely terse, and had been sent by special delivery.

Will you wire Miskatonic University at Arkham, Massachusetts to ascertain if there is available for study a photostatic copy of a book known as the *Necronomicon*, by an Arabian writer who signs himself Abdul Alhazred? Make inquiry also for the *Pnakotic Manuscripts* and the *Book of Eibon*, and determine whether it is possible to purchase through one of the local bookstores a copy of *The Outsider and Others*, by H. P. Lovecraft, published by Arkham House last year. I believe that these books individually and collectively may be helpful in determining just what it is that haunts this place. For there *is* something, make no mistake about that; I am convinced of it, and when I tell you that I believe it has lived here not for years, but for centuries—perhaps even before the time of man—you will understand that I may be on the threshold of great discoveries.

Startling as this letter was, the third and last was even more so. For an interval of a fortnight went by between the second and third letters, and it was apparent that something had happened to threaten Professor Gardner's composure, for his third letter was even in this selected excerpt marked by extreme perturbation.

Everything evil here .... I don't know whether it is the Black Goat With a Thousand Young or the Faceless One and/or something more that rides the wind. For God's sake ... those accursed fragments! ... Something in the lake, too, and at night the sounds! How still, and then suddenly those horrible flutes, those watery ululations! Not a bird, not an animal, then— only those ghastly sounds. And the voices! ... Or is it but dream? Is it my own voice I hear in the darkness? ...

I found myself increasingly shaken as I read those excerpts. Certain implications and hints lodged between the lines of what Professor Gardner had written were suggestive of terrible, ageless evil, and I felt that there was opening up before Laird Dorgan and myself an adventure so incredible, so bizarre, and so unbelievably dangerous that we might well not return to tell it. Yet even then there was a lurking doubt in my mind that we would say anything about what we found at Rick's Lake.

"What do you say?" asked Laird impatiently.

"I'm going."

"Good! Everything's ready. I've even got a Dictaphone and batteries enough to run it. I've arranged for the sheriff of the county at Pashepaho to replace Gardner's notes, and leave everything just the way it was."

"A Dictaphone," I broke in. "What for?"

"Those sounds he wrote about—we can settle that for once and all. If they're to be heard, the Dictaphone will record them; if they're just imagination, it won't." He paused, his eyes very grave. "You know, Jack, we may not come out of this thing?"

"I know."

I did not say so, because I knew that Laird, too, felt the same way I did: that we were going like two dwarfed Davids to face an adversary greater than any Goliath, an adversary invisible and unknown, who bore no name and was shrouded in legend and fear, a dweller not only in the darkness of the wood but in that greater darkness which the mind of man has sought to explore since his dawn.

II

SHERIFF Cowan was at the lodge when we arrived. Old Peter was with him. The sheriff was a tall, saturnine individual clearly of Yankee stock; though representing the fourth generation of his family in the area, he spoke with a twang which doubtless had persisted from generation to generation. The half-breed was a dark-skinned, ill-kempt fellow; he had a way of saying little and from time to time grinned or snickered as at some secret joke.

"I brung up express that come some time past for the professor," said the sheriff. "From some place in Massachusetts was one of 'em, and the other from down near Madison. Didn't seem t' me 'twas worth sendin' back. So I took and brung 'em with the keys. Don't know that you fellers'll git any-w'eres. My posse and me went through the hull woods, didn't see a thing."

"You ain't tellin' 'em everything," put in the half-breed, grinning.

"Ain't no more to tell."

"What about that carvin'?"

The sheriff shrugged irritably. "Damn it, Peter, that ain't got nothin' to do with the professor's disappearance."

"He made a drawin' of it, didn't he?"

So pressed, the sheriff confided that two members of his posse had stumbled upon a great slab of rock in the center of the wood; it was mossy and overgrown, but there was upon it an odd drawing, plainly as old as the forest—probably the work of one of the primitive Indian tribes once known to inhabit northern Wisconsin before the Dacotah Sioux and the Winnebago—

Old Peter grunted with contempt. "No Indian drawing."

The sheriff shook this off and went on. The drawing represented some kind of creature, but no one could tell what it was; it was certainly not a man, but on the other hand, it did not seem to be hairy, like a beast. Moreover, the unknown artist had forgotten to put in a face.

"'N beside it there wuz two things," said the half-breed.

"Don't pay no attention to him," said the sheriff then.

"What two things?" demanded Laird.

"Jest things," replied the half-breed snickering. "Heh, heh! Ain't no other way to tell it—warn't human, warn't animal, jest things."

Cowan was irritated. He became suddenly brusque; he ordered the half-breed to keep still, and went on to say that if we needed him, he would be at his office in Pashepaho. He did not explain how we were to make contact with him, since there was no telephone at the lodge, but plainly he had no high regard for the legends abounding about the area into which we had ventured with such determination. The half-breed regarded us with an almost stolid indifference, broken only by his sly grin from time to time, and his dark eyes examined our luggage with keen speculation and interest. Laird met his gaze occasionally, and each time Old Peter indolently shifted his eyes. The sheriff went on talking; the notes and drawings the missing man had made were on the desk he had used in the big room which made up almost the entire ground floor of the lodge, just where he had found them; they were the property of the State of Wisconsin and were to be returned to the sheriff's office when we had finished with them. At the threshold he turned for a parting shot to say he hoped we would not be staying too long, because, "While I ain't givin' in to any of them crazy ideas—it jest ain't been so healthy for some of the people who came here."

"The half-breed knows or suspects something," said Laird at once. "We'll have to get in touch with him sometime when the sheriff's not around."

"Didn't Gardner write that he was pretty close-mouthed when it came to concrete data?"

"Yes, but he indicated the way out. Firewater."

We went to work and settled ourselves, storing our food supplies, setting up the Dictaphone, getting things into readiness for a stay of at least a fortnight; our supplies were sufficient for this length of time, and if we had to remain longer, we could always go into Pashepaho for more food. Moreover, Laird had brought fully two dozen Dictaphone cylinders, so that we had plenty of them for an indefinite time, particularly since we did not intend to use them except when we slept—and this would not be often, for we had agreed that one of us would watch while the other took his rest, an arrangement we were not sanguine enough to believe would hold good without fail, hence the machine. It was not until after we had settled our belongings that we turned to the things the sheriff had brought and, meanwhile, we had ample opportunity to become aware of the very definite aura of the place.

For it was not imagination that there was a strange aura about the lodge and the grounds. It was not alone the brooding, almost sinister stillness, not alone the tall pines encroaching upon the lodge, not alone the blue-black waters of the lake, but something more than that: a hushed, almost menacing air of waiting, a kind of aloof assurance that was ominous—as one might imagine a hawk might feel leisurely cruising above prey it knows will not escape its talons. Nor was this a fleeting impression, for it was obvious almost at once, and it grew with sure steadiness throughout the hour or so that we worked there; moreover, it was so plainly to be felt, that Laird commented upon it as if he had long ago accepted it, and knew that I too had done so! Yet there was nothing primary to which this could be attributed. There are thousands of lakes like Rick's in northern Wisconsin and Minnesota, and while many of them are not in forest areas, those which are do not differ greatly in their physical aspects from Rick's, so there was nothing in the appearance of the place which at all contributed to the brooding sense of horror which seemed to invade us from outside. Indeed, the setting was rather the opposite; under the afternoon sunlight, the old lodge, the lake, the high forest all around had a pleasant air of seclusion—an air which made the contrast with the intangible aura of evil all the more pointed and fearsome. The fragrance of the pines together with the freshness of the water served, too, to emphasize the intangible mood of menace.

We turned at last to the material left on Professor Gardner's desk. The express packages contained, as expected, a copy of *The Outsider and Others*, by H. P. Lovecraft, shipped by the publishers, and photostatic copies of manuscript and printed pages taken from the *R'lyeh Text* and Ludvig Prinn's *De Vermis Mysteriis*—apparently sent for to supplement the earlier data dispatched to the professor by the librarian of Miskatonic University, for we found among the material brought back by the sheriff certain pages from the *Necronomicon*, in the translation by Olaus Wormius, and likewise from the *Pnakotic Manuscripts*. But it was not these pages, which for the most part were unintelligible to us, which held our attention. It was the fragmentary notes left by Professor Gardner.

It was quite evident that he had not had time to do more than put down such questions and thoughts as had occurred to him, and, while there was little assimilation manifest, yet there was about what he had written a certain terrible suggestiveness which grew to colossal proportions as everything he had not put down became obvious.

> Is the slab a) only an ancient ruin, b) a marker similar to a tomb, c) or a focal point for Him? If the latter, from outside? Or from beneath? (NB: Nothing to show that the thing has been disturbed.)

> Cthulhu or Kthulhut. In Rick's Lake? Subterrene passage to Superior and the sea via the St. Lawrence? (NB: Except for the aviator's story, nothing to show that the Thing has anything to do with the water. Probably not one of the water beings.)

> Hastur. But manifestations do not seem to have been of air beings either.

Yog-Sothoth. Of earth certainly—but he is not the "Dweller in Darkness." (NB: The Thing, whatever it is, must be of the earth deities, even though it travels in time and space. It could possibly be more than one, of which only the earth being is occasionally visible. Ithaqua, perhaps?)

"Dweller in Darkness." Could He be the same as the Blind, Faceless One? He could be truly said to be dwelling in darkness. Nyarlathotep? Or Shub-Niggurath?

What of fire? There must be a deity here, too. But no mention. (NB: Presumably, if the Earth and Water Beings oppose those of Air, then they must oppose those of Fire as well. Yet there is evidence here and there to show that there is more constant struggle between Air and Water Beings than between those of Earth and Air. Abdul Alhazred is damnably obscure in places. There is no clue as to the identity of Cthugha in that terrible footnote.)

Partier says I am on the wrong track. I'm not convinced. Whoever it is that plays the music in the night is a master of hellish cadence and rhythm. And, yes, of cacophony. (Cf. Bierce and Chambers.)

That was all.
"What incredible gibberish!" I exclaimed.
And yet—and yet I knew instinctively it was not gibberish. Strange things had happened here, things which demanded an explanation which was not terrestrial; and here, in Gardner's handwriting, was evidence to show that he had not only arrived at the same conclusion, but passed it. However it might sound, Gardner had written it in all seriousness, and clearly for his own use alone, since only the vaguest and most suggestive outline seemed apparent. Moreover, the notes had had a startling effect on Laird; he had gone quite pale, and now stood looking down as if he could not believe what he had seen.
"What is it?" I asked.
"Jack—he was in contact with Partier."
"It doesn't register," I answered, but even as I spoke I remembered the hush-hush that had attended the severing of old Professor Partier's connection with the University of Wisconsin. It had been given out to the press that the old man had been somewhat too liberal in his lectures in anthropology—that is, that he had "Communistic leanings!"—which everyone who knew Partier realized was far from the facts. But he had said strange things in his lectures, he had talked of horrible, forbidden matters, and it had been thought best to let him out quietly. Unfortunately, Partier went out trumpeting in his contemptuous manner, and it had been difficult to hush the matter up satisfactorily.
"He's living down in Wausau now," said Laird.

"Do you suppose he could translate all this?" I asked and knew that I had echoed the thought in Laird's mind.

"He's almost a day away by car. We'll copy these notes, and if nothing happens—if we can't discover anything, we'll go to see him."

If nothing happened—!

If the lodge by day had seemed brooding in an air of ominousness, by night it seemed surcharged with menace. Moreover, events began to take place with disarming and insidious suddenness, beginning in mid-evening, when Laird and I were sitting over those curious photostats sent out by Miskatonic University in lieu of the books and manuscripts themselves, which were far too valuable to permit out of their haven. The first manifestation was so simple that for some time neither of us noticed its strangeness. It was simply the sound in the trees as of rising wind, the growing song among the pines. The night was warm, and all the windows of the lodge stood open. Laird commented on the wind, and went on giving voice to his perplexity regarding the fragments before us. Not until half an hour had gone by and the sound of the wind had risen to the proportions of a gale did it occur to Laird that something was wrong, and he looked up, his eyes going from one open window to another in growing apprehension. Then I, too, became aware.

Despite the tumult of the wind, no draft of air had circulated in the room, not one of the light curtains at the window was so much as trembling!

With one simultaneous movement, both of us stepped out upon the broad verandah of the lodge.

There was no wind, no breath of air stirring to touch our hands and faces. There was only the sound in the forest. Both of us looked up to where the pines were silhouetted against the starswept heavens, expecting their tops would be bending before a high gale, but there was no movement whatever; the pines stood still, motionless; and the sound as of wind continued from all around us. We stood on the verandah for half an hour, vainly attempting to determine the source of the sound—and then, as unobtrusively as it had begun, it stopped!

The hour was now approaching midnight, and Laird prepared for bed; he had slept little the previous night, and we had agreed that I was to take the first watch until four in the morning. Neither of us said much about the sound in the pines, but what was said indicated a desire to believe that there was a natural explanation for the phenomenon, if we could establish a point of contact for understanding. It was inevitable, I suppose, that even in the face of all the curious facts which had come to our attention, there should still be an earnest wish to find a natural explanation. Certainly the oldest fear and the greatest fear to which man is prey is fear of the unknown; anything capable of rationalization and explanation cannot be feared; but it was growing hourly more patent that we were facing something which defied all known rationales and credos, but hinged upon a system of belief that antedated even primitive man, and indeed, as scattered hints within the photostat pages from Miskatonic University suggested, antedated even Earth itself. And there was always that brooding terror, the ominous suggestion of menace from something far beyond the grasp of such puny intelligence as man's.

Thus it was with some trepidation that I prepared for my vigil. After Laird had gone to his room, which was at the head of the stairs, with a door opening upon a railed-in balcony looking down into the lodge room where I sat with the book by Lovecraft, reading here and there in its pages, I settled down to a kind of apprehensive waiting. It was not that I was afraid of what might take place, but rather that I was afraid that what took place might be beyond my understanding. However, as the minutes ticked past, I became engrossed in *The Outsider and Others*, with its hellish suggestions of aeon-old evil, of entities co-existent with all time and coterminous with all space, and began to understand, however vaguely, a relation between the writings of this *fantasiste* and the curious notes Professor Gardner had made. The most disturbing factor in this cognizance was the knowledge that Professor Gardner had made his notes independent of the book I now read, since it had arrived after his disappearance. Moreover, though there were certain keys to what Gardner had written in the first material he had received from Miskatonic University, there was growing now a mass of evidence to indicate that the professor had had access to some other source of information.

What was that source? Could he have learned something from Old Peter? Hardly likely. Could he have gone to Partier? It was not impossible that he had done so, though he had not imparted this information to Laird. Yet it was not to be ruled out that he had made contact with still another source of which there was no hint among his notes.

It was while I was engaged in this engrossing speculation that I became conscious of the music. It may actually have been sounding for some time before I heard it, but I do not think so. It was a curious melody that was being played, beginning as something lulling and harmonious, and then subtly becoming cacophonous and demoniac, rising in tempo, though all the time coming as from a great distance. I listened to it with growing astonishment; I was not at first aware of that sense of evil which fell upon me the moment I stepped outside and became cognizant that the music emanated from the depths of the dark forest. There, too, I was sharply conscious of its weirdness; the melody was unearthly, utterly bizarre and foreign, and the instruments which were being used seemed to be flutes, or certainly some variation of flutes.

Up to that moment there was no really alarming manifestation. That is, there was nothing but the suggestiveness of the two events which had taken place to inspire fear. There was, in short, always a good possibility that there might be a natural explanation about the sound as of wind and that of music.

But now, suddenly, there occurred something so utterly horrible, something so fraught with terror, that I was at once made prey to the most terrible fear known to man, a surging primitive horror of the unknown, of something from outside—for if I had had doubts about the things suggested by Gardner's notes and the material accompanying them, I knew instinctively that they were unfounded, for the sound that succeeded the strains of that unearthly music was of such a nature that it defied description, and defies it even now. It was simply a ghastly ululation, made by no beast known to man, and certainly by no man. It rose to an awful crescendo and fell away into a silence that was the more terrible for this soul-searing crying. It began with a two-note call, twice repeated, a frightful sound: *"Ygnaiih! Ygnaiih!"* and then became a triumphant wailing cry that ululated out of the forest and into the dark night like the hideous voice of the pit itself: *"Eh-ya-ya-ya-yahaaahaaahaaahaaa-ah-ah-ah-ngh'aaaa-ngh'aaa-ya-ya-yaaa ...."*

I stood for a minute absolutely frozen to the verandah. I could not have uttered a sound if it had been necessary to save my life. The voice had ceased, but the trees still seemed to echo its frightful syllables. I heard Laird tumble from his bed, I heard him running down the stairs calling my name, but I could not answer. He came out on the verandah and caught hold of my arm.

"Good God! What was that?"

"Did you hear it?"

"I heard enough."

We stood waiting for it to sound again, but there was no repetition of it. Nor was there a repetition of the music. We returned to the sitting room and waited there, neither of us able to sleep.

But there was not another manifestation of any kind throughout the remainder of that night!

III

THE occurrences of that first night more than anything else decided our direction on the following day. For, realizing that we were too ill-informed to cope with any understanding with what was taking place, Laird set the Dictaphone for that second night, and we started out for Wausau and Professor Partier, planning to return on the following day. With forethought, Laird carried with him our copy of the notes Gardner had left, skeletal as they were.

Professor Partier, at first reluctant to see us, admitted us finally to his study in the heart of the Wisconsin city, and cleared books and papers from two chairs so that we could sit down. Though he had the appearance of an old man and wore a long white beard, and a fringe of white hair straggled from under his black skull cap, he was as agile as a young man; he was thin, his fingers were bony, his face gaunt, with deep, black eyes, and his features were set in an expression that was one of profound cynicism, disdainful, almost contemptuous, and he made no effort to make us comfortable, beyond providing places for us to sit. He recognized Laird as Professor Gardner's secretary, said brusquely that he was a busy man preparing what would doubtless be his last book for his publishers, and he would be obliged to us if we would state the object of our visit as concisely as possible.

"What do you know of Cthulhu?" asked Laird bluntly.

The professor's reaction was astonishing. From an old man whose entire attitude had been one of superiority and aloof disdain, he became instantly wary and alert; with exaggerated care he put down the pencil he had been holding, his eyes never once left Laird's face, and he leaned forward a little over his desk.

"So," he said, "you come to me." He laughed then, a laugh which was like the cackling of some centenarian. "You come to me to ask about Cthulhu. Why?"

Laird explained curtly that we were bent upon discovering what had happened to Professor Gardner. He told as much as he thought necessary, while the old man closed his eyes, picked up his pencil once more and, tapping gently with it, listened with marked care, prompting Laird from time to time. When he had finished, Professor Partier opened his eyes slowly and looked from one to the other of us with an expression that was not unlike one of pity mixed with pain.

"So he mentioned me, did he? But I had no contact with him other than one telephone call." He pursed his lips. "He had more reference to an earlier controversy than to his discoveries at Rick's Lake. I would like now to give you a little advice."

"That's what we came for."

"Go away from that place, and forget all about it."

Laird shook his head in determination.

Partier estimated him, his dark eyes challenging his decision; but Laird did not falter. He had embarked upon this venture, and he meant to see it through.

"These are not forces with which common men have been accustomed to deal," said the old man then. "We are frankly not equipped to do so." He began then, without other preamble, to talk of matters so far removed from the mundane as to be almost beyond conception. Indeed, it was some time before I began to comprehend what he was hinting at, for his concept was so broad and breathtaking that it was difficult for anyone accustomed to so prosaic an existence as mine to grasp. Perhaps it was because Partier began obliquely by suggesting that it was not Cthulhu or his minions who haunted Rick's Lake, but clearly another; the existence of the slab and what was carved upon it clearly indicated the nature of the being who dwelled there from time to time. Professor Gardner had in final analysis got on to the right path, despite thinking that Partier did not believe it. Who was the Blind, Faceless One but Nyarlathotep? Certainly not Shub-Niggurath, the Black Goat of a Thousand Young.

Here Laird interrupted him to press for something more understandable, and then at last, realizing that we knew nothing, the professor went on, still in that vaguely irritable oblique manner, to expound mythology—a mythology of prehuman life not only on the Earth, but on the stars of all the universe. "We know nothing," he repeated from time to time. "We know nothing at all. But there are certain signs, certain shunned places. Rick's Lake is one of them." He spoke of beings whose very names were awesome—of the Elder Gods who live on Betelgeuse, remote in time and space, who had cast out into space the Great Old Ones, led by Azathoth and Yog-Sothoth, and numbering among them the primal spawn of the amphibious Cthulhu, the bat-like followers of Hastur the Unspeakable, of Lloigor, Zhar, and Ithaqua, who walked the winds and interstellar space, the earth beings, Nyarlathotep and Shub-Niggurath—the evil beings who sought always to triumph once more over the Elder Gods, who had shut them out or imprisoned them—as Cthulhu long ago slept in the ocean realm of R'lyeh, as Hastur was imprisoned upon a black star near Aldebaran in the Hyades. Long before human beings walked the Earth, the conflict between the Elder Gods and the Great Old Ones had taken place; from time to time the Old Ones had made a resurgence toward power, sometimes to be stopped by direct interference by the Elder Gods, but more often by the agency of human or nonhuman beings serving to bring about a conflict among the beings of the elements, for, as Gardner's notes indicated, the evil Old Ones were elemental forces. And every time there had been a resurgence, the mark of it had been left deep upon man's memory—though every attempt was made to eliminate the evidence and quiet survivors.

"What happened at Innsmouth, Massachusetts, for instance?" he asked tensely. "What took place at Dunwich? In the wilds of Vermont? At the old Tuttle house on the Aylesbury Pike? What of the mysterious cult of Cthulhu, and the utterly strange voyage of exploration to the Mountains of Madness? What beings dwelt on the hidden and shunned Plateau of Leng?

And what of Kadath in the Cold Waste? Lovecraft knew! Gardner and many another have sought to discover those secrets, to link the incredible happenings of the planet—but it is not desired by the Old Ones that mere men shall know too much. Be warned!"

He took up Gardner's notes without giving either of us a chance to say anything and studied them, putting on a pair of gold-rimmed spectacles which made him look more ancient than ever, and going on talking, more to himself than to us, saying that it was held that the Old Ones had achieved a higher degree of development in some aspects of science than was hitherto believed possible, but that, of course, nothing was *known*. The way in which he consistently emphasized this indicated very clearly that only a fool or an idiot would disbelieve, proof or no proof. But in the next sentence, he admitted that there was certain proof—the revolting and bestial plaque bearing a representation of a hellish monstrosity walking on the winds above the earth found in the hand of Josiah Alwyn when his body was discovered on a small Pacific island months after his incredible disappearance from his home in Wisconsin; the drawings made by Professor Gardner—and, even more than anything else, that curious slab of carven stones in the forest at Rick's Lake.

"Cthugha," he murmured then, wonderingly. "I've not read the footnote to which he makes reference. And there's nothing in Lovecraft." He shook his head. "No, I don't know." He looked up. "Can you frighten something out of the half-breed?"

"We've thought of that," admitted Laird.

"Well, now, I advise a try. It seems evident that he knows something—it may be nothing but an exaggeration to which his more or less primitive mind has lent itself; but on the other hand—who can say?"

More than this Professor Partier could not or would not tell us. Moreover, Laird was reluctant to ask, for there was obviously a damnably disturbing connection between what he had revealed, however incredible it might be, and what Professor Gardner had written.

Our visit, however, despite its inconclusiveness—or perhaps because of it—had a curious effect on us. The very indefiniteness of the professor's summary and comments, coupled with such fragmentary and disjointed evidence which had come to us independently of Partier, sobered us and increased Laird's determination to get to the bottom of the mystery surrounding Gardner's disappearance, a mystery which had now become enlarged to encompass the greater mystery of Rick's Lake and the forest around it.

On the following day we returned to Pashepaho, and, as luck would have it, we passed Old Peter on the road leading from town. Laird slowed down, backed up, and leaned out to meet the old fellow's speculative gaze.

"Lift?"

"Reckon so."

Old Peter got in and sat on the edge of the seat until Laird unceremoniously produced a flask and offered it to him; then his eyes lit up. He took it eagerly and drank deeply, while Laird made small talk about life in the north woods and encouraged the half-breed to talk about the mineral deposits he thought he could find in the vicinity of Rick's Lake. In this way some distance was covered, and, during this time, the half-breed retained the flask, handing it back at last when it was almost empty. He was not intoxicated in the strictest sense of the word, but he was uninhibited, and he made no protest when we took the lake road without stopping to let him out, though when he saw the lodge and knew where he was, he said thickly that he was off his route, and had to be getting back before dark.

He would have started back immediately, but Laird persuaded him to come in with the promise that he would mix him a drink.

He did. He mixed him as stiff a drink as he could, and Peter downed it.

Not until he had begun to feel its effects did Laird turn to the subject of what Peter knew about the mystery of the Rick's Lake country, and instantly then the half-breed became close-mouthed, mumbling that he would say nothing, he had seen nothing, it was all a mistake, his eyes shifting from one to the other of us. Laird persisted. He had seen the slab of carven stone, hadn't he? Yes—reluctantly. Would he take us to it? Peter shook his head violently. Not now. It was nearly dark, it might be dark before they could return.

But Laird was adamant, and finally the half-breed, convinced by Laird's insistence that they could return to the lodge and even to Pashepaho, if Peter liked, before darkness fell, consented to lead us to the slab. Then, despite his unsteadiness, he set off swiftly into the woods along a lane that could hardly be called a trail, so faint it was, and loped along steadily for almost a mile before he drew up short and, standing behind a tree, as if he were afraid of being seen, pointed shakily to a little open spot surrounded by high trees at enough of a distance that ample sky was visible overhead.

"There—that's it."

The slab was only partly visible, for moss had grown over much of it. Laird, however, was at the moment only secondarily interested in it; it was manifest that the half-breed stood in mortal terror of the spot and wished only to escape.

"How would you like to spend the night here, Peter?" asked Laird.

The half-breed shot a frightened glance at him. "Me? Gawd, no!"

Suddenly Laird's voice steeled. "Unless you tell us what it was you saw here, that's what you're going to do."

The half-breed was not so much the worse for liquor that he could not foresee events—the possibility that Laird and I might overcome him and tie him to a tree at the edge of this open space. Plainly, he considered a bolt for it, but he knew that in his condition he could not outrun us.

"Don't make me tell," he said. "It ain't supposed to be told. I ain't never told no one—not even the professor."

"We want to know, Peter," said Laird with no less menace.

The half-breed began to shake; he turned and looked at the slab as if he thought at any moment an inimical being might rise from it and advance upon him with lethal intent. "I can't, I can't," he muttered, and then, forcing his bloodshot eyes to meet Laird's once more, he said in a low voice, "I don't know what it was. Gawd! It was awful. It was a Thing—didn't have no face, hollered there till I thought my eardrums'd bust, and them things that was with it—Gawd!" He shuddered and backed away from the tree, toward us. "Honest t' Gawd, I seen it there one night. It jist come, seems like, out of the air and there it was a-singin' and a-wailin' and them things playin' that damn' music. I guess I was crazy for a while afore I got away." His voice broke, his vivid memory recreated what he had seen; he turned, shouting harshly, "Let's git outa here!" and ran back the way we had come, weaving among the trees.

Laird and I ran after him, catching up easily, Laird reassuring him that we would take him out of the woods in the car, and he would be well away from the forest's edge before darkness overtook him. He was as convinced as I that there was nothing imagined about the half-breed's account, that he had indeed told us all he knew; and he was silent all the way back from the highway to which we took Old Peter, pressing five dollars upon him so that he could forget what he had seen in liquor if he were so inclined.

"What do you think?" asked Laird when we reached the lodge once more.

I shook my head.

"That wailing night before last," said Laird. "The sounds Professor Gardner heard—and now this. It ties up—damnably, horribly." He turned on me with intense and fixed urgency. "Jack, are you game to visit that slab tonight?"

"Certainly."

"We'll do it."

It was not until we were inside the lodge that we thought of the Dictaphone, and then Laird prepared at once to play whatever had been recorded back to us. Here at least, he reflected, was nothing dependent in any way upon anyone's imagination; here was the product of the machine, pure and simple, and everyone of intelligence knew full well that machines were far more dependable than men, having neither nerves nor imagination, knowing neither fear nor hope. I think that at most we counted upon hearing a repetition of the sounds of the previous night; not in our wildest dreams did we look forward to what we did actually hear, for the record mounted from the prosaic to the incredible, from the incredible to the horrible, and at last to a cataclysmic revelation that left us completely cut away from every credo of normal existence.

It began with the occasional singing of loons and owls, followed by a period of silence. Then there was once more that familiar rushing sound, as of wind in the trees, and this was followed by the curious cacophonous piping of flutes. Then there was recorded a series of sounds, which I put down here exactly as we heard them in that unforgettable evening hour:

Ygnaiih! Ygnaiih! EEE-ya-ya-ya-yahaahaahaa-ah-ah-ah-ngh'aaa-ngh'aaa-ya-ya-yaaa! (In a voice that was neither human nor bestial, but yet of both.)

(An increased tempo in the music becoming more wild and demoniac.)

Mighty Messenger—Nyarlathotep ... from the world of Seven Suns to his earth place, the Wood of N'gai, whither may come Him Who Is Not to be Named. ... There shall be abundance of those from the Black Goat of the Woods, the Goat With the Thousand Young .... (In a voice that was curiously human.)

(A succession of odd sounds, as if audience-response: a buzzing and humming, as of telegraph wires.)

Iä! Iä! Shub-Niggurath! Ygnaiih! Ygnaiih! EEE-yaa-yaa-haa-haaa-haaaa! (In the original voice neither human nor beast, yet both.)

Ithaqua shall serve thee, Father of the million favored ones, and Zhar shall be summoned from Arcturus, by the command of 'Umr At-Tawil, Guardian of the Gate. ... Ye shall unite in praise of Azathoth, of Great Cthulhu, of Tsathoggua .... (The human voice again.)

Go forth in his form or in whatever form chosen in the guise of man, and destroy that which may lead them to us. ... (The half-bestial, half-human voice once more.)

(An interlude of furious piping, accompanied once again by a sound as of the flapping of great wings.)

Ygnaiih! Y'bthnk ... h'ehye-n'grkdl'lh .... Iä! Iä! Iä! (Like a chorus.)

These sounds had been spaced in such a way that it seemed as if the beings giving rise to them were moving about within or around the lodge, and the last choral chanting faded away, as if the creatures were departing. Indeed, there followed such an interval of silence that Laird had actually moved to shut off the machine when once again a voice came from it. But the voice that now emanated from the Dictaphone was one which, simply because of its nature, brought to a climax all the horror so cumulative in what had gone before it; for whatever had been implied by the half-bestial bellowings and chants, the horribly suggestive conversation in accented English, that which now came from the Dictaphone was unutterably terrible.

> *Dorgan! Laird Dorgan! Can you hear me?*

A hoarse, urgent whisper calling out to my companion, who sat white-faced now, staring at the machine above which his hand was still poised. Our eyes met. It was not the appeal, it was not everything that had gone before, it was the identity of that voice—*for it was the voice of Professor Upton Gardner!* But we had no time to ponder this, for the Dictaphone went mechanically on.

> Listen to me! Leave this place. Forget. But before you go, summon Cthugha. For centuries this has been the place where evil beings from outermost cosmos have touched upon Earth. I know. I am theirs. They have taken me, as they took Piregard and many others—all who came unwarily within their wood and whom they did not at once destroy. It is His wood—the Wood of N'gai, the terrestrial abode of the Blind, Faceless One, the Howler in the Night, the Dweller in Darkness, Nyarlathotep, who fears only Cthugha. I have been with him in the star spaces. I have been on the shunned Plateau of Leng—to Kadath in the Cold Waste, beyond the Gates of the Silver Key, even to Kythamil near Arcturus and Mnar, to N'kai and the Lake of Hali, to K'n-Yan and fabled Carcosa, to Yaddith and Y'ha-nthlei near Innsmouth, to Yoth and Yuggoth, and from far off I have looked upon Zothique, from the eye of Algol. When Fomalhaut has topped the trees, call forth to Cthugha in these words, thrice repeated: *Ph'nglui mglw'nafh Cthugha Fomalhaut n'gha-ghaa naf'l thagn. Iä! Cthugha!* When He has come, go swiftly, lest you too be destroyed. For it is fitting that this accursed spot be blasted so that Nyarlathotep comes no more out of interstellar space. Do you hear me, Dorgan? Do you hear me? Dorgan! Laird Dorgan!

There was a sudden sound of sharp protest, followed by a scuffling and tearing noise, as if Gardner had been forcibly removed, and then silence, utter and complete!

For a few moments longer Laird let the record run, but there was nothing more. Finally he started it over, saying tensely, "I think we'd better copy that as best we can. You take every other speech, and let's both copy that formula from Gardner."

"Was it …?"

"I'd know his voice anywhere," he said shortly.

"He's alive then?"

He looked at me, his eyes narrowed. "We don't know that."

"But his voice!"

He shook his head, for the sounds were coming forth once more, and both of us had to bend to the task of copying, which was easier than it promised to be for the spaces between speeches were great enough to enable us to copy without undue haste. The language of the chants and the words to Cthugha enunciated by Gardner's voice offered extreme difficulty, but by means of repeated playings, we managed to put down the approximate equivalent of the sounds. When finally we had finished, Laird shut the Dictaphone off and looked at me with quizzical and troubled eyes, grave with concern and uncertainty. I said nothing; what we had just heard, added to everything that had gone before, left us no alternative. There was room for doubt about legends, beliefs, and the like—but the infallible record of the Dictaphone was conclusive even if it did no more than verify half-heard credos—for it was true, there was still nothing definite; it was as if the whole were so completely beyond the comprehension of man that only in the oblique suggestion of its individual parts could something like understanding be achieved, as if the entirety were too unspeakably soul-searing for the mind of man to withstand.

"Fomalhaut rises almost at sunset—a little before, I think," mused Laird—clearly, like myself, he had accepted what we had heard without challenge other than the mystery surrounding its meaning. "It should be above the horizon, because it doesn't pass near enough to the zenith in this latitude to appear above these pines—at approximately an hour after darkness falls. Say nine-thirty or so."

"You aren't thinking of trying it tonight?" I asked. "After all—what does it mean? Who or what is Cthugha?"

"I don't know any more than you. And I'm not trying it tonight. You've forgotten the slab. Are you still game to go out there—after this?"

I nodded. I did not trust myself to speak, but I was not consumed by any eagerness whatever to dare the darkness that lingered like a living entity within the forest surrounding Rick's Lake.

Laird looked at his watch, and then at me, his eyes burning now with a kind of feverish determination, as if he were forcing himself to take this final step to face the unknown being whose manifestations had made the wood its own. If he expected me to hesitate, he was disappointed; however beset by fear I might be, I would not show it. I got up and went out of the lodge at his side.

IV

THERE are aspects of hidden life, exterior as well as of the depths of the mind, that are better kept secret and away from the awareness of common man; for there lurk in dark places of the earth terrible desiderata, horrible revenants belonging to a stratum of the subconscious which is mercifully beyond the apprehension of common man—indeed, there are aspects of creation so grotesquely shuddersome that the very sight of them would blast the sanity of the beholder. Fortunately, it is not possible even to bring back in anything but suggestion what we saw on the slab in the forest at Rick's Lake that night in October, for the thing was so unbelievable, transcending all known laws of science, that adequate words for its description have no existence in the language.

We arrived at the belt of trees around the slab while afterglow yet lingered in the western heavens, and by the illumination of a flashlight Laird carried, we examined the face of the slab itself, and the carving on it: of a vast, amorphous creature, drawn by an artist who evidently lacked sufficient imagination to etch the creature's face, for it had none, bearing only a curious, cone-like head which even in stone seemed to have a fluidity which was unnerving; moreover, the creature was depicted as having both tentacle-like appendages and hands—or growths similar to hands, not only two, but several; so that it seemed both human and non-human in its structure. Beside it had been carved two squat squid-like figures from a part of which—presumably the heads, though no outline was definitive—projected what must certainly have been instruments of some kind, for the strange, repugnant attendants appeared to be playing them.

Our examination was necessarily hurried, for we did not want to risk being seen here by whatever might come, and it may be that in the circumstances, imagination got the better of us. But I do not think so. It is difficult to maintain that consistently, sitting here at my desk, removed in space and time from what happened there; but I maintain it. Despite the quickened awareness and irrational fear of the unknown which obsessed both of us, we kept a determined open-mindedness about every aspect of the problem we had chosen to solve. If anything, I have erred in this account on the side of science over that of imagination. In the plain light of reason, the carvings on that stone slab were not only obscene, but bestial and frightening beyond measure, particularly in the light of what Partier had hinted, and what Gardner's notes and the material from Miskatonic University had vaguely outlined, and even if time had permitted, it is doubtful if we could have looked long upon them.

We retreated to a spot comparatively near the way we must take to return to the lodge, and yet not too far from the open place where the slab lay, so that we might see clearly and still remain hidden in a place easy of access to the return path. There we took our stand and waited in that chilling hush of an October evening, while Stygian darkness encompassed us, and only one or two stars twinkled high overhead, miraculously visible among the towering treetops.

According to Laird's watch, we waited exactly an hour and ten minutes before the sound as of wind began, and at once there was a manifestation which had about it all the trappings of the supernatural; for no sooner had the rushing sound begun, than the slab we had so quickly quitted began to glow—at first so indistinguishably that it seemed an illusion, and then with a phosphorescence of increasing brilliance, until it gave off such a glow that it was as if a pillar of light extended upward into the heavens. This was the second curious circumstance—the light followed the outlines of the slab, and flowed upward; it was not diffused and dispersed around the glade and into the woods, but shone heavenward with the insistence of a directed beam. Simultaneously, the very air seemed charged with evil; all around us lay thickly such an aura of fearsomeness that it rapidly became impossible to remain free of it. It was apparent that by some means unknown to us the rushing sound as of wind which now filled the air was not only associated with the broad beam of light flowing upward, *but was caused by it*; moreover, as we watched, the intensity and color of the light varied constantly, changing from a blinding white to a lambent green, from green to a kind of lavender; occasionally it was so intensely brilliant that it was necessary to avert our eyes, but for the most part it could be looked at without hurt to our eyes.

As suddenly as it had begun, the rushing sound stopped, the light became diffuse and dim; and almost immediately the weird piping as of flutes smote upon our ears. It came not from around us, but from *above*, and with one accord, both of us turned to look as far into heaven as the now fading light would permit.

Just what took place then before our eyes I cannot explain. Was it actually something that came hurtling down—streaming down, rather?—for the masses were shapeless—or was it the product of an imagination that proved singularly uniform when later Laird and I found opportunity to compare notes? The illusion of great black things streaking down in the path of that light was so great that we glanced back at the slab.

What we saw there sent us screaming voicelessly from that hellish spot.

For, where but a moment before there had been nothing, there was now a gigantic protoplasmic mass, a colossal being who towered upward toward the stars, and whose actual physical being was in constant flux; and flanking it on either side were two lesser beings, equally amorphous, holding pipes or flutes in appendages and making that demoniac music which echoed and reechoed in the enclosing forest. But the thing on the slab, the Dweller in Darkness, was the ultimate in horror; for from its mass of amorphous flesh there grew at will before our eyes tentacles, claws, hands, and withdrew again; the mass itself diminished and swelled effortlessly, and where its head was and its features should have been there was only a blank facelessness all the more horrible because even as we looked there rose from its blind mass a low ululation in that half-bestial, half-human voice so familiar to us from the record made in the night!

We fled, I say, so shaken that it was only by a supreme effort of will that we were able to take flight in the right direction. Behind us the voice rose, the blasphemous voice of Nyarlathotep, the Blind, Faceless One, the Mighty Messenger, even while there rang in the channels of memory the frightened words of the half-breed, Old Peter—*It was a Thing—didn't have no face, hollered there till I thought my eardrums'd bust, and them things that was with it—Gawd!*—echoed there while the voice of that Being from outermost space shrieked and gibbered to the hellish music of the hideous attending flute-players, rising to ululate through the forest and leave its mark forever in memory!

Ygnaiih! Ygnaiih! EEE-yayayayayaaa-haaahaaahaaahaaa-ngh'aaa-ngh'aaa-ya-ya-yaaa!

Then all was still.

Yet, incredible as it may seem, the ultimate horror awaited us.

For we had gone but halfway to the lodge when we were simultaneously aware of something following; behind us rose a hideous, horribly suggestive *sloshing* sound, as if the amorphous entity had left the slab which in some remote time must have been erected by its worshipers, and were pursuing us. Obsessed by abysmal fright, we ran as neither of us has ever run before, and we were almost upon the lodge before we were aware that the sloshing sound, the trembling and shuddering of the earth—as if some gigantic being walked upon it—had ceased, and in their stead came only the calm, unhurried tread of footsteps.

But the footsteps were not our own! And in the aura of unreality, the fearsome outsideness in which we walked and breathed, the terrible suggestiveness of those footsteps was almost maddening!

We reached the lodge, lit a lamp, and sank into chairs to await whatever it was that was coming so steadily, unhurriedly on, mounting the verandah steps, putting its hand on the knob of the door, swinging the door open—

It was Professor Gardner who stood there!

For one cataclysmic moment, we sat open-mouthed and gazed at him as at a man returned from the dead.

Then Laird sprang up, crying, "Professor Gardner!"

The professor smiled reservedly, and put one hand up to shade his eyes. "If you don't mind, I'd like the light dimmed. I've been in the dark for so long ...."

Laird turned to do his bidding without question, and he came forward into the room, walking with the ease and poise of a man who is as sure of himself as if he had never vanished from the face of the earth more than three months before, as if he had not made a frantic appeal to us during the night just past, as if—

I glanced at Laird; his hand was still at the lamp, but his fingers were no longer turning down the wick, simply holding to it, while he gazed down unseeing. I looked over at Professor Gardner; he sat with his head turned from the lights, his eyes closed, a little smile playing about his lips; at that moment he looked precisely as I had often seen him look at the University Club in Madison, and it was as if everything that had taken place here at the lodge were but an evil dream.

But it was not a dream!

"You were gone last night?" asked the professor.

"Yes. But, of course, we had the Dictaphone."

"Ah. You heard something then?"

"Would you like to hear the record, sir?"

"Yes, I would."

Laird went over and put it on the machine to play it again, and we sat in silence, listening to everything upon it, no one saying anything until it had been completed. Then the professor slowly turned his head.

"What do you make of it?"

"I don't know what to make of it, sir," answered Laird. "The speeches are too disjointed—except for yours. There seems to be some coherence there."

Suddenly, without warning, the room was surcharged with menace; it was but a momentary impression, but Laird felt it as keenly as I did, for he started noticeably. He was taking the record from the machine when the professor spoke again.

"It doesn't occur to you that you may be the victim of a hoax?"

"No."

"And if I told you that I had found it possible to make every sound that was registered on that record?"

Laird looked at him for a full minute before replying in a low voice that of course, Professor Gardner had been investigating the phenomena of Rick's Lake woods for a far longer time than we had, and if he said so—

A harsh laugh escaped the professor. "Entirely natural phenomena, my boy! There's a mineral deposit under that grotesque slab in the woods; it gives off light and also a miasma that is productive of hallucinations. It's as simple as that. As for the various disappearances—sheer folly, human failing, nothing more, but with the air of coincidence. I came here with high hopes of verifying some of the nonsense to which old Partier lent himself long ago—but—" He smiled disdainfully, shook his head, and extended his hand. "Let me have the record, Laird."

Without question, Laird gave Professor Gardner the record. The older man took it and was bringing it up before his eyes when he jogged his elbow and, with a sharp cry of pain, dropped it. It broke into dozens of pieces on the floor of the lodge.

"Oh!" cried the professor. "I'm sorry." He turned his eyes on Laird. "But then—since I can duplicate it any time for you from what I've learned about the lore of this place, by way of Partier's mouthings—" He shrugged.

"It doesn't matter," said Laird quietly.

"Do you mean to say that everything on that record was just your imagination, Professor?" I broke in. "Even that chant for the summoning of Cthugha?"

The older man's eyes turned on me; his smile was sardonic. "Cthugha? What do you suppose he or that is but the figment of someone's imagination? And the inference—my dear boy, use your head. You have before you the clear inference that Cthugha has his abode on Fomalhaut which is twenty-seven light years away, and that, if this chant is thrice repeated when Fomalhaut has risen, Cthugha will appear to somehow render this place no longer habitable by man or outside entity. How do you suppose that could be accomplished?"

"Why, by something akin to thought-transference," replied Laird doggedly. "It's not unreasonable to suppose that if we were to direct thoughts toward Fomalhaut that something there might receive them—granting that there might be life there. Thought is instant. And that they in turn may be so highly developed that dematerialization and rematerialization might be as swift as thought."

"My boy—are you serious?" The older man's voice revealed his contempt.

"You asked."

"Well, then, as the hypothetical answer to a theoretical problem, I can overlook that."

"Frankly," I said again, disregarding a curious negative shaking of Laird's head, "I don't think that what we saw in the forest tonight was just hallucination—caused by a miasma rising out of the earth or otherwise."

The effect of this statement was extraordinary. Visibly, the professor made every effort to control himself; his reactions were precisely those of a savant challenged by a cretin in one of his classes. After a few moments he controlled himself and said only, "You've been there then. I suppose it's too late to make you believe otherwise—"

"I've always been open to conviction, sir, and I lean to the scientific method," said Laird.

Professor Gardner put his hand over his eyes and said, "I'm tired. I noticed last night when I was here that you're in my old room, Laird—so I'll take the room next to you, opposite Jack's."

He went up the stairs as if nothing had happened between the last time he had occupied the lodge and this.

V

THE rest of the story—and the culmination of that apocalyptic night—are soon told.

I could not have been asleep for more than an hour—the time was one in the morning—when I was awakened by Laird. He stood beside my bed fully dressed and in a tense voice ordered me to get up and dress, to pack whatever essentials I had brought, and be ready for anything. Nor would he permit me to put on a light to do so, though he carried a small pocket-flash, and used it sparingly. To all my questions, he cautioned me to wait.

When I had finished, he led the way out of the room with a whispered, "Come."

He went directly to the room into which Professor Gardner had disappeared. By the light of his flash, it was evident that the bed had not been touched; moreover, in the faint film of dust that lay on the floor, it was clear that Professor Gardner had walked into the room, over to a chair beside the window, and out again.

"Never touched the bed, you see," whispered Laird.

"But why?"

Laird gripped my arm, hard. "Do you remember what Partier hinted—what we saw in the woods—the protoplasmic, amorphousness of the thing? And what the record said?"

"But Gardner told us—" I protested.

Without a further word, he turned. I followed him downstairs, where he paused at the table where we had worked and flashed the light upon it. I was surprised into making a startled exclamation which Laird hushed instantly. For the table was bare of everything but the copy of *The Outsider and Others* and three copies of *Weird Tales*, a magazine containing stories supplementing those in the book by the eccentric Providence genius, Lovecraft. All Gardner's notes, all our own notations, the photostats from Miskatonic University—everything was gone!

"He took them," said Laird. "No one else could have done so."

"Where did he go?"

"Back to the place from which he came." He turned on me, his eyes gleaming in the reflected glow of the flashlight. "Do you understand what that means, Jack?"

I shook my head.

"*They* know we've been there, *they* know we've seen and learned too much—"

"But how?"

"You told them."

"I? Good God, man, are you mad? How could I have told them?"

"Here, in this lodge, tonight—you yourself gave the show away, and I hate to think of what might happen now. We've got to get away."

For one moment all the events of the past few days seemed to fuse into an unintelligible mass; Laird's urgency was unmistakable, and yet the thing that he suggested was so utterly unbelievable that its contemplation even for so fleeting a moment threw my thoughts into the extremest confusion.

Laird was talking now, quickly. "Don't you think it odd—how he came back? How he came out of the woods *after* that hellish thing we saw there—not before? And the questions he asked—the drift of those questions. And how he managed to break the record—our one scientific proof of something? And now, the disappearance of all the notes—of everything that might point to substantiation of what he called 'Partier's nonsense?'"

"But if we are to believe what he told us—"

He broke in before I could finish. "One of them was right. Either the voice on the record calling to me—or the man who was here tonight."

"The man—"

But whatever I wanted to say was stilled by Laird's harsh, "*Listen!*"

From outside, from the depths of that horror-haunted dark, the earth-haven of the dweller in darkness, came once more, for the second time that night, the weirdly beautiful yet cacophonous strains of flute-like music, rising and falling, accompanied by a kind of chanted ululation, and by the sound as of great wings flapping.

"Yes, I hear," I whispered.

"*Listen closely!*"

Even as he spoke, I understood. There was something more—the sounds from the forest were not only rising and falling—*they were approaching!*

"Now do you believe me?" demanded Laird. "*They're coming for us!*" He turned on me. "The chant!"

"What chant?" I fumbled stupidly.

"The Cthugha chant—do you remember it?"

"I took it down. I've got it here."

For an instant I was afraid that this, too, might have been taken from us, but it was not; it was in my pocket where I had left it. With shaking hands, Laird tore the paper from my grasp.

"*Ph'nglui mglw'nafh Cthugha Fomalhaut n'gha-ghaa naf'l thagn! Iä! Cthugha!* " he said, running to the verandah, myself at his heels.

Out of the woods came the bestial voice of the dweller in the dark. "*Ee-ya-ya-haa-haahaaa! Ygnaiih! Ygnaiih!*"

"*Ph'nglui mglw'nafh Cthugha Fomalhaut n'gha-ghaa naf'l thagn! Iä! Cthugha!* " repeated Laird for the second time.

Still the ghastly melee of sounds from the woods came on, in no way diminished, rising now to supreme heights of terror-fraught fury, with the bestial voice of the thing from the slab added to the wild, mad music of the pipes, and the sound as of wings.

Then, once more, Laird repeated the primal words of the chant.

On the instant that the final guttural sound had left his lips, there began a sequence of events no human eye was ever destined to witness. For suddenly the darkness was gone, giving way to a fearsome amber glow; simultaneously the flute-like music ceased, and in its place rose cries of rage and terror. Then there appeared thousands of tiny points of light—not only on and among the trees, but on the earth itself, on the lodge and the car standing before it. For still a further moment we were rooted to the spot, and then it was borne in upon us that the myriad points of light were *living entities of flame!* For wherever they touched, fire sprang up, seeing which, Laird rushed into the lodge for such of our things as he could carry forth before the holocaust made it impossible for us to escape Rick's Lake.

He came running out—our bags had been downstairs—gasping that it was too late to take the Dictaphone or anything else, and together we dashed toward the car, shielding our eyes a little from the blinding light all around. But even though we had shielded our eyes, it was impossible not to see the great amorphous shapes streaming skyward from this accursed place, nor the equally great being hovering like a cloud of living fire above the trees. So much we saw, before the frightful struggle to escape the burning woods forced us to forget mercifully the other details of that terrible, maddened flight.

Horrible as were the things that took place in the darkness of the forest at Rick's Lake, there was something more cataclysmic still, something so blasphemously conclusive that even now I shudder and tremble uncontrollably to think if it. For in that brief dash to the car, I saw something that explained Laird's doubt, I saw what had made him take heed of the voice on the record and not of the thing that came to us as Professor Gardner. The keys were there before, but I did not understand; even Laird had not fully believed. Yet it was given to us—we did not know. "It is not desired by the Old Ones that mere man shall know too much," Partier had said. That terrible voice on the record had hinted even more clearly: *Go forth in his form or in whatever form chosen in the guise of man, and destroy that which may lead them to us.* Destroy that which may lead them to us! Our record, the notes, the photostats from Miskatonic University, yes, and even Laird and myself! And the thing had gone forth, for it was Nyarlathotep, the Mighty Messenger, the Dweller in Darkness who had gone forth and who had returned into the forest to send his minions back to us. It was he who had come from interstellar space even as Cthugha, the fire-being, had come from Fomalhaut upon the utterance of the command that woke him from his eon-long sleep upon that amber star, the command that Gardner, the living-dead captive of the terrible Nyarlathotep had discovered in those fantastic travelings in space and time; and it was he who returned whence he had come, with his earth-haven now forever rendered useless for him with its destruction by the minions of Cthugha!

I know, and Laird knows. We never speak of it.

If we had had any doubt, despite everything that had gone before, we could not forget that final, soul-searing discovery, the thing we saw when we shielded our eyes from the flames all around and looked away from those beings in the heavens, the line of footprints that led away from the lodge in the direction of that hellish slab deep in the black forest, *the footprints that began in the soft soil beyond the verandah in the shape of a man's footprints, and changed with each step into a hideously suggestive imprint made by a creature of incredible shape and weight, with variations of outline and size so grotesque as to have been incomprehensible to anyone who had not seen the thing on the slab—and beside them, torn and rent as if by an expanding force, the clothing that had once belonged to Professor Gardner, left piece by piece along the trail back into the woods, the trail taken by the hellish monstrosity that had come out of the night, the Dweller in Darkness who had visited us in the shape and guise of Professor Gardner!*

THIS story, which first appeared in *Fantastic Stories of Imagination* for February 1963, was one of the few Cthulhu Mythos tales anyone produced during the sixties. Few remember it today. I had never heard of it till Fred Blosser tipped me off to it. You will note how the story makes good use of themes and sequences from various familiar tales by Lovecraft and Bloch. We start out in Bloch's "The Secret of Sebek", tip our hat to "The Skull of the Marquis de Sade", slink through the streets with "Pickman's Model", and descend the stairs with "The Grinning Ghoul" down into "The Festival." On the whole the story provides a glimpse of what HPL denied us in "The Rats in the Walls", "those grinning caverns of earth's centre where Nyarlathotep, the mad faceless god, howls blindly in the darkness."

It is a fine patchwork, where you have to look pretty hard to spot the seams. Warner may seem from this description to have mortared together a pile of literary bricks, but if so, I have already misled you. I trace out what I guess to be his sources just to highlight the quality of what he has built with them. As you will see, the tale is anything but pat and predictable.

In its original publication, the piece bore the following introduction about the author:

> The hold that H. P. Lovecraft exerts from beyond the grave on followers of fantasy seems to grow stronger through the years. This story, by a New Orleans newspaperman, grew out of his admiration for Lovecraft, and his determination to keep alive the HPL style by using it in fanciful letters to his friends. This was the only letter written. But it weaves a spell worthy of the master.

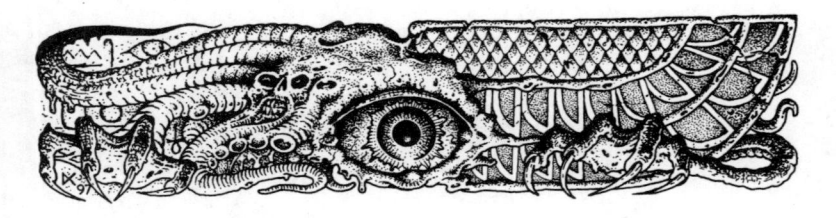

The Titan in the Crypt

by J. G. Warner

DEAR Jim,

I am sending this by special delivery so it should get to you by the day after tomorrow. I shall follow it by no more than a day. You must take me in for a time until I get my bearings, and can determine on which side of the balance my mind lies.

I know you would receive me without so much as a preparing letter. I am writing this, rather, to keep my own sanity, which has been pushed to the brink by the final horror that has just befallen me. You are the only person I know who would even listen to such a story as I have to tell. You must believe it and help me escape. You can, if anyone or anything can. But I doubt whether I can get away, ultimately.

You remember Tessier, the fat old furniture dealer. It all began with him. He drank a lot, you know, and talked pretty wildly; you seemed rather interested in him, although it seemed to me that his queer hints and insinuations were only the product of an oversensitive imagination nurtured in New Orleans. Well, Tessier remarked that he knew a lot about things you were interested in—your folklore and mythology, of course—after you left last summer. He never would say just what, but kept telling me to wait. I must say that he got me pretty interested.

Two days ago he called me. He was drunk, worse than usual. It was the last night of Mardi Gras, but I hadn't made any plans, and he insisted that I come to his store. He said that he was finally ready to show me the secret he had been talking about, and kept apologizing and bemoaning the fact that you weren't here. Thank God you weren't.

Well, since I really hadn't anything to do, and it would give me a chance to get rid of Tessier and his dark mutterings, I conceded. I left the apartment and started fighting my way through the wild carnival crowds. It was not more than five blocks from my apartment to Tessier's on Royal, but it took me more than half an hour to get there.

You've never seen the French Quarter on a carnival night, Jim. It's mad; the streets are roped off, crowds so thick you can hardly move. Drunks lurch into you and women tug your sleeve—it's really rather unpleasant unless you're in the mood, and I wasn't. The din was deafening, and the old wrought-iron galleries were sagging beneath the weight of the celebrants dancing on them. The streets are so narrow that the people on the galleries could nearly join hands across the packed street. It was terribly hot and muggy, and a rather unpleasant smell was coming off the Mississippi. It's only a few blocks from Royal, you know, and when the Quarter isn't so noisy you can hear the cow-like lowing of the ships' horns.

I WAS in a decidedly foul mood when I finally got to Tessier's pretentious antique furniture store. You were never there, were you? It's the usual thing for the Rue Royal—lots of glass with all those polished gold buckets and vulgar stone statues piled in careless disarray. The old fool was waiting inside under a little porcelain lamp and when he saw me at the door, he waddled to unlock it.

He was almost overpoweringly drunk, and had the air of a man about to uncover the secrets of the universe. I was suddenly beset by an overwhelming urge to turn around and go home, but before I could act he had bolted the door and was leading me to the rear of his shop.

Tessier looked even worse under the lamp, surrounded by all those ominous big stone nymphs and birds and ancient chairs. A gross, revolting soapstone Buddha two feet high peered down from a filing cabinet at us with a vapidly inscrutable expression. The old antique seller was in really bad shape. He hadn't even attempted to shave for a couple of days and there was a yellow tinge under the normal sickly grayish cast of his hog-jowled face. He acted alternately frightened and excited as he pulled me into a dimly lit back room, like a child hugging itself in some pleasurable yet dreaded anticipation.

"This is the night—the night, you know," he tittered, and began fumbling into some sort of closet. I didn't think this sort of statement was worth an answer, so after a moment he went on.

"You'll find a lot of things to startle you about New Orleans tonight, Paul. You'd never believe it if I told you, and you'd probably have babbled it, so that's why I didn't tell you until tonight, so you can see for yourself.

"But you must never speak to anyone of what you will see down there tonight. Never. You'll see what I mean. God, if they should ever learn I brought you ...."

I was growing impatient. "What's all this about, Tessier? And what's that?" He had brought two strange, musty-looking dun-colored robes with loose cowls from the closet.

"Put it on," he said, handing one of the mildewed things to me.

"Paul, you won't believe this until you see it, but I'll tell you now, because we can't talk, not even whisper, once we get there. Remember that. They might notice you.

"The French Quarter is two centuries or more old, you know. There's a hundred blocks of it now but you only know half of it. The rest of it's down there," he said, almost shouting, and pointing at his feet. "Only about fifty people know this, and you'll be surprised who they are.

"Yes, there's something down there, under these crumbling buildings and banquettes that have been here since white men were here. But it's been down there long before that, long before there was a Vieux Carré, and probably even before there were Indians. It's probably been there forever.

"You didn't think the old town was built here, in the middle of a Godforsaken swamp, for nothing, did you? Not when it's a lot better for a town site a little farther up the river.

"We all go down there, once a year, the last night of Carnival. Our fathers did, and their fathers before them, and theirs, and God knows who else before that. I don't know why we go down there now, really, but we do, and when you see who else goes down, maybe you'll think it's gotten us results. You'll see some pretty rough things, Paul, and I hope you won't give yourself away."

"For God's sake, man, what are you talking about?" I demanded, thoroughly disgusted now. "What's down there?"

"Catacombs," he croaked. "Miles of them. Nobody's been through them all, that we know of, and we don't know how far or how deep they go, but they seem to cover all the Quarter—underneath."

Well, Jim, this was the first concrete statement of the night, and you'll understand that it was enough to make me pull on the evil-smelling old robe and pull the cowl over my head, as Tessier did.

"It's nearly time now. We must go, and remember, whatever you do, don't say a word once we step out this door. Keep absolutely quiet and don't stare. If anybody notices you aren't one of us, God help me—and you."

WITH that, he doused the lights and opened a rear door. The blackness of the night made it seem nearly light within the store. Tessier looked up at me and in the dimness at the door his disgusting face was almost pitiful with a fearfulness that was beginning to pervade it. I think he was starting to wish he hadn't brought me, and I was about to offer to leave, when an overpowering stench of whiskey floated into my nostrils, gagging me, and I pushed him out the door.

We were in a small, rundown courtyard, piled around with boxes and crates and old packing and stuffing. Tessier tugged at the flowing sleeve of my cassock and I started after him through the blackness.

We passed out through the little courtyard and into a long, high-walled passageway. The din of the celebration burst afresh into my ears, and above the walls and the rooftops of the old town we were creeping through, the lights offered an eerie glow. Raucous, obscene, and wildly incongruous music shrieked at us from the nearby Bourbon Street dives as we walked silently through the deserted, musty outdoor corridor. The walk led to an old wooden door, and through that we went into another courtyard. It was pitch black at eye-level but I could hear the bubbling of a fountain nearby over the roar of the crowds in the streets outside.

Tessier opened a protesting door and we were on a side street, Conti I think it was. It is the last place-memory I have of that night. Nobody took notice of us, with more strangely costumed figures to be seen anywhere during Mardi Gras, and we slipped across the street and into another doorway.

We didn't, I don't think, cross another street. But it seems that Tessier, growing surprisingly steadier in that oppressively hot, dank air, led me through an endless series of courtyards, passages, plank doors and private alleys until I was perfectly lost. I guess we must have crossed a street somewhere. I remember I never lost sight of the dim glow above the crumbling rooftops, and I could always hear the laughing, milling crowds in the streets.

It seemed we had been threading our way through those ancient galleried courtyards for more than half an hour when Tessier suddenly pushed open a door and only blackness looked out. We went in and he shut the door and for long moments I couldn't see a thing. Then, just as I was growing accustomed to the utter darkness, the door opened again and three more hooded and cowled figures slunk in.

As best I could tell, Jim, the place was an old slave-quarters; it had only one big room and another small floor above; but we were there only long enough for Tessier to light a soaked rag on the end of a club-like piece of wood and he was bearing one of those torches so beloved of the pulp magazine artists.

Then he walked to the middle of the room and began tugging at a ring on the floor. One of the three strangers went to help him. I glanced around enough to see that the place was falling apart, the two windows boarded up.

THEN Tessier was tugging at my sleeve. The other three had already gone down the hole that their efforts had opened. Now Tessier was ready to descend into the square-shaped hole in the brick floor. There wasn't a ladder there. Rather, there were steps, hewn and placed into the immemorially soggy ground. Tessier went down and motioned for me to pull the door shut above me as I followed. I was groping for the lid to the trap when I noticed that I could no longer hear the carnival revelers. Then I pulled the trap door shut above me and it clanged into place with a startling boom that was answered by an echo from the bowels of the earth.

I had never known it before, but apparently I suffer from claustrophobia. No doubt it was enhanced by the utter weirdness of everything I had been doing and everything I had seen for the past hour, but when the door shut over my head and I looked down at the fire-lit, endless steps running into the worm-riddled earth, an icy chill settled behind my forehead and I had to fight off the advance guard of panic.

The three persons that had descended before us were already out of sight, but I fancied I could hear footsteps echoing back through that terrible moldy tunnel. The slightest noise produced unerringly somber results in that nether world.

Tessier was pulling at me again, and we began the descent. His torch cast shadows about us. I could see that the walls of the sharply declining hole were earthen; it was not shored up in any manner that I could discern. The steps were of stone, worn unaccountably smooth at the edges, since Tessier told me this eerie pilgrimage was made only once a year, on the last day of Carnival. I wondered how this seemingly small amount of stone could produce such perfect echoes.

Down and down we went, Jim, until my legs were about to give out. Tessier was clutching at the earth, and now we had gone so far down that it was fairly oozing with slime and wetness, and revolting green slime on the steps made the descent treacherous. Every so often we passed holes nearly a foot large in the walls, and they reminded me of the little worm passages in a spadeful of upturned earth.

The indescribably foul odor that seemed almost to ooze visibly from the black earthen walls was becoming unbearable and I feared I would fall on the slippery steps and retch, when the steps suddenly halted and Tessier's torch flared out in a large, high-ceilinged earth chamber.

THE chamber was like an overturned bowl, and must have been twenty feet high at its peak, and probably twenty feet across. It was like an eldritch fearsome vestibule, for six black openings had been cut into the circular walls. Tessier walked to the center of the earthen room and looked about, a puzzled expression on his fat features, while great drops of moisture oozed from the blackish-yellow ceiling and dripped on his mouldering cassock. Then he nodded to himself and started into one of the six openings, beckoning me to follow with a jerk of his flaming torch.

We entered the slightly round door and I found myself peering down an almost—as far as I could tell from Tessier's torch—illimitable catacomb. The old fool had been speaking the truth. The French Quarter was undermined with these sinister dank tunnels, although I have no idea how far below the gay carnival crowds we were.

Tessier, apparently sober now and growing increasingly agitated, waddled as briskly as he could down the slightly concave floor of the round catacomb. I found it hardly high enough to stand erect, and began walking with a stoop, but even so something wet and wholly loathsome seeped through the cowl into my hair and down my face occasionally.

The catacomb wasn't as long as I must have thought, for we hadn't walked long before some sort of noise seemed to float to our ears over the drum-like beats of our footsteps. The stone had stopped with the steps, and all about us was bloated earth now, but still those perfect reproductions of every sound struck our ears like mocking laughter. Strange growths tugged at my cowl and my head was soggy with clinging lumps of swollen dirt as we forged on; soon the cowl was pushed back and my hair was growing matted with that unnameable excretion of the earth that dripped on it.

All the time the buzzing grew louder, and soon I seemed to detect a glow of light far down the catacomb we were following, far beyond the feeble reach of Tessier's faggot. Still we kept on that soggy path in the tunnel, although at intervals of about twenty paces new catacombs yawned blackly at us from either side; it is a wonder we were not lost forever in that murky awfulness below New Orleans. Better perhaps for me that we had been.

The noise grew louder, and the glow brighter, and my fear, thrust back by ever-present conscious effort, surged back in a great wave when from a side catacomb belched a soggy thump as I passed—a thump almost inaudible, giving the impression of fathomless distance. I nearly cried out, but Tessier did not falter; apparently the growing growl from ahead had drowned that awful flopping sound from his ears.

I was staggering, nearly sick with a fear that I could hardly hold in my stomach, when the end of the catacomb appeared and I saw a milling crowd of the cowled figures. Thirty more paces to the blazingly lighted door and I almost fainted when I saw black hands bigger than a man reaching down for the hooded forms.

A PARALYZING, sickening horror gripped me when I saw those two great ebony hands cupping down as if to reach under the crowd of tan-robed men, but in another instant I realized that those gruesome claws were part of a terrible titan statue that hovered like a monstrous demon of death over the illimitable chamber and its occupants. As the terrible fright poured from me like an outgoing tide, leaving me weak and queasy, I gazed awestruck at that chamber, at the great black figure that dominated it—that was it, almost, and the sinister group gathered under the fearful shadow of the giant.

The chamber was so vast that the torches held on poles not far from the mouth of the catacomb in which we stood, and ranging far back until they were only little evil stars, seemed to illuminate only fractions of it. Jim, it seemed to me to cover more than a square mile; of course I can't be sure since I couldn't see the far reaches of the dome-shaped, although oblong, earthen grotto, and my mental state then was admittedly wretched.

In the center, under that breathtaking, all-encompassing figure, stood about fifty persons, dressed like Tessier and me. When I saw some of their faces, I could hardly believe it, just as Tessier had warned. The very contemporary fathers of the city of New Orleans stood there, looking rather ridiculous, their uncomfortably smiling faces peering from the shadows of their cowls.

I will not name the men I saw. Great politicians, whose reputations were not of the highest but certainly spoke of nothing like this; financial and shipping barons; university heads—you'd really be shocked there, Jim—mingling with sinister-visaged, ill-reputed but vaguely affluent dwellers of the French Quarter, about whose lives a strange aura of mystery had been attached in that sane world somewhere above us.

They were talking among one another, somewhat self-consciously it seemed, and their faces bore rather embarrassed grins, as if they didn't want to be there, saw no reason for it, and felt silly. Apparently, Jim, they had no conception of what that eyeless thing was that stooped high above them.

The titan stone statue had its feet somewhere in the black recesses of the vast chamber, an egg-shaped auditorium about two hundred feet high at its apex, which was almost directly above us. There at the crown was that bloated head, yet the knee of that great black figure was dimly visible in the shadows, far, far away, slightly bent. The other knee was invisible in the blackness. Its arms were bowed and outstretched downward, bent at the elbows, and appeared about to scoop up us all. The whole great figure gave the impression of a vast black demon hunter, running in city-spanning strides, snatching up its victims in its black, slime-dripping paws.

There above us, Jim, bore down that head for which you have searched the world over; I recognized it from your talks, although neither your words nor mine could describe its blank awfulness. You hunted for years to no avail, but I, God help me, found it.

HIGH above us, yet it must have been a hundred yards across, was a head without a face—a great, ebony head with no features save long, pointed ears almost like wings.

Hurtling over us in his slime-dripping foulness was the Mighty Messenger, the Crawling Chaos from the blackness below the nighted pyramids. Forgotten for centuries upon centuries, buried with civilizations older than man, here he was below the heart of New Orleans, and these great men were vapid fools beneath him, they who would have fled screaming had they known what that magnificently wrought stone colossus represented.

It was set into the bowels of the earth, only a giant bas-relief, and it seemed to nearly cover all of the great chamber's ceiling and part of its sides.

My eyes caught, over the heads of the milling crowd beneath the statue, stone steps rising out of the foul earth and leading to a slimy altar between the outstretched hands of the black god.

My senses still reel when I think of that sight—the flickering torches lighting the end of the vast egglike chamber with its sloping walls hewn from the dirt, and that hideous black giant loping bestially out of the black reaches of the chamber, faceless, reaching impersonally out for us.

Tessier nudged me back to what remained of my senses. I looked down at him and he bore an abjectly fearful, pleading expression. His fat little face conveyed to me perfectly the idea that if it should be discovered that an outsider was in this great dank chamber of horrors, neither of us would ever see the daylight world again.

We joined the group of men moving about the wet stone altar, men who should have been leading the gay Mardi Gras revels somewhere above us instead of lurking furtively under flickering torches in this huge subterranean chamber.

AS far as the eye could follow the walls of the chamber, more catacombs opened, so many I could not begin to count them. In a moment of startling lucidity, I wondered whether I should ever feel safe again in the French Quarter, or all of New Orleans for that matter, knowing the vast emptiness that lay beneath its crust. The remembrance of this thought now makes me want to scream.

The voices of the crowd, gathered round the altar, seemed by the strange acoustics of that accursed nether world to come from everywhere, from even the very unseen feet of the thing that hovered above. Drops of moisture, falling as if from the sky, plopped with revolting little thuds upon us. I stood among the hooded visitors to the depths, and tried to make myself inconspicuous. They seemed to be waiting for something, and the babble swelled when a lone hooded figure came out of the entryway catacomb with a bulky package beneath his arms, wrapped in coarse brown paper.

The man was one of New Orleans' leading morticians. Apparently, whatever he had brought in the package was what had been awaited, for the voices died and perfect silence filled the chamber, except for the plops falling from the great ceiling above. Gathering his robes about him, he started up the wide slippery flight of stairs to the altar, and in the dancing light of the torches the fingers of the black thing seemed to twitch.

He placed the package on the altar and began a high, wailing sort of song-chant. I could make out nothing of what he said, and it seemed to be repeated almost simultaneously everywhere in the vast sunken room. I watched with a sick dread as his hands began to fumble with the knots in the shop cord that held the package together.

The paper fell open and as I strained morbidly to see what was between those titanic black hands, the horror descended upon me.

A muffled roar welled up from the far reaches of the blasted cavern, from the feet of the Mighty Messenger, and grew louder and louder like a vast bowling ball rumbling down a giant's alley toward cowering ten-pins. The faces of the crowd whitened and the last thing I saw was the mortician with his hands wildly outstretched; then a colossal blast of wind blew me from my feet and plunged the great cavern into the blackness of bottomless hell.

I seemed to fall into the very abyss of terror, terror so great that saliva choked me and I clutched myself into a quivering, mindless ball there on the foul dank floor. The coldness of death gripped my brain and I know not how long I lay there trembling and drooling like a stricken idiot.

WHEN thought returned to me the great cave was soundless. I dared not open my eyes for a wild fear of what might be before them. Slowly I relaxed my aching muscles and listened for some sound, something. But there was nothing—nothing at all where there had been fifty people. Even the incessant drip from the ceiling far above me was no more. Then panic came surging back—where was I? Was I still in the cavern? How long had abject terror held me senseless?

Timidly I made an effort to open my eyes. I couldn't at first—the very muscles seemed locked. Then, slowly, they seemed to part; it felt like an infinity. Then they must have been open, but I saw nothing. Only blackness.

My first thought was blindness. I moved my hand until it was before my face, but I could see nothing. I could see no more with my eyes open than I could with them closed.

The noise of rising from that miserable floor sounded like the clash of doom in the utter silence, but nothing touched me. I took a step. Nothing happened—only the sound of the footfall. It seemed like one step was taken everywhere in that great cave. I looked up where I had last seen that faceless evil, but here was only blackness, the blackness of the pit.

I began stepping forward into the blackness, gingerly, my hands in front of me like a blind man. Maybe I was blind. I had no matches, no way to make a light to try to see. Then my hands touched slimy stone and I knew at least that I was still in the great chamber, at the foot of the altar between the hands of the giant. I recoiled from that thing and remembrance of the package on the altar.

I turned, gropingly. I could not even think of what had happened to the others—to Tessier, who had brought a stranger into their midst. I began walking toward the wall upon which the entry catacomb opened—or toward where I thought it was. Then I remembered dismally that the catacomb to the slave quarters in the old town was only one of seemingly hundreds that opened into the chamber, and that I should probably die of hunger before I could even explore part of the first one I found.

But I kept walking, growing more bold in my steps as I grew used to utter blackness, keeping one hand before me. The hand gouged into the pulpy wall, and I sidled to my right, feeling all the while for an opening. Then my hand hit an empty spot—I felt gingerly around for the roof of the catacomb and jerked my hand away in disgust when I realized it was in one of those evil foot-wide holes.

I KEPT going, and the next pocket my hand found proved to be a catacomb. Whether it was the one to the surface, or whether there were others which also led to the surface, I could not know. I entered.

After I had gone a few steps, I noticed that the sounds of my footsteps were more normal in the close confines of the tunnel than they had been in that time-eroded chamber. Then my head, the cowl fallen from it, slid into the roof of the catacomb and furrowed into that repulsive slimy mud. I began to walk with a slight stoop.

The catacomb seemed to take no curves, or at least they were very gradual ones, for only occasionally did I seem to stagger into the wall and recoil from its shocking pulpiness. I do not know how long I must have walked—all thoughts of time were far from my grasp—before it seemed that sight was dimly returning, faintly and blueishly.

A pale blue gas seemed to escape weakly from the moss-ridden walls of that infernal passageway, and I could see very dimly, not close at hand, but at a distance of many paces. The sight was limited to a faint recognition of the slightly tubular outlines of the benighted subterranean pathway.

On and on I went, and in the moldy coolness I grew calmer, and it seemed that the drippings from the ceiling that plagued our entry were not to be found in this tunnel. But the abysmal stench of the first one, a smell of things eon-dead and decaying, like the river of time suddenly run dry, clung all about me, and breathing was a laborious thing.

As I walked, I seemed to become aware of a sense of tension, of cosmic apprehension, as though the catacombs were holding their breath. So strongly did this feeling grip me that I almost unconsciously began to hold my breath, even more than the foul odor made necessary. I held my breath as I walked, then expended it and drew a new lungful, like a child playing at hide-and-go-seek. Then I caught myself walking along with catlike steps, almost on my toes. I found myself listening with all my senses, joining the catacombs in their brooding alertness.

I tiptoed drunkenly down that ghastly tunnel, straining my ears as if I were trying to hear the expectancy of the walls. I jumped and rammed my head into the slimy soft roof when I trod on something that crunched under my foot. I didn't shout, but I started to run, and then the noise of my running frightened me worse than ever, so I gripped myself and resumed walking. I looked over my shoulder, timidly, apprehensively, into the blue light, now glimmering about where I had been when I walked on that thing that crunched. But all I could see was something small which reflected the blue light a fraction brighter than the floor.

AS I walked, my heart pumping loudly, I could almost hear it too. I listened. I listened because the walls and the ceiling and the floor of that earthen catacomb were listening with a malign expectancy. They were waiting and listening for something; the very air about me seemed alive.

Then it came.

I felt it first. The earth was trembling around me—above me, at my side, but mainly under my feet. It was trembling like the skin of a slowly beaten drum. As I stood rooted with the now familiar sick fear caressing me, I expected the walls to begin crumbling. It began slightly, ever so slightly, but even then it seemed hideous because the very catacomb itself seemed to tense and draw up. The booming rhythmic vibrations increased, and increased, and then I heard it and screamed.

It sounded at first like the distant throbbing of a drum, but when it grew a little louder I knew what it was, and it was worse than what I had feared. A wave of cosmic terror shot through my body at the sound of those obscene loping footsteps, the footsteps of a hunting beast.

I fought the terror that was clutching at my brain and stiffened and felt the cool sucking mud at the top of my head. The mud carried the vibrations of those awful padding footfalls that grew louder and the vibrations grew stronger.

I know only this, Jim, and I knew it as I stood there trembling with an ague of terror. No sane, living man ever saw the thing that was hurrying down that catacomb after me. There weren't two feet, there were four. And they didn't run in the greyhound gallop of two and two. No, each of those unnameable paws came down in turn—one ... two ... three ... four ... one ... two ... three ... four, and the space between the shock of the footsteps as they grew near was too damnably far apart. And as it came closer, that mind-blasting, space-eating loping, like that of some fiend-wrought wolf of hell, the very catacomb around me bounced and trembled and squished, and the noise of that hunting creature's pads was like muffled cannon's roar. And then came the thought that sent me reeling, screaming like a stricken animal into a panicked flight.

What manner of thing, star-sent or earth-begotten, could make such dreadfully loud footsteps and cause the very earth to tremble, and still be small enough to course through a tunnel in which I could not stand erect?

I remember no more of that catacomb clearly. I remember only a wild, careening run, bouncing and staggering through that fiend-cursed catacomb, screaming in terror as the footsteps of my monstrous pursuer grew into my ears until I thought I was being buffeted by thunder—running, running forever, falling, crawling, staggering up, whimpering like a lost child and smelling a charnel smell of long sealed tombs freshly opened like a hot searing blast and then suddenly I fell, fell and sank into murky tepid water that blanketed my brain.

I RECOVERED in a waterfront doctor's office where my stomach was being pumped of the things I had swallowed. The doctor said I was otherwise fit and when he had finished wrenching my intestines, I staggered home.

I had been pulled out of the Mississippi River at the Barracks Street wharf at dawn, nearly drowned. Apparently I had fallen into some underground reach or pool of the mother of rivers, and had floated into the channel which sane men see. I tried to sleep when I got home, but I couldn't and still haven't. The thought of what lay beneath me was too awful.

The morning paper was at my door, and I fetched it when I realized sleep would not come, and may never come again. I opened the door and looked out at the sweaty dawn, at the last staggering remnants of the last night of Carnival, at the streamers and confetti and torn masks and glass trinkets scattered over Chartres Street, the leftovers of revelry, and I seemed to feel better.

But then I glanced at the paper and choked with shock. There, on the front page, was a photograph of a high city official reviewing a Mardi Gras krewe parade, a parade held well after the time I had seen him gazing up at the gruesome altar somewhere below me now.

My loathing for the French Quarter became so great then that within a few hours I had packed my suitcase and had taken a room uptown in the Garden District, the staid oak-lined old Garden District. It seemed to refresh me. But last night, the first night in that little room in the great old mansion, as I almost began to doze, it seemed that I felt the ground trembling below me with great shuddering footsteps ....

I snapped to attention and the sensation was gone. My nerves were wrecked. It was then that I began to toy with the idea of visiting you.

I made up my mind in a flash an hour ago when the landlady came and told me she was sorry, but that I should have to move.

I asked her why, and she told me that her house was suddenly and unaccountably sinking into the earth.

ROBERT Bloch, faithful acolyte of Luveh-Keraph, mystic priest of cryptic Bast, used the magic he learned from Saracen wizards to transmute various items of Lovecraftian lore into wholly new nightmares. "Fane of the Black Pharaoh" (*Weird Tales*, December 1937) creatively combined Lovecraft's tantalizing mention of the Pharaoh Nephren-Ka and his blasphemies in "The Haunter of the Dark" with the long-lived Pharaoh Kephren from "Under the Pyramids" (published as "Imprisoned with the Pharaohs"). The basic *fabula* of "Under the Pyramids" and "Fane of the Black Pharaoh" is the same: A naive Westerner in search of secrets is led by a dubious and inscrutable Egyptian (who turns out to be an *ancient* Egyptian, whether by age or by race) into an unknown tomb far underground, where he is to meet his doom.

The apparent influence of "Under the Pyramids" on "Fane of the Black Pharaoh" might also provide a clue as to the origin of a puzzling item in the latter story, the reference to the "Blind Apes" in the tomb of Nephren-Ka. Can this item have been suggested by this passage from "Under the Pyramids?"

> I would give much, in view of my experience and of certain Bedouin whisperings discredited or unknown in Cairo, to know what has developed in connexion with a certain well in a transverse galley where statues of the Pharaoh were found in curious juxtaposition to the statues of baboons.

In "Under the Pyramids" Lovecraft reveals the Sphinx to be no mere artistic fantasy—it was a *sculpture from life*. Who was the model? Lovecraft dubs the creature the Unknown God of the Dead. Bloch has decided it must have been Nyarlathotep, though in this story we will not meet him in that form. Nyarlathotep the Sphinx appears in "The Faceless God."

In a move that perhaps out-Lovecrafts Lovecraft, Bloch even assimilates Nephren-Ka to Cthulhu! The Black Pharaoh, a priest like Cthulhu, is said to lie "dead" in his tomb till the circling millennia return to an auspicious time for him to rise. Here we must think inevitably of Robert E. Howard's Kathulos ("Skull-Face"), a character quite similar to Nephren-Ka as Bloch conceived him, and whom Howard and Lovecraft agreed should be identified somehow with Cthulhu. "It would be amusing to identify your Kathulos with my Cthulhu—indeed, I may so adopt him in some future black allusion" (August 14, 1930). He did, in "The Whisperer in Darkness", right next to another Howard name: "L'mur-Kathulos, Bran."

If Bloch managed to hybridize two Lovecraft stories into a unique mix of his own—the present story—then how appropriate that Archie Goodwin in turn took up "Fane of the Black Pharaoh" itself and combined parts of it with elements from "The Skull of the Marquis de Sade" and "The Shambler from the Stars" to concoct the wonderful story "Collector's Edition" (illustrated by Steve Ditko) in *Creepy* #10, August 1966.

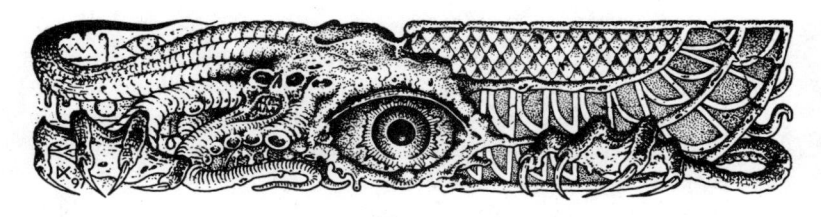

Fane of the Black Pharaoh

by Robert Bloch

"LIAR!" said Captain Cartaret.

The dark man did not move, but beneath the shadows of his burnoose a scowl slithered across a contorted countenance. But when he stepped forward into the lamplight, he smiled.

"That is a harsh epithet, *effendi*," purred the dark man.

Captain Cartaret stared at his midnight visitor with quizzical appraisal.

"A deserved one, I think," he observed. "Consider the facts. You come to my door at midnight, uninvited and unknown. You tell me some long rigmarole about secret vaults below Cairo, and then voluntarily offer to lead me there."

"That is correct," assented the Arab, blandly. He met the glance of the scholarly captain calmly.

"Why should you do this?" pursued Cartaret. "If your story is true, and you do possess so manifestly absurd a secret, why should you come to me? Why not claim the glory of discovery yourself?"

"I told you, *effendi*," said the Arab. "That is against the law of our brotherhood. It is not written that I should do so. And knowing of your interest in these things, I came to offer you the privilege."

"You came to pump me for my information; no doubt that's what you mean," retorted the captain, acidly. "You beggars have some devilishly clever ways of getting underground information, don't you? So far as I know, you're here to find out how much I've already learned, so that you and your fanatic thugs can knife me if I know too much."

"Ah!" The dark stranger suddenly leaned forward and peered into the white man's face. "Then you admit that what I tell you is not wholly strange—you do know something of this place already?"

"Suppose I do," said the captain, unflinching. "That doesn't prove that you're a philanthropic guide to what I'm seeking. More likely you want to pump me, as I said, then dispose of me and get the goods for yourself. No, your story is too thin. Why, you haven't even told me your name."

"My name?" The Arab smiled. "That does not matter. What does matter is your distrust of me. But, since you have admitted at last that you do know about the crypt of Nephren-Ka, perhaps I can show you something that may prove my own knowledge."

He thrust a lean hand under his robe and drew forth a curious object of dull, black metal. This he flung casually on the table, so that it lay in a fan of lamplight.

Captain Cartaret bent forward and peered at the queer, metallic thing. His thin, usually pale face now glowed with unconcealed excitement. He grasped the black object with twitching fingers.

"The Seal of Nephren-Ka!" he whispered. When he raised his eyes to the inscrutable Arab's once more, they shone with mingled incredulity and belief.

"It's true, then—what you say," the captain breathed. "You could obtain this only from the Secret Place; the Place of the Blind Apes where—"

"Nephren-Ka bindeth up the threads of truth." The smiling Arab finished the quotation for him.

"You, too, have read the *Necronomicon*, then." Cartaret looked stunned. "But there are only six complete versions, and I thought the nearest was in the British Museum."

The Arab's smile broadened. "My fellow-countryman, Alhazred, left many legacies among his own people," he said, softly. "There is wisdom available to all who know where to seek it."

For a moment there was silence in the room. Cartaret gazed at the black Seal, and the Arab scrutinized him in turn. The thoughts of both were far away. At last the thin, elderly white man looked up with a quick grimace of determination.

"I believe your story," he said. "Lead me."

The Arab, with a satisfied shrug, took a chair, unbidden, at the side of his host. From that moment he assumed complete psychic mastery of the situation.

"First, you must tell me what you know," he commanded. "Then I shall reveal the rest."

Cartaret, unconscious of the other's dominance, complied. He told the stranger his story in an abstracted manner, while his eyes never swerved from the cryptic black amulet on the table. It was almost as though he were hypnotized by the queer talisman. The Arab said nothing, though there was a gay gloating in his fanatical eyes.

Cartaret spoke of his youth, of his wartime service in Egypt and subsequent station in Mesopotamia. It was here that the captain had first become interested in archaeology and the shadowy realms of the occult which surrounded it. From the vast desert of Arabia had come intriguing tales as old as time—furtive fables of mystic Irem, city of ancient dread, and the lost legends of vanished empires. He had spoken to the dreaming dervishes whose hashish visions revealed secrets of forgotten days, and had explored certain reputedly ghoul-ridden tombs and burrows in the ruins of an older Damascus than recorded history knows.

In time, his retirement had brought him to Egypt. Here in Cairo there was access to still more secret lore. Egypt, land of lurid curses and lost kings, has ever harbored mad myths in its age-old shadows. Cartaret had learned of priests and pharaohs; of olden oracles, forgotten sphinxes, fabulous pyramids, titanic tombs. Civilization was but a cobweb surface upon the sleeping face of Eternal Mystery. Here, beneath the inscrutable shadows of the pyramids, the old gods still stalked in the old ways. The ghosts of Set, Ra, Osiris, and Bubastis lurked in desert ways; Horus, Isis, and Sebek yet dwelt in the ruins of Thebes and Memphis, or bided in the crumbling tombs below the Valley of Kings.

Nowhere had the past survived as it did in ageless Egypt. With every mummy, the Egyptologists uncovered a curse; the solving of each ancient secret merely uncovered a deeper, more perplexing riddle. Who built the pylons of the temples? Why did the old kings rear the pyramids? How did they work such marvels? Were their curses potent still? Where vanished the priests of Egypt?

These and a thousand other unanswered questions intrigued the mind of Captain Cartaret. In his new-found leisure he read and studied, talked with scientists and savants. Ever the quest of primal knowledge beckoned him on to blacker brinks; he could slake his thirsty soul only in stranger secrets, more dangerous discoveries.

Many of the reputable authorities he knew were open in their confessed opinion that it was not well for meddlers to pry too deeply beneath the surface. Curses had come true with puzzling promptness, and warning prophecies had been fulfilled with a vengeance. It was not good to profane the shrines of the old dark gods who still dwelt within the land.

But the terrible lure of the forgotten and the forbidden was a pulsing virus in Cartaret's blood. When he heard the legend of Nephren-Ka, he naturally investigated.

Nephren-Ka, according to authoritative knowledge, was merely a mythical figure. He was purported to have been a Pharaoh of no known dynasty, a priestly usurper of the throne. The most common fables placed his reign in almost biblical times. He was said to have been the last and greatest of that Egyptian cult of priest-sorcerers who for a time transformed the recognized religion into a dark and terrible thing. This cult, led by the arch-hierophants of Bubastis, Anubis, and Sebek, viewed their gods as the representatives of actual Hidden Beings—monstrous beast-men who shambled on Earth in primal days. They accorded worship to the Elder One who is known to myth as Nyarlathotep, the "Mighty Messenger." This abominable deity was said to confer wizard's power upon receiving human sacrifices, and while the evil priests reigned supreme they temporarily transformed the religion of Egypt into a bloody shambles. With anthropomancy and necrophilism they sought terrible boons from their demons.

The tale goes that Nephren-Ka, on the throne, renounced all religion save that of Nyarlathotep. He sought the power of prophecy, and built temples to the Blind Apes of Truth. His utterly atrocious sacrifices at length provoked a revolt, and it is said that the infamous Pharaoh was at last dethroned. According to this account, the new ruler and his people immediately destroyed all vestiges of the former reign, demolished all temples and idols of Nyarlathotep, and drove out the wicked priests who prostituted their faith to the carnivorous Bubastis, Anubis, and Sebek. The *Book of the Dead* was then amended so that all references to the Pharaoh Nephren-Ka and his accursed cults were deleted.

Thus, argues the legend, the furtive faith was lost to reputable history. As to Nephren-Ka himself, a strange account is given of his end.

The story ran that the dethroned Pharaoh fled to a spot adjacent to what is now the modern city of Cairo. Here it was his intention to embark with his remaining followers for a "westward isle." Historians believe that this "isle" was Britain, where some of the fleeing priests of Bubastis actually settled.

But the Pharaoh was attacked and surrounded, his escape blocked. It was then that he had constructed a secret underground tomb, in which he caused himself and his followers to be interred alive. With him, in this vivisepulture, he took all his treasure and magical secrets, so that nothing would remain for his enemies to profit by. So cleverly did his remaining devotees contrive this secret crypt that the attackers were never able to discover the resting-place of the Black Pharaoh.

Thus the legend rests. According to common currency, the fable was handed down by the few remaining priests who actually stayed on the surface to seal the secret place; they and their descendants were believed to have perpetuated the story and the old faith of evil.

Following up this exceedingly unusual story, Cartaret delved into the old tomes of the time. During a trip to London he was fortunate enough to be allowed an inspection of the unhallowed and archaic *Necronomicon* of Abdul Alhazred. In it were further emendations. One of his influential friends in the Home Office, hearing of his interest, managed to obtain for him a portion of Ludvig Prinn's evil and blasphemous *De Vermis Mysteriis*, known more familiarly to students of recondite arcana as *Mysteries of the Worm*. Here, in that greatly disputed chapter on oriental myth entitled "Saracenic Rituals", Cartaret found still more concrete elaborations of the Nephren-Ka tale.

Prinn, who consorted with the mediaeval seers and prophets of Saracen times in Egypt, gave a good deal of prominence to the whispered hints of Alexandrian necromancers and adepts. They knew the story of Nephren-Ka, and alluded to him as the Black Pharaoh.

Prinn's account of the Pharaoh's death was much more elaborate. He claimed that the secret tomb lay directly beneath Cairo itself, and professed to believe that it had been opened and reached. He hinted at the cult survival mentioned in the popular tales; spoke of a renegade group of descendants whose priestly ancestors had interred the rest alive. They were said to perpetuate the evil faith, and to act as guardians of the dead Nephren-Ka and his buried brethren, lest some interloper discover and violate his resting-place in the crypt. After the regular cycle of seven thousand years, the Black Pharaoh and his band would then arise once more, and restore the dark glory of the ancient faith.

The crypt itself, if Prinn is to be believed, was a most unusual place. Nephren-Ka's servants and slaves had built him a mighty sepulcher, and the burrows were filled with the rich treasure of his reign. All of the sacred images were there, and the jeweled books of esoteric wisdom reposed within.

Most peculiarly did the account dwell on Nephren-Ka's search for the Truth and the Power of Prophecy. It was said that before he died down in the darkness, he conjured up the earthly image of Nyarlathotep in a final gigantic sacrifice, and that the god granted him his desires. Nephren-Ka had stood before the images of the Blind Apes of Truth and received the gift of divination over the gory bodies of a hundred willing victims. Then, in nightmare manner, Prinn recounts that the entombed Pharaoh wandered among his dead companions and inscribed on the twisted walls of his tomb the secrets of the future. In pictures and ideographs he wrote the history of days to come, reveling in omniscient knowledge till the end. He scrawled the destinies of kings to come, painted the triumphs and the dooms of unborn empires. Then, as the blackness of death shrouded his sight, and palsy wrenched the brush from his fingers, he betook himself in peace to his sarcophagus, and there died.

So said Ludvig Prinn, he that consorted with ancient seers. Nephren-Ka lay in his buried burrows, guarded by the priestly cult that still survived on Earth, and further protected by enchantments in his tomb below. He had fulfilled his desires at the end—he had known Truth, and written the lore of the future on the nighted walls of his own catacomb.

Cartaret had read all this with conflicting emotions. How he would like to find that tomb, if it existed! What a sensation—he would revolutionize anthropology, ethnology!

Of course, the legend had its absurd points. Cartaret, for all his research, was not superstitious. He didn't believe the bogus balderdash about Nyarlathotep, the Blind Apes of Truth, or the priestly cult. That part about the gift of prophecy was sheer drivel.

Such things were commonplace. There were many savants who had attempted to prove that the pyramids, in their geometrical construction, were archaeological and architectural prophecies of days to come. With elaborate and convincing skill, they attempted to show that, symbolically interpreted, the great tombs held the key to history, that they allegorically foretold the Middle Ages, the Renaissance, the Great War.

This, Cartaret believed, was rubbish. And the utterly absurd notion that a dying fanatic had been gifted with prophetic power and had scrawled the future history of the world on his tomb as a last gesture before death—that was impossible to swallow.

Nevertheless, despite his skeptical attitude, Captain Cartaret wanted to find the tomb, if it existed. He had returned to Egypt with that intention, and had immediately set to work. So far he had a number of clues and hints. If the machinery of his investigation did not collapse, it was now only a matter of days before he would discover the actual entrance to the spot itself. Then he intended to enlist proper governmental aid and make his discovery public to all.

This much he now told the silent Arab who had come out of the night with a strange proposal and a weird credential: the seal of the Black Pharaoh, Nephren-Ka.

When Cartaret finished his summary, he glanced at the dark stranger in interrogation.

"What next?" he asked.

"Follow me," said the other, urbanely. "I shall lead you to the spot you seek."

"Now?" gasped Cartaret. The other nodded.

"But—it's too sudden! I mean, the whole thing is like a dream. You come out of the night, unbidden and unknown, show me the Seal, and graciously offer to grant me my desires. Why? It doesn't make sense."

"This makes sense." The grave Arab indicated the black Seal.

"Yes," admitted Cartaret. "But—how can I trust you? Why must I go now? Wouldn't it be wiser to wait, and get the proper authorities behind us? Won't there be need of excavation; aren't there necessary instruments to take?"

"No." The other spread his palms upward. "Just come."

"Look here." Cartaret's suspicion crystallized in his sharp tones. "How do I know this isn't a trap? Why should you come to me this way? Who the devil are you?"

"Patience." The dark man smiled. "I shall explain all. I have listened to your accounts of the 'legend' with great interest, and while your facts are clear, your own view of them is mistaken. The 'legend' you have learned of is true—all of it. Nephren-Ka *did* write the future on the walls of his tomb when he died; he *did* possess the power of divination, and the priests who buried him formed a cult which *did* survive."

"Yes?" Cartaret was impressed, despite himself.

"I am one of those priests." The words stabbed like swords in the white man's brain.

"Do not look so shocked. It is the truth. I am a descendant of the original cult of Nephren-Ka, one of those inner initiates who have kept the legend alive. I worship the Power which the Black Pharaoh received, and I worship the god Nyarlathotep who accorded that Power to him. To us believers, the most sacred truth lies in the hieroglyphs inscribed by the divinely gifted Pharaoh before he died. Throughout the ages, we guardian priests have watched history unfold, and always it has agreed with the ideographs on those tunneled walls. We believe.

"It is because of our belief that I have sought you out. For within the secret crypt of the Black Pharaoh it is written upon the walls of the future that you shall descend there."

Stunned silence.

"Do you mean to say," Cartaret gasped, "that those pictures *show* me discovering the spot?"

"They do," assented the dark man, slowly. "That is why I came to you unbidden. You shall come with me and fulfill the prophecy tonight, as it is written."

"Suppose I don't come?" flashed Captain Cartaret, suddenly. "What about your prophecy then?"

The Arab smiled. "You'll come," he said. "You know that."

Cartaret realized that it was so. Nothing could keep him away from this amazing discovery. A thought struck him.

"If this wall really records the details of the future," he began, "perhaps you can tell me a little about my own coming history. Will this discovery make me famous? Will I return again to the spot? Is it written that I am to bring the secret of Nephren-Ka to light?"

The dark man looked grave. "That I do not know," he admitted. "I neglected to tell you something about the Walls of Truth. My ancestor—he who first descended into the secret spot after it had been sealed, he who first looked upon the work of prophecy—did a needful thing. Deeming that such wisdom was not for lesser mortals, he piously covered the walls with concealing tapestry. Thus none might look upon the future too far. As time passed, the tapestry was drawn back to keep pace with the actual events of history, and always they have coincided with the hieroglyphs. Through the ages, it has always been the duty of one priest to descend to the secret tomb each day and draw back the tapestry so as to reveal the events of the day that follows. Now, during my life, that is my mission. My fellows devote their time to the needful rites of worship in hidden places. I alone descend the concealed passage daily and draw back the curtain on the Walls of Truth. When I die, another will take my place. Understand me—the writing does not minutely concern every single event; merely those which affect the history and destiny of Egypt itself. Today, my friend, it was revealed that you should descend and enter into the place of your desire. What the morrow holds in store for you I cannot say, until the curtain is drawn once more."

Cartaret sighed. "I suppose that there is nothing else left but for me to go, then." His eagerness was ill dissembled. The dark man observed this at once, and smiled cynically while he strode to the door.

"Follow me," he commanded.

TO Captain Cartaret that walk through the moonlit streets of Cairo was blurred in chaotic dream. His guide led him into labyrinths of looming shadows; they wandered through the twisted native quarters and passed through a maze of unfamiliar alleys and thoroughfares. Cartaret strode mechanically at the dark stranger's heels, his thoughts avid for the great triumph to come.

He hardly noticed their passage through a dingy courtyard; when his companion drew up before an ancient well and pressed a niche revealing the passage beneath, he followed him as a matter of course. From somewhere the Arab had produced a flashlight. Its faint beam almost rebounded from the murk of the inky tunnel.

Together they descended a thousand stairs, into the ageless and eternal darkness that broods beneath. Like a blind man, Cartaret stumbled down—down into the depths of three thousand vanished years.

The temple was entered—the subterranean temple-tomb of Nephren-Ka. Through silver gates the priest passed, his dazed companion following behind. Cartaret stood in a vast chamber, the niched walls of which were lined with sarcophagi.

"They hold the mummies of the interred priests and servants," explained his guide.

Strange were the mummy-cases of Nephren-Ka's followers, not like those known to Egyptology. The carven covers bore no recognized, conventional features as was the usual custom; instead they presented the strange, grinning countenances of demons and creatures of fable. Jeweled eyes stared mockingly from the black visages of gargoyles spawned in a sculptor's nightmare. From every side of the room those eyes shone through the shadows—unwinking, unchanging, omniscient in this little world of the dead.

Cartaret stirred uneasily. Emerald eyes of death, ruby eyes of malevolence, yellow orbs of mockery—everywhere they confronted him. He was glad when his guide led him forward at last, so that the incongruous rays of the flashlight shone on the entrance beyond. A moment later his relief was dissipated by the sight of a new horror confronting him at the inner doorway.

Two gigantic figures shambled there, guarding either side of the opening—two monstrous, troglodytic figures. Great gorillas they were—enormous apes, carved in simian semblance from black stone. They faced the doorway, squatting on mighty haunches, their huge, hairy arms upraised in menace. Their glittering faces were brutally alive; they grinned, barefanged, with idiotic glee. And they were blind—eyeless and blind.

There was a terrible allegory in these figures which Cartaret knew only too well. The blind apes were Destiny personified—a hulking, mindless Destiny whose sightless, stupid gropings trampled on the dreams of men and altered their lives by aimless flailings of purposeless paws. Thus did they control reality.

These were the Blind Apes of Truth, according to the ancient legend; the symbols of the old gods worshiped by Nephren-Ka.

Cartaret thought of the myths once more, and trembled. If tales were true, Nephren-Ka had offered up that final mighty sacrifice upon the obscene laps of these evil idols—offered them up to Nyarlathotep, and buried the dead in the mummy-cases set here in the niches. Then he had gone on to his own sepulcher within.

The guide proceeded stolidly past the looming figures. Cartaret, dissembling his dismay, started to follow. For a moment his feet refused to cross that gruesomely guarded threshold into the room beyond. He stared upward to the eyeless, ogreish faces that leered down from dizzying heights, with the feeling that he walked in realms of sheer nightmare. But the huge arms beckoned him on; the unseeing faces were convulsed in a smile of mocking invitation.

The legends were true. The tomb existed. Would it not be better to turn back now, seek some aid, and return again to this spot? Besides, what unguessed terror might not lair in the realms beyond; what horror spawn in the sable shadows of Nephren-Ka's inner, secret sepulcher? All reason urged him to call out to the strange priest and retreat to safety.

But the voice of reason was a hushed and awe-stricken whisper here in the brooding burrows of the past. This was a realm of ancient shadow, where antique evil ruled. Here the incredible was real, and there was a potent fascination in fear itself.

Cartaret knew that he must go on; curiosity, cupidity, the lust for concealed knowledge—all impelled him. And the Blind Apes grinned their challenge, or command.

THE priest entered the third chamber, and Cartaret followed. Crossing the threshold, he plunged into an abyss of unreality.

The room was lighted by braziers set in a thousand stations; their glow bathed the enormous burrow with fiery luminance. Captain Cartaret, his head reeling from the heat and mephitic miasma of the place, was thus able to see the entire extent of this incredible cavern.

Seemingly endless, a vast corridor stretched on a downward slant into the earth beyond—a vast corridor, utterly barren, save for the winking red braziers along the walls. Their flaming reflections cast grotesque shadows that glimmered with unnatural life. Cartaret felt as though he were gazing on the entrance to Karneter—the mythical underworld of Egyptian lore.

"Here we are," said his guide, softly.

The unexpected sound of a human voice was startling. For some reason, it frightened Cartaret more than he cared to admit; he had fallen into a vague acceptance of these scenes as being part of a fantastic dream. Now, the concrete clarity of a spoken word only confirmed an eerie reality.

Yes, here they were, in the spot of legend, the place known to Alhazred, Prinn, and all the dark delvers into unhallowed history. The tale of Nephren-Ka was true, and if so, what about the rest of the strange priest's statements? What about the Walls of Truth, on which the Black Pharaoh had recorded the future, had foretold Cartaret's own advent on the secret spot?

As if in answer to these inner whispers, the guide smiled.

"Come, Captain Cartaret; do you not wish to examine the walls more closely?"

The captain did not wish to examine the walls; desperately, he did not. For they, if in existence, would confirm the ghastly horror that gave them being. If they existed, it meant that the whole evil legend was real; that Nephren-Ka, Black Pharaoh of Egypt, had indeed sacrificed to the dread dark gods, and that they had answered his prayer. Captain Cartaret did not greatly wish to believe in such utterly blasphemous abominations as Nyarlathotep.

He sparred for time.

"Where is the tomb of Nephren-Ka himself?" he asked. "Where are the treasure and the ancient books?"

The guide extended a lean forefinger.

"At the end of this hall," he exclaimed.

Peering down the infinity of lighted walls, Cartaret indeed fancied that his eyes could detect a dark blur of objects in the dim distance.

"Let us go there," he said.

The guide shrugged. He turned, and his feet moved over the velvet dust. Cartaret followed, as if drugged.

"The walls," he thought. "I must not look at the walls. The Walls of Truth. The Black Pharaoh sold his soul to Nyarlathotep and received the gift of prophecy. Before he died here he wrote the future of Egypt on the walls. I must not look, lest I believe. I must not know."

Red lights glittered on either side. Step after step, light after light. Glare, gloom, glare, gloom, glare.

The lights beckoned, enticed, attracted. "Look at us," they commanded. "See, dare to see all."

Cartaret followed his silent conductor.

"Look!" flashed the lights.

Cartaret's eyes grew glassy. His head throbbed. The gleaming of the lights was mesmeric; they hypnotized with their allure.

"Look!"

Would this great hall never end? No; there were thousands of feet to go.

"Look!" challenged the leaping lights.

Red serpent eyes in the underground dark; eyes of tempters, bringers of black knowledge.

"Look! Wisdom! Know!" winked the lights.

They flamed in Cartaret's brain. Why not look—it was so easy? Why fear?

Why? his dazed mind repeated the question. Each following flare of fire weakened the question.

At last, Cartaret looked.

Mad minutes passed before he was able to speak. Then he mumbled in a voice audible only to himself.

"True," he whispered. "All true."

He stared at the towering wall to his left, limned in red radiance. It was an interminable Bayeux tapestry carved in stone. The drawing was crude, in black and white, but it *frightened*. This was no ordinary Egyptian picture-writing; it was not the fantastic, symbolical style of ordinary hieroglyphics. That was the terrible part: Nephren-Ka was a realist. His men looked like men, his buildings were buildings. There was nothing here but a representation of stark reality, and it was dreadful to see.

For at the point where Cartaret first summoned courage to gaze he stared at an unmistakable tableau involving Crusaders and Saracens.

Crusaders of the Thirteenth Century—yet Nephren-Ka had then been dust for nearly two thousand years!

The pictures were small, yet vivid and distinct; they seemed to flow along quite effortlessly on the wall, one scene blending into another as though they had been drawn in unbroken continuity. It was as though the artist had not stopped once during his work; as though he had untiringly proceeded to cover this gigantic hall in a single supernatural effort.

That was it—a single *supernatural* effort!

Cartaret could not doubt. Rationalize all he would, it was impossible to believe that these drawings were trumped up by any group of artists. It was one man's work. And the unerring horrid consistency of it, the calculated picturization of the most vital and important phases of Egyptian history could have been set down in such accurate order only by a historical authority or a prophet. Nephren-Ka had been given the gift of prophecy. And so ....

As he ruminated in growing dread, Cartaret and his guide proceeded. Now that he had looked, a Medusan fascination held the man's eyes to the wall. He walked with history tonight—history and red nightmare. Flaming figures leered from every side.

He saw the rise of the Mameluke Empire, looked on the despots and the tyrants of the East. Not all of what he saw was familiar to Cartaret, for history has its forgotten pages. Besides, the scenes changed and varied at almost every step, and it was quite confusing. There was one picture interspersed with an Alexandrian court motif which depicted a catacomb evidently in some vaults beneath the city. Here were gathered a number of men in robes which bore a curious similarity to those of Cartaret's present guide. They were conversing with a tall, white-bearded man whose crudely drawn figure seemed to exude an uncanny aura of black and baleful power.

"Ludvig Prinn," said the guide, softly, noting Cartaret's stare. "He mingled with our priests, you know."

For some reason the depiction of this almost legendary seer stirred Cartaret more deeply than any hitherto revealed terror. The casual inclusion of the infamous sorcerer in the procession of actual history hinted at dire things; it was as though Cartaret had read a prosaic biography of Satan in *Who's Who*.

Nevertheless, with a sort of heartsick craving his eyes continued to search the walls as they walked onward to the still indeterminate end of the long red-illumed chamber in which Nephren-Ka was interred. The guide—priest, now, for Cartaret no longer doubted—proceeded softly, but stole covert glances at the white man as he led the way.

Captain Cartaret walked through a dream. Only the walls were real now: the Walls of Truth. He saw the Ottomans rise and flourish, looked on forgotten battles and unremembered kings. Often there recurred in the sequence a scene depicting the priests of Nephren-Ka's own furtive cult. They were shown amidst the disquieting surroundings of catacombs and tombs, engaged in unsavory occupations and revolting pleasures. The camera-film of time rolled on; Captain Cartaret and his companion walked on. Still the walls told their story.

There was one small division of the wall which portrayed the priests conducting a man in Elizabethan costume through what seemed to be a pyramid. It was eerie to see the gallant in his finery pictured amidst the ruins of ancient Egypt, and it was very dreadful indeed almost to watch, like an unseen observer, when a stealthy priest knifed the Englishman in the back as he bent over a mummy-case.

What now impressed Cartaret was the infinitude of detail in each pictured fragment. The features of all the men were almost photographically exact; the drawing, while crude, was life-like and realistic. Even the furniture and background of every scene were correct. There was no doubting the authenticity of it all, and no doubting the veracity thereby implied. But—what was worse—there was no doubting that this work could not have been done by any normal artist, however learned, unless he had seen it all.

Nephren-Ka had seen it all in prophetic vision, after his sacrifice to Nyarlathotep.

Cartaret was looking at truths inspired by a demon ....

On and on, to the flaming fane of worship and death at the end of the hall. History progressed as he walked. Now he was looking at a period of Egyptian lore that was almost contemporary. The figure of Napoleon appeared.

The battle of Aboukir ... the massacre of the pyramids ... the downfall of the Mameluke horsemen ... the entrance to Cairo ....

Once again, a catacomb with priests. And three figures, white men, in French military regalia of the period. The priests were leading them into a red room. The Frenchmen were surprised, overcome, slaughtered.

It was vaguely familiar. Cartaret was recalling what he knew of Napoleon's commission; he had appointed savants and scientists to investigate the tombs and pyramids of the land. The Rosetta stone had been discovered, and other things. Quite likely the three men shown had blundered onto a mystery the priests of Nephren-Ka had not wanted to have unveiled. Hence they had been lured to death as the walls showed. It was quite familiar—but there was *another* familiarity which Cartaret could not place.

They moved on, and the years rushed by in panorama. The Turks, the English, Gordon, the plundering of the pyramids, the World War. And every so often, a picture of the priests of Nephren-Ka and a strange white man in some catacomb or vault. Always the white man died. It was all *familiar*.

Cartaret looked up, and saw that he and the priest were very near to the blackness at the end of the great fiery hall. Only a hundred steps or so, in fact. The priest, face hidden in his burnoose, was beckoning him on.

Cartaret looked at the wall. The pictures were almost ended. But no—just ahead was a great curtain of crimson velvet on a ceiling rack which ran off into the blackness and reappeared from shadows on the opposite side of the room to cover that wall.

"The future," explained his guide. And Captain Cartaret remembered that the priest had told how each day he drew back the curtain a bit so that the future was always revealed just one day ahead. He remembered something else, and hastily glanced at the last visible section of the Wall of Truth next to the curtain. He gasped.

It was true! Almost as though gazing into a miniature mirror he found himself staring into *his own face!*

Line for line, feature for feature, posture for posture, he and the priest of Nephren-Ka were shown standing together in this red chamber just as they were now.

The red chamber ... familiarity. The Elizabethan man with the priests of Nephren-Ka were in a catacomb when the man was murdered. The French scientists were in a red chamber when they died. Other later Egyptologists had been shown in a red chamber with the priests, and they too had been slain. The red chamber! Not familiarity but *similarity*! They had been in *this chamber*! And now he stood here, with a priest of Nephren-Ka. The others had died because they had known too much. Too much about what—Nephren-Ka?

A terrible suspicion began to formulate into hideous reality. The priests of Nephren-Ka protected their own. This tomb of their dead leaders was also their fane, their temple. When intruders stumbled onto the secret, they lured them down here and killed them lest others learn too much.

Had not he come in the same way?

The priest stood silent as he gazed at the Wall of Truth.

"Midnight," he said softly. "I must draw back the curtain to reveal yet another day before we go on. You expressed a wish, Captain Cartaret, to see what the future holds in store for you. Now that wish shall be granted."

With a sweeping gesture, he flung the curtain back along the wall for a foot. Then he moved, swiftly.

One hand leapt from the burnoose. A gleaming knife flashed through the air, drawing red fire from the lamps, then sank into Cartaret's back, drawing redder blood.

With a single groan, the white man fell. In his eyes there was a look of supreme horror, not born of death alone. For as he fell, Captain Cartaret read his future on the Walls of Truth, and it confirmed a madness that could not be.

As Captain Cartaret died he looked at the picture of his next hours of existence and *saw himself being knifed by the priest of Nephren-Ka.*

The priest vanished from the silent tomb, just as the last flicker of dying eyes showed to Cartaret the picture of a still white body—*his body*—lying in death before the Wall of Truth.

THIS was Lin Carter's first attempt at a novel, written about 1952-53. Like many first-time writers, as he later told me, he had underestimated the length required by most publishers for a novel, and yet it was too long for inclusion as a short story in your average anthology. So it languished for years in his files. Some time later he began a more complete rewrite, but his anticipated word count shows that he planned to lengthen it by only 1700 words. My guess as to why he did not try to inflate it to novel length was that he had successfully placed another early novella, *The Flame of Iridar*, as half of a Belmont Double and hoped he might do the same with a new version of *Curse of the Black Pharaoh*. In any case, he dropped the project. The new version broke off after only the twenty-fifth typed page. The present publication is accordingly a hybrid, using the revised beginning and reverting to the first draft. I have reconciled the minor inconsistencies which existed in the text.

It is clear enough that the Black Pharaoh is supposed to be the same one you're thinking of, but Carter does not use the name. He has chosen instead to identify the pharaoh as Khetep/Khotep, apparently intended as Khety, a local self-styled "king" at Dura during the 9th Dynasty (2130-2080 B.C.), when central authority was giving way to local strongmen. Khety proclaimed himself king and built his own pyramid. During the same period we also hear of a local nomarch, Ankhtify, who felt at liberty to annex a neighboring district even as he acknowledged the nominal authority of an otherwise unknown pharaoh called Neferkare (= *Nepher-Ka*-Ra!).

Similarly, instead of a direct reference to Nyarlathotep, Carter invokes Iao-Thaumungazoth, a name cobbled together from *Iao*, a Hellenistic version of the Hebrew divine name *Yah* (much used in Hellenistic Egyptian magic) and the Greek *thaumazo*, "to marvel." It is the name of the most terrible of the three primal lords of Lin Carter's Lemuria—Yamath, Lord of Flame; Slidith, Lord of Blood; and Iao-Thamungazoth, Lord of Chaos (in *Thongor in the City of Magicians*, 1968).

A name that *will* ring a familiar bell, though, is that of Anton Zarnak, the young Carter's combination of Van Helsing and Jules de Grandin. Here he reprises Edward van Sloan's role in *The Mummy*. Lin retrieved Zarnak many years later for a pair of Mythos stories, "Perchance to Dream" (see *The Xothic Legend Cycle*) and "Dead of Night" (*The Book of Iod*). He had by then realized he needed to make Zarnak's persona a bit more exotic, though the occult sleuth's sanctum sanctorum remained pretty much as Carter describes it here. The Gnostic amulets, books like Mather's edition of *The Greater Key of Solomon*, and the grotesque wooden mask of Yama, king of devils, all bedecked Lin's own apartment as long as he lived. Anton Zarnak was the alter ego of the old as well as the young Lin Carter.

Curse of the Black Pharaoh

by Lin Carter

Chapter 1

Death in the Night

Permit not Thou to come nigh unto me Him that would attack me in the House of Darkness.
—*Book of the Dead*

THE long afternoon's drive down into Middlesex was comfortable enough but uneventful. Brant dozed a little, smoked, stared out of the window at green fields and woods and farms, alone with his thoughts. Time and again he dug out the London newspapers and read the front-page articles again; by now he had virtually committed them to memory. The journalistic phraseology differed, a little, from paper to paper. The *Times* treated it more from the obituary angle, the *Express* played up the sensationalism. The *Graphic*, however, struck a middle tone:

"PHARAOH'S CURSE" CLAIMS 5th VICTIM!
Weird Death of Archaeologist
Scotland Yard to Investigate

LON. Sept. 29—Professor Clive Carrington, renowned expert on ancient Egypt, was discovered murdered in his bed at 2 a.m. this morning in his Hampton Court residence by a manservant. Police physicians, called to the scene, pronounced the famous Egyptologist dead under what an official spokesman termed "extremely mysterious circumstances", but details were not at once released to the press. Trustees of the Carrington Museum announced this morning that Scotland Yard would inquire into the circumstances surrounding the Professor's demise, hinting at suspicions of foul play. Professor Carrington returned to this country from Cairo only last month, where he had led the Carrington-Shenstone expedition to the discovery of the so-called "lost pyramid" containing the mummified remains of Khotep, or Khetep, a pharaoh of the sixth dynasty. It will be recalled by the public that four other individuals associated with the ill-fated but successful expedition have succumbed to "accidents" of one kind or another: two young students who accompanied the Professor and the Earl of Shenstone to Upper Egypt, as well as two native workmen hired by a local *dragoman*. No satisfactory explanation has yet been made public as to—

"Excuse me, sir; we're here."

Brant looked up as the chauffeur spoke, glanced at the tall gateposts and the avenue of century-old elms, and stuffed the newspapers in his briefcase with a gruff nod. He brushed pipe-ash from his rumpled tweed suit, straightening the garments, as the limousine drew up before an imposing facade. Wilfrith Hall had been constructed during the reign of Edward II, but little of its original Plantagenet architecture had survived the extensive "restorations" made by one of Lord Shenstone's ancestors in the early years of Victoria's reign. It was a hideous mock-Gothic pile with false crenelations and walls of massive, ivy-shrouded fieldstone. It looked both uncomfortable and somber, heaped up against the gold and scarlet sunset, with thick woods spread out behind it and dark, shaggy hills looming beyond. Something in the scene touched a nerve in Brant's strong, straight body. He repressed a small, inexplicable shudder.

"Inspector Brant?"

"That's right." Climbing out of the long Bentley he looked up to the top of the steps where a slender, vaguely effeminate man of forty-odd, dressed in black, old-fashioned pince-nez spectacles clamped to the thin bridge of his nose, stood awaiting him.

"My name is Crithers, his lordship's secretary. Will you come this way, please? Hambleton will see to your bags," he said, gesturing to the chauffeur.

Brant allowed himself to be conducted into the main hall of the estate, a gloomy, high-raftered corridor lined with bad ancestral portraits and dusty stuffed heads. Suits of eighteenth-century armor were pedestaled in poorly lit niches along the length of the hall.

The secretary was silent, but Brant felt the need to speak, so he said, awkwardly, "It was thoughtful of Lord Shenstone to have his car sent for me. It was waiting when I arrived; good thing, too—I would have had the devil's own time getting a cab at the station."

Crithers nodded stiffly, indicating a door. "His lordship is very anxious to greet you, Inspector. In here, if you please."

Brant rapped his knuckles on the mahogany panel, turned the knob, and entered the room. A tall, heavy figure turned from French windows which gave forth on a view of dark woods and fields, drowned now in purple shadows.

"Come in, come in, Inspector! Thank you, Crithers; that will be all. Whiskey and soda, Inspector—?"

"Brant, sir. Yes, thank you."

Shenstone busied himself with a cut-glass decanter and the soda bottle. Brant sank into a comfortably overstuffed chair, glancing around at the room. It was large and long, the walls marched with rows of books, leather bindings, the gleam of gold. Tables were strewn with a clutter of interesting objects. An *ushabti* tomb figurine of blue enamel served as a paperweight to a stack of demotic parchment scrolls. A tray of neatly labeled potsherds stood between the E. A. Wallis Budge *Hieroglyphic Dictionary* and a small idol of green paste, a repulsively saurian figure, redolent of leering malignancy, which represented Sebek the crocodile god. A funerary stele of black basalt, inscribed with hieroglyphs in white and scarlet, rested against a German blackletter text of the *Kronstedt Papyrus*. Canopic jars hewn from crysolite and feldspar, the brown and crumbling mummies of sacred cats, ibises and serpents, were jumbled about a tall *mibkharah* incense-burner of fretted silverwork.

"There we are; your health, Inspector!"

Brant accepted the glass, took a grateful swallow, and dug out his pipe and tobacco pouch. For the first time he got a clear look at the face of his host. In so doing, he received an unnerving shock. Although he had never met the Earl before, Lord Shenstone was a figure of considerable repute in his scholarly field and his likeness was familiar to Brant from frequent appearances in the magazines. An amazing alteration had taken place—it was as if he had aged thirty years!

Despite the deep bronze hue the fierce Egyptian sun had worked on his lean, commanding features, he had a sickly, greenish pallor. The keen lines of his strong visage had *blurred*—become loose, flabby. The once-sharp eyes were weak, uncertain: They were bleared with the rheum of a man goaded beyond his endurance, unable to sleep, to rest. He had the look of a man aged horribly beyond his natural years—or of a man haunted night and day by some hideous fear too terrible to be given a name. Something of the horror he felt must have showed in Brant's eyes, for the Earl spoke, weary amusement in his tones.

"You see it too, eh?"

"Good heavens, sir, what—"

Shenstone cut him off with a lifted hand. "I know how I must look; I saw it written in the faces of the reporters who interviewed us when we docked. I see it in the eyes of my servants, who are too polite to ask, but cross themselves when they think I do not see, and give out that my health has been impaired by the nervous exhaustion of the expedition. Brant, I—"

He broke off and sat still for a long moment, hunched over his drink. Then: "We found an awful thing in Egypt. ... We stumbled upon a ghastly horror that was covered up and forgotten ages since ... we pried open a rightful cesspool of ancient evil, and all in the name of science. *Science!*" he repeated with a mirthless laugh. "Well, God help us, we're paying for it now, every last one of us!"

"My Lord, you must not—"

Shenstone shook his head. "Say it, man. I look like someone in mortal fear of death, don't I? Well, you're right; I am. The fear is with me every minute of the night and day; it's with me now, as we sit talking here, hovering at my shoulder like a cold shadow, casting its sickly gloom into my very heart."

Brant uttered a gruff cough. "Lord Shenstone, believe me, I know how you feel. The murder of your old friend and colleague was a ghastly crime—but it was just that, a crime, and nothing more. This is the twentieth century, after all. Oh, the cheap press has raked up all this 'Pharaoh's Curse' nonsense, but it doesn't change matters. Surely you, a philanthropist, a man of science and learning, give no credence to these foolish superstitions—"

"'Superstitions?' I wonder ...." Shenstone stared unseeingly across the room, where the inscrutable visage of a green-painted Osiris priest smiled back at him across the ages from a cartonnage death mask found in a Theban necropolis. "Egypt is old ... *old*," he whispered, his lean, aristocratic face haunted by a shadow of some nameless fear. "A mighty civilization ruled there, once, in time's forgotten dawn. Their deeds were prodigious, their works awesome, and their monuments have outlasted the aeons. The wisdom they possessed has been a legend for seven thousand years; down the numberless centuries their myths have echoed, whispering of powers beyond nature, of an evil transcending the world, of dim, inchoate gods beyond the simple figures they cut in eternal granite ... *and something killed those five men.*"

The words hung in the air, heavy, formidable, posing a question to which reason and logic and science—all the formal half-truths by which modern science supports civilization—can offer no answer.

"Something killed them," Shenstone whispered. "Something whose ancient rest we disturbed when we broke the immemorial silence of the Valley of Hodesh with our shovels and spades. Something that is awake now, out there in the darkness, somewhere: an ancient, accursed, and evil thing, animated by but one single purpose—to track down and murder those who broke that ancient silence and disturbed the sleep of the ages."

His voice sank to a sharp whisper which pierced Brant with its cold message of horror.

"It has killed five times already. God help me, Brant! *I am the next victim!*"

Chapter 2

Secret out of Time

> It was a Thing of great Mystery, which had never before been seen or looked upon.
>
> —*Papyrus of Mu*, XXI

SHENSTONE seemed anxious to relieve his mind before an attentive, sympathetic audience. Brant let him tell his story in his own way, taking occasional notes on a small pad held unobtrusively on his lap. The older man made them both another whiskey, settled into his chair again, and launched into a rambling, curious tale.

It's not very likely that you have ever heard of the "Temple of Darkness" (he said); few have. And fewer still believe the legend. At any rate, I should explain the Egyptians had a strange custom of naming the pyramids wherein they buried their ancient kings. Take the Gizeh group for example; the Great Pyramid itself is called "the Horizon of Cheops", and the third pyramid, built a bit later, they know by the title "Divine-is-Mycerinius." One pyramid in particular has long interested us specialists. Its name is "the Temple of Darkness of Khotep", and it interests us because it has never been found. It was built a very long time ago, at the end of the sixth dynasty; and that is indeed very old, even in Egypt, where things are measured in millennia rather than centuries. We know it was built because of references to it in those inscriptions which have been translated, but we don't know exactly when it was built, or exactly where. From its name, a good guess places it in the decline of the sixth dynasty, because Khotep, or Khetep, was the last king of that dynasty. Where he erected his tomb was never known. That was the idea, of course, as you must know. Entering a pyramid was difficult enough, what with secret doors and false passageways; but even so they were usually robbed. Hide the tomb away where no one could find it, and you had a good chance of escaping even from the tomb-robbers. Early Egyptologists, not finding Khotep's tomb with the others of his remote dynasty, took to calling it "the Lost Pyramid"; the name was a bit sensational, but it caught on.

Whether it was or was not a pyramid was also a matter of conjecture. Only pharaohs of the fourth through the twelfth dynasties built the mysterious and impressive monuments we call, after the Greeks, "pyramids"— those man-made mountains of eternal stone that brood through the ages amidst the trackless sands of a desert only slightly more ancient than are they. The pyramids are pretty much all in the same area: those of Khufu, or Cheops, Mycerinius and Chephren, which are called the "Pyramids of

Gizeh", stand on a high, rocky plateau, the next to northernmost of the series of pyramidal tombs which center about the site of Memphis, which in those days was the capital of the Two Lands. I can give you some hint of their incredible age by explaining that the city of Memphis ceased to be the capital of Egypt rather more than four *thousand* years ago.

They make quite an imposing spectacle, especially the three very ancient pyramids at Gizeh, which are much larger than the rest. There they rise in a row, from the Great Pyramid itself, to the second pyramid, that of Chephren, followed by the pyramid of Mycerinius, built about seven hundred years before the fall of Memphis, and smaller than its mighty neighbors. It stands near the Sphinx itself, which was built on the edge of the Gizeh plateau and just east of the second pyramid. Scattered in the desert about and extending into the south are the other pyramids, smaller and of less importance and more "recent"—if you can call anything whose age can be measured in dozens of centuries "recent"—a whole valley-full of pyramids, in fact, with the brown Nile glittering away to the east and the famous step-pyramid of King Zoser barely in sight, at Sakkara on the horizon.

Beyond the Memphian group rise the pyramids of later kings, Senusert I and his successor, and Amenemhat III, and the old pyramid of Meydum, the name of whose royal builder is open to dispute. But the pyramid of Khotep, the Lost Pyramid they call "Temple of Darkness", is not among the Memphians, nor in the deserts to the south. No man on earth knew where it had been built long, long ago, when the world was young, and not yet free from the shadows of an aeon-old horror older than the planet itself.

Two years ago I was vacationing in Cairo with my niece, Miss Adrienne Haldane, daughter of my dead younger brother, Sir Bertram. To our suite at Shepheard's one evening, as the haunting cry of the *muezzin* rang out over the rooftops from the old minarets of the Caliphate, came my old professor from Cambridge, Clive Carrington. We had seen little of each other since our school days, but he had won a prodigious reputation in archaeology and his monographs on the Eleusinian Mysteries and the lost rituals of Serapis and the chronology of Manetho had won him the admiration of the savants of Europe. He was as excited as a boy of twenty when he came bursting in the door, his dinner clothes rumpled, his tie askew, a pottery jar of uncertain antiquity tucked under one arm.

"Ruthven!" he cried, mopping his bald brow with an immense bandana, his white goatee waggling with excitement. "It's a godsend that you're in Egypt, too—the one man in Europe with the experience I need, who can also lay his hand on ready cash!" I sat him down and thrust a drink on him and asked what he was talking about. "What am I talking about— what *could* I be talking about!" he shrilled. "The Lost Pyramid, of course— *Khotep's* pyramid—see?" And, with that, he set down the pottery jar he carried, whisked a roll of parchment from its mouth, and spread it out flat on the table. It was reed-papyrus, brown and withered with age—and reed-papyrus has not been made in Egypt since the Ptolemys. The inscription was in hieratic, with the cartouches picked out in red and black and azure, still fresh and bright despite the centuries which had weathered most of the rows of hieroglyphs almost to illegibility. Despite the fading of the glyphs, I could make out several rows at top and bottom, and in the center there was a map of sorts—and a very ancient one it was, for east was at the top instead of south, which is how the later dynasties oriented their maps. Carrington was babbling away excitedly, jabbing his thumb at this line and that. "See, here's the Nile, of course—the Third Cataract, here—and this spot down here must be the oasis of Wadi Hassur, according to the chaps at the Geographical Society. But look here, just over to the west, this oval—can you read the inscription? I'll read it for you—faded, of course, but under the infrared you can make it out—'the Secret Valley of Hodesh.'"

There was a sheer ecstasy in his voice as he recited that mystic phrase with relish and delight written all over his face.

The Secret Valley of Hodesh ....

I wish now I had never heard those words from any living man.

According to what little information tradition had preserved concerning the Lost Pyramid, the last resting-place of Khotep—"the Black Pharaoh" was the name they had for him, and it was foul and shuddersome things they whispered of his reign, too—his pyramid was hidden in a place called the Secret Valley of Hodesh. But no map of Egypt, ancient or modern, bore a valley of that name, and the name itself, although vaguely Semitic, was in no language known to men of today, and was meaningless in Egyptian. I was puzzled, intrigued—before long, fascinated. I listened to Carrington's account of finding the scroll. He had long known the papyrus map existed, he explained: It was mentioned in the last treatise written by the Gaon Saadia, a medieval Hebrew mystic. Another reference to it he found in an early manuscript of the *Sepher Yetzirah*, a work of the ancient Kaballah. A copy of the Hodesh map was rumored to exist in the library of the Greek Patriarchate in Jerusalem, but it proved to be a forgery. Finally, Carrington heard that the papyrus was for sale in the Rue Fuad in Alexandria. A native dealer in antiquities of the quasilegal variety (by which euphemism is meant stolen goods) was said to have it for sale to the highest bidder. He learned this from the black market, a valuable source of information cultivated by every Egyptologist worth his salt, for the thriving trade in stolen antiquities had led many an otherwise scrupulous scientist to a great discovery. Carrington eventually tracked the man down, one Ibrihim, a dealer who worked out of a shabby little shop in a back alley behind El-Azhar Mosque in Cairo.

Needless to say, Carrington had by now infected me with his own enthusiasm. Although I was in Egypt on vacation, it was simplicity itself to have funds transferred from my London banker and mount an expedition. Time was of the essence, for the *Khamsin* season was not far off, and unless we departed almost at once we should have to delay our excavations until the following year. Two young students who had studied under Carrington happened along; they were on vacation themselves, and we signed them on with great dispatch. Native workmen were hired; a steam yacht was procured to carry us up the Nile. My niece would have liked to have accompanied us but had to return to Switzerland, where she is in school. Thank heavens she had nothing to do with this filthy business!

We sailed from Cairo to Khartoum deep in the Sudan, beyond the Third Cataract. There we moored the yacht, hired camel teams, and struck off over the desert into the west. Soon we were off the map, in an obscure corner of Egypt little-known, for the reason that it had hardly even been explored. No one knows much of the Hodesh Valley region of Egypt, for few have ever had reason to go there. There is simply nothing there to draw anyone—empty desert and barren, rocky hills, and silence—the eternal, cryptic silence that broods in the forgotten waste-places of the earth.

We literally went off the map, bound for a valley no one had visited for four thousand years. *And from that journey, four of us would never return* ....

Chapter 3

Into the Unknown

Millions of years minister into him, and millions of years hold him in fear.
—*Book of the Dead*, LXXVIII

THERE is terror and dread in that vast and eternal desert (Shenstone continued after a moment). I sometimes feel man was not meant to navigate those drear and awful wastes of limitless sand. The silence of the desert is like the silence of a gigantic tomb in which all human hopes and dreams and aspirations sink, are swallowed and destroyed. There is a quality of mystery, too, in that silence—an element of the unexplained and the inexplicable. A weird enigma clings to the star-lit silence of the eternal pyramids, within whose secret chambers are withered husks of ancient kings who sleep the ages by, spiced and hung about with amulets, the names of awful and shadowy gods upon their unspeaking tongues.

The natives felt it from the first. They were uneasy, restless, whispering amongst themselves. We paid little attention at the time, and if we noticed it at all, we put their uneasiness down to simple superstition. There are many civilizations that hesitate to disturb the kingly dead.

I wonder now if they did not have some premonition of our goal. The pharaoh Khotep has a vile reputation and the evil of his reign lingered for many centuries in legend and tradition. There is a grim and ominous passage in the *Ku-Nepesht Papyrus* that speaks of him: Like Akhenaten, ages later, he was a heretic against the Gods of the Nile, turning from their worship to give homage before the dark fanes of those even more ancient Ones whose names we are not meant to utter aloud. He was a searcher into forbidden mysteries, a seeker-out of the cryptic lore of an arcane wisdom that even now is not entirely dead. Unlike Akhenaten, who was content to worship his own god while Egypt followed her ancient ways, Khotep sealed the temples, perverted the priesthood to his own worship of darkness. His reign was a dark age—thousands died on the scarlet altars of the hellish Forces he strove to evoke. The *Ku-Nepesht Papyrus* whispers that he dared have unholy traffic with "Those That Slumber Not", and bartered to Them his hope of the afterlife in the Second World for vast necromantic power in this life, and immortality in the flesh; so, at least, the legend goes. He had from his black gods some sort of magical talisman of great authority and power—the "Star of Set", the legends call it, employing the name of the traitor god in the context of Satan. With this talisman his power was gigantic, but his gods turned against him in the end; for all his fancied immortality he died, and his body was prepared according to the ancient rites and was interred by his followers in the Secret Valley. But the legends say more—it hints that his spirit is somehow earthbound—"And his *ka* went not to Karneter the divine land but lingereth to this hour in his tomb," says the papyrus. He was the last king of a black, accursed dynasty—the same tainted blood that ran in Khotep's veins spawned Queen Nitocris as well, Nitocris the Ghoul-Queen, Thomas Moore's dark "Lady of the Pyramid." The tale of her hideous revenge upon her enemies you may recall from the darkest pages of Herodotus.

With his death the dynasty was brought down and Egypt entered into a true dark age whose chronicles are lost: a bloody time of riot and insurrection and civil war. We know almost nothing of that period; it is one of those mysterious "blank spots" in the history of immemorial Egypt. With this black legendry of horror and sorcery and human sacrifice enshrouding the name of Khotep the Black Pharaoh, it is no wonder the native bearers and workmen shrank before the chill breath of dread as we approached the Secret Valley, if indeed they had any inkling of *whose* tomb we planned to desecrate.

We reached the vicinity of the Valley by the 23rd. Here the desert gives way to steep and rocky hills, a tortuous labyrinth of sheer and vertiginous cliffs wherein an exploring party could wander for weeks. The scroll Carrington had bought off Ibrihim the curio-seller warned that the Valley was cunningly concealed and could only be entered "in the hour when Sothis ascendeth, for then will the Seven Scorpions point the way." We had no way of knowing what this cryptic phrase meant, but Carrington thought it referred to a sign carven in the rock.

For hours we wandered through a maze of steep rock-walls, over meandering trails bestrewn with jagged flints—trails that could as well have led to the inferno of Dante as to the Lost Pyramid. Then night fell and the stars emerged, diamonds of icy fire, dazzling against a sky of jet-black velvet. Among them was the Dog Star, Sirius: The Egyptians call it Sothis. Sothis, the Dog Star ... my mind wandered strange trails, even as my body wove between sheer walls of splintered rock ... I thought of Anubis, the jackal-headed Lord of Death, whose mythos is so curiously akin to the old Transylvanian *cultus* of the "Lord of Wolves" ... *and then we heard the jackals, baying in the hills!*

The brilliant white spark of Sirius rose above the horizon. A lean yellow scimitar of a moon hung low over the rocky peaks like a sword of Damocles suspended over our heads. Sirius rose, and—

Carrington seized my arm in a crushing grip.

Before us on the sheer rock wall *seven scorpions burned!*

The breath caught in my throat. I leaned forward, heart hammering, to study the weird symbol. Seven scorpions, painted on the smooth stone, blazing with an eerie green phosphorescence in the dim glory of the light from the dog star. How the trick was worked, I cannot say; but I knew what it was—the Sign of the Seven Scorpions—the dreaded and aeon-ancient symbol of the pharaohs of the sixth dynasty. With it the old, demon-haunted kings sealed their tombs and sepulchers, warning away desecrators. It was the Seal of Death and its meaning was simple: Death would befall those who went past the row of luminous, ghostly symbols!

We had come too far to turn back now. Carrington plunged ahead, following the narrow way that twisted between the rock walls. The natives moaned and wept, eyeballs rolling whitely in the dimness; I forced them ahead of me at gun-point. In a deathly silence, we followed the winding path until ....

We stood on the top of a pass through the hills. Below us a deep valley yawned blackly. At the very center of the depression, its base invisible in the darkness, its peak lifted against the stars, it stood. The Lost Pyramid—the Temple of Darkness—the last resting-place of the Black Pharaoh!

Four thousand years of wind and rain and sun had weathered it, crumbling away the limestone facing. But the portal stood sealed, as best as we could see in the darkness. Sphinxes crouched before it like ghastly watchdogs guarding a forbidden door.

In a curious mood of anticlimax, we made our way down into the Secret Valley and made camp for the night, and slept. Uneasy were my slumbers, and my dreams were ... troubled.

With dawn we began excavation. The approach to the pyramid was an avenue lined with black diorite sphinxes, shockingly lifelike and strangely deformed. As we approached and saw them clearly we understood why. They were dog-headed—a gaunt herd of leering, canocephalic monstrosities that grinned down at us, fangs bared, muzzles wrinkled in a snarl, unearthly menace gleaming in their stony eyes.

The entrance to the pyramid was framed with huge pillars of an unfamiliar purple stone. The portal itself was sealed with two unbroken leaves of massive granite fastened together with the Seal of the Scorpions for a final warning. They were exquisitely worked in fine gold, the seven spiked tails woven together in a barbed knot. We tried to remove the Seal intact, but it proved impossible, so Carrington smashed it to fragments with his axe after making a photograph. As he smashed the Seal, I thought a shadow passed over the face of the sun; the shattering of the Seal rang and echoed weirdly in the stony silence of the dead valley. The natives pried the granite portal open and we went in, Carrington and I, and the two students, Collins and Mazzeo. If only we had turned back in that moment, those two brave young men would still be alive, I suppose ....

The transition from suffocating heat and blinding sun without to cool, musty darkness within was stunning. We stood and gasped for breath for a long moment, for the air was vitiated. The natives broke open the inner door, although I had to threaten them with my pistol before they would move. As the inner door was pierced, a thick, disgusting stench assaulted our nostrils—the dead, stale air of the unsealed tomb, heavy with dust and ancient rottenness, I suppose. Collins bent aside, retching, gasping for breath; Mazzeo stood breathing shallowly, fighting against the impulse to be sick. Truly, the stench was charnel—unspeakably vile—not just the reek of ancient decay, but a musky, fetid smell like a nest of snakes. Carrington and I were accustomed to the soul-unheaving stench of newly opened tombs, but even we were shaken.

We went on, though. It was only the *natron*, the spiced corruption old tombs emit; surely, it was only that. But my soul shuddered deep within me, as if it knew the stench of cosmic vileness.

Our flashlight cut a swath through ebon gloom. The stone pave underfoot was thick with undisturbed dust. Our beams played along the wall: The last illumination in this place of gloom of corruption had been oil-soaked torches held up by the hands of priests, forty centuries ago. We murmured to each other, echoes booming strangely in the enclosed space: The last sound to echo here had been voices raised to chant the mighty Hymn of Interment in the language of antique and mystic Khem.

The ghosts of lost, pharaonic grandeur haunted this dead place. We were somber, silent in their presence.

There was something strange about those walls.

The usual "pyramid texts" were absent here—the portraiture of kneeling servitors, the representations of the ancient gods, the recital of the deeds and glories of the dead king. One symbol, repeated endlessly, and one symbol only, was painted down the narrow hall. It was the *ankh*, the Cross of Life, but oddly different—and then it struck me. The looped cross, curved in white, was here but *reversed*. And painted in jet black!

It was not the *crux ansata*, the Cross of Life.

The inverted cross, dead black, was the *crux mors*.

The Cross of Death!

Chapter 4

The Thing That Glowed

Hail, soul, thou mighty one of terror! Verily, I am here. I have come. And I behold thee.

—*Book of the Dead*, IX

WE stood at the entrance to the King's Chamber now. The natives, trembling with palsied terror, chipped away with mortar. One of them gasped in pain as his chisel slipped, gashing his hand. We sent him outside for first aid. The possibility of infection here was slight, but no point in risking it.

Stone by stone fell away. We were breathless with excitement, tense with the drama of the moment: An unopened tomb, its royal treasures intact, is the dream of the Egyptologist. And, like most human dreams, seldom attained.

At last we cleared the rubble away and stepped into the sepulchral chamber. I felt a weird sensation of pressure, of *weight*; it was as if we stood miles deep within the bowels of the earth. The crushing burden of thousands of tons of stone weighed down our souls in the blackness of the vault. We turned the torches up.

For some peculiar reason, I thought of those lines from the seventh tablet of the *Gilgamesh Epic* written down in eldritch Babylon, the most ancient poem in the world:

> Descend ... into the House of Darkness .... To the house which none
> leave who have betrodden it .... To the house whose inhabitants do with-
> out light, where dust is their nourishment and clay their food. ... They
> see not the light, who dwell in the darkness. In the House of Dust ...
> there do dwell the mighty ones, who from the days of old ruled this land.

Odd, how scraps of things you read years ago can pop into your mind in moments of suspense and great excitement!

We turned the torches still brighter and shone them about us.

The sarcophagus of the Black Pharaoh was hewn of black marble, massively proportioned, covered with graven hieroglyphic inscriptions. There could be no longer any doubt of what we had found, for among the rows of glyphs I spotted the cartouche of Khotep itself, picked out in scarlet enamel.

Carrington was staring at the wall behind the sarcophagus itself. A blurred figure, curiously difficult for the eye to make out, was painted there; but the paint seemed to have been eaten away, as if some mold or fungoid infection had spoiled the paint. At any rate, the figure was smeared and hard to see—but hunched, deformed somehow, not quite human. An enormous cartouche was painted in clear black to either side of the blurred painting. Carrington read it aloud in strange, halting tones:

"Iao-Thaumungazoth—"

Something in the acoustics of the vault made the uncouth name ring out much more loudly than he had expected. He started wildly and paled as the curious name boomed out in the dead silence.

Iao-Thaumungazoth—a strange name! Again, it was not Egyptian. Perhaps it was the name of the black god of madness and evil Khotep had worshiped with dreadful rites, who can say? At any rate, I doubt a human voice had spoken it aloud for ages ....

As the echoes of the name faded away, I started suddenly and Carrington and I exchanged a queer glance. Suddenly my flesh turned cold and crept on my bones. For I had heard, or thought I had heard, a weird, awful sound—inexplicable, but terrifying. A sluggish, sleepy shifting of enormous weight within some deep and hollow place. It was almost as if the mummy had *stirred* within his sarcophagus of black marble; or perhaps the sound came from deeper down, far below us, in the depths of the abyss at the bottom of the earth. It was as if Something that had long slept stirred in its sleep at the mention of its Name ....

An involuntary exclamation rose to my lips, but I stifled it. Collins and Mazzeo looked at each other, faces pale and tense and drawn. Surely, the sound had been nothing—my imagination, nothing more.

Carrington set the trembling natives to prying off the stone lid of the sarcophagus as he played his light about the walls of the chamber. One wall held a painted bas-relief. It depicted a tall, kingly form—the pharaoh himself, obviously, in all his imperial accouterments, the leopard skin, the *uraeus* crown, arms crossed upon his chest, bearing the crook and flail. The same oddly realistic, curiously lifelike, strangely unconventionalized art style could be seen in the pharaoh's portrait, just as we had noticed it in those gaunt, crouching malignancies that passed for sphinxes outside the pyramid.

I stared up at the gaunt, stiff figure portrayed on the wall. It was the face of the pharaoh that caught and held my attention—regal, cold, aristocratic, with lines of cruelty around the thin-lipped mouth. I noticed that, blasphemously, instead of the red and white double crown of a king, he wore the triple crown of a god. And by some uncanny trick of the painter's art, his burning eyes which glared down at us seemed to bore directly into my own; he seemed to frown down upon us, the outlanders, the desecrators of his tomb, the would-be thieves of his treasure. There was cold, malignant menace in that burning gaze.

I tore my eyes away and stood there, unaccountably feeling a shudder rise up within me. Carrington, who seemed to feel nothing of this air of cold menace, was busily setting up his camera to photograph the wall paintings.

Collins and Mazzeo were set to work prying loose the lid of the sarcophagus. After a time the heavy slab was slid aside, revealing the gilded wooden coffin. It glittered with vivid hues as bright and fresh as if they had been painted yesterday, and not millennia ago. The upper part of the coffin was worked into a representation of the pharaoh's face, and we noted with surprise that the eyes were pictured as if *closed*, and that, from the center of his forehead, a *third eye*—open—glared up at us.

"The third eye of astral vision," Carrington muttered excitedly. "That means he was an adept of black magic." Gingerly breaking the seals, he opened and removed the coffin lid.

A curious stillness fell over us all, standing there in the light of the electric torches. The wooden lid, bright with gold leaf and rich with covered enamels and inlaid gems, slid away.

And we saw the mummy for the first time!

The gaunt cadaver was tightly wrapped from head to foot in spiced linen bandages which time had withered into dirty brown strips of crumbling cloth, splotched here and there where the preservative gums had leaked through to stain the bandages. The wrappings over the face had rotted away, exposing the ghastly skull-like face of the thing. The dry flesh had shrunk back to the bone like cracked and peeling leather. Here and there it had grown scaly and leprous with decay, and on the brow it had rotted away entirely, exposing the brown bare bone of the skull.

The lips had shriveled, and the gums, exposing naked teeth like long canine fangs bared in a mirthless grin or a snarl of savage defiance. The nose had fallen in, leaving a hideous, rotting hole in the center of the face—

Collins gave a strangled gasp. "Look! The *eyes*—"

They were half open; the skin, as it had shrunk and died, had peeled back the lids and we could see the dead, dry, yellowish eyeballs, which had congealed into a hard jelly. The torches wavered in our trembling hands, casting flickering shadows over the ghastly skull-face, making the shrunken, decayed features seem to move, dry wrinkled lips to writhe in a soundless snarl, the lids of the eyes to twitch ....

Carrington was puttering about within the coffin. "Strange!" he grumbled. "No sign of Canopic jars bearing the preserved internal organs, and there are none of the usual protective amulets about the corpse ... the Amulet of the Pillow that should be under the neck ... no sign of the Tet amulet that permits the deceased to reconstitute his body in the Second Life ... no heart scarab ... no *urchat* ... nothing but the Shen amulet, laid here on the breast, to give the body everlasting life. I don't understand it," he grouched, casting the rays of his lamp about the walls of the burial chamber. "No Canopic jars anywhere; it's as if they prepared the corpse, leaving the brain and heart and viscera intact—"

"What's this?" I stooped to remove a small black box clasped between the crossed hands of the mummy, which seemed to hug the small casket to its bony breast.

We tried to disengage the small black box from the grasp of the mummy, but found it unexpectedly difficult: It was almost as if the dead thing clung jealously to its treasure. At length we tore the small casket from the grip of those rotting paws—ripping loose, in the process, some of the bandages that bound the arms to the breast. The loosened wrappings fell away, exposing the hands of the thing—grisly, decayed talons, clawed like some predatory vulture.

The box was small and almost square, carved of sandalwood and painted with hard black enamel. Its only decoration was a symbol inlaid in bright gold, which I recognized as the hieroglyphic for Set the Destroyer.

"The Sign of Set," Carrington breathed curiously, "and look—the god is holding the *crux mors*—do you suppose they buried the pharaoh with the Star of Set?" His whispered words reverberated through the hollow vault in the sibilant echoes. We crowded near, eager to gaze upon the necromantic jewel, the fabulous talisman. Carrington fumbled with the sealed box but it was fastened in some mysterious manner and he could not find the catch, or even the jointure of the lid.

Suddenly a hoarse cry rang out and we spun around to see young Collins tumble forward in a dead faint. Tucking the black case with the Set hieroglyph worked in gold into his pocket, Carrington knelt to examine the boy. He was white as paper, head lolling loosely, eyes rolled up glassily. It might have been the vitiated air of the vault, or the stench of the preservative gums and tomb natron; anyway, we carried him out of the vault and into the open air under the blinding glare of noon. We set him down in the shade of the gate of purple pylons and Carrington forced a few drops of brandy between his lips. He gagged, coughed, and started around blinking. Then—

"It *moved*," he panted. "I saw it move—when you were trying to open the little black box. One of those rotting claws—*twitched!*"

Carrington soothed him. "Nonsense, my boy, you had a touch of the heat, nothing more. The thing's been dead for thousands of years. Touch of the heat, the closeness, the dead air—bit of rest is what you need. Mahmoud! Help the young *effendi* to his tent."

"Nevertheless ... I saw it move," Collins whispered from white lips.

Chapter 5

The Hand of Death

Deliver thou him from the worms which live upon bodies of men and women and feed upon their blood.
—*Nekhtu-Amen Papyrus*

SHENSTONE poured himself another whiskey with slender hands that shook. Brant declined, and watched as the Earl downed it in swift, shuddering gulps, his face a grey mask of strain in the deepening gloom that now shrouded the book-lined room.

Almost from the first moment we entered the pyramid, disaster haunted us (Shenstone resumed). An hour or so later, the first accident occurred. We had rigged up a crane and pulley and were lifting the sarcophagus of black marble out of the portal of the pyramid into the open air. Old Mahmoud Reis was steadying the massive thing, walking along beneath. A rope snapped—something went wrong—the sarcophagus fell, the lid jarring off, the coffin lid too—crushing Mahmoud's legs under the weight of the marble mass. He screamed—terribly—and for long, long minutes we strove to lift the sarcophagus and free his poor, crushed, mangled legs—and all the while the face of the mummy leered at us in grinning, skull-like mockery from the open coffin—grinned, while the hot red heart-blood of the old fellow streamed down his tortured limbs and *dripped upon the dead withered husk*. Faugh! It was horrible! (Shenstone shuddered in a quick spasm of disgust.)

The blood dripped down, besplattering the mummy's chest and face— dribbling down into those grinning jaws, falling between the brown, bared fangs, half-parted in a frozen snarl. Dripped—dripped—*feeding the dead thing with hot blood!* We freed Mahmoud Reis at last, but he died within minutes. I held his tired old head cradled in my lap.

"I warned you—*effendi*—the mummy's curse!" he panted. "Beware—*effendi*—beware the Curse of Khotep! I—die—*Allah!*—*Allah! Allahu akbar!*"

And he died in my arms. "Yes, Mahmoud Reis—old friend!" I cried softly, "*Allahu akbar!* God is great. Go with God, old friend, *ma'salama*, Mahmoud Reis, goodby!"

We buried the old fellow that evening, far toward an end of that accursed valley, where the shadow of the Lost Pyramid could not touch his grave. The next day we removed some of the tomb figures—including a splendid nine-foot figure of Anubis in green basalt, and some funerary urns of alabaster, porcelain, chrysolite and faience. But then Yussuf Ahmad—the boy who cut his hand opening the inner portal—came down with something. Great putrescent leaking sores all over his face and hands. Young Collins, the boy who fainted in the tomb, was next to catch the plague. Alarmed, we hurried back toward Khartoum, bearing with us the sarcophagus, the mummy, and the movables. But Yussuf Ahmad died of the strange plague before we were out of sight of the Sealed Valley, and Collins only lasted another day. He died there in the desert, in the sudden purple dusk of Lower Egypt, and we buried him under the shifting sands. Other members of our party were stricken with the putrescent running sores, and at Khartoum we were all hospitalized. Another native died of the ghastly plague-like illness while we were being rushed to Cairo for treatment there. In all, four of us died.

In Cairo, another series of ominous and peculiar accidents haunted our footsteps. A mysterious fire broke out in the warehouse where the antiquities were stored. The night-watchman managed to pass the alarm before it had spread very far, and the treasures were recovered undamaged. Then a few days later, some thief broke into the warehouse—although we could never ascertain how he made his entry. But the treasures were disturbed—as if someone had searched through them for something that was not there. This was particularly curious, as nothing whatsoever was taken—it was almost as if the thief, not finding the particular thing he sought, left abruptly, disappointed.

By this time we were all in a state of nerves—and the newspapers had gotten hold of the "Pharaoh's Curse" story and were spreading it. We left Egypt as soon as humanly possible and returned to England, arriving last month. Clive was jealously guarding the Star of Set by carrying it on his person—he had not let the black box, which continued to resist all our efforts to open it, out of his sight since it was removed from the mummy's grasp.

And then, the end, as you know. Poor Clive—dying in such a terrible way—

"TELL me exactly what happened, from your point of view," Brant urged.

"Well, I actually know very little; I was here in Wilfrith when the murder occurred. Clive spent yesterday afternoon with me here, going over the documents. When he left, I persuaded him to leave the Star of Set with me—I had a theory about the manner in which the box was fastened."

"Then the talisman is here, in this house, at this moment?" Inspector Brant asked. Lord Shenstone nodded.

"In my safe. What with all the excitement, I've had no chance to try my theory and attempt to open the box. I'll show it to you in a moment: I am almost done with my unhappy story.

"As you no doubt know, Professor Carrington returned to London yesterday evening. As I understand it, he worked for a little while in his office at the Museum, then, as the watchman was going his rounds, Clive accompanied the man—old Pipkin. It seems a thief broke into the Museum—at any rate, a rear window was smashed open, as were the heavy steel mesh fastened over the aperture and the grill of iron bars."

"Yes," Inspector Brant nodded. "The mesh was torn off with terrific strength. And the bars were bent awry. But go on, tell me all you know."

"Quite so," continued Shenstone, lighting another cigarette. "Well, it seems the thief attacked Clive, injuring him in the throat. As I understand it, his throat was—*torn*—torn out, as if by some spiked steel weapon, like an iron mace. And the night-watchman, believed by the police to have been in league with the thief, had vanished. But again, nothing was taken. The jewels and treasures were intact, although again the thief had searched through them, without apparently finding the thing he sought, whatever it may be."

"Nothing taken," Inspector Brant interrupted quietly, "except one thing!"

"Yes. Yes, one thing is missing. *The mummy itself.* And that is another mystery—and I am exhausted with trying to fathom it!"

"That is everything you know?" Brant asked, glancing over the closely written pages of his pocket notebook.

"That is everything. A complete puzzle from beginning to end."

Inspector Brant brooded. "Five men dead. One of accidental injury. Three of some unknown disease. The last, the victim of an unknown assailant. The last is the one that interests me. It is riddled with contradictions. Why rob a museum, and overlook priceless treasures of gold and gems—to steal a *mummy*! A valuable antiquity, yes, but worth only a fraction of the value of a handful of gems. And clumsy to transport. How did they get it away?"

"Through the broken window, obviously," Shenstone said.

"Yes, but *why?* If Pipkin the caretaker was an accomplice, why not simply unlock the door? Why struggle with an unwielding, stiff, heavy burden—strive to push it out a window—when all you have to do is to simply unlock a door? And another mystery—why kill Professor Carrington at all? Burglars and thieves, my Lord, do not kill. It would be foolish. A slug in the head and tie you up with a gag in your mouth—yes. But murder? Never! Too dangerous. The risk is too great."

"I hadn't thought of that aspect of the crime," Shenstone admitted, nervously.

"Another thing. The method of the murder. How are men killed? A knife in the back—a cracked skull from a cosh or gun-butt. But *this!* I saw the Professor's body at the morgue this morning. His throat was torn out by some wild beast—or so it looked."

"A steel mace, perhaps—" Lord Shenstone said.

"A rather—uncommon—weapon, wouldn't you say, sir? *Does the Carrington Museum have a medieval wing?*"

The question jolted the Earl visibly.

"Great God, I hadn't thought of that!" he gasped. "Why, no! No medieval department at all! Nothing but Eastern antiquities—Mesopotamian relics, Egyptian, Indian, and so on. Where could the murderer have obtained such a weapon?"

"Precisely. Now, as you related your story, I've been thinking of all sorts of explanations. One is that the thief sought the Star of Set—a priceless jewel, no doubt worth many thousand pounds—did not find it since it was in your possession at the time—was disturbed in his search by Professor Carrington, and slew him to avoid an alarm. This is good as far as it goes, but does *not* explain why he—or they, there must have been more than one, the mummy was too heavy for one man to carry—this does not, I say, explain why they took the mummy at all. Unless there was something concealed in the mummy itself, something so valuable that it made the gems lying about worthless by comparison."

"I suppose that is possible," Lord Shenstone said.

"But we have no direct evidence to that effect. It looks to me as if the thief—or thieves—is after the Star of Set. Twice your collection of treasure has been searched through—with nothing taken—and each time the only thing of value missing from the collection was the talisman."

An almost visible atmosphere seemed to grow in the room, like a clammy, clinging fog.

"Then—I dread what will happen when the thief learns I have the Star in my possession," Shenstone said softly.

Inspector Brant closed his notebook, and rubbed his lean jaw with one bronzed hand. "I wish it was as simple as plain thievery," he said. "But I suspect there is something darker here."

"The curse?"

Brant nodded. "The curse. I am not a superstitious man. But in my work I have seen things—heard of things—experienced them myself—that make me realize that sometimes—"

He broke off, staring thoughtfully into the shadows. Then he raised his gaze to look the Earl in the eyes.

"I know of only one man in Europe who can help you," he said slowly.

"Yes? Who? Tell me, man!"

"Have you ever heard of a man called—"

Brant broke off. At that precise moment a telephone rang, the shrill and unexpected sound jarring them both. Shenstone snatched up the receiver from a near table.

"Yes? Oh, Crithers. Yes; one moment."

Turning, he said, "For you, Inspector. Scotland Yard."

Brant took the instrument from his hand.

"Brant here. Yes, Mailey. *What?* Oh, good work!"

He covered the receiver with one hand, and said to Shenstone: "My assistant, calling. *They've found Pipkin, the caretaker!*"

Lord Shenstone gasped.

"Wonderful! Excellent news. Was he—alive?"

"One moment," said Brant, turning back to the telephone. "Yes, old man, still here. Was the caretaker alive? What? Oh … I see. You're sure? Where is he? We'll be there at once."

He hung up, turning.

"Well? Well? Alive?"

Brant looked at Shenstone somberly.

"Alive—but completely *mad!*"

Chapter 6

The Eyes of the Mummy

THE following morning found Inspector Brant and Lord Shenstone in London. They drove from Wilfrith Hall in Shenstone's black Rolls Royce limousine, Shenstone carrying in a locked attaché case the black box containing the Star of Set. This was contrary to Brant's advice, for he felt the talisman would be far more secure locked away in Shenstone's safe, but the Earl insisted. He would not let the necromantic jewel out of his hands.

Brant checked in at the Yard and made his report to Commander Nils Eaton, his immediate superior, while turning over his pocket notebook to Lt. Barker of the stenographic department for transcript. Then, wasting as little time as was possible, Brant and Lord Shenstone drove up Martyn

Street, down Gardner, and crosstown to the Hasse Street station, where Pipkin had been arrested and was being held for psychiatric observation.

"We tracked him into Soho, and found him holed up in a ratty little flat under an assumed name," Gareth Mailey, his assistant, reported as he led Inspector Brant and Lord Shenstone to the cell. "He was a nervous wreck—completely off, mad as a hatter. We had to take him out in a straitjacket."

"Can't believe old Pipkin was mixed up in this mess," the Earl muttered, as they descended in the lift. "I've known the old chap for thirteen years. Completely dedicated to the Museum—would have laid down his life for Professor Carrington, I'd have sworn."

"Well, we'll soon discover his side of the story—this is the cell?" Brant inquired. Mailey nodded, and the constable unlocked the door and they went in.

Old Pipkin, a little dried-up gnome of a man with a wispy white beard framing his ruddy, apple-cheeked face, was curled up on the cot when they entered, his face turned to the wall, arms secured in the straitjacket, his hunched shoulders and frail, bent form redolent of hopeless misery.

He straightened with a start as the door clanged open, jerked a face of livid fear in their direction, and relaxed as he recognized Lord Shenstone.

"Oh, yer Lordship! It's you! I was afraid it was—" he quavered, his pale, lined face working, rheumy eyes red with sleeplessness.

"Who were you afraid it was?" Brant inquired, as Shenstone helped the old man to a more comfortable position and adjusted a pillow behind his head.

"*'Im*, Officer—*'IM!*"

"Who do you mean by 'Him?'"

"'Im what done it—'im what done in the Perfessor, that's 'oo I mean," the old fellow quavered, and then, turning to the sympathetic face of Lord Shenstone, he moaned, "Oh, yer Lordship, ye'll believe me, won't ye? It were awful—*awful*—an' I couldn't do a single thing to stop 'im—I was that petrified, I was!"

"Come, come now, Pipkin, old fellow, of course I'll believe you. So will this gentleman here; it's Inspector Brant, come down from Scotland Yard to listen. We're here to help you—we want to know what happened."

The tired old man took a deep breath, then let it out in a long shivering sigh.

"I told it all a-ready, to *'im*," he said, nodding at Gareth Mailey. "'*E* didn't believe me—thought I were *mad*, 'e did!"

Then he turned piteously to Shenstone again: "But I'm *not* mad, ye'r Lordship, I tell ye I saw it with me own eyes!"

"Tell us what you saw—everything, mind you, no matter what it was," Inspector Brant said in a firm, calm voice, bending down to pat the old man's quivering, hunched shoulders. "Just tell us the truth, and nothing bad will happen to you. Don't be afraid. We're all anxious to help you—but we must know what happened."

The old man gazed up at him with red, rheumy eyes that seemed haunted and desperate with some vague, shadowy fear.

"Well, I'll tell ye then, everthin', jist as it happened. I was makin' me rounds at the Museum, jist as I always do—night before last, it was. The Perfessor was in 'is office workin' away. When I comes by, he pokes 'is head out and sez: 'That late, eh Pips?' ('E always called me Pips.) 'I'll be leavin' soon—soon's I takes these things back to the storeroom.' So 'imself and I go down to the storeroom—where the new mummy is, ye understand, an' all the gauds and trinkets 'e jist brought back overseas. H'about one in the mornin' it was, or thereabouts. Well, we goes in, and I stays by the door while th' Perfessor takes me lantern and goes in: 'H'I won't be but a minute, Pips,' 'e sez, 'H'I'll just put these perpyrus rolls back, 'n' I wants ta copy one cartoushy off'n the coffin's lid.' Se 'e goes in, leavin' me standin' there in the dark by th' door. Perfessor sets th' lantern down on a packin' case, and puts them scrolls with th' others. Ye'll understand that all this while, th' mummy was in 'is wooden case, leant up against th' wall. Perfessor takes off th' lid and puts it down atop one of them cases and takes some papers out o' 'is pocket, leanin' over, startin' ta trace one of them cartoushy-things. From where I'm standing, th' light strikes up inta th' mummy's rottin' face—I kin see it now, awful it were—an' then—*an' then!—*"

His audience leaned closer to the shrinking little figure on the cot. "Yes, yes? What happened then?" Shenstone asked.

Pipkin shrieked: "*The eyes!* The eyes o' the mummy!"

"What about them, man?!"

Pipkin drew another long, shuddering breath: "H'as I watched, they began t' open—slow, slow, them dry wrinkled old lids, jerkin' up—*'e was alive, I tell you!* Alive!—an' 'is eyes glaring, wide open—I couldn't move, couldn't speak! Them eyes peerin' around, searchin' the room, wild, mad eyes, like some animal, blazin', burnin'—pits o' yellow fire. Then 'e spies th' Perfessor bendin' over in front of 'im. An' bares 'is awful teeth like a big cat snarlin'—*an' 'is hands move—tearin' loose—the rottin' ole bandages a-snappin' an' a-breakin'*—and all th' time I wuz leanin' there h'against th' door, shakin' like a palsy had me—couldn't speak, 'n' Perfessor there, busy wid 'is drawrin', payin' no mind.

"An' them awful hands was loose, openin' 'n' closin' like th' 'orrid claws o' some fearsome bird—'n' I couldn't speak a word t' save me wretched life—'n' th' Perfessor not noticin' nary a thing! An' then th' mummy reaches down—'is awful, mad eyes a'glarin'—'n' grabs Perfessor by 'is shoulder—'n' I kin hear 'im gasp an' 'e straightens up 'n' sees th' mummy's face—'n' 'e screams—screams like a stuck pig!—an' then th' thing reaches out an' seizes 'im by 'is scrawny ole throat *an' tears it out wid that awful claw! Blood—blood pours out like a hose—all over th' dead thing what ain't dead but oughta be!"*

It was still as death in the grim little cell, silent as the grave except for Pipkin's hysterical, wheezing sobs. A line from the *Nu-Pesht Papyrus* ran through Inspector Brant's mind—a line Lord Shenstone had read for him the night before—

And dark things walked that had no right to live.

"What happened—after that?" Brant asked.

"'E shakes th' Perfessor, shakes 'im like a cat shakin' a dead rat—all th' time blood is spewin' out all over everthin'—and 'e drops 'im. An' 'e stands there a bit, peerin' around wid those mad glarin' eyes—'e spies th' jewels an' paws through 'em like 'e's lookin' fer somethin', but 'e don't find it an' that makes 'im mad—'e raises up 'is awful skull-head an' snarls wid rage (all the time makin' no sound, like as if 'e can't talk)—an' then he looks over at th' door where I'm standin', leanin' there in th' dark, half-dead in me terror—'n' for a little I think 'e's comin' over to me, but 'e doesn't. An' then he starts toward th' tother door, leadin' out back—shuffles along slow 'n' ponderous-like, jerky an' slow, 'is bloody paws danglin' down, allweez peerin' from side t' side wid those blazin' yellow eyes. Then 'e goes out an' I cain't see 'im no more but I kin *hear* 'im, shufflin', shufflin' along—then 'e starts bangin' at somethin'—th' windee at th' back—beatin' at it an' worryin' at it like a wild beast tryin' t' git out—glass crashin' and iron bars crunchin' as he bends 'em out o' th' concrete—I kin hear 'im rippin' away th' steel mesh like h'it were paper—an' then I kin move and all I kin think is: *Run! Run! Run!*—I go scrabblin' down the hall, bashin' inta cases an' fallin' down an' then I'm up against th' front door, an' I grabs me keys—an' all th' time I kin hear th' mummy smashin' and smashin' at the back windee an' I'm thinkin' 'e 'eard me an' *any minute now 'e'll be after me!* So I lets meself out an' locks th' door behind me—an' I *run! I run!*—I don't know where I'm going, but I run like that thing wuz at me 'eels!

"H'it's about two in th' mornin' now—streets empty—a cold wind creepin' down th' street 'n' th' fog comin' in, th' wind twistin' it inta clammy yellow ghosts—not a soul in sight—but I knows by now that dead thing must be through th' windee 'n' out in th' alley behind th' Museum—for all I know, 'e's after me already—so I run, an' run, an' run, til I cain't see, cain't breathe, th' clammy yellow fog clutching at me wid long wispy fingers as I run—an' then—an' then—I dunno what happent. May be I went off me coconut, or passed out, but sometime in th' mornin' I finds meself in Soho. I'm all mud and wet from head t' foot, 'n' half dead from fright, but I got some money on me, an' I rents me a room in one o' them bummy little places—the mummy cain't never find me there—I locks th' door an' sits there listenin' an' ever time somebody goes up or down th' hall,

I think: *It's 'im! It's 'im! 'E found me!*—an' then, later on, I tried to sleep but ever time I closed me pore eyes, I sees 'im, snarlin' and glarin' wid them mad eyes like yellow pits of hell-fire, wid th' Perfessor's blood dribblin' down 'is gory paws all over 'im—an' then th' police come and got me ...."

There was silence when the old man's story was done. Mailey finished taking notes, and closed and pocketed his notebook with a snap. Brant exchanged a long, wordless look with Shenstone. Pipkin glanced at their faces.

"Oh, ye don't believe me, ye don't! Ye don't!" he cried wildly. "Ye think I'm mad, too, like t'others! They think I'm mad, but I'm not mad! I saw it, I tell ye! *Wid me own eyes, I saw it! I swear it! Oh Gawd, won't anybody believe me?! I saw it!*"

They left the cell, while a doctor came and gave the old man something to quiet him. In a few moments the wild raving screams died away and the doctor emerged, locking the cell behind him.

"That will make him sleep, and give him a good long rest, which is something he needs. I am Doctor Foley, the psychiatrist examining the prisoner," he introduced himself.

They acknowledged the introduction, and Inspector Brant said, "Tell me, doctor, what's your opinion?"

Doctor Foley smiled whimsically. "You mean, is he insane? Difficult question to answer, Inspector. Technically—at the moment—yes, he is insane. But, understand, I mean his wrought-up state, the extreme nervous tension and hysteria. As for the truth or lack of truth in his wild story—that I cannot say. But the man has suffered some tremendous shock—his nerves have given way."

Shenstone inquired, "Will he recover?"

"With sound sleep, rest, good food, yes—he will recover from the state he is now in. But, if he is mad in the clinical sense—if his story is the product of a deranged mind—that will be another matter."

They went upstairs to the lounge for coffee.

"You've heard his story, then?" Brant asked. The doctor nodded.

"He tells it to everyone who comes within earshot."

"And what do you think of it?"

Doctor Foley gave a wry smile: "What could I possibly think of it? The man claims to have seen a mummy, dead for thousands of years, come to life and tear, mangle, and murder a man. I am a scientist and, as such, disbelieve in the existence of the supernatural. What could I possibly think of such a story, except that it comes from a feverish, hysteric mind suffering from some terrific nervous shock?"

They finished their coffee, and the doctor left. Shenstone turned to Inspector Brant and asked, "What do we do now?"

Brant said, "The story is wild—mad, if you like—but I somehow feel the old fellow was telling the truth. It seems impossible, but—I have experienced strange things before, during the course of my work—things that seemed impossible."

Shenstone smiled shakily. "I thought you disbelieved in the supernatural, Inspector?"

Brant said, "I do! But we are arguing about words. Whatever exists—however unusual and weird—whatever occurs—however impossible it may seem—*must be natural*. If it happens, in nature, then it is a part of nature; the supernatural is a contradiction in terms. The occurrence may obey strange laws—laws about which we know very little, but natural laws nevertheless. The event may be rare, but the phenomenon is natural. Only a few pioneering minds may know the existence of the law, but it is a natural law, just the same."

The Earl shivered. "I hope you are right, but what are we to do?"

Brant brooded over his pipe. "Last night in Wilfrith Hall, I was about to say something, when the call about Pipkin's capture interrupted."

"Yes?"

"I was about to ask you a question. I'll ask that question now. Have you ever heard of a man called—*Dr. Anton Zarnak?*"

Chapter 7

The Monster-Killer

YOU mean—Zarnak the 'Monster-Killer?'" Lord Shenstone asked, incredulously.

"So the newspapers call him," Brant replied, quietly.

"Why, yes, I've heard of him, of course. Some sort of charlatan, isn't he? Cultist, or something?"

"Cultist—perhaps; but, charlatan? No. A brilliant scientist—although his theories have caused him to be laughed out of his profession. He probably knows more about Chaldean cuneiform, Egyptian hieroglyphics, and Old Sanskrit—than you or I know about the English language! Speaks eleven languages fluently. He studied philosophy, metaphysics, and psychology at the Sorbonne, and had his Doctor of Philosophy degree from there. He has a degree in theology, too, and a degree in medicine. He practiced medicine for some years—until the accident that changed his life."

"Accident?"

"Yes. He was practicing in some Balkan country—perhaps it was in Transylvania—when his wife and baby son were slain by a werewolf—"

"*Werewolf?* Oh, come now, Inspector, *really*—"

"Yes, *werewolf*," Brant insisted, doggedly. "In case you don't know, it's a medically recognized (although extremely rare) malady. The disease is called lycanthropy. However, this horrible accident ruined Zarnak's life and career. He traced the monster down and destroyed it, and since then he has devoted his life to seeking and slaying such abnormal monstrosities."

"What could he know about our pharaoh's curse?"

"He has traveled extensively in the Near East. I happen to know he spent some years in Egypt, as a matter of fact. If there is any man in the world who could help, Dr. Zarnak is that man."

"You say he was discredited by the medical profession?"

"Yes. He published several papers on lycanthropy and vampirism, but his theories were too radical, too advanced. Orthodox medical science ridiculed him. But he is not interested in fame. His one burning interest lies in tracing down and stamping out these pockets of nightmare and black superstition."

"How do you know so much about the man? Friend of yours?"

"I am honored to say that he is. We first met three years ago, when I was involved in the 'Vampire of London' case. He gave Scotland Yard the benefit of his amazing scholarship. I admire the man. He is one of the most brilliant intellects in Europe. A man of immense physical endurance and utter courage, selfless in his devotion to humanity; a man of the most extraordinary learning in odd, out-of-the-way by-paths of human knowledge."

"Does he reside here, in London?" Shenstone asked.

"He travels about the world extensively, but keeps quarters in several cities ready for him day or night, all year round. He has a flat near here in Half Moon Street. I happen to know he is here in London at this moment; he arrived a week or so ago from India, and I remember reading an interview with him published in the papers. If you are willing, I'll ring him up."

"Inspector, I am in your hands. If you believe this Dr. Zarnak can help me, I will be happy to pay whatever fee he asks."

"Dr. Zarnak does not care about fees or payments. But I appreciate your urgency. I'll call him at once."

DR. Anton Zarnak not only was in, he invited them to attend him in his quarters at their earliest convenience. Leaving Gareth Mailey to report to the Yard, and instructing him to call them at Zarnak's number if anything at all peculiar came up, Brant and Lord Shenstone left the station. The black limousine carried them through Piccadilly ... past Hyde Park Corner with its playing children and baby carriages ... up to the curb before the house in Half Moon Street. The doctor's landlady, Mrs. Hecht, let them in: a small, rosy, plump, and motherly woman, whom Dr. Zarnak called "the greatest unconscious medium in Europe."

"Why, Inspector Brant—upon my word!"

"Good afternoon, Mrs. Hecht! It's a pleasure to see you again. This is Earl Shenstone of Wilfrith Hall."

She made a curtsy. "Your Lordship's servant, I am sure. Well, Mr. Brant, sir, it's been years. My! it's good to have the Doctor back at home, and gentlemen calling again, just like in the old days. But here I am, keeping you down here with my silly talk, and the both of you waitin' to see the good Doctor. Just you go right up, Inspector, you remember the way, top of the stairs and to the right. He's waiting to see you."

They went up the stairs, knocked on the door to the right of the landing, and received no answer, but, after a moment, pushed the unlocked door open and entered a large low-ceilinged cozy room with a fine stone fireplace and oak-paneled walls crowded with books of every sort and description. Books new and books old; books in English, French, German, Greek, Latin, Sanskrit, Arabic—books bound in leather, cloth, and paper, and others, rarer and more curious, bound in carven wood, animal skins such as leopard, or serpent-hide; a few very ancient volumes covered in old metal, inlaid with colored enamel and set with gems.

Books of magic, demonology, and witchcraft there were in plenty. The *Sword of Moses*, in M. Gaster's translation of 1896, and a *Key of Solomon* in Mather's London edition of 1889 (the edition from which the blacker portions were expurgated by the editor). There was an Old French manuscript of the *Lemegeton*, dating from the seventeenth century, with its infernal hierarchy of the Seventy-two Princes of Hell; the chaotic *Liber Spirituum*; the hysteric *Mystical City* of Agrada; a version of the infamous *Grand Grimoire* in the edition of Antonio Venitiana del Rabina; and the nightmarish *Pseudomonarchia Daemonum* of Wierus, Amsterdam, 1660.

Still other volumes testified to the wide range of their owner's intellectual interests. The *Poimandres* of Hermes Trismegistus and the *Visions of Zosimus*; R. A. Dart's *Proto-Human Inhabitants of Southern Africa* and Caton-Thompson's *The Zimbabwe Culture*; editions of Porphyry, Proclus, Psellus, and Paracelsus; a work by Rhases, the medieval Persian alchemist, the *Book of Secrets*. Here, too, was a bound manuscript of Pretorius' *Homunculi* and a rare copy of van Helsing's *The Vampire in Transylvania*.

Glass-lidded tables along one wall disclosed curiosities from the far corners of the earth. Cuneiform tablets of baked clay, carven Gnostic jewels, Egyptian *ushabti* figurines, a gold flask of holy water from the Sacred Well of Zamzam in Mecca, soapstone bird figures from Great Zimbabwe in Southern Rhodesia, talismans, pentacles and zodiacal charts from all of Europe. Along the wall under the darkly draped windows Maori idols shouldered Chinese josses. A grotesque Tibetan mask of Yama, King of Devils, hung above a *barbut*, or stringed Persian lute, upon one wall, while a limestone *stele* of the Kassite King, Helishipak II, from twelfth century B.C. Susa hung on another. An aromatic lamp of perforated silver from Damascus hung from the ceiling in one corner, just above hideous idols of the two Aztec goddesses, Centeotl and Tlaloc. It was a crowded, fascinating, bewildering room.

"Gentlemen! I beg your pardon for keeping you waiting like this. Unfortunately I was detained, putting through a cablegram to Dr. Yussuf Bey at the University of Alexandria!"

The tall, lean, aristocratic figure of Dr. Anton Zarnak entered from an adjoining room and came over to them, uttering polite apologies. His name had a tang of the foreign, but no trace of it could be ascertained either in his dress or his face. He was faultless: attired in black, his immaculate costume setting off his slender, noble form admirably. He was (Shenstone surmised) perhaps forty, with smoothly brushed iron-gray hair rising from a sharp widow's peak in his broad, intellectual brow. His eyes were black, magnetic, alert and commanding; his nose, a thin blade. He was close-shaven, lean-jawed; his face bore a peculiar pallor, and there was a twist of bitterness in his thin lips, a shadow of melancholy in his dark eyes.

In one hand he carried a small, light, black briefcase, which was never far from his person, day or night. He set it down now to shake hands with Inspector Brant and Lord Shenstone.

"Brant, I can't tell you how great a pleasure it is to see you after these years! Lord Shenstone, welcome to my humble quarters—let me take these books away so that you gentlemen may seat yourselves," Dr. Zarnak said, removing from two chairs Anrich's work on the Mysteries, and a bound volume of the *Naassene Document*.

"Not at all, Doctor. Upon my word, we've been admiring your collection of books. I swear there are some rarities here."

Zarnak permitted himself a rare smile. "Yes, my Lord—if, as the Greek mythographers assert, the hero Cadmus was the inventor of books, then I own myself one of the old fellow's most devoted disciples. However, the Egyptians claim Thoth"—(he nodded at a lead statue of the ibis-headed Egyptian god of learning, standing atop his mantelpiece)—"as the true inventor of books, so perhaps I am in his following, instead."

Shenstone smiled; he instinctively liked the man from first meeting. "An interesting statuette, Doctor. Unusual to find a *leaden* figure of Thoth—metal of Saturn, isn't it?"

Anton Zarnak gave him a bright, unwinking gaze of sudden interest.

"I was aware of your archaeological interests, my Lord, but I did not know you were a student of the Mysteries, as well."

"I must confess I am not; however, I, too, am a lover of books, with a range of interests perhaps less discriminating than yours."

Zarnak bowed slightly, in acknowledgment of the compliment, and continued: "Gentlemen, let us proceed at once to the problem. Brant, you may light up that filthy briar of yours. I want to hear everything about the Carrington-Shenstone Expedition—even those details that may not seem, to your criminological mind, relevant to the five murders."

"Then you know why we are here?" Shenstone inquired, with surprise.

"Certainly, my Lord. And I am very happy Brant rang me up. If he hadn't, I would probably have contacted you myself. I am an assiduous reader of the newspapers, as well as of their more distinguished cousin, the book. Now—let me hear everything."

Dr. Zarnak sprawled out in his great overstuffed chair, one leg comfortably hooked over the arm of it, while Shenstone and Brant, alternately, related the story of the ill-fated archaeological expedition. He made no comment during the story; indeed, he did not even look at them. His eyes half-hooded under drooping, sleepy lids did not even watch them, but stared instead into the dark cavity of the fireplace. With the slender, tapering fingers of one lean hand he rubbed his forehead absently, listening intently. From time to time he tapped one forefinger along the bridge of his nose—a habitual gesture. He made but two comments during the narration: the first, when Brant stumbled over the names of the three dark gods written on the lid of Khotep's sarcophagus.

He said: "Call them gods, if you wish. Yet: 'If Gods do evil then they are not Gods,' as Great-grandfather Euripides somewhere says. Go on."

The second interruption, a question, came as Lord Shenstone was describing the conditions of the mummy. Zarnak raised his head and asked: "No protective amulets about the mummy at all?"

Shenstone said: "Only the Amulet of the Shen."

"The Shen, of course, but—the tablet under the mummy's head, the hypocephalus, that was missing, too?"

Shenstone nodded. Zarnak inquired, "I take it you have not unwrapped the mummy—you do not know if it underwent evisceration or was interred with intact organs?"

Shenstone shook his leonine mane. "There were no Canopic jars, and, at the time, Clive remarked the mummy had probably not been eviscerated."

Zarnak nodded, thoughtfully. "The Ceremony of the Vulture," he mused.

"Eh?"

Zarnak roused himself. "Sometimes—under certain circumstances—a mummy was entombed with all organs intact. This was most frequently done when the deceased had no desire to enter the Second Life. I very much doubt if Khotep wished to visit the Hall of Judgment and stand before the Weigher of Hearts. Go on, please."

As the lengthening shadows of mid-afternoon gradually filled Half Moon Street with premonitions of gathering darkness, they completed the long, mystery-filled, tragedy-haunted tale. As they fell silent, and Zarnak in his great chair stared broodingly into the dark fireplace, Lord Shenstone blurted, "Can you help us, Doctor?"

Zarnak stirred. "Eh? Oh, yes, of course. Your pardon, I was thinking—"

"You have knowledge of Egyptian magic, then?" Shenstone persisted.

"I confess to some learning in the lore of that enigmatic and ancient kingdom, yes," Zarnak said, wryly. "I am, however, no *Magister* in the Egyptian rites. I have studied those 'Twelve Chapters' of the *Book of the Dead* that reveal the Names of Power; I have mastery over certain of the *hekau*, that is the Words. I am one of the few men living who has explored the secret caverns below the Ninth Pyramid. I have undertaken certain researches within the pyramids of Gizeh, those antique monuments, weary and old with a thousand years of history behind them when young Tut-Ankh-Amen ascended the Golden Throne of Thebes. And, perhaps more than any other European, I know the truth behind those strangely persistent myths of subterranean passages burrowed beneath the Sphinx, leading down, down, down to depths hinted at in weird legends found only in the most ancient and mouldering of papyrus scrolls. Yes, I can help you. But I can *promise* nothing!"

At that instant, the telephone rang.

Brant was at it in seconds. "I left your number with Mailey," he said. "They were to call me, at the Yard, if anything came up. Pardon me. Yes? Brant here. Yes—what—*good God!* The same way? Yes. Where? Mannix Lane, where it runs into the Thames? I understand. No—I'll ring you, if I need you. Carry on."

He hung up and turned to them.

"What has happened?" Doctor Zarnak inquired.

"They've found another body," Brant said, tensely.

"Oh, God," Shenstone groaned.

"Where?"

"At the end of Mannix Lane, where it ends by the Thames. A dock workman, throat torn out, just as Professor Carrington was murdered."

Zarnak sprang to his feet, crossed over to the bookcase, and pulled out a street map of London and the suburbs.

"When was this man killed?"

"Sometime this morning, about the time we entered London. Mailey says he wasn't discovered until noon, or thereabouts. Expression of unbelieving horror stamped on his face, frozen there in death."

"Yes—yes—" Zarnak said eagerly, tracing his forefinger over the map. He lifted his proud head and regarded them solemnly.

"Gentlemen: The monster is leaving London."

"How?"

"On the Thames, I should think. If you check, you will most probably find a small boat missing. The mummy may have abandoned it by now, however. Look—"

He called them to his side, and traced a straight line with his forefinger.

"Here is the Carrington Museum—and here is Mannix Lane. You see? He is going in an almost straight line. I may venture to guess, my Lord, that your Wilfrith Hall lies somewhere—here?" He extended the straight line beyond London, through the suburbs, and into the country.

Shenstone said: "Yes! Yes! Wilfrith is—here, exactly."

"Ah, yes. He hasn't got too far to go, then."

"Why do you think the mummy is going to Wilfrith Hall?" Brant said, puzzled.

"Extrapolation, my dear Brant. However, let me remind you that—while we do not know the exact degree of the mummy's powers—he doubtless thinks the Star of Set is still at Lord Shenstone's estate."

"The Star of Set?"

"Exactly. He has sought twice the tomb treasures without finding it. Now I believe he is trying for Wilfrith Hall."

Shenstone rubbed his brow, wearily.

"Why is he so anxious to recover the Star, I wonder?"

"Why, indeed," Doctor Zarnak said dryly: "He did, after all, sell his soul—in a sense—to get it. Another reason, and perhaps an even better one, is that *his soul is undoubtedly imprisoned within it.*"

Brant barked, "What?"

"Yes! When we finally get around to examining this mysterious gem—which we shall have to do, very shortly—we shall, I doubt not, find the *ka* of the pharaoh imprisoned within it."

"Good Lord!"

"As you say. And, unfortunately, there is an even stronger reason for the mummy's desire to recover the gem—and a powerful reason why we must at all costs prevent him from *ever* recovering it."

"What is that?"

"Simply, that the gem is a talisman of terrific potency, the symbol of his previous mastery of supernatural powers. At present the mummy is functioning at only a fraction of his power—sheer physical strength and the everlasting life in the body, for which he bargained away his chances of the Afterlife. If he ever gains possession of the jewel, he will recover the stupendous magical powers he once possessed, to enable him to exert complete dominion over one of the most prodigious empires the world has ever known. At present he is limited in the scope of his powers—he must walk overland, physically, to gain Wilfrith Hall. With the Star in his hands, he could command the forces of nature—he could bend the laws of space and time to his malignant will!"

The telephone rang once again, startling them all. Zarnak seized it.

"Zarnak here. Yes, yes—what? I see." He hung up, grimly.

"What—now?" Shenstone demanded.

Zarnak said, softly, "Time is running out, my friends. It is later than we think. Lord Shenstone, your niece, Miss Haldane, is on her way to Wilfrith. She sent a telegram at one o'clock. Your secretary, Mr. Crithers, just notified Scotland Yard."

"Good Lord—and the mummy is on his way there, too!"

"Yes," said Zarnak, grimly.

"Can we intercept her—head her off—a message—"

"Impossible—she will be there within two hours, according to her telegram. We must move swiftly, gentlemen, to prevent another tragedy. Lord Shenstone—does the Carrington possess, in its Egyptian Collection, such a thing as an *Ur-Hekau?*"

"Why, no, they do not."

Zarnak's mouth twisted bitterly.

"A great pity, it is one of the things I need most," he said, softly.

Shenstone brightened: "But—I know the British Museum has one, from the Tomb of Nectanebus. I know one of the Trustees of the B. M., Lord Corbenek—"

Zarnak's eyes flashed: "The *Rod of Nectanebus*—this is more fortunate than I had dared to hope! Very well—come, gentlemen, we must bustle! Bustle! You, my Lord, will come with me to the home of Lord Corbenek, then to the British Museum to acquire the Rod. ... I have everything else I will need"—(he patted the small black valise beside his chair)—"here. Brant: We do not need you. You take the fastest car Scotland Yard owns and attempt to turn the girl off, keep her away from Wilfrith Hall, if possible. Also call the Hall; warn them of what is approaching. Tell them—I do not think guns will do much good, but the mummy will be afraid of fire and light. It will be dark soon. Tell Crithers to keep all the lights blazing, and the windows locked, but to keep the drapes drawn back—the mummy will hesitate to enter a bright-lit room. Keep all the servants upstairs—locked in. And tell them to—pray."

He snapped up his valise and headed for the door, with Shenstone in tow.

"Swiftly, gentlemen. We have much work to do, and little time to accomplish it in, if we are to succeed with excellence, and we must not be afraid to sweat a little. Remember the so-wise words of Great-grandfather Hesiod: 'Before the gates of Excellence, the High Gods have placed—sweat!'"

Chapter 8

Adrienne

A STORM was gathering in the sultry night. All day there had brooded sullenly over this country landscape an electric tension; now, toward evening, dark thunderheads piled slowly in the west and a damp ever-stronger wind whistled just above the treetops. Leaves swished uneasily, and through the harsh, lurid red glow of sunset could be seen the ominous, gathering weight of rain-heavy clouds spilling overhead, riding the hissing wind.

As the horse-drawn carriage clattered over Beresford Brook and began its long race through Wilfrith Wood, Adrienne Haldane tried to complete her book. She had begun it early that morning to alleviate the monotony of the long train trip, and had only a few chapters to go. It was a Gothic novel of supernatural menace, prescribed reading for her course in the English novel, and she had intended to read it during her seashore vacation with her roommates. But newspaper scare-heads, speculating on the possible candidacy of her uncle, Lord Shenstone, as the next victim of the mysterious "Pharaoh's Curse", disturbed her plans. She was in the last stages of packing yesterday evening, and ready to depart to meet her roommates at Brighton, when news of Professor Carrington's grisly and uncanny murder aroused her fears for her uncle's safety. On the spur of the moment, she had completely changed her vacation plans (always the prerogative of a woman) and decided to spend the vacation week at Wilfrith Hall.

Lord Shenstone was her only living relative, and in the years after the death of her father, Sir Bertram, the lonely Earl had to a very large degree taken a father's place in her affections, and she herself had become almost a daughter in his mind.

Her annoyance, on arriving in the small town of Beresford and finding the town's one ancient taxicab undergoing repairs, had not been lightened when her repeated phone calls to Wilfrith Hall brought the news that Lord Shenstone's car was in London. There was no means for her to reach Wilfrith Hall, except by the antiquated coach-and-four kept in service by the owner of the local riding stable, which he obligingly put at her disposal.

As the coach rumbled across the wooden bridge and rattled into the long, twisting, tree-lined drive through Wilfrith Woods, Adrienne put aside her novel with a small, petulant frown and stared through the coach window at the gloomy view of heavy trees whipping past, against a turgid, ominous, and scarlet-lit sky. It was useless to attempt to concentrate any longer on her book: She was too worried about her uncle. Her phone call from the Beresford Inn had, it seems, arrived only a little while after the arrival of her telegram, announcing her impending arrival. Now she would reach

Wilfrith—but with her uncle in London, mysteriously accompanied by an inspector from Scotland Yard! Rather than easing her fears for Shenstone's safety, this increased them. At first she had paid little attention to the wild newspaper speculations, but the news of Professor Carrington's death, together with the surprising information that Scotland Yard, at least, considered the state of Lord Shenstone's danger sufficient to warrant assigning an inspector to investigate, alarmed her exceedingly.

These thoughts filled her mind as the racing carriage sped through the winding ways of the gloomy forest, and the Gothic novel in her lap was forgotten. In a way, she quite resembled a typical heroine of Radcliffian romance: her fearful young beauty, set in the gloomy scene of the antique coach; foam-flecked horses speeding toward the old mansion before the storm broke; the dark, brooding forest with its whipping trees and deep shadows; and the windswept sky of fading scarlet light, piled with darkling storm clouds. She was twenty, a slender, exquisite slip of a girl with superb skin of pallid, delicate gold and great strange eyes of jade green. Her smooth, unwaving hair was burnished red-copper, worn in a page-boy bob. It followed the delicate contours of her small, proud head like a golden helmet. Her nose was small and straight and her chin tiny and rounded, but with a stubborn small strength.

She was not tall, and very slender, yet with small, firm, proudly lifting breasts and long, lovely legs. She had a delicate, tiny waist and full swelling hips. There was something about her that contradicted everything else. Her youth and apparent daintiness were contradicted by her robust health and well stocked mind. Her pallid, heart-shaped face with great wistful eyes gave little evidence of her provocative, subtle, delicately malicious, and cat-like purring voice and laugh. She was a tiny bundle of contradictions, but a breathtaking one.

She was thinking of Jane Street and Anne Lovell, her roommates, and their long-planned vacation together, now reversed by her sudden whim—when a dazzling flare of sudden lightning made her catch her breath in a small, stifled shriek. The storm had not yet broken, but it was only moments away. The coachman from the livery stable was whipping his team, but his efforts would most probably go unrewarded, and they would not reach their goal before the downpour.

Adrienne shivered—whether from the damp chill in the wind, the gloomy darkness of the forest with the storm hanging over it, or the half-forgotten Gothic novel in her lap, she did not know. Somehow, she very strongly wished she were already in the warmth and light of Wilfrith Hall, this very moment.

Then the storm came down—a blinding flare of lightning, a deafening concussion of thunder, and sheets of cold wet rain that lashed against the windows of the musty coach and drummed on the top. And then the coachmen—*screamed*.

She leaned forward, half-opened the window, and called: "What's the matter?"

Tom, from the livery stable, bent around and said, "Nothing, Miss. Best close the windy afore you get soaked. Old Mitch here thought he saw a ghost, or somethin' up ahead."

He grinned through the rain. His partner's voice came through the hiss of rain, surly but frightened: "Weren't no ghost—looked like a dead man—walkin'. Just my nerves, Miss, didn't mean ter frighten ye."

She closed the window and sat back.

A dead man—walking?

It was raining in a deluge now, and lightning flashed above almost continuously. The alternate cold white electric flare and following inky darkness were like the flickering of a great white wing. Adrienne shivered again and drew the warm jacket of her green and brown plaid suit more closely about her. The carriage bucked from side to side.

She peered out of the opposite window into the rain-soaked dark. Suddenly lightning flared—*and Adrienne screamed!*

By the long flare she had seen a terrible sight. Standing directly opposite, staring at her with glaring yellow eyes, was a tall, gaunt figure amid the dark foliage, wrapped in brown and rotting bandages, with the hideous head of a peeling skull.

The coach whipped by and the figure vanished from sight. Half-fainting, Adrienne sank back.

"What is it, Miss?" the coachman called.

"I—I saw it, too!"

Old Mr. Mitchell and Tom exchanged fearful glances, as all the shadowy brood of country superstitions rose in their blood.

"Le's get out o' here!" Mitchell said, and began urging the horses on to greater speed with his whip. The coach rocketed along the curving road between frowning walls of wet trees, through slimy mud and black puddles, through the almost palpable walls of roaring wind and stinging rain.

Then another prolonged blaze of lightning lit the black sky, and by its unearthly light Adrienne could see the grisly figure. It was hurling itself through the woods, keeping pace with the racing coach-and-four, plunging through the trees like some indestructible Juggernaut. Adrienne saw a branch whip right across the glaring eyes of the thing, but it never paused or faltered, but crashed on as if it could feel no pain. Then the darkness came down, and the terrible thing vanished from sight.

"I saw it again!" she called.

The two men glanced fearfully from side to side, as the coach swung around a sharp, dizzy curve through the pelting storm. Adrienne clung to the seat to hold her balance in the wildly swaying coach.

Then—suddenly—the coach staggered, slewed around, and came to a lurching halt. Adrienne tore open the door and peered out. Young Tom sprang down from his seat and went around to the front of the horses.

"What happened?" she cried.

"It's old Judy, she slipped in that there puddle," he called.

Adrienne gazed around at the menacing gloom of the woods.

"Is she—all right?"

He got to his feet, and shook his head.

"Lamed herself when she fell," he yelled over the booming detonations of thunder.

"Kin we get on?" Mitchell cried from his place. "We be almost to th' Hall—jest a little further now."

"Yes, but we go slow," his partner said, climbing back to his place beside him.

The coach started up again, but slowly, slowly, as the old horse limped along, favoring her bad leg. Rain drummed against the coach top and lashed the windows. The two coachmen hunched themselves down under their blanket and pulled their dripping hat brims further down across their eyes.

Old Mitch felt the coach sag to an extra weight, and an instant later a hand clutched his knee.

He looked down. Holding his leg in an iron grip was a hand whose peeling, leprous flesh had rotted almost to the bone. Long claw-like fingernails sprouted from the fingers like the spurs of a vulture. From wrist on down the arm was tightly wrapped in brown dirty bandages, now wet with streaming rain. He gasped and raised his eyes to stare directly into the skull-face of the mummy—two glaring mad eyes like pits of yellow, raging fire ... nose rotted away leaving a black hole ... through gaps in the linen wrappings terrible glimpses of the decayed, withered face could be seen ... and the hideous, silently snarling bared brown fangs ....

He cried out, "*Tom!*" before the other paw reached up and ripped out his throat. Belching forth a flood of scarlet gore, he toppled between the horses. Tom skewed around, white face staring with horror and disbelief, automatically pulling in the reins and halting the horses.

"*Run, Miss! Run!*" he shrieked, beating a clubbed fist at the rotting face. Then one clawed hand closed brutal fingers over his free hand, and the other stretched for his face.

Adrienne ripped the door open and sprang out of the coach into the stinging rain. The coach swayed as Tom fought with the monster, now clearly limned in a lightning flash, now drowned in pouring darkness. The horses screamed and bucked, sensing the nearness of the dead but living thing.

She hovered for one moment—but there was nothing she could do for him. Then she turned and plunged into the rainswept darkness, running for her very life. In a moment the coach was left behind a sharp turn in the road. She ran on, slipping and staggering in the mud, her white face lashed by the stinging blows of the rain, the angry, shrieking wind tugging at her soaked dress. At any moment she expected to feel the dreadful weight of the mummy's hand on her shoulder. She—*ran!*

Luckily she had worn "sensible" Oxfords, instead of her high heels. But her mind was not concerned with that; her only thoughts were of the lights and safety and strong walls of Wilfrith Hall. She expected to see it through the streaming curtains of the rain around every bend and turn of the road. She ran on and on, till every breath seared and rasped in her lungs like fire.

Then—behind her—an ominous sound, louder than the wind. The *splish! splosh!* of another pair of feet, running. Had Tom beaten off the monster? She turned and saw in another flare of lightning the gigantic form of the mummy, stalking after her.

Without thinking, her actions dictated by some automatic instinct for survival, she turned suddenly into the underbrush and vanished between the trees. The mummy halted, swinging his terrible head to and fro like a maddened, frustrated beast. Then it, too, entered the inky blackness, and vanished between the close-packed trees.

Here in the dense woods the darkness was absolute. Adrienne lost all sense of direction. Unable to see, scarcely able to think, she only knew she must keep moving. She staggered and fell, tripping over an invisible root. Picking herself up and ignoring the sting of a scraped knee, she stumbled on. She blundered into trees, caught her hair in rough branches, fell, and fell again, struggling on in terror. Now and then she stopped to listen and catch her breath. But it was impossible to hear if the mummy was struggling after her or not, for whatever sounds the monster must have made were drowned and lost in the bellow of thunder, shriek of wind, and constant rustle of breeze-whipped branches and dripping leaves.

Many times she came to the end of her strength, and thought she could go no farther. But each time she staggered to her feet again, spurred on by the knowledge of the nearness of the Hall, with its warmth and bright lights and fortress-like walls. She blundered on through the dripping black forest.

Suddenly—ahead—the lights of Wilfrith Hall! With renewed vigor she plunged ahead, fighting her way through the clinging bushes. She had almost reached the very edge of the woods, when a terrible, tall figure stepped from behind a tree and stood motionless between her and the lights of safety.

The mummy!

Chapter 9

Duel with the Mummy!

INSPECTOR James Brant sped from Half Moon Street to Scotland Yard, leaving Lord Shenstone and Dr. Zarnak behind, busied at their preparations for an occult attack on the monster.

Brant's first thought was a telegram to Beresford to have Miss Haldane warned, when she arrived, not to venture on to Wilfrith Hall. Unfortunately (he was informed), a violent storm brewing in the south had disrupted temporarily all long-distance communications. This untimely storm also destroyed his plans for making the journey to Wilfrith Hall by plane, for he was an accomplished pilot and could have reached the country estate by air in a minute fraction of the time it would take to accomplish the same destination by train.

"What about a car?" Mailey asked, as Brant paced up and down in his office at the Yard, like a caged lion.

"Car?"

"There's a fine racer in the shop," Mailey informed him. "A Bentley Sixteen. Commander Eaton had a racing engine installed in her. She can beat anything on the road."

"That might just be the answer," Brant said, smacking his fist into his palm. "At least it's worth a try. I can't just stay up here, with that girl in danger. I wonder—"

Gareth Mailey grinned.

"Anyone would think you were blotto on the lass!"

Brant flushed. College, the War, and then the Yard had left him little free time for women.

"Don't be a bloody fool. I've never even seen the girl. Listen: Tell the Chief I'm taking the Bentley. If Dr. Zarnak calls, tell him I'm on my way to Wilfrith."

Mailey made a mock salute. "Right-o, boss. I'll hold the forth here. Or do you want my strong right arm with you?"

"You can do me more good right here," Brant said. "My right arm is strong enough!"

Mailey assumed an injured air. "Not like mine, old boy. My strength is as the strength of ten, because my heart is pure. *Ouch!*"

His quotation broken off by having his hat pulled suddenly down over his face, Mailey removed the offending headpiece and grinned after his departing friend.

"Good luck, old man," he said softly. "I guess you'll need it!"

The Bentley was in the shop, luckily enough, and Brant requisitioned it from Steve Weyland, the shop's chief mechanic.

"There's a quicker route than going by Beresford," Weyland told the younger man as busy mechanics filled the racing engine with high-octane petrol. With oil-stained fingers he traced out a straight overland route on one of the maps tacked to the wall. Inspector Brant hastily memorized the way as the old mechanic counseled him on the vagaries and whims of the powerful racing car. He thanked the master mechanic and his team, and tooled the powerful machine out into the street.

Turning on the siren to obtain right of way, he gunned the motor and sped through London, taking dangerous curves with reckless courage that ignored all hazards in favor of *speed—speed—speed!*

Soon he left London behind and was roaring through the crowded suburbs. Walls of blank brick flashed past. His unlighted pipe clamped firmly between his teeth, he stared ahead, never taking his eyes from the road, except to steal periodic glances at the lighted dial of the timepiece on the dashboard. Swiftly, the miles unrolled behind him. The great machine responded to his every touch like a superbly trained horse. It seemed to draw strength and speed from some deep well of unlimited resources.

Once in the country, he pressed the pedal to the floor and held it there. The Bentley leaped ahead like a spurred stallion. They raced through the gathering gloom. Overhead, lightning flickered on and off among the high-piling thunderheads as the scarlet light of sunset faded. The great car ate the miles.

As he drove, his mind busied itself on many questions. The entire mystery was puzzling and frightening to him. The uncanny and occult nature of the monster rose perpetually to plague him. Inspector James Brant was a hard-headed, practical, and scientifically minded young materialist. The depth and range of his experience in wartime service and peacetime crime-fighting had taught him much about purely human evil—but the supernatural malignancy of his adversary was a new experience for him.

It was the cryptic and baffling mystery of the Myrdstone Witch-Cult that had introduced him to the terrible knowledge that supernatural evil existed in the twentieth century, and that primordial terrors that should have vanished when the light of the Renaissance dissolved the midnight shadows of the Dark Ages, still survived into our enlightened, modern age. Remembering that cesspool of sinister menace and unclean foulness that had defiled Myrdstone moor, and was only dispelled when Dr. Zarnak exercised his extraordinary knowledge of such ancient mysteries, Brant saw grim reasons for accepting the full import of the "Pharaoh's Curse."

The reek of immemorial decay—the ancient corruption of decadent Egypt, which even in the dawn of history had been called "The Black

Land"—these apocalyptic horrors sometimes lingered far beyond their natural deaths—or were revived in bestial and nightmarish avatars. Strange survivals of earlier, darker aeons yet lingered on in dim neglected corners of the earth; unclean rituals and antediluvian rites were yet celebrated in remote and nightmare-haunted places of the world; and hellish Things already ancient when the very hills were young still found their furtive worshipers ....

There were, besides, strange rumors and whispered scandals that hinted at the prodigious power of the ancient demon-gods, that they yet had the strength to slay. Brant remembered the sensational Tut-Ankh-Amen curse, and the more recent Paut Temple terrors. No, Egypt's ancient magic could still strike after the dust of ages had settled over the rotting bones of her devil-priests and death-obsessed god-kings. The black, unholy witchery of that vast, shadowy Empire of the Dawn whose mighty splendors are now but memories lingering in the hollow eye sockets of the dry and cracking skulls of her antique Pharaohs—*lived today!*

The storm broke, and gusts of rain hissed over the gleaming hood of the racing Bentley. Brant shook off these eldritch, unwholesome speculations and bent his full concentration on the road. So heavily did the rain pour down that visibility dwindled to mere feet before his headlamps. The howling darkness closed about the speeding machine; the whole world shrank down to a few cubic feet of musty air within the car. All around, a mad, chaotic void of roaring wind and flying sheets of rain. The lonely country road unreeled straight before him: no traffic, no stoplights. He flashed along the miles, attention bent on the wet, slippery road, every faculty focused in preparation for sudden and treacherous curves.

His thoughts turned to the unknown girl he was racing to protect. Perhaps the jesting words of Gareth Mailey, hours before back in the black stone halls of that citadel on the embankment, had buried a hint in his unconscious mind—but for whatever reason, he found himself imagining what she looked like ... wondering what sort of a person she was ....

Lightning flared in the black heavens, lighting for a split second a mad scene of billowing, boiling clouds. Thunder boomed and long echoes went gobbling down the sky. The wind screamed madly, like a racked victim of some unholy inquisition.

At last the leafy edges of Wilfrith Woods appeared, lit by his lights. He slowed, crawling across the bridge, and began maneuvering the tortuous twists and turns of the forest road, slimy with mud and puddles of black water. Wilfrith Hall was only moments away—

What was that black thing that loomed up out of the rain, lit by a flash of scarlet lightning? He jammed on the brakes and clutched the wheel as the car skidded wildly in the slime. It was a carriage, lurched over on one broken wheel. What—?

He grabbed up a flashlight and sprang out. Instantly a stunning blow of rushing wind made him stagger. Buffeted by the howling gale, half-drowned with the lashing rain, he clawed open the carriage and flashed his light inside. Nothing—an abandoned book, now water-soaked. Across the flyleaf a pen had inscribed neatly: *Adrienne*.

Brant slammed the door and staggered through the slushy mud to the front of the carriage. The horses had, for some reason, apparently bolted, dragging the carriage part way into the ditch, then torn loose of their restraints and run away—or so the broken straps attested. No sign of the coachman?

Brant flashed his light around and stopped short. Half underneath the wheels, a black, sodden body lay, squelched in mud. In the blaze of the electric torch, the dead face stared straight into Brant's eyes: white as chalk, lips baring the teeth in a frozen, soundless shriek. He knelt and tried to examine the body. The throat was torn out and long ribbons of flesh, clawed loose, were mingled with the blood and water.

The mark of the mummy!

Inspector Brant left the body and played his torch along the brink of the gushing ditch. Half in and half out of the water he found another body. His heart rose in his mouth—but it, too, was the corpse of a man. Dead, this time, by slightly different means. His neck was broken. His head had been twisted around to the rear of the body, as a bored child will maltreat an old doll—and the body had been flung carelessly into a ditch, as if the mangler had tired of its plaything—

And—the girl?

Inspector Brant's lips curled back in a fighting snarl. He flashed his light into the wood, but the darkness there was impenetrable. He began sprinting along the road toward Wilfrith Hall, skirting the ditch, flashing his light from side to side.

Nothing. No sign, no clue, no evidence that anyone—a living, terrified girl, fleeing for her life and very sanity, or a dead, unliving but monstrously animated Thing—had passed this way.

Then—a scream!

At the sound, Brant stopped dead, questing with all senses. Where had that shrill call of unbearable panic come from? Ahead? He raced along the road—and suddenly the frowning walls of the great Hall loomed up.

And there, ahead, on the borders of the wood, he saw—

The mummy.

It was very tall, topping even his six-foot-one by a half-foot. The withered bandages were dribbling with water. Brant was not given to museum-going and had never seen a mummy before, but somehow he had always pictured them as tiny, dried husks of humanity. But this was—monstrous! It loomed there against the trees, a powerful, ape-like form, huge, hulking. He could not see its face for the head was turned, gazing into the thick underbrush. The scream must have come from there, for Brant saw no one else on the road. Had she shrieked under the grip of mangling paws, or in terror as the mummy stepped before her?

Brant sprang forward, seized the mummy by one massive shoulder, and pulled it about. It staggered off balance and lurched drunkenly—and he saw the terrible face. The scaly, parchment flesh shrunk to reveal the lines of the skull; the reptilian lips withered back to a perpetual snarl, exposing the unnaturally long, canine fangs; the mad eyes, like pits of hell-fire.

As the mummy reached for him, Brant drew his weapon and fired from the hip. It was a war souvenir, a powerful German Luger, glistening with oil and hair-triggered for speed. The ugly snout belched blue fire and filled the pouring darkness with the sharp stench of gunpowder, stronger even than the repellent stink of decay from the mummy's body.

It staggered as the pellet of red-hot lead hammered into its chest. Brant could see, by the lights of Wilfrith Hall, that fragments of shrivelled flesh and black shreds of cloth spun away into the night as a small black puncture marked the rotting chest of the Thing.

But that did not stop it. The mummy came on again, raising its rotting, blood-soaked talons. Brant retreated before the monster's remorseless advance, hammering away at the grisly figure. Bolt after bolt of blue flame exploded from the Luger, ripping through and through the stalking thing, without stopping it.

Brant felt the stirrings of real fear. Never before had he confronted an enemy that hot lead could not kill. Even the Myrdstone Witches could be slain, but this creature—*would not die!*

He retreated further along the edge of the wood, aiming more carefully. His bullets ripped and tore through the places where vital organs and important muscles were, all without even slowing the remorseless advance of the undying mummy. Whatever mysterious magical power animated those long-dead limbs could not be killed with bullets.

Strange, mad duel! Brant was to live it over and over again in his dreams. The ballet-like slow stalking advance of the monster, and his slow, step-by-step retreat. The howling wind, and lashing rain; the bellowing thunder and unearthly flare of lightning, here between the black, dripping forest and the frowning, Gothic walls of the old house—fit setting for a duel of ancient magic and modern gunpowder! A scene from the nightmare pages of Poe or Hoffmann! A theme for the half-mad talents of a drug-intoxicated Baudelaire!

Then Brant recalled nine half-forgotten words from the lips of Dr. Zarnak, far away in London—words spoken, it seemed to his dazed mind, ages and ages ago, in a scene of warmth and light and safety wide removed from this eldritch wood, this demoniac storm, and this dream-like duel with a monster dead over four thousand years ago—words that fanned the spark of hope within him to a quick fire:

"... *the mummy will be afraid of fire and light.*"

LIGHT!

Brant turned and, bringing the torch around, directed a dazzling beam of incandescent white light straight into the eyes of the mummy!

It staggered—stopped—slowly raised its rotting, ragged arms to shade the lidless eyes from the merciless blast of pure light. Greatly daring, Brant stepped to the side and beamed it in the eyes again. It shook its monstrous skull-head like a tormented, helpless bear, covering this new angle. He jumped around to the other side, directing the electric ray directly into the face of the thing.

Now the duel was re-enacted, with positions reversed! It was Brant who advanced remorselessly, and the monster who retreated before the strange weapon. Step by step, Brant forced the maddened thing back until it stood helpless against a giant oak. Then he lifted his revolver slowly, planning to put a stream of flaming lead right through the skull, exploding that evil, withered brain. *Then* let the monster walk! If it could live through that, he would hold it at bay with his torch, while he carefully blew off every fragment of the head—

The monster did not wait to bear the test. Unable to endure the blinding ray a moment longer, it flung wide its mighty arms—dashing the pistol from Brant's hand and half-striking him to earth as well, so prodigious was its awful strength—and, turning, plunged into the woods.

He picked up the pistol, wiping away the mud. He could hear the creature crashing through the forest: The sounds were fainter and fainter. ... It had gone.

He walked back to where he had met the mummy, sick and shaken with release of the awful tension of the battle.

Adrienne Haldane fell, fainting into his arms.

The first round was—theirs!

But who would win—the second?

Chapter 10

Besieged by the Mummy!

WHEN Crithers at last answered the persistent ringing of the bell, he found an amazing sight. Brant, bearing Adrienne in his arms, shouldered past him into the front hall and made for the library.

"Inspector! What—"

Laying the girl down on a sofa near the fire, Brant snapped, "No time for explanations now, man. Get some brandy—and a towel. *Quick*, man!"

Crithers closed his mouth, which was gaping with astonishment, and hurried to do the Inspector's bidding. He handed a towel and a glass of liquor to Brant, saying, "But that's Miss Haldane! Whatever happened?—an accident?—shall I call Dr.—"

"She's all right. I'll take care of her; a shock. Listen, Crithers. This is important. Lock and bolt all doors—all windows—in the entire house. Do you understand?"

"Very well, sir."

"How strongly are the windows guarded?" Brant asked.

"The ground floor windows, sir, with the exception of these library windows, are covered with steel grills. Lord Shenstone wanted to protect his art collection against possible burglary, and had the bars put on last summer. The upstairs windows, however, are not barred."

"Excellent! Now listen, Crithers. Have the servants turn on *all the lights in the house*. Upstairs and down, as well. Tell them to draw back the curtains or shutters, or whatever, so that the windows are completely open to view from outdoors. *All* lights, you understand; every light in every room. And get those doors and windows locked! Quickly!"

Whatever faults he may have possessed, procrastination was not part of Crithers' character. He instantly drew the library curtains back and locked the great French doors, turning on all lights in the room. Then he left, to see the same done in all other rooms.

Brant bent his attention to the girl. She was soaking wet, and still in a faint, but seemed otherwise unharmed. She lay there on the sofa, an appealing vision of young womanhood. Warm red lips half-parted; smooth hair like a red-bronze-gold helmet, clinging wetly to the delicate lines of her brow. Her golden skin was white, deathly, but it added to—rather than impaired—her exciting beauty. He wiped the cold rain from her face and throat with awkward, gentle dabs of the folded towel. Then, supporting her head on his arm, he slightly lifted her, holding the goblet of brandy to her lips, and forced a few drops down her throat.

She coughed, choking on the fiery fluid. And opened her eyes, staring directly into his own.

Her jade green eyes, enormous in her pallid face, were wide with terror—which faded into dumb surprise.

"Here: Drink this."

With eyes still fixed on his face, she accepted more of the brandy, coughed a little.

He was staring at her, unaware of his fixed, rude gaze. As a faint flush rose in her cheeks, he realized, and tore his eyes away, slightly embarrassed.

"Drink some more—"

"Thank you, that's enough." (Her voice was soft and mellow, with a clear strong tone to it—*Lovely*, he thought to himself.)

"Who are you?" she asked, taking the towel from him, and, shrugging out of her soaked jacket, rubbing her slender arms.

He flushed. "Oh—sorry—I should have—the name is Brant, Inspector Brant. Scotland Yard."

She nodded, and glanced around the room. Then she began toweling her wet hair, vigorously.

"How did I get here? Did you carry me?"

(Was there a faint undertone of malicious mockery in her voice?)

Brant said: "Yes, I—I mean, you fainted."

"I remember now." She began rubbing her wet legs, staring thoughtfully at him, with her silky hair a-tangle (which he thought quite striking). "You fought—*It*—off with your gun."

He nodded. "It's gone now," he said, reassuringly.

She shivered a little.

"What—was it?"

He told her, awkwardly, knowing his bald narrative sounded like the ravings of a madman. But she listened gravely. Having seen the mummy herself, she was willing to accept even the fantastic story he gave her.

"Gone for—good? Or will it return?"

Since she was through with the towel, he took it from her and began drying himself as she drank off the rest of the brandy and lit herself a cigarette.

"Probably not for good, Miss. But Dr. Zarnak said light would drive it away, and perhaps it won't enter the house tonight—"

"Dr. Zarnak?" she interrupted, leaning forward eagerly. "You mean, Zarnak the Monster-Killer?"

"Yes," he said, somewhat surprised, "that's the man. Do you know him?"

She shook her head, tousled hair flying and catching glints of gold radiance from the firelight. "If you mean, have I ever met him *personally*—no. But I've read all about him in the newspapers, and he's one of my heroes. And he's actually helping Uncle Ruthven? That means he'll be coming here?"

Brant nodded. "Tomorrow, most probably. I doubt if they'll make it tonight, with this storm."

She sobered. "And the monster? Do you think it would be safe for them driving on the forest road, with that—that *Thing*—wandering loose?"

He lit a rare cigarette and took a glass of brandy, saying, "Oh, I think they'll be safe enough in a motor-car. I abandoned mine where your carriage was left."

She raised sudden, enormous eyes. "Oh!"

Startled, he lowered the glass. "What?"

"Forgive me—but I just happened to think—you must be the same Inspector Brant that accompanied Zarnak on the Myrdstone Moor Witchcraft case—?"

He said yes, uncomfortably.

"Why—then, *you're* one of my heroes, too!" she crowed. "How very exciting!"

He flushed again, feeling himself sixteen kinds of a fool.

"I—well, I really did very little, Miss. It was Dr. Zarnak who handled everything, he cleared up the mystery. I was just sort of along. In fact, I had made a pure muddle of the whole case, by the time he came into it."

She regarded him with a slight, a *very* slight, small smile and said, sweetly, "How very modest of you, Inspector. The true modesty of a real-life hero. How lucky we are to have both you and the Doctor helping my uncle on this case."

He grunted something, not knowing what, and sat there twisting his cigarette furiously between his blunt, strong fingers, trying to think of something to say.

Then, abruptly (and characteristically) her mood changed. She half turned and stared out into the howling storm that raged and bellowed with unabated vigor beyond the tall French doors. In firelit profile, he could not help noticing how her proud high young breasts thrust out against the wet cloth of her white blouse.

She shivered a little. "To think, out there somewhere, that thing is wandering about, perhaps prowling around the house this very instant. It's—*horrible*. I wish your bullets had killed it."

He started to speak, then broke off as Crithers came in.

"Beg pardon, sir, and Miss. I've followed your instructions to the very letter, Inspector. The house is secure."

Brant rose to his feet.

"Well done, Crithers. Tell me—where is the telephone?"

"There's one on the table there, sir, by his Lordship's chair. But I'm afraid you'll find the instrument out of operation. This storm seems to have severed our communications with the outside world, sir."

"Very well. Nothing we can do about that. I doubt if we could summon outside help on a night like this, anyway, storm or no storm."

Crithers looked puzzled.

"Sir? Outside—help?"

Brant suddenly realized that the man knew nothing of the dreadful menace that lurked around the old house on this wild night. Well, there was really no reason to alarm him, or the rest of the servants, either. Let him remain puzzled.

"No matter, Crithers. Uh—Miss Haldane, I suggest you get out of those wet clothes and have a hot bath. Perhaps a bite of supper—I'm sure the kitchen can put something together. Then you might as well retire for the night—in one of the upstairs bedrooms."

"Yes, Inspector," the girl said, demurely.

He flushed again. Damn the girl! She possessed the strange power to make him appear an utter fool!

"Crithers, if you will have someone bring me a dry suit of clothes. Here, in the library. And, perhaps, some supper, too. Anything—don't go to any fuss."

"Certainly, sir. A pleasure."

"And tell me—has his Lordship any guns about the place—in shooting condition? Heavy guns—rifles?"

Crithers looked more puzzled than ever, but he nodded, pointing to a glass case against a further wall.

"Yes, sir. That case holds a selection of my lord's hunting rifles. For big game. His Lordship has been on several safaris in central and southern Africa, and keeps the weapons in firing condition."

Brant strode over and examined the gleaming array of deadly weapons, feeling a new flow of confidence pour through him. He spotted a heavy-duty Magnum Express rifle.

"Excellent, excellent. If you'll be so kind as to find me some ammunition for that," he said, pointing out the Magnum, "then that will be all."

Adrienne asked, "Then you are planning to spend the night in the library, Inspector?"

"Yes."

She drifted across the room to join Crithers at the door. As she passed near him, she gave him a quick, sly upward glance and breathed, *"How heroic!"*

He flushed scarlet.

Crithers held the door for her; she paused on the sill, and turned to him with another abrupt change of mood.

In a quiet voice, sober, completely serious, she said, "Good luck."

She was not mocking him now. He grinned, for the first time, and said firmly, "Thanks. Perhaps I won't need any."

She stood looking at him for a moment. Then—

"Perhaps. I hope not. But good luck, anyway. And goodnight. And—Inspector?"

"Yes, Miss Haldane?"

A flash of the familiar feline witchery lit up her jade eyes. In a voice demure but amused, she said, "Do you have a Christian name, Inspector? I do: It's Adrienne."

He felt himself turning red again.

"Yes: James."

"Thank you. Then, goodnight. And—thank you for what you did"—she nodded toward the road—"for what you did out there."

"I was happy—" he started to say. But she was gone.

An hour later, Brant began his vigil. Dry now, and in clean clothes lent from Lord Shenstone's wardrobe, with some warm supper in him and the loaded Magnum ready, Brant was prepared for any event that might befall. Adrienne Haldane had retired to one of the bedrooms upstairs, with the door locked at his suggestion. Crithers, acting upon Brant's directions, had seen to it that all the servants in the house were also ensconced in upstairs bedrooms, locked in. In case the mummy made an attempt on the house that night, there was no need to involve the servants in any danger.

Brant did not know whether to expect the mummy to strike again that night, or not. There was no way of telling. Surely, however, if the monster *did* attempt to enter Wilfrith Hall that night, he would have to come through the library windows, as all the other ground-floor windows were barred.

And if he came—Brant was ready for him!

Grinning at the thought, the Inspector patted the oiled barrel of the powerful elephant gun propped against his chair. If this rifle could stop a rhino or a bull elephant in full charge—it should prove powerful enough to blast the monster to smithereens!

But probably his strongest weapon was the blinding light that blazed from every room in Wilfrith Hall. That would probably prove sufficient defense against the monster. Brant slowly stuffed and lit his briar, listening to the bellow and shriek of the storm. This very moment, he reflected grimly, those glaring mad eyes that had stared blindly through the impenetrable gloom of four thousand years of black Egyptian night were staring hungrily at the blazing lights of Wilfrith Hall. The undying mummy was, perhaps, prowling about the Hall this very moment—seeking some loophole in the barrier of insupportable light.

Wilfrith Hall was like a beleaguered fortress, Brant thought, with a chill of uneasiness and premonition—

And then the lights went out.

Chapter 11

The Duel in the Dark

BRANT sprang to his feet, and in so doing heard the rifle fall to the floor. The sudden transition from blazing lights to absolute and unrelieved darkness was stunning. For a moment he stood there, thinking rapidly—then a flare of lightning filled the room with white electric glare, winking out again, and followed by a long rolling concussion of thunder.

Obviously the storm must have knocked down a power line, he thought. He turned toward the fireplace to stir up the coals with the poker. No doubt Crithers could scare up some candelabra—even an oil lamp—but these would not help. It was the blinding glare of the electric lights that had shielded the fortress that this house had become.

And now the walls were down.

He stirred the coals and added some wood, and was half turning to replace the poker when—

Crash!

Outlined against the flicker of lightning, the huge black tattered figure of the mummy smashed through the tall French windows and sprang into the room. Shards of glass sprinkled the floor, glinting redly in the firelight—fragments of broken wood scattered over the carpet, and the wet, dripping figure of the monster stood before him.

Brant swung the poker, aiming at the mummy's head—but the monster deflected it with a lifted arm. He swung again, but the mummy seized the poker, twisted it from his grasp, and flung it across the room. Brant heard it smash a glass case and fall to the floor.

The mummy reached for him—Brant jumped back, scrambling for the Magnum. His sense of direction was lost in the inky gloom: He could not even find the chair. He crouched there on the floor, his heart pounding so loudly it seemed to him the mummy should be able to hear it. His palms were wet with sweat, and he could feel trickles of perspiration down over his ribs, wet against his shirt. He had never been so frightened in his life.

The mummy moved, clattered against a table. Startled, Brant jumped over by the wall, and stood breathless with pounding pulse against the wall of books. In the jet darkness he could make out nothing but the vague red glow of the fire, a dim smudge of gore-colored light somewhere across the room. The fire's light was too faint to enable him to pick out any object in the room. Then he heard the mummy move again, and a vase smash. He seized the opportunity to run for the door, the noise of his movements covered by the crash.

But his direction was more confused than he had thought—instead of the door, he found another wall of books. Sweating, gasping for breath, he stood there straining his eyes to pick out some landmark in the gloom by which to orient himself. It was like some terrible nightmare, this being trapped in the impenetrable darkness with a mad thing—neither of you able to see the other.

Then he heard a thud near—very near—*and the firelight caught the eyes of the mummy, and lit them like the eyes of a beast.* It glared terribly, from side to side, like an animal questing for the scent of its prey. Brant shrank against the wall—and his elbow moved, dislodging a heavy book which struck the floor with a thud startlingly loud in the thick silence. The mummy snapped its head around and lunged at the sound.

Brant sprang away, his position revealed, but the mummy moved too quickly. One rotting paw closed over his collar—the other lifted for his throat. Brant struggled in the mummy's grasp, striking the horrible head with a balled fist. Then, thinking with a lightning swiftness he did not know he possessed, he seized his own shirt collar and tore down the front of his shirt, popping the buttons. He wriggled out of his torn shirt with one sinuous motion and flung himself across the room, leaving the monster holding the empty piece of cloth. He got to the fireplace and was reaching for a piece of burning wood—*"The mummy will be afraid of fire,"* Zarnak had said—when the monster was upon him again.

Now its awful, snarling skull-face was visible in the red light—eyes two glaring pits of yellow fire—firelight glinting redly from bared canine fangs and patches of bare bone along brow and cheek. He could see the scaly foulness of the decayed and shriveled flesh, and the shrunken, dry, reptilian lips drawn back over the grinning tusks.

With a horrible, soundless hiss of rage, it struck at him with one mighty arm, catching him on the shoulder and knocking him half the length of the room, away from the fire. He sprawled gasping on the carpet, breath knocked out of him. As he struggled to get up his fingers encountered oiled metal.

The rifle!

He snatched up the Magnum, leveled it at the mummy, whose advancing figure was plainly outlined against the red glow of the fire, and touched the trigger.

The rifle went off—a flash of fire that lit the room with an unearthly yellow-blue flare for a second. The impact knocked Brant sprawling. The sound of the explosion was deafening in the confines of the room. Echoes whipped and rumbled from wall to wall. The sharp stench of cordite filled the room. Brant scrambled to his feet again.

But the mummy only staggered. It lurched drunkenly for a moment, then recovered its balance and stood there before the fire.

And in the glow, Brant saw something that made his flesh chill and crawl. A panic-fear of the supernatural went over him like a spray of iced water—

The wood was catching fire now, and its blaze was growing brighter. The mummy was only a black silhouette before the blaze, *but in the monster's chest Brant could see a ragged spot of scarlet fire. The rifle had not killed or even slowed the mummy, but it had torn a hole completely through its chest, through which Brant could see the fireplace!*

He gasped—shuddered—hurled the rifle at the mummy's head, and sprang for the door. In the stronger firelight he could see the glint of the knob. In seconds he was out in the hall, and had locked the door to the library. Here it was completely dark—Brant could not even see his hand before his face—but he felt his way along the hall to the foot of the staircase which led to the bedrooms upstairs.

Should he flee, hoping the hardwood door would keep the mummy out?

His question was answered for him. Like a raging cat, the mummy attacked the door. It hammered with insane rage, smashing through a panel.

"What is it—what's happening?"

Brant turned. Adrienne Haldane, in a filmy nylon nightgown, holding a kerosene lamp in one hand, was coming down the stairs, followed by Crithers in a plaid bathrobe.

Brant gestured fiercely.

"Back! Upstairs quickly! It's breaking through the door—"

With a terrific crash the mummy tore the door off the hinges and stood in the doorway, a tattered black figure outlined with firelight, eyes glowing horribly. It spotted Brant by the staircase and headed for him.

Adrienne screamed—and without thinking, flung the kerosene lamp at the monster's head. It struck his shoulder, smashed, and burning oil ran down its chest and arms. Wet from the rain though it was, the mummy's body caught fire—blazed up—lighting the hall like some horrible human torch designed to illuminate a Nero's feast.

They stood, gasping at the sight. The mummy struck at his flaming body with flailing hands—then turned and rushed into the library again, through the broken windows, flung itself into the pouring rain, and vanished from sight.

Adrienne, half fainting, fell into Brant's arms. At the top of the stairs, the servants clustered, murmuring in fright. Crithers clung to the banister, his face the color of wax.

"Tell them it's all right now," Brant said, gesturing with his free arm. "Tell them to get back in bed, and lock their doors." Then he turned to Adrienne, smoothing back the golden hair from her cheeks.

"It's over now, Adrienne. The mummy's gone. Don't be afraid."

She leaned against him, shuddering a little, nestling into his arm.

"I'm—not going to faint. Is it—*really* gone?"

Brant nodded, gently.

"We're even now," he said. "I saved your life in the forest—and you just saved my life, by throwing that lamp at the thing."

She disengaged herself, and drew the nightgown about her throat.

"I—is it dead?"

"Perhaps. I don't know. The rain will probably put the fire out. But I think we've seen the last of it for tonight. You'd better go back to bed now. I'll stay down here for what's left of the night."

"Yes, Inspector." She looked at him demurely, her fear gone now.

"Oh, Inspector—"

"Yes?"

Little lights of mischief danced and sparkled in her jade eyes.

"Thank you for remembering my first name!"

THE power failure was only a temporary one, for within the hour the lights flickered once or twice and then continued to burn steadily. The room was a shambles. Brant, in another clean shirt borrowed from Crithers, and with a pot of hot black coffee to help him stay awake, set about putting the room to rights again. The one French window through which the monster had come was a shattered ruin, and the Inspector could do nothing about it. But the rest of the room was soon put back in order, and Brant settled down to the rest of his long vigil.

It was a slim chance that the burning oil had destroyed the mummy. Brant could not know for sure. The creature had plunged back into the icy deluge of the rain mere seconds after being set on fire by the lamp. It might be lying out there in the storm now, a dead, charred black thing. Or it might still be prowling about the old house, kept at bay by the barrier of the blazing lights, or the memory of searing fire.

Whatever the reason, the mummy did not attempt to enter the mansion again that night. Along toward morning the fury of the storm somewhat abated. Brant kept himself awake with fresh coffee, alert for every sound. The sluicing rain died to a drizzle ... then to mere drops. Finally, toward sunrise, the storm clouds rolled away, having exhausted their fury. The morning sky was clear and pure; only feathery wisps of cloud touched by the first rays of dawn married the blue expanse.

With the full light of day, Brant allowed himself to fall into a deep slumber at last. But his dreams were not nightmares of the undying monster out of black and ancient Egypt—but dreams of the clear oval face of a lovely girl. A girl with huge jade green eyes, and hair like a slim golden helmet, and a smile that wavered between gentleness and feline mockery.

Chapter 12

The Secret of the Talisman

WITH morning, Dr. Zarnak and Lord Shenstone arrived from London, the storm having impeded their progress and caused them to spend the night at an inn some miles away from Wilfrith Hall. They were vastly relieved to learn that while the mummy had fulfilled their fears and attempted to enter the Hall, it had been beaten back without causing any greater damage than a broken door and a smashed window.

"But I wish you could have stayed out of this, my dear," the Earl said to Adrienne Haldane. "This filthy business is no place for a young woman."

"I was anxious to see how you were," she explained. "Those newspaper stories about the 'Pharaoh's Curse' and 'Who Will Be the Next Victim' had me frightened for you."

He hugged her affectionately.

"Sweet of you to say that, my dear. But still—with that unholy *thing* lurking around the Hall—I don't mind telling you, when Dr. Zarnak and I were driving in this morning, and saw the coach and the bodies, I—well, we were certain the Monster had done you some harm. I'd feel much better if you were out of here, out of this whole mess."

"Now Uncle Ruthven," Adrienne said, "you mustn't be so silly! Goodness—you make me sound like some delicate schoolgirl. Why, after all, I've gone on safaris with you and Professor Carrington, and expeditions to Central Asia and India—"

She broke off, a glint of mischief twinkling in her eyes.

"And besides, if I *hadn't* come, I'd have never met the famous Dr. Anton Zarnak! Doctor, I've been one of your ardent fans for years. In fact, I had a sort of schoolgirl crush on you, some years ago. I cut out all those newspaper stories about the Witchcraft on Myrdstone Moor, and pasted them up in a scrapbook!"

The doctor, lean and aristocratic in immaculate black, his small black bag by his side, bowed slightly in recognition of her compliment.

"Thank you very much, Miss Haldane. I am delighted if my little 'cases' have afforded you any amusement and vicarious excitement. Unfortunately, it is far safer to read about them in the daily news journals than to find yourself a real-life actor in one. I must agree with your uncle. You would be safer elsewhere."

"But you *can't* send me away now, Dr. Zarnak—Uncle Ruthven! Not right in the middle of things! And besides—would it be safe to drive through Wilfrith Woods again? My coach was attacked last night, and the car could very well be attacked today, driving me to the station."

"Now, Adrienne—" Lord Shenstone protested.

Dr. Zarnak pursed his lips. "Perhaps your niece is right. At any rate, we have the whole day ahead of us, and your car can take her to Beresford Station at any time. Right now, I'm sure we are all hungry for breakfast—I confess myself to be virtually famished. And if Inspector Brant has slept sufficiently, I am very eager to question him about last night's attacks."

So they adjourned to the breakfast room, where a red-eyed and yawning Inspector Brant soon joined them. Happy to have their master with them once again, Josephine the cook and Maurice the footman piled the table high with a truly festive meal. Hot toast and marmalade. Bacon and eggs, waffles and ham. Freshly squeezed orange juice, hot coffee steaming in a silver urn, muffins and biscuits dripping with melted butter—it was a repast to be remembered, and they plunged in with enthusiasm.

As they ate, Brant related in full detail the story of the terrible night of storm and fear. He described his breakneck trip from London, the discovery of the abandoned coach and the two corpses. He related how he drove the mummy away with his electric torch, and rescued Adrienne Haldane from the black woods. The long, tense vigil in the library, when a barrier of blazing windows held the mad monster at bay. Then, the power failure—the harrowing duel in the dark, the failure of the Magnum to stop the dreadful thing that would not die. When he told how Adrienne had driven off the monster by hurling the flaming lamp at it, her uncle beamed on her affectionately. When he told his breathless audience of his long night's wait in the library, and the failure of the mummy to reappear, Dr. Zarnak, brooding eyes half-hooded with long lids, sat tapping the slim bridge of his nose with a forefinger.

"I doubt if the creature has been destroyed," he said at length. "The drenching rain would have extinguished the fire without any difficulty."

"But you don't think it will attack during the daytime?" the Earl asked.

"Definitely not. The sunlight will keep it deep under cover—in Wilfrith Woods, no doubt. No, during the daylight hours, the mummy of Khotep will be in a comatose state. Only with sunset will it revive to trouble us once again. And this time—we shall be ready!"

He touched the black attaché case which was never out of his sight.

"I have everything we will require—here!"

Shenstone pushed back his plate, heaving a deep sigh.

"I sincerely hope so, Doctor. This unholy business has me at my wits' end."

"Never fear. With the materials from the British Museum, which your friend Lord Corbenek so kindly lent us, and certain weapons of my own, we shall be more than a match for the pharaoh's mummy."

"How do you expect to destroy the mummy?" Adrienne asked.

"By using the greatest weapon God has given us, Miss Haldane," he said, smiling faintly. "Courage, faith, strength, and the greatest gift of all,"—he touched his high, pallid brow with one slender forefinger—"intelligence!"

Then, pushing back his chair and rising to his feet, Dr. Zarnak said, "But first we have one bit of unfinished business to complete. Something we have been intending to do, and have been delayed from doing, by the pressure and rapidity of events, for far too long."

"And what is that?" Brant asked, finishing off his cup of steaming coffee.

"The Star of Set!"

The four of them adjourned to the library, where Madden the gardener and general handyman had pieced together makeshift repairs on the broken door and the shattered windows. There, once they were seated, Dr. Zarnak produced the small black case incised with the dreadful hieroglyph of Set, the Destroyer.

"The key to the mystery lies in this small black box that has not been opened in four thousand years," Dr. Zarnak said quietly. "But first, my Lord, I must briefly examine the tomb objects from the Lost Pyramid. I believe you told me that most of the small movables were here, rather than in the museum?"

"Yes, Doctor." Shenstone rose and went over to a wall where a large oil painting hung against the wooden paneling. He moved the frame to one side, disclosing a combination safe built into the wall.

"The tomb objects are here, for further study. Only the jewels and treasure were taken to the Carrington, where they might be under guard." He opened the safe and removed a number of objects, carefully wrapped in cloth. Placing them on a long table littered with books, he stepped aside to allow Dr. Zarnak to examine them.

Zarnak looked them over quickly.

"Ah, yes, here is the Shen. You said it was in the cenotaph, on the body, as usual? Very good. And the tablet, the Hypocephalus, that was missing?"

Shenstone nodded. "Also, there were no Canopic jars. Only this small stoppered vase of feldspar," he said, indicating a small squat container which Zarnak carefully unwrapped and held to the light. Small glyphs were inked upon one side.

"The cartouches of the Dark Gods—the same as on the lid of the sarcophagus!" Zarnak exclaimed.

"Yes, I suppose so."

"You have not opened it?"

"No, not yet," Shenstone replied.

With careful fingers, Zarnak removed the stopper. A black, inky oil, viscous and half congealed with age, scummed the inside of the vase. Its odor was unspeakably vile—redolent of the nauseous vapors of the grave.

Zarnak made a face.

"*Faugh!* Take this and have it destroyed at once. Do not burn it, by any means. But if you have any ammonia in the house, have the oil diluted with a good measure of that fluid and poured down the drain. Have the container scoured with boiling water."

Shenstone took it from him gingerly and rang for a servant.

"Certainly—but what is it?"

"A rare oil secreted by the Cynonycteris, or 'pyramid bat.' The creature has a small leaf-shaped gland beside the snout that secretes this foul substance. It is the chief ingredient of that terrible incense which is never named in the magical writings of Egypt—it was used in disgusting ceremonials which I shall not attempt to describe, such as one which I shall veil in the antiseptic scholarly Greek of *anthropomancy*. When mixed with a certain juice, as this phial was, the juice of the leaf of an Egyptian herb, the *tannah*-plant, it was used in preserving the mummies according to the Ceremony of the Vulture. *Ahh!* Take it out and have it destroyed at once! This indescribable stench stifles the very soul!"

Presently a servant came, received careful instructions, and removed the stinking vase to destroy the oil.

"Do you wish to examine the rest of the tomb objects?"

Doctor Zarnak shook his head.

"It is no longer necessary. Now I know for certain that the pharaoh's body was preserved according to the disgusting Vulture Ceremony. With this knowledge, I know how to destroy the mummy, I am certain—almost. One can never be positive in these dark matters, but I feel sure. ... We shall see. Now for the Star of Set."

Shenstone replaced the tomb objects in his safe, locked it, and moved the painting back to its original position. Dr. Zarnak examined the small black box with delicate fingers.

"*Can* you open the case?" Adrienne asked, leaning forward eagerly. A slight frown creased the Doctor's pale brow under the sharp widow's peak of smooth dark hair.

"I believe so—yes, just a moment, now—they were clever, hellishly clever, these old artisans—the catch is concealed under the Sign of Set—"

A smile of satisfaction lit the pallor of his perfectly chiseled features. "Ah!"

Click.

The panel which bore the golden hieroglyph slid to one side under the firm pressure of Zarnak's surgical fingers.

"There we are! *The Star of Set!*"

The talisman was a large faceted crystal of black glass, or some substance like obsidian. It was cut into twelve five-sided facets which caught the light and glittered evilly as the Doctor turned the jewel between his long fingers. The other three leaned forward eagerly, clustering about him.

"See! Each side of the gem is engraved with a cartouche!" the Doctor pointed out.

Shenstone nodded. "Yes—the three names of the Dark Gods, just as they were inscribed on the feldspar vase of incense oil, and carven upon the lid of the black marble sarcophagus. But what are the other names?"

Dr. Zarnak turned the evil gem in his hand. It cast an oily glitter over his face as he examined it closely.

"The names of the avatars of the Three. Each of the Xin (as the Demon-Gods are named) were worshiped in three avatars. My friends, with this knowledge at our command—we have pierced behind the veil! We possess the lore that is the key to the Allegory of Set, the Destroyer!"

"But—I don't understand!" Adrienne protested.

Zarnak smiled briefly as he inserted the talisman back within its small black coffin.

"Naturally, Miss Haldane, I do not expect you to know the most closely guarded secrets of the Nilotic pantheon! Even that immemorially ancient book, the *Kitab al-Mayyitun* (that is to say, the 'Book of the Dead'), veils this wisdom in the protective obscurity of symbology and allegory. And that mighty document was already thought to be of considerable antiquity, even in the reign of the Pharaoh Semti, of the First Dynasty—nearly five thousand years ago!"

"I must confess I don't understand, myself," Shenstone said. "And I have been a close student of the Theban Recension of the *Book of the Dead*. Please explain, Doctor."

Zarnak sat back and placed his elbows on the arms of the chair, with his fingertips together, resting his pointed chin on his thumbs.

"Very well. You must understand that it is an ancient belief in the Near East that every being—man, god or demon—has several names. His birth-name (what we would call his 'legal' name), and others, including the most important of all, his *Psychonomen*, his 'soul-name', i.e., his true name, the name of his soul as it came to Earth, fresh from the hands of God. When your great traveler and scholar, Sir Richard Francis Burton, rendered the *Alf Laylah wa Laylah* into English prose as 'The Thousand and One Nights', he gave an explanatory footnote to the effect that every *djinn*, or evil spirit, bore his 'true' name written on his forehead, and that whoever read it had power over the spirit and could destroy him. This belief persisted throughout the East. You will find it among the Hebrew mystics who sought in the Kaballah to discover the Secret and Holy Names of God, which (they believed) the prophet Moses had been given upon Sinai, when the Ten Commandments were handed down, and which he had concealed by means of a cypher within the Pentateuch. With the possession of these Divine Names, the Kabbalists asserted that they could command the Demons of the Pit—or the Angels of the Seven Heavens—and, I suppose, even the Divinity itself.

"This belief was shared by the ancient Egyptians. I have spoken before of the *hekau*, the Words or Names of Power. Some of them are revealed in a certain section of the *Book of the Dead*, in Twelve Chapters. Others are given in the *Pyramid Texts*, and some in certain necromantic papyri. With the possession of the Three Names of the Three Avatars of the Three Dark Lords, a vast *lacuna* in our grasp of Egyptian demonology is closed. A vast gap in our learning has been bridged!"

Brant said: "Does this mean you are now equipped to do battle with the mummy?"

"With the Names of Power, and armed with the *Ur-Hekau* from the British Museum—the very Rod of Nectanebus himself—I am indeed prepared to duel with the monster. The battle will begin when the darkness falls. And I *must* win! The Star of Set is now here in this house. Once the mummy gains possession of that potent and malignant talisman, civilization itself may be in danger."

A grim expression passed over Zarnak's pale and noble features.

"But above all things, we must not give way to fear. 'Fear is the chink in our armour through which the Opponent strikes,' as Great-grandfather Pythagoras somewhere says ...."

Chapter 13

Calm Before the Storm

FOR the desperate little band of adventurers in Wilfrith Hall, the day dragged along with almost unendurable slowness. It was a clear, bright day. As if wanting to make up for the fierce storm of last night, Nature spread a clear blue sky above the landscape, set a few small white clouds adrift upon it, and drenched the land with bright warm sunshine.

The beautiful day was not, however, untainted with a certain aura of repressed fear and brooding menace. The dark mass of Wilfrith Hall seemed somehow ominously still during the long hours of daylight. Perhaps it was only due to the imagination of the adventurers, wrought as they were to a high pitch of tension by the suspense of waiting until sundown, when the battle with the forces of darkness would begin—but the gloomy tangle of dense-packed trees seemed to exude an almost visible, almost tangible radiation of lurking, slumbering malignancy.

They all felt it. Adrienne Haldane, searching through the library for a book sufficiently interesting to engage her attention, found herself staring across the driveway at the dark wall of ancient oaks. She felt a cold chill run over her body ... as if with some sense beyond the usual five, she detected the lurking, brooding, slumbering Power that was hidden within the shadowy depths of that old forest.

Inspector James Brant, wandering restlessly through the halls of the huge estate, caught himself half-consciously wondering if it would be possible to seek the mummy out, in whatever secret lair it had found for itself within the heart of the woods, and, while the monster was still in its comatose state, immobilized by the power of the Sun—destroy it!

The idea sounded at least worth a try, and he wondered in what part of the old mansion Dr. Zarnak and Lord Shenstone had secreted themselves.

Zarnak and his host were in the grand hall of the building, whiling away the slow hours by examining the archaeological treasures the Earl had collected during his many expeditions and safaris into the little-explored portions of the earth. In Shenstone, the mysterious doctor had found a kindred spirit: a man of learning and science who, like himself, had for many years found his curiosity and imagination stirred by the dark and little-known areas of man's history on this planet.

They were engaged in examining a plaster cast of the Easter Island tablets, those peculiar wooden plates inscribed in a language unknown to any people of the world, the mysterious and cryptic records of a mighty race long vanished into the mists of time, whose origins, attainments, and ultimate end remained an insoluble enigma to this very hour.

Even absorbed as they were by their discussion of the lost Easter Island people, their weird and gigantic stone monuments, and the other unsolved secrets of that far-off and mystery-haunted region of the Pacific, such as the peculiar and unexplained ruins called Nan-Matal and Matalania upon the island of Ponape—even as they discussed with animation and keen, scholarly interest these age-old mysteries, neither could for one moment forget the slowly approaching terror with which they would be face to face in a mere matter of hours. And both could feel (even here behind many walls, far out of sight of the forest) a cold aura of mystery that brooded upon the old house, and waited for the moment of moonrise, the signal for its release ....

Adrienne stifled a little cry as the library door cracked open. James Brant came in, hesitated for a moment, seeing her, and then came in, saying apologetically, "I didn't mean to startle you, Miss Haldane. I didn't know that anyone was in here—"

She smiled. "That's all right, Inspector. You didn't really frighten me. I was sitting here in Uncle's chair, trying to get interested in a book, and I guess my attention was wandering—I didn't hear you come down the hall."

She stirred restlessly and put the book on the little table beside her chair.

"It's pretty hard to get interested in Mr. Wodehouse, with that—that *thing* out there, waiting for nightfall—waiting for *us!*"

Brant said, forcefully, "That's nonsense, Miss Haldane! Keep it out of your mind—don't even think about it! Remember what the Doctor said about letting *fear* weaken us. You just let the Doctor and me worry about the monster—I've seen Zarnak in tight spots before, and he's cool and level-headed. If anybody can stop this thing, it's the Doctor, so don't you worry."

She smiled faintly.

"All right. I won't. Do you—have a cigarette?"

He lit a cigarette for her, and then one for himself, and half sat in the window seat, glancing out at the sun-bathed landscape.

"As a matter of fact," he continued, after a few moments, "I originally started in here, thinking I might find the Doctor looking at your uncle's books, or something. I have an idea that it might be worth a chance trying to go after the mummy now—right now—while it's half-unconscious. Remember, this morning Dr. Zarnak said the mummy would be in a comatose state during the daylight hours? Well, if we went out into the woods now we might catch it and could kill it before it awoke—"

Something in the serious tone of his voice aroused the imp in Adrienne. She smiled and said, impudently, *"How heroic!"*

Brant stifled a grunt, flushed brick-red, opened his mouth to make a remark—then, catching her wide-eyed innocent gaze, he saw the sparkle of merry devilment dancing in her wonderful jade green eyes—and he grinned.

It was the first time she had ever seen him smile, and it was a transformation. His habitually grim, wooden expression (that went so perfectly with his leather-brown tanned face and strong jaw) suddenly lightened, and the lopsided, boyish grin changed his whole appearance. It was, for Adrienne, a sort of revelation. She liked what she saw, very much. But she refrained from showing it.

The mood between them had broken, and they laughed together.

"Why don't you ever call me 'Adrienne?'" she asked.

"I don't know," he said, frankly. "Why don't you call me 'James?'"

"A pact!" she flashed. "A James for an Adrienne!"

"It's a deal," he said, grinning.

She cocked her small, gold-helmeted head on one side, stroked her small, stubborn chin with a slender finger, and regarded him mockingly.

"No ... I think you are more of a 'Jim' than a 'James.' 'Jameses' are so *stuffy*. Not quite as much as 'Georges' or 'Herberts', but still ... stuffy."

"I'm afraid I am rather a bit stuffy," he confessed.

"Are you?" she asked. "Goodness, I would never have guessed."

"You're making fun of me again," he remarked, good-naturedly. "But I don't mind—I like amusing children." And, strangely enough, he really *didn't* mind. This sort of banal, pointless small talk had always bored and infuriated him. Many girls talked this way—but for some reason he found himself enjoying it—

"*Children*, is it? My gosh, then you must be old as Methuselah!" Adrienne retorted. "You no doubt have great-great-great-grandchildren by now!"

"As a matter of fact," he said, with careful carelessness, "I'm not even married."

"Really?" she asked, serious again. "Why not?"

He shrugged.

"No particular reason. Just never found the right one, I guess. Went into the Service right after college—a boy's school it was, too—then the Yard, once the Yanks came in and helped us lick the Jerries. Never had much time for women, somehow."

Adrienne extinguished her cigarette in the ashtray, carefully not looking at the Inspector.

"I'm not married or engaged, either," she said, in a clear and very distinct voice.

There was a long moment or two of complete silence.

He said: "Miss Hal—Adrienne—where exactly is it that you go to school?"

She told him.

He put out his cigarette and started to stuff his pipe.

"Do you—uh—ever get into London?"

"Oh yes. Holidays, and vacations, sometimes. I have an old aunt who lives on Crothering Place. I sometimes visit her."

He caught her wandering gaze and made her look at him.

"Of course, you must understand, I don't have very much time free."

"Yes," she said.

"The Yard keeps me rather busy."

"Yes."

"But if you *are* up in London sometime—and I *can* manage to get a few hours off—I'd very much like to take you to dinner—if you would like to, I mean ...."

"Yes, I'd like that."

They smiled into each other's eyes for a while in silence. It wasn't that they couldn't think of anything to say. It was more as if they had found a special new way of saying it.

Slowly the long hours dragged away toward evening. The adventurers lunched together rather late, as they wanted to be alert and in readiness for the attack of the mummy by sundown, and probably would not have dinner. At the meal they discussed strategy. Dr. Zarnak, with his customary reticence, refused to give any details of the magical methods he intended to employ against the monster, but gave full instructions on the part each of them was to play in the forthcoming battle. He then left the table to spend the afternoon in solitude, preparing himself for combat with the powers of evil.

Left to their own devices, Lord Shenstone showed Inspector Brant the art treasures of Wilfrith Hall, accompanied by his niece. The upstairs hall was lined with family portraits, some of them by distinguished seventeenth- and eighteenth-century court painters like Lupoff, Pollard, and Ehrlich.

They strolled down solemn rows of cracking, time-faded old portraits. The Earl gave his guests a guided tour: This Shenstone had been a "widely read" poet; that one, a naval hero in the War of 1812; this one over here, a famous foreign minister. At one point he was surprised to notice that Brant was unobtrusively holding Adrienne's left hand in his. The young woman did not seem to object. The Earl suppressed a quiet smile and beamed benevolently on the stalwart young Scotland Yard inspector, who at that moment was perusing conscientiously the stern visage of a Lord Chief Justice Shenstone. Lord Shenstone looked again at Adrienne Haldane's demure and happy face—and, quite suddenly, discovered an urgent errand that demanded his immediate presence below. With profuse apologies, he left them to their own devices.

It is quite possible that they did not even notice he was gone.

Inevitably, the long shadows of late afternoon crept across the land, until Wilfrith Hall was drowned in purple dusk. The sun stood a little above the western hills, bathing the country in deep red light. Heavy storm clouds were building their dark towers in the eastern skies, even as they had the night before. Ominous piles of deep black vapor billowed and accumulated above the dim horizon, lit with tiny flickers of scarlet lightning.

Nature herself was preparing a suitable stage set for the final battle between the forces of light and the powers of darkness.

Chapter 14

Zarnak Fails

SHORTLY before sundown, the adventurers met in the library. This room, that had seen several important preliminaries, was to be the stage of the last combat. They were all present, including Adrienne Haldane, who insisted with her stubborn determination that she would not miss this final act of their adventure.

Dr. Anton Zarnak, calm and self-possessed, was dressed in his habitual black, but with two unusual additions to his costume. About his throat, a slender silver chain suspended a small *ankh* against his chest. The looped cross of life was made of polished silver, mirror-bright. His head was covered with an Egyptian headdress of stiff, starched linen, banded with thick stripes of alternating gold and white, and an antique gold *uraeus* encircled his brows. Somehow this costume did not appear ridiculous. The lean, chiseled nobility of his pallid features assumed a shadow of lost pharaonic grandeur. He looked like a hierophant of the ancient mysteries, a phantom out of vanished time, summoned to the present day to do combat with primordial evil from the days when the world was young.

Bidding his companions to observe absolute silence, no matter what occurred, he commenced his strange and lonely battle. From his black attaché case, he selected a small faience box filled with a blue powder. After presenting the box to the four cardinal directions, he scattered it on the floor by the French windows, in the form of a large circle. It was through the windows that the mummy would come, as soon as the hour of sunset came.

Then he removed the *Ur-Hekau* from his case. It was a sinuous wooden rod topped by a horned ram's head, crowned with the *uraeus*. It was very ancient, and the wood was ebony black. An almost-palpable aura of power seemed to emanate from the Mighty Staff of Enchantments, like a thrilling vibration, supersonic but sensible, agitating the air in the room.

With the rod, he saluted the four cardinal directions, speaking aloud the names of their tutelary guardians, according to the Egyptian mysteries.

"*Meatha!*"

"*Hafi! Hapi!*"

"*Tuamutef!*"

"*Qebhsennuf!*"

Then he set alight the tall *sib-kharah*, the incense burner of fretted silver belonging to Lord Shenstone. The pungent fragrance of some perfume unknown to his fascinated audience floated in wisps of smoke through the slowly darkening room.

Holding the Rod of Nectanebus in both hands, he spoke these words in a solemn, chanting voice:

"Hail unto thee, Thoth, favorite of Ra the Lord of Might! Hail to thee, Thoth, the mighty one of the Words of Power! Hail to thee, who art in the Boat of The Millions of Years, the Lord of Wisdom, the Scribe of the Divine Ones! Thou Lord of Brightness who illuminates the Gods, hail to thee. Moon, Thoth, Bull of Hermopolis! Thou who establisheth the Thrones of the Gods, thou who art intimate in Their Mysteries, thou Judger of Men. Let us praise the Lord Thoth, the Balance in the Weighing of Souls: Let us praise his Name who loves those who avoid evil, and from whom all evil flees. Thou, the remembrancer of Time and Eternity, who madest Osiris victorious over his enemies, make thou me to be victorious over mine enemy!"

There was a hush of complete silence over the room as Dr. Zarnak finished speaking. In that silence they waited. Tension gathered in the room, a taut throbbing suspense that was almost tangible. Zarnak opened the wall safe, removed the black box that contained the Star of Set, and placed it just beyond the edge of the circle of blue powder.

The trap was baited.

They waited, and as the long moments dragged by, the storm broke outside. A deafening crash of long booming thunder went rolling down the sunset sky, and stinging cold rain lashed against the windows. Storm clouds spilled over and covered the sky in a dome of impenetrable darkness, smothering the sunset's crimson embers. Then a dazzling flare of lightning lit the storm-whipped landscape, and by its momentary light they caught a terrifying glimpse of something standing beyond the French windows, a dark, looming shape, silhouetted against the flare.

Glass shattered, and the thing was in the room with them. Adrienne gasped, trying not to shriek. Brant's arm tightened protectively around the girl's slim shoulders, and his other hand gripped tightly the butt of the pistol in his jacket pocket.

The mummy was in the room. Zarnak moved with lightning speed, touching a match to the ring of powder. It flared into life and surrounded the looming figure in a circle of blue flame. The creature stood as if paralyzed, frozen within the ring of flame. Like some great, blinded beast, it swung its massive head from side to side, examining the strange circular prison that surrounded it. By the mysterious blue light, the four persons in the room could see the hideous figure plainly. The arm and shoulder had been charred black by the flaming oil in the lamp Adrienne had flung at the monster the night before. They could plainly see the horrible hole through the chest, framed in ragged tatters, withered, leathery flesh and decaying cloth, where the Magnum bullet had torn its way last night. The monster's head was clearly seen: the massive skull-head, the scaly shrunken flesh clinging to the bone beneath, the tatters and scraps of funeral bandages dangling about the glaring eyes and silently snarling mouth with its array of grisly, brown fangs.

Zarnak spoke: "I know thee, and I know thy name, and I know the name of the Gods that guardeth thee. Thy name is in my mouth, and I will utter it. Thou art THU-TU, the Doubly Evil One. Thou art AMAM, the Devourer. Thou art SAATET-TA, the Darkener of the Earth."

The mummy bared its dry fangs in a grimace of snarling menace. It tried to move, but the ring of flame engaged it as if in invisible walls. It struggled against this prison of magic, beating against the empty air with the massive mace of its clubbed fist.

Zarnak spoke: "Thou art dead, and thy followers are dead, and thy name is dead upon the lips of men. Be thou, therefore, dead and depart from the Lands of the Living! Thou art dead, and the Gods thou worshipped are dead, and the Demons that served thee are dead. Be thou, therefore, dead and get thee from this place down into the Lands of the Dead!"

A blinding flash of lightning lit the fantastic scene. Rain slashed the broken panes of glass. A demon of wind howled and shrieked about the house. The mummy struggled madly to break through the invisible cell that imprisoned it.

Zarnak spoke: "Go thou down to thy punishment. Go thou down to Karneter, to the Divine Land. Go thou down before Osiris. Go thou down before the Throne of Judgment, where thy black heart shall be weighed in the balance against the Feather of Truth!"

He lifted the *Ur-Hekau*, which had been held down to his side, pointed it at the mummy, and opened his mouth to speak—

But another flare of lightning lit the room, and the mummy's blazing eyes caught sight of the black box containing the Star of Set, which stood just beyond the circle of magic. A rigor of malevolent rage convulsed the skull-face—*and then the broken windows were swept inward by the fury of the storm, which suddenly lashed the house with redoubled strength!* A blast of icy wind and stinging rain swept the room, and the circle flickered and died before its force. Suddenly free, the mummy seized the black box and sprang out into the storm, vanishing into the roaring chaos of water and wind!

Brant jumped up, pulling out his revolver.

"Quick!" Shenstone cried. "The thing mustn't escape! It'll open the box, and then—"

Zarnak took command, his voice cracking like a whip. "Brant! Shenstone! Follow me—we must not let the mummy get away. Miss Haldane, stay here."

He turned and hurled himself out the French windows into the storm, followed by the two men. In a split second the storm had swallowed them up, and Adrienne was left in the room alone, her face a white frozen mask of shock.

The girl stood there for long moments, her hands held to her cheeks, staring through the open windows into the howling storm-torn night. The vibrations of the supernatural struggle died away, and the cold aura of malignancy and tension faded out of the air, and the room became nothing more or less than another ordinary room. It seemed incredible that anything of mystery and strangeness could have occurred in such prosaic surroundings.

Then Adrienne Haldane awoke from her shock. She moved quickly. She snatched a rifle from the glass case of weapons across the room, the very same Magnum with which Inspector James Brant had battled with the living mummy the night before. She cracked the breech and peered within. The lock was empty; she pulled open a drawer, found the box of Magnum shells, and fitted them into the oiled rifle, then snapped the lock again and clicked off the safety. She had accompanied her uncle on several safaris and archaeological expeditions, and knew exactly how to use this weapon. Without wasting time or extra motion, she slipped into her jacket, put the powerful elephant gun in the bend of her arm, went out through the windows into the storm, and vanished into the howling darkness.

She was not going to stand by and see her friends in peril while she stood behind in safety. She was going to stand with Dr. Zarnak and Lord Shenstone—and Inspector James Brant—and face whatever danger awaited them, together.

And now the room was completely empty.

Chapter 15

The Last Incantation

THE storm raged. The sky was a black mass of whirling vapor. The land cowered under the lashing of the cold rain. Thunder bellowed down the sky like a barrage of cannons. Lightning flared and flamed, lighting the tortured trees with flashes of scarlet light.

By its intermittent glare, Zarnak, Brant, and Shenstone tracked the monster. It did not head for the woods, but out into the fields away from Wilfrith Hall. The sparsely grassed ground was turned into a plain of black mud by the chill downpour, and the dragging feet of the monster left great ruts by which its progress could be tracked.

"It wants to—get away from the house—so that it can open the box without—interference—" Zarnak shouted, his voice scattered by the gusts of wind.

"Looks like it's—heading for the river," Shenstone yelled. The noise of the storm was deafening.

The ground was climbing now, rising steadily under their feet. A litter of stones impeded their advance, but it also slowed the mummy, who could not be very far ahead of them.

"The ground—rises—to a cliff—overlooking the Pevent," Shenstone shouted, cupping his hands about his mouth so as to be heard over the roar of thunder. "The monster—seems to be—heading there."

Dr. Zarnak nodded. His headdress was torn away; his black hair streamed with rain, which ran down his taut, white face.

"God—grant—we reach the mummy—before it opens the box, and—releases the Star of Set!" he shouted.

"What will happen—if we are too late—to stop him?" Brant cried.

"The mummy of—Khotep—will regain all—the powers he once—had. We will be—helpless to—destroy him!" Zarnak shouted in reply.

Just then the scarlet lightning revealed the cliff above them. Near the top they could see the ragged form of the living mummy, slowly ascending the heights. His progress was slower than theirs, since he held the box containing the Star in one hand, and could only use one hand to climb with.

"Hurry! We must hurry—in time!" Thunder drowned some of Zarnak's words, but his urgency was communicated to his companions. They redoubled their speed, slipping and sliding in their struggle to climb over the wet black boulders. It seemed as if the forces of nature themselves opposed them—as if the very elements fought on the side of their terrible opponent. The rough and broken boulders stood like stumbling blocks in their path, and they were forced to climb over them with infinite effort, their hands slipping on the wet, dripping rock. The invisible hands of the wind clutched at their clothing, tore at their hands, stung and buffeted their faces, striving to hold them back. The hissing spray of the rain lashed at their eyes, blinding them, and soaked their garments, weighing them down. Between the boulders, a liquid sea of oily black mud clung suckingly to their shoes. They were dazzled by the glare of the incessant lightning; deafened by the explosions of thunder; stunned by the fury of the onslaught of the storm. Still they struggled on, pitting their stubborn and unyielding small store of human strength against the black and demoniac rage of elemental nature.

"He's on—the cliff!" Shenstone panted. Zarnak lifted his head and stared up.

They were very close to the top now. Here the rocks fell away and the cliff narrowed to a sharp, arrow-pointed ledge some ten or fifteen feet square, that overhung the river below. Brant looked down. Seventy feet below them the roaring flood of the river raged against the rocks and dashed itself in fury upon the sheer climbing wall of rock. The storm-tortured Pevent was a boiling chaos of ink-black water, seething around the sharp fangs of the rocks, laced with a bubbling white foam. The wind-whipped waves of cold black water crashed again and again against the foot of the cliff and exploded into clouds of flying, icy spray. Clinging to the wet boulder, Brant shuddered. It was like a scene from the darker pages of Dante's *Inferno*. The raving black waters that foamed around the fangs of rock far below were like the grim punishment reserved for those souls burdened and befouled with some Sin of Sins too terrible even to bear a name. *A man falling from this height would live mere seconds*, he thought.

Lightning split the sky above them, and a detonation of thunder boomed across the sky from cloud to cloud. By the long, slowly fading flare of the lightning they could plainly see the black, dripping figure of the mummy, only a dozen yards from where they clung to the tumbled boulders.

It was unspeakably hideous. Wind whipped the tatters of ragged bandages around its massive form. Water slithered through the soaked, rotten rags of ancient linen, whose gaps revealed the glistening black withered flesh of the living dead thing before them. Tattered, charred, storm-lashed, it was yet an engine of indomitable strength—a fury-driven mechanism of stupendous energy. From whatever pit of Hell it derived its strength, the terrible half-life that drove and animated the centuries-dead corpse was not yet exhausted.

It stood there on the ultimate lip of the cliff, overhanging the black chasm of furious waters, pillar-like legs spread and braced against the half-solid impact of the screaming wind. Its eyes were balls of yellow hell-fire, blazing within the black, sunken sockets of its skull-like head. It menaced them, lifting one mighty arm above its head, threatening with balled fist. The other hand clutched to the ragged chest the black box that held the ominous talisman.

Clinging to the rock, Dr. Zarnak leveled the Rod of Nectanebus at the black figure. He began to chant loudly, over the roar of wind and rain:

"Mayest thou never exist,
May thy Ka never exist,
May thy body never exist,
Mayest thou never exist!"

With a sudden thrill of amazement, Brant and Shenstone saw that a vague blue glow shimmered now about the tip of the Wand of Power, a flickering nimbus of sapphire light.

"May thy limbs never exist,
May thy bones never exist,
May thy flesh never exist,
Mayest thou never exist!"

The mummy lowered its arm and began to fumble with the black box, clutching it in one withered hand. With clumsy, rotting claws it strove to release the cunning catch and open the case. Zarnak's chanting voice droned on:

"May thy form never exist,
May thy attributes never exist,
May thy powers never exist,
Mayest thou never exist!"

The blue aura strengthened about the tip of the *Ur-Hekau*. It burned against the black night like a small azure star, no longer flickering and wavering, but burning steady now, and gathering strength moment by moment, growing brighter and brighter.

"May thy mind never exist,
May thy strength never exist,
May thy words never exist,
Mayest thou never exist!"

Brant saw with a sudden shock that the mummy had stopped striving to unlock the black box. With a sudden grip of strength, the talons closed about the case. The enameled wood splintered, crumpled, and to Brant's horror he saw the mummy lift in one claw *the Star of Set!* It glittered with baleful light above the dark. The mummy held it triumphantly above him, clasped in one claw. He glared in arrogant victory over the crouched figures of his enemies—

Crack!

A rifle shot from behind them hissed past their ears. The Star of Set shattered to a thousand glittering splinters in the moment of impact. The mummy's claw closed over—empty air!

"May thy place never exist,
May thy tomb never exist,
May thy chambers never exist,
Mayest thou never exist!"

Brant craned his head and looked behind. A few feet away, Adrienne Haldane knelt on a flat-topped boulder, with a smoking Magnum rifle in her hands. The echoes of the shot bounced from rock to rock. The girl's pale face was a white oval against the raging darkness. Tremulously, she smiled at him.

"May thy memory never exist,
May thy name never exist,
May thy deeds never exist,
Mayest thou never exist!"

The monster fumbled in the empty air, but the Star of Set was gone. Only the hollow and mocking wind whistled through its groping talons. As if suddenly weakened, it swayed in the grip of the howling wind, knees buckling, head drooping drunkenly against the charred chest.

"May thy Ka never exist,
May thy Sekhem never exist,
May thy Ren never exist,
Mayest thou never exist!"

The light about the tip of the Staff of Enchantments was a blinding ball of seething blue fire now. It blazed against the night, taut and quivering with some mysterious energy. By its strong and steady light, Zarnak's face was a stern mask of grim retribution.

"May thy Khu never exist,
May thy Ba never exist,
May thy Khaibit never exist,
Mayest thou never exist!"

The mummy swayed drunkenly on the edge of the abyss, its arms groping for support. The burning glare of its yellow beast-eyes dimmed, as if filmed with an opaque shell of age. The unquenchable life force that animated the monster seemed to ebb and fade, like a candle going out.

"Mayest thou never exist,
May thy Khat never exist,
May thy Sahu never exist,
Mayest thou never exist!"

The curse-litany of Apophis ended. A sudden stillness drew a sphere of tense silence about the little group. They could no longer hear the clamor of the storm. The blue fire about the tip of the Sceptre of Light—suddenly snapped out. They crouched in complete darkness. Brant drew his breath, and held it.

Then Zarnak stood up to his full height, and cried aloud a mighty phrase of power—

The darkness was split by a gigantic bolt of lightning! It clove apart the blackness with a blast of dazzling blue light. The bolt caught the mummy full in the chest and drove it to his knees with the impact. For a long, blinding moment it writhed and snapped, spitting long jagged sparks of electric flame, quivering like a serpent of fire between heaven and earth. Then the bolt vanished and the world shook to the detonation of a mighty burst of echoing thunder.

The mummy's figure emerged, wrapped in a holocaust of fire. Flames raged and tore from its body and limbs, and its head was a mass of fire. For a second the flaming figure tottered on the brink of the cliff—then the ledge shivered into fragments, and the figure was hurled into the abyss of the storm. They saw the flaming body fall down through the darkness in a long, fiery arc, cleaving the blackness like a blazing meteor. Then the fiery form vanished from sight as its fires were extinguished in the swirl of foaming, black water that lashed the base of the cliff. They stood at the summit, watching the seething, icy flood far below. Adrienne had joined them and clung to Brant wordlessly. His arm was strong about her trembling shoulders.

"I think the storm is letting up," Doctor Zarnak said.

Indeed, the turbulence of clouds was thinning away, and even as they looked the full moon emerged from a rift in the vapors, and shone forth on the night, clean, pure, and serene and far from earthly troubles.

The Epilogue

THE special delivery letter that Mrs. Hecht laid on his desk consisted of an engraved parchment card. Below the crest of Shenstone was this inscription:

>Ruthven, Eighth Earl Shenstone
>Requests the Honor of Your Attendance
>Upon the Occasion of the
>Marriage of His Niece
>Miss Adrienne Morgana Haldane
>to
>Mr. James Malcolm Brant
>On the Fifteenth of This Month
>In Saint Wilfrith's Church, Beresford

"And will there be a reply, Doctor?" Mrs. Hecht asked. Dr. Anton Zarnak shook his head.

"I shall answer with a letter. Thank you—oh, and Mrs. Hecht."

"Yes, Doctor?"

"Would you be so kind as to telephone Sir Ian MacHeath? I shall be unable to meet him for our appointment on the fifteenth."

"Yes, Doctor."

Dr. Zarnak built a steeple of his long fingers, rested his pointed chin on the tips, and regarded his landlady with a gentle, thoughtful look.

"Will that be all, Doctor?"

"Yes, I believe so."

He then allowed a rare smile to flicker about the corners of his thin lips, and lighten briefly the melancholy pallor of his features.

"If he asks a reason, you may tell him this. 'Although marriages are created in Heaven above, they must be celebrated here on Earth, below,' as Great-grandfather Apollodorus somewhere remarks. That will be all, and good night."

STEVE Miller, rather like the characters in the following story, unearthed this artifact from the files of obscure, early Lovecraft fanzines (*The Atavar* [no, that's not a misprint] #1, October 1946). There the piece appeared under the transparent pseudonym "Robert Roch", apparently the Nyarlathotepic mask of *Atavar*'s editor John Cockcroft.

I will have more to say on the story by way of comparing it with Rahman and Rahman's "The Temple of Nephren-Ka", but for the moment, let us turn to the question of where Lovecraft came up with the Nephren-Ka concept. I am willing to bet he derived it from the entry for "Papyrus of Setna" in Lewis Spence's *Encyclopaedia of Occultism*, which we know he owned. This text tells of Prince Setna Kha-em-ust, son of Rameses II; the papyrus was found under the head of a mummy in the Memphis necropolis. The prince was himself an accomplished necromancer and learned of

> a magic book containing two spells written by the hand of Thoth himself. ... He who repeated the first spell bewitched thereby heaven and earth and the realm of night, the mountains and the depth of the sea. ... He who read the second spell should have power to resume his earthly shape, even though he dwelt in the grave. ... Setna inquired where this book was to be found, and learned that it was lying in the tomb of Nefer-ka-Ptah ..., and that any attempt to take away the book would certainly meet with obstinate resistance. These difficulties did not withhold Setna from the adventure. He entered the tomb of Nefer-ka-Ptah, where he found not only the dead man, but the Ka of his wife Ahuri and their son, though these latter had been buried in Koptos.

He bore the scroll away with him, but, after a liaison with a comely witch, ill fortune followed, and "at length, the prince recognized and repented of the sacrilege he had committed in carrying off the book, and brought it back to Nefer-ka-Ptah" (364-365).

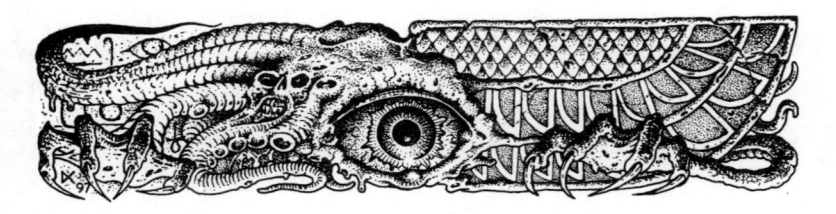

The Curse of Nephren-Ka

by John Cockcroft

THE burning sun beat cruelly down upon the scorching sands. The party trudged wearily on, their goal dimly in sight on the distant horizon.

For days the Vanguard Archaeological Expedition had continued its tiresome trek across the dreary wasteland that was the Egyptian desert, stopping only to obtain snatches of much-needed food and sleep. The object of their journey was the fabulous tomb-pyramid of ancient Nephren-Ka, within whose maze of chambers and corridors, somewhere, was cached hordes of jewels and gold in such vast amounts as to stagger the imagination.

Nathan Karr, curator of the Wentworth Memorial Museum and one of the two leaders of the expedition, was visibly worried. He tramped along in troubled silence.

"What's the trouble, Nat?" asked his partner, Dan Foley. "There's something bothering you, isn't there?"

"Yes, there is, Dan," replied Karr nervously. "It's that damned curse that's supposed to be attached to Nephren-Ka's tomb. There may be something to that legend."

"Nonsense," snorted Foley. "Preposterous! Nat, you don't really believe in that poppycock, do you? Nobody but a fool would even give it a second thought!"

"I don't know," brooded Karr. "In those days, the days of the ancient Egyptians, people knew a great deal about certain arts and methods that have not been handed down to modern times. Certain forms of black magic and sorcery were among these arts. You know what happened to the members of the Tut-Ankeh-Ammen expedition—well—"

"Coincidence," interrupted Foley, "sheer coincidence. Pretty soon you'll be saying that you believe in fairy stories! But enough of this talk for a while, Nat; it isn't doing your nerves any good at all."

"I suppose you're right. But I can't seem to get it off my mind," remarked Karr.

His mind flashed back to that day, two months before, when he had first heard of Nephren-Ka and his pyramid. He had come to the museum on that day, just as he had every day for the past twenty years. It had been a perfectly normal day—until the phone rang. He had answered it and a strange voice, thick with foreign accent, had explained that if he wanted some information on a hitherto-undiscovered pyramid, to come to his apartment, he had named an address, immediately. "Time is of the utmost importance, so proceed with the greatest of haste," the voice had rasped.

Naturally Karr had been interested, inasmuch as the Wentworth Memorial Museum was devoted mainly to objects of an archaeological nature.

Upon arriving at the designated place, he had found it to be a cheap rooming house down in the waterfront district. He had gone up to the room and knocked. Nothing had happened; no sound had stirred from within. He had knocked again, louder this time. Still no response. Trying the door and finding it unlocked, he had gone in.

An exclamation of surprise had escaped his lips as his eyes had taken in the form of a short dark man sprawled upon the dingy uncarpeted floor. Quickly he had stooped over and felt the man's heart. He was dead. Then Karr had noticed the small feathered shaft of a dart protruding from the small of the man's back.

He had gotten up and made a quick search of the room. On a small rickety table on the far side, he had espied a sheaf of papers which he had quickly glanced through. He had noted with satisfaction that they contained numerous hieroglyphics. Hurriedly stuffing the sheaf into his breast pocket, he had dashed out of the building.

Several days later he had brought the papers to the attention of Dan Foley, expert Egyptologist and translator. Together they had spent many days deciphering the manuscript.

They had learned of Nephren-Ka, who had lived in primal times, long before the first Egyptian was born. He was said to have been in close relationship with the dread being, Nyarlathotep. The manuscript was rather vague, but spoke of a vast and bountiful treasure hoard—and of a curse: "Whosoever shall desecrate the tomb of Nephren-Ka, shall die by violence at the hands of the host of the tomb, who shall at the time of desecration assume a form similar to that of the trespasser."

A month later the expedition in search of the tomb was underway.

THE day dawned bright and torrid as the party finally made their way up to the pyramid. It had been farther off than they had assumed, due to the fact that it was of far more gigantic bulk than they had imagined. It towered skyward for fully 1500 feet and was at least 2000 feet on a side at the base. It differed from any pyramid that any of the party had seen in that it appeared to be composed of a single solid block of stone. What blasphemous mockery of the natural laws of space and time could have built so vast a monolith?

The stone itself was of a type never before seen on the face of this earth. It was a dark, opalescent stone with little specks of silver and blood-red interspersed over the marble-smooth surface. Karr had a strange clammy sensation as he touched the polished stone.

After exploring the exterior for several hours, Foley and Karr entered the tomb, armed with electric torches, spare batteries, and automatics. They took also the map of the interior of the pyramid that was among the papers that had caused the start of the expedition.

Traversing the labyrinth of passageways for a considerable time, they came upon a sealed chamber upon whose door were hieroglyphs denoting the chamber as the charnel room.

After some deliberation, during which Karr tried desperately to dissuade Foley from entering, Foley drew his automatic and made short work of the seal. Both leaned on the door, which slowly swung open with a groan that echoed from the very depths of Hell. Immediately they were met with a foul miasmic odor, reeking with mustiness and decay. A cloud of dust welled up and drifted noisomely out of the door.

Karr pointed his flash into the bowels of the crypt and was momentarily blinded as the bright beam was dazzlingly thrown back from pile after pile of precious stones. There was every conceivable kind and variety of gem, including some that neither had ever gazed upon before this moment.

In the center of the vault was a bejeweled altar upon which rested the mummy case.

Foley ran forward with eager hands and rapidly brushed aside the two-inch layer of dust that lay like a shroud over the stone casket. He paused momentarily as he viewed the monstrous figure depicted upon the lid, then he fumbled around in an effort to open the coffin.

"Well, I'll be damned!" exclaimed Foley in amazement. "Why—the seal—it's broken! How could it be? We're the first to enter the crypt!"

"Darned if I know," replied Karr, with equal intensity. "Here, I'll help you lift the lid."

Both were astounded at what they saw as the heavy slab finally gave way beneath their combined efforts.

"God!" cried Foley. "The casket is empty! The mummy is not here!" He turned about to face Karr.

"Oh, yes, the mummy's here all right," Karr answered calmly. He reached down to his pocket and withdrew his automatic. Seven shots rang out. A bullet-riddled body crumpled to the floor.

With a ghastly chuckle that reverberated within the moldy walls of the crypt, Nephren-Ka ripped to shreds the clothing that had bound him and crawled up to his coffin. Once more he resumed his interrupted sleep.

FOR a long time, Cthulhu Mythos fans had no easy access to Robert Bloch's "Fane of the Black Pharaoh" and knew of that potentate only what is said in passing in Lovecraft's "The Haunter of the Dark." These few words were easily evocative enough to provide inspiration for glosses such as this one. This accounts for why no notice is taken in this (or the following) story of Nephren-Ka's devil's bargain with Nyarlathotep to gain knowledge of the future. This is all to the good, since otherwise we should no doubt suffer endless reiterations of the theme. Having said that, let us hasten to admit that this is no guarantee of avoiding redundancy, since, as you cannot help but notice, though "The Temple of Nephren-Ka" (*Fantasy Crossroads* #10/11, March 1977) was written without knowledge of Cockcroft's "The Curse of Nephren-Ka", the two stories are parallel to an astonishing degree. Yet there is an interesting difference.

The stories have exactly the same basic fabula, or plot embryo, which seems almost to be dictated by the choice of topic. In the Rahmans' tale there is genuine development along the syntagmic axis. Rahman and Rahman manage to cover their tracks, leaving clues but leading us a merry chase. By contrast, Cockcroft has created a "narrative of substitutions" (see Tzvetan Todorov, "The Quest of Narrative" in his *The Poetics of Prose*, and Stanley Fish, "Structuralist Homiletics" in his *Is There a Text in This Class?*) in which the sequential scenes are merely contiguous, not consequential. There is no real horizontal movement along the syntagmic axis; instead the movement is along the paradigmatic axis, a vertical juggling of options from the menu of equivalent symbols. Rather than one episode leading into another, causing another, as in "The Temple of Nephren-Ka", in "The Curse of Nephren-Ka" one episode is merely next to another, and they could almost be reshuffled in any order. They are all cameos containing the whole story in miniature, essentially equivalent to one another. Once we learn that one character's name is "Nathan Karr", we have the whole thing in a nutshell. Once we read the terms of the ancient curse, again, there's a thumbnail sketch of the whole. At the climax, well, we have one of those endings that Fritz Leiber wisely called "confirmational", not "revelational." In other words, "no reader can have failed to guess it." In precisely the same way, as Monika Hellwig once observed, we have the resurrection of Jesus depicted three times in Matthew's Gospel: at Bethlehem, on the Mount of Transfiguration, and at the empty tomb. There is no real progression at all. You are just moving from one stained glass window to the next. As Derrida says (not without certain criticisms; see "Force and Signification" in his *Writing and Difference*), such a narrative simply makes manifest what most hide: the static simultaneity of narrative structure, the unmoving, already written plot, which only gains the illusion of temporal passage by virtue of our page-after-page reading of the text. The ending is already there on the last page, no matter whether we are on page one or page fifty.

By the way, notice the name of Private Carnot, surely a relative of the unscrupulous Dr. Carnoti as he appears in the Arkham House text of Bloch's "The Faceless God."

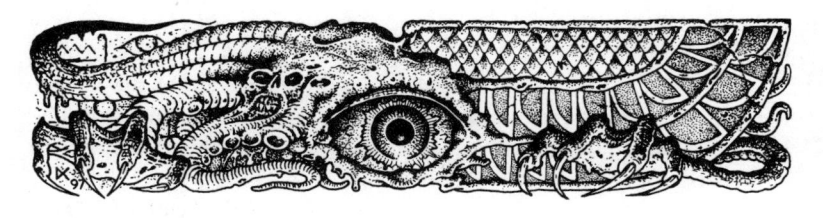

The Temple of Nephren-Ka

By Philip J. Rahman and Glenn A. Rahman

(dedicated to Robert Bloch)

LT. Degreve stood motionless, resting his hand on an ancient column while his eyes adjusted to the shadowy tunnel. Slowly, the cool basaltic walls seemed to catch the dim light of the lanterns that had been set up that morning, and the murky passage materialized.

Degreve strode down the long colonnade with sharp, quick steps. Dr. Brumaire had sketches and measurements enough for one day, he thought. If they did not pack up now, they would have to end their ride back to the garrison in El Fayium by dark.

"Brumaire!"

The lieutenant's tone had not been loud, but the dusky gray stone caught his voice and sent it rebounding. Degreve scanned the black shadows of the myriad pillars that flanked either side of the ageless fane. Brumaire was nowhere to be seen. Degreve waited a moment for the familiar shuffle of the old doctor's feet to sound on the hard, stone floor from behind the massive idol that dominated the temple, or out of one of the dark alcoves hidden amid the pillars.

Degreve snorted. The doddering old fool must be lost in his work again. The lieutenant stepped further into the ancient hall and glanced fleetingly on the stone titan that sat enthroned at the end of the colonnade. The unsteady light of the torches and lamps played over the falcon-headed god, casting liquid shadows that endowed the stiff features of the idol with a discomforting illusion of life.

"Brumaire!" he called again, more sharply.

The echoes fairly exploded, startling the young officer with the violence of their retort. The lieutenant swallowed a breath of air and waited for the verbal thunder to recede. As the last echoes died, a jarring clatter of heavy boots sounded behind him.

The lieutenant spun on his heels toward the entrance of the temple. Rushing into it came the lumbering figure of his private, Carnot, and their guide, a slight fellow called Farabi. Pvt. Carnot hastily saluted and after an awkward pause inquired after the shouting.

"That fool Brumaire is either asleep or deaf," said the lieutenant. "Find him and tell him we are leaving immediately." Carnot saluted hastily and shuffled off into the shadows.

The oppressive atmosphere of the temple had put an edge on Degreve's growing impatience and a scowl hardened his features. He turned at the sound of returning feet.

"He is not here, Lieutenant," reported the French private.

"Not here? Impossible!" Degreve waved Carnot away. "Search the temple again!"

"If I might speak, *effendi*," Farabi whispered. "I warned Dr. Brumaire of the evil reputation of this valley and the temple it conceals.

"The shrines of the ancient kings are abominations in the sight of Allah and are haunted by unclean spirits and evil djinn. To linger here is to put your body, mind, and soul in terrible peril, for those wretched few the djinn do not put to death, the Black Messenger enters and makes his own."

Carnot's voice echoed from the back of the oblong temple, hushing the words of Farabi.

"Lieutenant," the private called, "I've found Brumaire's notebook!"

The massive infantryman looked like a small child beneath the huge granite statue of the falcon-headed god. Near the idol glowed a set of several lanterns that had been moved there to illuminate the hieroglyphic inscription on its base.

Degreve flipped through the doctor's notes and frowned. There was nothing in it but meaningless transcriptions, the last of them abandoned half finished. They searched about the base of the stone god and then examined the walls for any concealed passageway the doctor might have accidentally discovered.

"There is a trick used by certain tomb robbers," offered Farabi reluctantly. "It is said that often a small draft may be detected from concealed tunnels if a torch is passed slowly across the wall where it is hidden."

"Well, do so," snapped Degreve, ordering Carnot to fetch three torches from their supplies. When the private returned, the lieutenant thrust one into the Arab's brown hand and took another for himself. The guide stepped toward the north wall, while Pvt. Carnot inexpertly checked the east wall behind the statue.

Lt. Degreve passed his torch around the corners of the plinth and altar of the idol. The torch revealed nothing but dusty shards of shattered vessels, broken by past looters. Quietly he cursed the missing scholar for his carelessness, himself for not posting Private Carnot to watch Brumaire, and General Bonaparte for ever encouraging civilians to join his Egyptian expedition. Brumaire was a man not without influence; it would look very bad if he did not return with him.

"*Effendi*!" called the Egyptian excitedly. "Observe." Farabi passed the torch slowly across the roughly carved stones. There was a faint stir at one point, hardly noticeable. He passed the brand back and forth slowly as the slight flicker repeated itself again at the same point along the wall.

The deft hands of the Egyptian felt the stones for some kind of hidden catch. He pressed on a smaller block with a bas-relief of an eye. A sly grin touched his lips; the block gave way. The eye slid six inches into the block and then stopped. Farabi returned to the spot where the torch had been disturbed and motioned the two soldiers to help him push.

A section of the wall swung freely on a pivot, releasing a stale, charnel draft from the black aperture revealed. The light of Farabi's torch disclosed a narrow doorway at the end of a short, roughly hewn corridor.

Lt. Degreve looked at Carnot and then back at Farabi in disbelief. He began to take an impetuous step over the threshold when Farabi's quick hand shot out and grabbed his arm.

"Have caution, *effendi*," he nervously warned the lieutenant. "If your doctor went down this passage, it could not have been of his own volition. The *fellahin* tell many terrible stories of men who have wandered near this place and not returned. This valley belongs to the archdemon, Iblis, and to forgotten gods older than he."

Degreve grunted for silence. He had no more respect for the superstitions of the *fellahin* than he did for the ancient heathens that had created the temple. He ordered Carnot to fetch the rest of the torches and a length of rope in case the doctor had fallen into a pit.

When all was prepared, Degreve entered the dark corridor first, followed by the reluctant Farabi, sandwiched between the lieutenant and Pvt. Carnot.

"Do not go before the light, and take care where you place your feet," counseled Farabi. "The old race of Egypt built many hidden pits and cunning deathfalls into their sacred temples to discourage thieves and desecraters."

Carefully moving the torch about the mouth of the tunnel, the young officer took a tentative step. He listened, but heard only the soft rustle of his two companions as they cautiously followed.

The corridor was short; they reached the narrow doorway with a dozen halting steps. Thrusting a torch before them, they peered into the secret chamber. The smooth, gesso-coated walls blazed orange in the torchlight, although their true color was a deep saffron. Crowded upon them were strange glyphs and fierce portraits of polymorphic deities. Towering over all was a terrible, divine sentinel carved of black granite. The ibis-headed god stood squarely confronting the three men, his arm stiffly extended as if to command them to abandon their sacrilegious intrusion.

Farabi's lemuroid eyes swelled in superstitious wonder as he prayed in Arabic that his young, foreign god, Allah, might shield him from the indignation of the Forgotten Ones.

Lt. Degreve shook off the awe that momentarily froze him and scanned the room for any sign of the missing scholar. It contained nothing but inscrutable frescoes and the mute tutelary. Behind the twelve-foot statue, buried in its quaking shadow, was an ornate bronze door stained with verdigris. As the torches were moved closer, they found it hung ajar. Three feet into the adjacent chamber loomed a rugged wall that ran from either wall and was flush with the ceiling. The stones were so poorly dressed and fitted as to suggest great haste in its erection.

Degreve was on the verge of conceding that Brumaire had been spirited off the earth by demons when he began to notice that the all-pervasive, mephitic stench seemed stronger in the blocked room.

"There, in the corner—a hole." Lt. Degreve moved his torch toward the roughly excavated opening in the southwest corner of the barricade.

"Brumaire must have gone through here," said Degreve, kneeling beside the opening.

"This is madness," said the Egyptian, his voice dry with fear. "Brumaire has been taken by ghouls. We must flee this place before the same fate befalls us."

Degreve scowled irritably; the boundaries of reality and myth, so basic and essential to a European, were totally lost upon the Moslem.

"Do you think I might persuade my captain that your superstitions are an excuse for failure in Bonaparte's army?"

"Die if you wish, *effendi*, but let me go back. This place is accursed; it bears the brand of the demon Iblis—the Black Messenger of Karneter, the Stealer of Souls."

"Legends! Can you utter nothing but legends?" the Frenchman snapped.

Degreve angrily drew his cavalry saber and held the tip menacingly at the throat of the paled guide.

"You will not leave here until we do. Until then, you will follow."

Lt. Degreve crouched beside the tunnel and explored its opening with his torch. The jagged hole shrank to a diameter of less than three feet before it passed through the thick wall.

"Send Farabi in after me," he ordered. "Shoot him if he tries to desert."

Degreve stood up and tried to catch his breath in the dense, funereal atmosphere of the chamber. Already, the narrow tunnel that opened by his feet was orange with the light of Farabi's torch. Then, as the smooth gesso walls caught his light, he noticed a dark silhouette sprawled on the floor of the chamber, perhaps thirty feet away.

Ordering his men to hurry, Lt. Degreve rushed to the prostrate, gangly figure of Dr. Brumaire, who lay lifelessly beside his extinguished torch. The young officer rolled the scholar onto his back and listened for his heartbeat. Seizing the doctor by his shoulders, he shook him to consciousness.

An eye flickered and the gray-bearded antiquarian moaned softly. For a long moment the doctor stared into the tense face of Lt. Degreve without seeming to recognize him.

"Forgive me—" he muttered, "this air—I must have passed out." Brumaire awkwardly felt about his coat and found his pince-nez.

Surrounding them in lurid colors and a style alien to any of the hieroglyphs or paintings they had previously glimpsed were scores of shocking murals.

In a large panel that commanded attention was depicted a spindly pharaoh on a tall, ornate throne. To him came men dressed differently than the Egyptians, a pale-skinned embassy with long, black hair that trailed to the base of their spines and tendrils that hung down in front of their ears and over their chests. The leader of the embassy, a prince who wore a plumed headdress, presented to the king a strange, black jewel of many facets that rested in a yellow box of odd geometry.

"What manner of place is this?" muttered the lieutenant, drinking in the vivid portraits and nightmarish scenes.

"They form a historical narrative," offered the doctor. "One so startling I am forced to connect it with legends of the heretical pharaoh, Nephren-Ka, whose terrible history is hinted of in the fragments of Manetho preserved by Africanus."

In a series of vignettes, slaves were seen erecting a new temple filled with crude, elongated idols of alien design. The images of the venerated gods of Egypt were smashed and cast from their pedestals and new, more terrifying gods elevated. In the new temple, the mad pharaoh was depicted brandishing a curved blade and putting slaves to death with the aid of scarlet-clad acolytes. Behind him towered a new figure, a dark man of cyclopean dimension, robed in blood red and of terrifying evil and unyielding visage.

"The pictures portray Nephren-Ka's abandonment of the traditional gods of Egypt for the Dark One. See how the old priests are blasted by the Dark One or fallen upon by his legion of subordinate demons."

These hordes were the most terrible images depicted. They filled the latter panels, attacking people, stealing children, and defiling the embalmed dead. Farabi recognized them as the most feared djinn of the desert, remembered even to his generation, and known to the Bedouin as *qutrubs*. In paintings that must have been even more abominable to the death-revering Egyptians, the scrawny, gibbonous ghouls crawled about performing nauseating acts of defilement and desecration.

They were hook-beaked, black and shaggy with apish bodies and long talons. With these, they ripped apart the cotton wrappings of royal mummies, dismembered them, and feasted on the dry fragments. In one insane mural the pharaoh was seen actually taking part in this necrophagia.

Tearing his eyes from the walls, Degreve turned once more to the bland, unmoved figure of Brumaire and demanded an explanation of how he had gotten to this hidden room of blasphemies.

The doctor paused to gather his thoughts. "The entrance was partly open. I noticed it while copying the inscription on the statue of Horus in the Hall of Pillars. I must have sprung some ancient trap—it closed behind me and I was forced to go forward until I found this room."

Degreve scowled in exasperation. He cursed his ill fortune that he should be assigned to watch over such a senile fool, who knew no responsibilities save his pointless research.

"I should have listened to Farabi and left you here to die."

While the lieutenant took the doctor to task, Pvt. Carnot decided to explore the strange chamber. It was a long room with a downward sloping floor ornamented with macabre mosaics whose themes were as grim as those of the murals. Toward the far end of the room was a curious structure shaped like a squat, truncated cone some eight feet in diameter. Upon examination, he found it to be some kind of shaft or well. He bent over to peer into its foul-smelling depth as Lt. Degreve called him back. Reluctantly, he turned to rejoin the company.

Farabi had already slipped back through the tunnel, eager to escape the horrible murals. Brumaire, still protesting that he should have more time to study the paintings, followed.

Carnot hurried to the lieutenant, reporting his find and muttering something about a rustling noise he heard issuing deep below the shaft.

"Nothing more than rats. Now, follow me."

When Degreve reached the other side, he handed his torch to Brumaire and offered his hand to help the unwieldy Carnot through the narrow opening.

Suddenly a strange pallor swept across the face of the private and he twisted his features in a hoarse scream. Carnot's hand closed crushing upon Degreve's. Carnot cried and jabbered for help, but he lost his grip on the startled lieutenant and slid into the black hole.

Degreve jerked back his torch from the doctor after cocking his pistol as the private's lunatic, guttural wails poured from the other side. As a shaggy hand reached through the tunnel, Degreve flung himself away from the opening, firing blindly. A shrill screech sounded that jarred the young officer out of his fear-inspired torpor. Seizing the old doctor by his wrist and screaming an inarticulate warning, he fled the walled-up room as unseen hands pulled the dead monstrosity back into the darkness.

With their hearts rising to their throats, the three men bolted through the saffron-colored room, through the narrow corridor, and back into the Hall of Pillars. Degreve caught a breath of what he hoped would be clean air, but was almost strangled by the intensity of the stench.

A shrill hoot assailed his ears at the same instant that a fetid black shadow leaped at him. The lieutenant staggered back as crooked talons ripped through the blue fabric of his jacket and gouged deeply into the flesh beneath. His stumble threw him against Brumaire, whose body steadied him long enough to allow him to bring his still-smoldering pistol down crushingly into the hideous beaked face of the scrawny thing of bone and coarse fur.

While Lt. Degreve pulled himself loose, Farabi gasped and was knocked to the floor as another creature leaped at his throat. The frailer Egyptian was fallen upon by yet more of the hellish beings lunging from the shadows.

Degreve struck wildly with his saber, first at his own reeking attackers and then at the obscenities that crouched over the fallen guide. Slowly, sanity rallied inside his brain and he leaned against the column for support when he realized the fight was over.

Brumaire bent over the prostate, bloody Farabi and slowly examined him. Degreve shut his eyes and turned from the sickening sight revealed in the dim light. The Egyptian lay twisted with his throat torn out; beside him lay one of the slain ghouls with his dagger buried deeply into its chest. About him sprawled two other slaughtered devils, more hideous in flesh than in a thousand tomb paintings. Shaggy, wattled, and vulture-beaked—Farabi had called them *qutrubs*, eaters of the dead.

Brumaire softly touched one of the dead ghouls and sighed.

"My poor slave," he said gently.

"What's the matter with you?" The fouled, clawed lieutenant looked at the venerable Parisian scholar. "Have you been driven mad?"

But when the man calmly looked up at him, he saw not the face of Brumaire, but a cruel, swarthy visage bearing an ironic, uncompromising smile. Degreve shrunk back toward the mouth of the accursed fane.

The dark man rose to his full height and followed after the lieutenant. "A pity you could not read the warning above the image of Thoth," he said.

The young officer whirled and bolted into the night. What he had brought out of the secret fane was not Brumaire but an undying devil. His hopes of escape shattered when he saw the slaughtered horses. He hurriedly loaded his pistol as he fled over the sand.

At the top of a dune he turned toward the entrance of the temple and pulled back the hammer of his weapon. For an instant his finger froze in astonishment as the dark, pursuing shape began to swell in the fainter light and take on a nightmarishly inhuman silhouette, but then the lieutenant saw no more as the powder exploded in his face and a sheath of fire burst from within him and enveloped his screaming body in roaring flames.

The dark man lingered at the edge of the conflagration, his features lean and reddened in the light of the blaze. The charred body broke and crumbled upon the sand.

Slowly the tall figure turned from the pyre and strode toward the mouth of the tunnel where the hook-beaked ghouls awaited him. He regarded them quietly in the dying glow of the cremation as they gathered about him in a dark mass. Then, as the night breeze scattered the remaining ashes of the invader, he motioned them silently and they followed him back into the temple of Nephren-Ka.

H IMSELF a wanderer and delver in exotic climes, Bob Culp was just the man to perpetrate the scholarly piece you are about to read. Lovecraft's antique horrors gained much of their effect from the genuineness of the scholarship with which he garnished them. Too often, attempts to emulate HPL in this respect fall flat simply because the authors do not do their homework, do not even know how to do their homework. Culp did. This story is only minimally a story at all, and that is not due to any lack of skill on Culp's part—just the reverse. He had the keen eye to see what some others do not, namely that, in a tale like "The Call of Cthulhu", Lovecraft embeds a story not so much in narrative discourse as in scholarly exposition. Thus the story events are distanced from the reader, since the reader seems to be reading the residue of the events, their echo, as in a nonfictional medium. Following this lead, Culp attests to Paul de Man's observation that even an exposition, an argument, is after all a kind of narrative, its train of thought a plot with an outcome. In fact, Culp's conclusion works both as a narrative climax and a scholarly conclusion, the former being smuggled skillfully within the latter.

On a different matter, Culp's own remarks, which prefaced "The Papyrus of Nephren-Ka" in the February 1975 mailing of the Esoteric Order of Dagon Amateur Press Association, bear quoting:

> In this tale I have striven to illustrate what I consider a felicitous trend for Lovecraftian "spin-offs", i.e., the development of some minor facet into an adjunct of the "mythos" that will enlarge its scope and in turn broaden the horizon for future stories. The possibilities are limitless, without shedding a drop of ichor or arousing Great Cthulhu from his slumber, whereas the pastiche offers constantly diminishing areas of development and resulting stagnation.

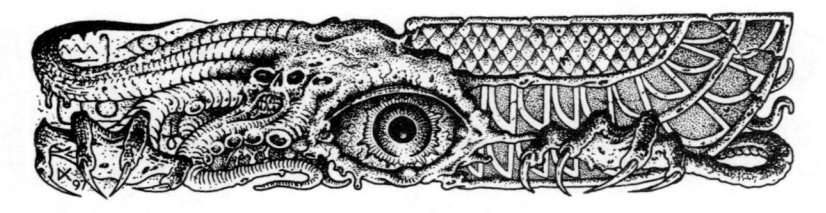

The Papyrus of Nephren-Ka

by Robert C. Culp

At the last from inner Egypt came the strange dark one ... wrapped in fabrics red as sunset flame.
—H. P. Lovecraft

THE date of the period when the land of Egypt was taken possession of by the race of people we are accustomed to call Egyptian is unknown. None of the researches which has been carried on by historians, philologists, anthropologists, and archaeologists has, up to the present, given any information from which the time of this event may be definitively established. Just as nothing is known of the period of the advent of the invaders, likewise nothing is known of the aboriginal people living there when they arrived.

The race to which the Egyptians known from mummies and statues belong and its characteristics establish that they were Caucasian. It is also certain that they brought a high level of civilization with them to the land commonly called *Kamt*, because of the dark color of the soil. It was also known by the name of *Ta-mera*, the "land of the inundation", as well as *Beqet* or *Baqet*, denoting Egypt as an olive-bearing land.

Over the history of Egypt there hangs a mystery greater than that which shrouds the origin and home of the Egyptians; of the period which preceded Menes, the first historical king of Egypt, nothing is known. According to Manetho a race of demigods ruled before the advent of Menes. These may possibly correspond with the *Shesu Heru,* or followers of Horus, as they are called in the Turin Papyrus, which list begins with the god-kings and ends with the rule of the Hyksos at the end of the XVIIth Dynasty, or about 1700 B.C. The work of Manetho of Sebennytus on Egyptian history is unfortunately lost. Composed during the reign of Ptolemy II, its extracts are preserved in Josephus and are the most valuable evidence which has been passed down, for Manetho by reason of his position as a priest and his knowledge of the Egyptian language had access to and was able to make use of the ancient literature in a way no other writer seems to have done.

Manetho's grouping of Egyptian kings into dynasties has been retained in Egyptological writings despite the lack of basis in actual practice. The ancient Egyptians made no such distinction. This fact is evident from the Tablets of Abydos and Sakkarah. The former gives the names of seventy-five kings beginning with Menes and ending with Seti I, the father of Rameses II; it is not a complete list and there is nothing to show why names are omitted. The latter, inscribed during the reign of Rameses II, gives the names of forty-seven kings, agreeing closely with the Tablet of Abydos. The Tablet of Karnak, inscribed during the reign of Thothmes III, contains the names of sixty-one kings, substantiating to a degree the lists of both Abydos and Sakkarah. All serve to some degree to resolve those instances where Manetho's list is corrupt.

Because the chronology has been and probably will be for some time a subject of conjecture and a variety of opinions, another approach to the problem was undertaken. The fixed points in Egyptian history are so few and the gaps between them so great that it was decided to investigate the possibility of codifying genealogical and dynastic tables through references in Egyptian funerary papyri. Accordingly, although this was to be a private endeavor, the cooperation of museums and known private collectors having such documents, unavailable through commercially published sources, was solicited. The response was gratifying, and as the volume of document copies began to accumulate, they were either translated or the accompanying translations verified. Then texts were transcribed onto magnetic tape in a format usable on any available electronic computer. Lists of individual names were standardized and references to predecessors and antecedents were carefully noted and likewise standardized. All references to the reigning personages or chronological markers were specifically coded as the record was created.

It soon became apparent that the greater bulk of the records pertained to persons of lesser nobility, with a predominance representing the priestly castes. While the transcription process was proceeding, a correlation program, providing for assembly and tabulation of data based on different variables, was written and compiled. At the point when the number of records transcribed was sufficient to be significant, a trial run was made. Here also the results were gratifying: Printing only the names, ages, and lengths of reign of referenced rulers in their respective chronological order, a great deal of similarity to the previously established records was noted. Succeeding listings filled more and more gaps, verifying many existing records and invalidating others, but most significantly pointing up a mystifying hiatus.

The last ruler in the Sixth Dynasty was Queen Nitaquert (Nitocris), who enlarged the pyramid of Mykerinos and covered it with slabs of granite. Her remains are believed to be interred in a fine basalt sarcophagus in a chamber near that of Mykerinos. Between her reign and that of the next king in the sequence, who would fall in accepted contexts in the Seventh Dynasty, there was an unexplained gap of approximately thirty to thirty-five years.

Of the period of the Seventh through the Eleventh dynasties nothing definite is known; the names of the kings who reigned cannot even be arranged accurately in chronological order. Toward the end of this period a number of kings, apparently of Theban origin, ruled; one named Menthuhetep is styled on a stele on the island of Konosso as the conqueror of thirteen nations. His name also appears on rocks beside the old road from Coptos to the Red Sea through the valley of Hammamat. The mightiest king seems to have been Seanchkara, who was able to send expeditions to the land of Punt, the land of the gods and specifically the home of the god Bes. These data were confirmed and a logical array was forthcoming of the names substantially as listed by Budge, beginning with "Ab" rather than "Men-ka Ra." *Ab* phonetically translates in many ways, but the hieroglyphs in the cartouche imply wisdom.

The lengthy process finally ran its course, the last available record was transcribed, the final statistical justification performed on the entire array, and the composite list was printed. There was yet the unexplained and unaccounted-for period of time, relatively minute but bafflingly stubborn.

A list of the document control numbers used to identify those immediately before and after the period was printed and those manuscripts themselves were isolated. The translations of each were painstakingly verified and all but one proved to have been accurately translated and transcribed. The Papyrus of Djed-Sobk-Iuf-Ankh ("Sebek speaks and he lives"), priest of Sebek, proved to be the exception. It is printed in black, and a series of figures placed in two registers follows a cyclic movement; those in the lower register, forming three vignettes, read from left to right toward a scarab over the head and arms of a figure representing the god Sebek, while those in the upper register are read from right to left toward a scarab encircled by a serpent. The other representations form a complete composition divided into seven vignettes. Closer examination revealed that they had been deliberately written in archaic priestly language, unintelligible and thus susceptible to misinterpretation by the uninitiated.

Presuming upon a friendship of long standing, a copy of the papyrus, the final tabulation, and a letter explaining the entire project as well as the problem were dispatched at once to an old-school Egyptologist then residing in Dar es Salaam. Before too long, a reply was forthcoming, which in essence stated that the papyrus originated in the ancient town of Shetet in

Medinet el-Fayum. To the north of the town, now known as El-Med'neh, are extensive mounds known to the inhabitants as Kiman Faris ("riders' hills"), covering about one-half acre and rising to a height of sixty-five feet. These now mark the site of ancient Crocodilopolis. The largest mound, known as Kom el-Kharyama, encloses the ruins of a large necropolis, in which during the last twenty years important numerous discoveries of papyri have been made, many of which were in the hands of a private collector. His collection included the very sarcophagus of this same priest. Coincidentally, the scholar was to depart shortly to undertake a short investigation of another matter at Edfu, and he declared himself willing to undertake an investigation of the matter of the Papyrus of Djed-Sobk-Iuf-Ankh at the same time. In conclusion he stated that a complete translation of the representations would be forwarded as soon as possible.

After a lengthy period of time, during which the chronology was refined, verified, and differences tabulated between it and established lists, the translation arrived. The priests of the cult of the crocodile god, never numerous, had, during the reign of Queen Nitocris, been appointed as tutors and guardians to a hitherto-unknown heir to the double *uraeus*. The assigned responsibilities were dutifully observed to the letter. However, after the death of the queen and the assumption of the throne by the unnamed heir, the priests had been relegated to relative obscurity. This had been predicted by the Queen Mother, who had also foreseen the downfall of the pharaoh. He, with his followers, worshiped strange gods older than even those anciently worshiped throughout the red and black lands. Mention of these on the walls of the Temple of Bek-h'det at Edfu is a matter of record, but the inclination has always been to consider them as references to deities in the normal though extensive pantheon, confused by the obscure priestly representations. Dark rites are prescribed, rituals of invocation and propitiation are formulized, but without exception direct references to specific names have been obliterated.

During the aforementioned excavations at El-Kharyama the tomb of an obscure priest had been discovered, whose date of interment had always been reckoned in the twenty-first dynasty—primarily because, though it had been discovered at a lower level, the others opened in the same area were of that period. The scroll definitely states that the priest known as Djed-Sobk-Iuf-Ankh was the guardian of the genealogical papyrus of the heretofore-unknown ruler and implies that after the cult had seen to the completion of their ward's tomb they had followed the instructions of Queen Nitocris and simply waited. When, as the Queen had predicted, the end came, they saw to the interment of the lord, obliterated all traces of its location, and dispersed to their respective homes. Since none of the excavation party had been able to interpret correctly the papyrus, it had rested in

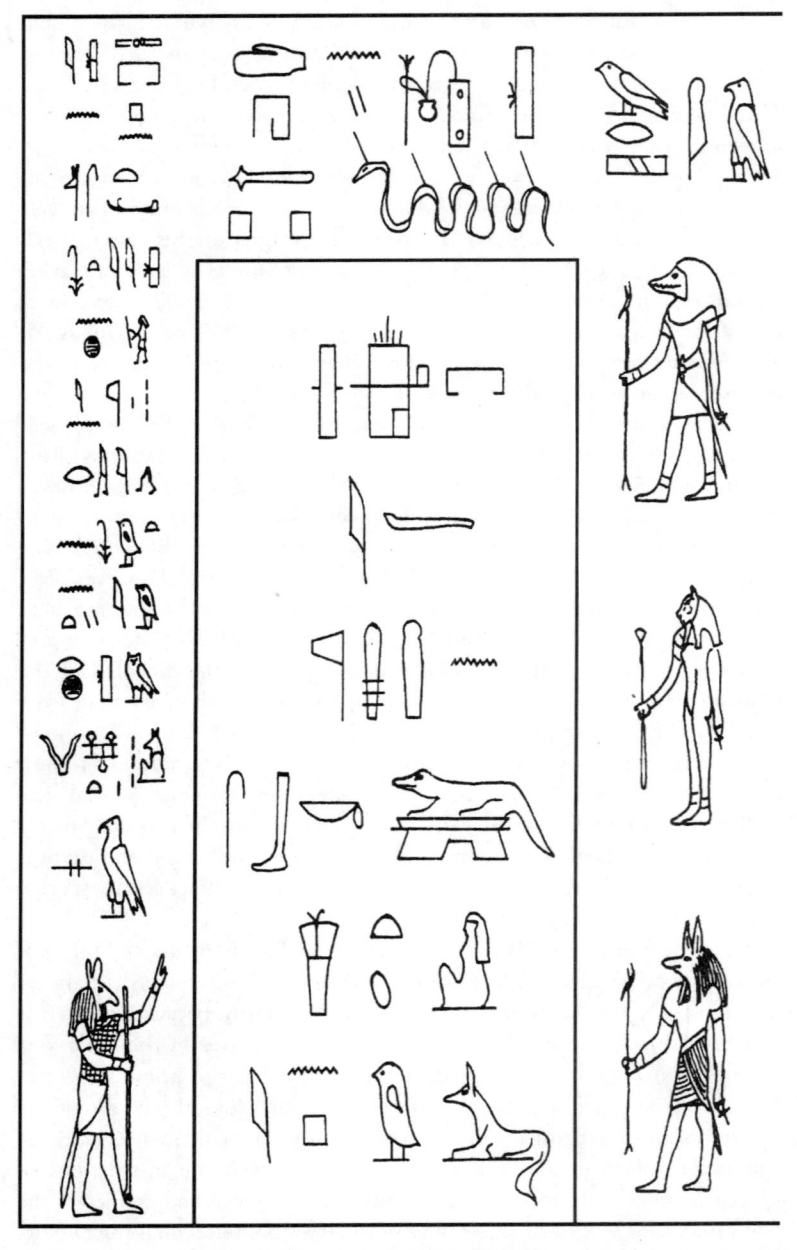

Papyrus of NPHRN-KA RA

The Papyrus of Nephren-Ka 221

Dynasty VI, Memphis B.C. 3140

the possession of the private collector until the time of his demise. It had then passed, in accordance with the provisions of his will, to the Kunsthistorisches Museum in Vienna. The item number is 3859 in their catalog, with length and width given as 2.187 meters and .153 meters respectively. (For more detail see Hans von Demel, *Der Totenpapyrus des Djed-Sobk-Iuf-Ankh*.)

It was now known that there had been another ruler after Queen Nitocris and before Ab, and that he had been deposed by total and outright rebellion of the priests, nobility, and *fellahin* because of the unprecedented bloodshed entailed in dark incantatory rites of propitiation and appeal to blasphemous and horrible demon-gods seemingly unsatiated by the rivers of blood that flowed from the temple altars. The entire population had been forced to perform debasing rites of ritual necrophilia, a perpetual degenerate Saturnalia. Yet there was no name, only references to "he whose name may never be spoken." The proscription decreed by Ab had been total and absolute. Many rulers in the past had attempted to obliterate the evidence of their predecessors, but none had succeeded to this extent. In fact, the annals had been so horrific as to be handed down from generation to generation secretly by word of mouth, and no records were kept of succession and genealogy until time or accident permanently laid the specter to rest. Hence the confusion of over seven hundred years in the history of Egypt. Temporarily in the record the lost pharaoh was put down simply as unknown; even though the gap in the lineage was accounted for, there was no corresponding name.

SO now there was nothing for us to do but wait. In due course a short letter arrived, merely saying that the small carpet we had so long desired had been procured and had been sent by air, on a date some two weeks previous. That same day the local airline agent called with the information that the carpet had arrived. Pick-up was arranged at once, and shortly the bundle was in our possession and opened. The prayer rug, though a rarity in itself, went practically unheeded, but there was no sign of the papyrus. Examination of the short but large-diameter piece of bamboo around which the carpet had been rolled revealed an all-but-imperceptible seam down the side: Inside lay the scroll. When unrolled it was found to have a tracing rolled up with it. On the tracing was a complete transliteration and the corresponding translation for each register of the various representations. Since it had been rolled up from the end rather than the beginning, it was necessary to restrain our impatience as the roll of ancient papyrus was rerolled in reverse. In the process only fleeting notice was taken of the translation, while we searched for the cartouche that would at last reveal the identity of the long-missing pharaoh. At last, at the beginning of the roll it lay before our gaze, challenging our credulity and to say the least shattering all conceptions of the demarcation of fact and fiction. The prenomen translated to Nephren-kha Ra, King of the North and South. The banner name unbelievably read *tehni Apep*, "dedicated by deed to Apep!" Apep, the personification of foulness, is the prime demon in the entire fantastic array of netherworld beings of the Egyptians, so fearful and abhorrent that special exorcism rituals were conducted in all temples daily to banish him. The balance of the banner name was more conventional, reading "King and High Priest of Sebek, Bubastis, and Anubis." The real puzzle lies in the same representation that confirms the owner's place in both the chronology and the lineage, for the name of the wretch's father is as enigmatic as had been the progeny.

Directly below the crocodile, opposite Kheperer the beetle god who created the world, approaching the winged orb with the *ut'at* eye of the moon, the first line reads, "Son of Nitocris and the divine messenger of the gods." Skip for the moment the second line and go to the third line, "lies in a tomb maintained in perpetuity"; fourth line, "which will remain a hidden place"; fifth line, "awaiting the arrival of"; and last line, "the Opener of the Way." For a finale, return to the second line and read the name of the sire of the infamous Nephren-kha: NYARLATHOTEP.

GARY Myers, whose collection *The House of the Worm* appeared from Arkham House in 1975, is a heretic. He proved his heretical character in that volume, and he only deepens his guilt here. As you will see, he found a way to harmonize the Lovecraft Mythos and the Derleth Mythos in a genuinely Lovecraftian way. As one of the relative few who have dared try to continue HPL's Dunsanian legacy, he was hailed by Lin Carter (in *Lovecraft: A Look behind the "Cthulhu Mythos"*, soon to be available in a new corrected and expanded edition from Borgo Press) as the most talented of the New Lovecraft Circle. That talent is on display in this story, "The Snout in the Alcove", which will be new to you even if you have read it in its original appearance in Lin Carter's *Year's Best Fantasy Stories: 3* (DAW Books, 1977), since it has been substantially rewritten for this appearance.

Of the tale, Myers explains: "This story ... was supposed to be my 'Dream-Quest', my scorched-earth farewell to the Lovecraftian dreamlands, and a Carteresque summation of my own take on the Cthulhu Mythos." Of course, it turned out that Gary would descend the seven thousand onyx steps more than once thereafter. This time he may really mean it, though, since he is at work on a series of modern-era tales of the Cthulhu Mythos.

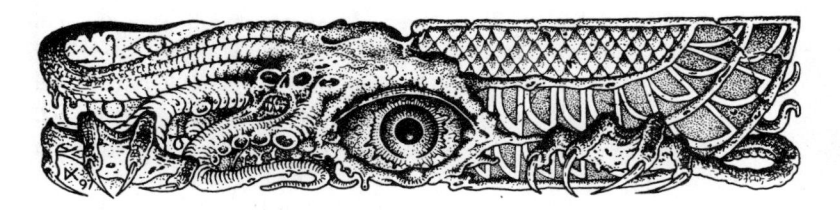

The Snout in the Alcove

by Gary Myers

I AWOKE from an evil dream to a strange alcove. A pointed arch was curtained with a tapestry. A lamp like the full moon depended from above. So dim was the lamp, and so gloomy the tapestry, that the rays of the one could light but feebly the design of the other.

Thinking to find in this design some clue to my whereabouts in space and time, I was turning out my pockets in a vain quest of matches when the curtains suddenly parted to admit a snout. A snout palely luminous and cloudily transparent. A snout in the shape of a long gray cone tapering to a clump of wriggling pinkish tentacles.

I threw myself down on my face.

But the attack I feared never came. Instead there came the far-off echo of excited voices and the sound of rapidly approaching feet. Then the dim light around me grew suddenly brighter, and I was helped to my feet by many pairs of reassuringly human hands. I found myself in a circle of seven young men in robes of simple white, seven young men with torches in their hands and looks of consternation on their faces.

Their demeanor was not unfriendly, yet they seemed to know no better what to make of me than I had known what to make of the snout. I thought to reassure them with a show of openness. No doubt, I said, they were pursuing the demon that had left me as they had found me. It had looked in on me and gone out again only seconds before they arrived. Indeed, it was probably due to their timely arrival that it had withdrawn so quickly, and that I had taken no more harm from its visit than a momentary fright. For this I was greatly in their debt. If they would continue in the same direction, they would soon overtake their quarry. But if they would increase my debt to them, they would not go without first telling me the name of this place to which my dreams had brought me.

If the young men were at all reassured by my speech, they did not show it at once. They stood a little apart from me and conferred together in quiet voices before one of them made me this reply. They were indeed on the trail of the demon, a monstrous agent of the outer dark which had been sent here by its dread masters to accomplish some unknown but undoubtedly evil purpose. They followed it to thwart that purpose by driving its agent back again to the darkness from whence it came. They had briefly entertained a suspicion that I myself was that demon, attempting to conceal its true identity within a borrowed form. But now that they had heard me speak, they realized that I was as human as they were. So there could be no harm in telling me that I found myself in the lower halls of the Temple of the Elder Ones at Ulthar.

Now it was my turn to look troubled, for Ulthar was not unknown to me. It was one of the more important towns in the dreamlands surrounding our waking world. This I had good reason to know, having visited these dreamlands on eleven former occasions. But it was my very knowledge of the place that made me so ill at ease. For I could not have become familiar with these dreamlands without also becoming familiar with their legends and their prophecies. And chief among these was one which foretold how presently the benign Elder Ones would be deposed by infinity's Other Gods, who would drag the world down a black spiral vortex to the central void where the demon sultan Azathoth gnaws hungrily in the dark; and how this doom would be prefigured horribly in the second coming of the crawling chaos Nyarlathotep. This prophecy, together with certain indications of its imminent fulfillment, had troubled me to such an extent that I had ended my eleventh visit with the solemn vow that it should be my last. And this was the place in which I found myself now!

But I said nothing of this to the priests. I only asked to be directed by the shortest way back to the waking world. Again they conferred among themselves, and again one spoke for all. He regretted that they could not answer me as completely as they would wish; but they were the merest neophytes of their order, and the mysteries of which I spoke were still unknown to them. But doubtless their patriarch could give me whatever information I desired. So I asked him how I might find this patriarch. He answered that if I would but follow him he would lead me to him now.

So it was that we parted from the others, and left them to resume their interrupted hunt while we found our own way to the upper regions of the temple. For my part I was very glad to be putting that haunt of demons behind me. For my fear of the snout had never left me. I had glimpsed it only partly and for the briefest space of time, yet even that brief partial glimpse had been enough to convince me that there were few things more terrible in all the world than the prospect of seeing the snout again. So long as we remained on the lower floors, that prospect seemed very near. But the higher we rose above them the more distant it became, until, by the time we reached the threshold of the temple's great hall, it seemed to have withdrawn from me completely.

The close quarters of the floors below had done nothing to prepare me for the airy grandeur above. There had been dark and narrow corridors winding between shut and forbidding doors. Here were light and openness, with golden lamps lowering from above on golden chains, and marble columns uplifting arches higher than the lamplight could reach. There had been echoing loneliness, with only the presence of my silent guide to temper the fear that loneliness entails. Here were gathered a multitude of people. These people were so still and silent that I almost did not notice them. Yet there they were, standing around the perimeter of the room like so many columns themselves, some of them singly and some in groups, but all of them perfectly motionless, all of them watching the center of the room in tense expectancy.

Here my guide took leave of me to confer with one of the silent watchers. The latter was likewise robed in white, but older and higher in rank; for his black beard was shot with gray, and the tall staff in his right hand was headed with the ankh of the priests of the Elder Ones. But I paid little attention to their interchange, being more interested in what the others were watching. In the center of the room was something that I took to be a chair, but it was so closely canopied and curtained that I could not be sure. Neither could I tell if anyone was seated within it. Facing this chair, if such it was, were three old men standing shoulder to shoulder. These were dressed like messengers in long gray cloaks much stained with mud and dust, and they leaned upon their priestly staves like men in the last stages of exhaustion. But their voices were still powerful, and one by one they addressed the hidden auditor in words that all could hear.

"For three months," said the first messenger, "has come to Celephais no ship out of cloud-fashioned Serannian where the sea meets the sky. For two months has come no caravan over the Tanarian Hills from Drinen in the East; and the last did not return to Drinen, but took ship westward over the Cerenarian Sea to Hlanith on the estuary of the river Oukranos. One month ago a sea of darkness rolled out of the East by night, even to the shoulders of the Tanarian Hills, and did not roll back at dawn. The darkness wailed with the voices of lost souls, and we of Celephais lit watch-fires on the heights, lest the rising floor roll over them and drown the land of Ooth-Nargai in its darkness and wailing. And when I took ship for Hlanith, a red-robed stranger was preaching heresy in the bazaar, and no man there but feared to lay hands on him."

"Many ships," said the second messenger, "came to Hlanith from the East in the month that is past, and poured into the streets of Hlanith an endless stream of tight-lipped mariners who started at every shadow. And many more ships were turned away to seek out other ports. And then for a while no more ships came. But four nights ago a last ship rowed out of the East, and she glowed eerily in the dark and smelled of the sea as no ship ever smelled of it before. We of Hlanith repelled her with long poles which sank deep into her spongy sides. On the next night she came again, and again we repelled her. And as the galley bore me up the Oukranos toward Thran, the strange ship was rowing into the harbor for the third time, with a red-robed stranger standing like an iron figurehead in the prow."

"We of Thran," said the third messenger, "awoke but yestermorn to find the water of Oukranos brackish and the flotsam of Hlanith awash against the marble wharves of Thran. And yestereve at the hour of dusk a red-robed stranger was stopped by the sentry before the eastern gate, until he should have told three dreams beyond belief and proved himself a dreamer worthy to pass the hundred gates of Thran. And what dreams he told to the sentry, I did not hear; but they who did hear fled screaming out of the northern and western and southern gates, and then we who did not hear fled also. And yesternight at midnight we looked eastward from the jasper terraces of Kiran, and saw the thousand gilded spires of Thran melt beneath the gibbous moon."

Here occurred a strange thing, a thing far stranger in its way than anything I had heard there. For as the third messenger ended his speech, a priest stepped forward from our midst and vanished between the curtains that surrounded the canopied chair. He remained thus hidden from our sight until we grew restive with waiting. And when at last he came out again it was to proclaim in a loud voice to all the assembly, "The audience is ended."

Of all the strange things spoken there, this was surely the strangest. We had looked for the occupant of the curtained seat to answer the speeches we had heard and allay somewhat the fears they had awakened. Instead he had turned us away without a word of explanation. The people muttered in their surprise and disappointment. I shared their surprise and disappointment, for I knew the import of the messages as well as they. When the others began to wander away, I could only stare stupidly after them. But then I felt a light touch on my elbow, and turning my head saw standing beside me the priest to whom my guide had spoken, the priest who had dismissed the assembly. "The patriarch will see you now," he said. And he led me to the curtained seat and parted the heavy curtains.

There was something deceptive about the appearance of those curtains, for what I had thought was barely wide enough to contain a chair I now found to encompass a great four-poster bed. But I was too experienced a dreamer to be much troubled by the vagaries of dream. An old priest half lay, half sat upon the counterpane, supported by many pillows. And I would have guessed that this was the patriarch I sought, by the amazing length of his snowy beard alone, or by the signs of an alien zodiac embroidered in silver upon his night-black robe. But I knew him at once by the weariness in his wrinkled face and the wisdom in his faded eyes: the aching weariness of a man fully three and a half centuries old, the troubled wisdom of an old disciple of Barzai the Wise. And I knelt at the bedside of the patriarch Atal and reverently kissed his wizened hand.

The old priest bade me rise from my knees, and even offered me a seat beside him on the edge of the mattress, an offer which I gratefully accepted. He regretted that the temple could not afford me greater hospitality; but the state of the world just then required that it function less like a temple than a fortress under siege, a situation which would certainly grow worse before it grew better, if it ever grew better at all. Yet even the strictest measures could not ensure the temple's security, as my experience with the demon had shown. Its presence alone had been enough to do them inestimable harm, by wounding the morale that was almost their only asset. But its timely discovery had prevented it from doing greater harm still, by learning and ultimately thwarting the plan on which all their hopes were pinned.

On which my hopes too were pinned. He knew already what I was there for, because the priest who had brought me to him had also told him my need. I had come to learn how one might escape from the utter end of the world. And I had done well to come to him; for he had been pondering exactly that question for the last century or more, and at last he believed he had found an answer. "And whether that answer is right," he said, "and the forces of darkness will be halted in their advance; or whether it is wrong, and those forces will trample us into the mire in their march toward hideous victory: In either case there is no time now to look for another. For the rumors of the second coming of the crawling chaos Nyarlathotep have been confirmed beyond any doubt, and it only remains to be seen whether man can contrive to prevent the doom of the world, even as did the Elder Ones when they and the world were young and only the Other Gods were old."

But before he would speak further on this matter, he would have me first declare what I knew of infinity's Other Gods. So I said I knew only what all men knew: that the Other Gods were the prankish servitors of the Elder Ones; that they had been disembodied by the Elder Ones to punish them for their prankishness; and that only the eternal vigilance of the Elder Ones, as symbolized in their Elder Sign, warded the prankishness of the Other Gods away from the habitations of man. But I saw from his face that this was the wrong answer.

So then I admitted to knowing what it was unlawful for any but a priest of the Elder Ones to know. "The Other Gods are the ultimate gods, who came to earth in a dim age of chaos before the Elder Ones were born.

The Other Gods were born in the black spiral vortex where time began, and they died when the cycle of eternity bore them too far from the primal chaos. But they will live again when the cycle of eternity bears them into the black spiral vortex where time will end, where the world and the stars will be devoured by the boundless demon sultan whose name no lips dare speak aloud.

"And the corollary is also true, that time will end when the Other Gods return. But when the young Elder Ones came down from the stars in their ships of cloud, they found the horrible dead bodies of the Other Gods and knew what they portended. And they wove potent spells between the bodies and the souls of the Other Gods, binding the bodies beneath the ground and banishing the souls beyond the orbit of the moon. And the first coming of the crawling chaos Nyarlathotep, the soul and messenger of the Other Gods, was thwarted by the spells of the Elder Ones.

"But too much of eternity has weakened those spells, and the terrible souls of the Other Gods have lowered like dark clouds upon even the lesser peaks of earth. And the senile Elder Ones, their spells long forgotten, have withdrawn into their onyx fortress atop unknown Kadath in the cold waste, there selfishly to prepare their last defense, or fatalistically to await the doom they have no longer any power to avert. And if the Elder Ones themselves despair, then where is there any hope for man?"

The old priest listened in silence to the end and solemnly nodded his venerable head. The situation certainly looked hopeless. Yet he believed that there was a hope, though eons of time and gulfs of space might conspire to keep us from it. His hope lay in something that Barzai the Wise had told his young disciple on the eve of their ill-fated ascent of forbidden Hatheg-Kla, over three centuries ago. "The worshipers of the Elder Ones know that the Elder Ones created man, and the priests of the Elder Ones know that man evolved unsupervised from the source and prototype of all earthly life, which the Elder Ones created and the elder records name Ubbo-Sathla. But what even the priests do not know, for only Barzai was ever able to decipher those frightful parts of the *Pnakotic Manuscripts* which are too ancient to be read, is that when the Elder Ones grew tired of creating life, they left their inconceivable wisdom, written on mighty tablets of star-quarried stone, in the keeping of Ubbo-Sathla. And it was Ubbo-Sathla whom the furry prehumans worshiped and the later Hyperboreans vilified by the name of Abhoth, the father and mother of all cosmic uncleanness. Abhoth laired beneath the mountain Voormithadreth on the continent of Hyperborea in the prehistory of the waking world. And it may be that the spells wherewith the Elder Ones once averted the doom of the world are preserved by Abhoth beneath the mountain Voormithadreth. This is my hope, and this is my plan: to go and seek them there."

I did not see fit to comment on his plan, or to give my opinion on the probable success or failure of its outcome. To do so would only have prolonged his inattention to the question that had never ceased to be uppermost in my mind, the question of my speedy return to the safety of the waking world. But when I tried to suggest this to Atal, he denied that these were separate questions, and asserted that my quickest way to the waking world was to accompany him on his quest of Voormithadreth. It was in vain that I tried to sway him. My participation in this venture, he said more than once, was absolutely vital to its success. "My priests and I are natives of dream. We can have little power in the waking world even if we can come there, which is by no means certain since the hidden ways between sleep and waking are mostly closed to us. But you are a native of the waking world, and those ways are not closed to you. And an experienced dreamer can cross the boundaries between the worlds as easily as cross a threshold.

"Besides," he added in a lower voice, "the ultimate fate of the dreamlands may touch you more closely than you know. For you have already vowed never to return here, and you have returned in spite of your vow. Then what is to prevent your returning again in the days and weeks to come? What is to prevent your returning to the demon-haunted corpse of a ruined world, to the soul-destroying emptiness of interstellar space, or to the howling maelstrom before the throne of One not to be named?"

What arguments had I to oppose this? I could only surrender my will to his and ask what I must do.

He answered, "On my dressing table you will find a casket. Within that casket, which is not locked, you will find a silver whistle. You must take the whistle from the casket and bring it here to me."

This sounded simple enough, but I had been behind these curtains and I knew that there was no dressing table to be found there. Yet when I parted the curtains I saw that the room behind them had changed. It was no longer a wide hall of hanging lamps and gleaming columns. It was more modest in its dimensions, and more comfortable in its appointments, with its carpeted floor and paneled walls illumined by homely candles, and its curtained windows shutting out the night. And it was without much surprise that I now saw standing against one paneled wall a dressing table with a small casket sitting upon it.

I went to the dressing table and opened the casket and took out the whistle it contained. Its silver was tarnished almost black, but not so black as to keep me from recognizing the singular stamp it bore: a hieroglyphic abomination of horns and wings and claws and a curling tail. And knowing what this whistle was used to summon, I was not a little disquieted when, having passed it from my hand to his, I saw him raise it to his bearded lips, and heard him sound one mournful note upon it.

"This also you must do," he said. "You must stand watch at the open window and tell me what you see there."

So I drew aside the curtains and opened the window wide and stood before it gazing into the darkness. At first there was little to report. Below were the pointed silhouettes of trees in a formal garden, above was the sky ablaze with summer stars. But then a distant caterwauling arose, and then some stars began to be blotted out: I thought by a dense cloud of bats, for the stars still blinked within its shifting outline, but its center was opaque. Larger and larger grew the cloud, until all the stars were blotted out, until the frenzied caterwauling was all but lost in a loud drumming as of many pairs of great, leathery wings. A dank, evil-smelling wind blew in through the window in fitful gusts, tossing the curtains about the room and shaking the candle flames.

"And now one last thing you must do to prepare for our departure. Our steeds are creatures of darkness and skittish as all such in the presence of light. Therefore you must extinguish the candles to entice these creatures closer."

So I started around the room, extinguishing one by one each trembling flame that came in my way. And with every candle I put out, the room grew so much darker. And the shadows that danced in the corners of the room, some of them went out with every candle, but those that remained grew so much bolder and stronger. And I knew that when the last candle was extinguished, only one shadow would remain; but that one shadow would be great enough to cover all in darkness.

But when the last candle was before me, and I leaned forward to blow it out, I saw something emerge from the darkness behind it. Something palely luminous and cloudily transparent. Something in the shape of a long gray cone tapering to a clump of wriggling pinkish tentacles.

But as I watched, the pale luminescence grew paler, and the cloudy transparency clearer, until there remained only my own pale face obscurely mirrored in the glass of a window pane.

I blew out the last candle.

IN this sonnet (which first appeared in *Crypt of Cthulhu* #86, Eastertide 1984) Richard L. Tierney drops several names familiar at least in a general way to most *Weird Tales* fans. One of them, Nitocris, who hosted a "vengeful feast", is mentioned in Lovecraft's "Under the Pyramids" (AKA "Imprisoned with the Pharaohs") as the "Ghoul Queen." Her feast is described there and at greater length in "The Vengeance of Nitocris" (*Weird Tales,* August 1928) by Thomas Lanier Williams (better known as Tennessee Williams!). Both Lovecraft and Williams got it from Herodotus' *Histories,* where we read:

> Next the priests read to me from a written record the names of three hundred and thirty monarchs, in the same number of generations, all of them Egyptians except eighteen, who were Ethiops, and one other, who was an Egyptian woman. This last had the same name—Nitocris—as the queen of Babylon. The story was that she ensnared to their deaths hundreds of Egyptians in revenge for the king her brother, whom his subjects had murdered and forced her to succeed; this she did by constructing an immense underground chamber, in which, under the pretense of opening it by an inaugural ceremony, she invited to a banquet all of the Egyptians whom she knew to be chiefly responsible for her brother's death; then, when the banquet was in full swing, she let the river in on them through a large concealed conduit-pipe. The only other thing I was told about her was that after this fearful revenge she flung herself into a room full of ashes, to escape her punishment. (Book II, translated by Aubrey de Selincourt, Penguin, 1954, p. 166)

Brian Lumley, too, mentions Nitocris in his "The Mirror of Nitocris" (which appears in *The Caller of the Black,* [Arkham House, 1971], *The Compleat Crow* [W. Paul Ganley, 1987], *Fruiting Bodies* [TOR 1993; Penguin 1993], and *Titus Crow* [TOR, 1997]).

The second stanza of "The Contemplative Sphinx" is largely based on Lovecraft's "Under the Pyramids." Tierney has used themes from that story also in his Simon of Gitta tale "The Treasure of Horemkhu" (*Pulse-Pounding Adventure Stories* #2, December 1987; and soon to be reprinted in the Chaosium Cthulhu Cycle collection *The Scroll of Thoth: Tales of Simon Magus and the Great Old Ones*).

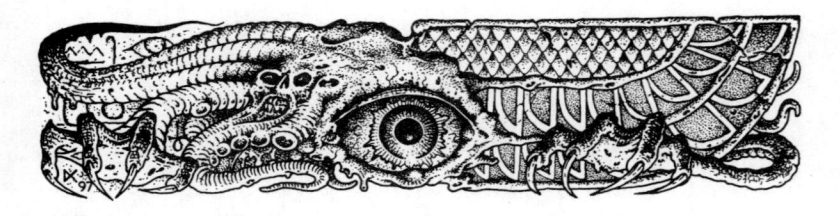

The Contemplative Sphinx

by Richard L. Tierney

Ten thousand centuries its eyes have known—
That contemplative Watcher of the East.
It saw Nitocris plot her vengeful feast
And watched dark Nephren-Ka ascend his throne.
Its stony flesh endured Set-Typhon's storm.
Its graven visage gazed across the sands
When savage beasts licked Nyarlathotep's hands
And Stygian lords did sorcerous rites perform.

To travellers who come to gaze and gape
'Tis said: "Five thousand years ago, not more,
King Kephren carved its lion-mighty shape."
But Bedouins yet recite the ancient lore
That its dark origins no man can know,
Nor those vast, columned caverns far below.

ANCIENT Egypt was the home of eldritch mysteries, both inscribed upon the glassy plains of the pyramids and hidden within and beneath them. It already had the reputation in ancient times, which is no doubt why Plato ascribed his allegory of Atlantis to a priest of mystic Egypt. My guess is that the priest in question was named Luveh-Keraph. Nineteenth-century Masonism indulged fantasies of secret initiations in hidden adyta below the sphinx, and all manner of occultist sects, not least the Order of the Golden Dawn and the Summit Lighthouse, have traced their supposed secrets and revelations to the same source. Old Egypt has, despite itself, become something of a diploma mill, one of those places you can write away to and buy a bogus degree, attesting the erudition you don't really have. Even so, the land of the brooding Sphinx has suffered approbation by eccentrics who seek to lend their delusions the profundity they so manifestly lack by claiming an ancient Egyptian pedigree for them.

The latest chapter in this pathetic saga is that of a discipline of misinformation called Afrocentrism (see Cheikh Anta Diop, *The African Origin of Civilization: Myth or Reality*, Lawrence Hill Books, 1974). One wonders at the perversity of bypassing the genuine glories of one's own heritage (see, for example, Margaret Shinnie, *Ancient African Kingdoms*, New American Library, 1970; or Patricia and Frederick McKissack, *The Royal Kingdoms of Ghana, Mali, and Songhay: Life in Medieval Africa*) to maintain falsely that the ancient Egyptians were black Africans. (On the whole question, see Mary Lefkowitz, *Not Out of Africa*, Basic Books, 1996; and Kwame Anthony Appiah, "Beyond Race: Fallacies of Reactive Afrocentrism", in *The Skeptic*, vol. 2, no. 4, 104-107.)

The trouble with all such claims, whether made by Aleister Crowley, Elizabeth Claire Voyant, or Leonard Jeffries, is that they are all fictitious. They are colorful and alluring, but not true. And thus they suffer even as fiction. As Camus said, their artistic creativity clips the wings of its own hatchling by forgetting its gratuitousness as fiction. Occultism and pseudohistory take themselves too seriously. No wonder we see a defter hand at work in *admitted* fictions set in ancient Egypt, whether Boris Karloff's *The Mummy* or Lovecraft's "Under the Pyramids". Robert Bloch, too, caught the fever fated unto all who violate King Tut's curse and delve into ancient fictive Egypt. Bloch wrote a whole series of marvelous Egyptian tales, some of them Cthulhu Mythos yarns, others not. The complete cycle is as follows: "The Faceless God", "The Opener of the Way", "The Brood of Bubastis", "Fane of the Black Pharaoh", "The Secret of Sebek", "The Eyes of the Mummy", and "Beetles."

These tales by Lovecraft and Bloch have themselves assumed the status of a canonical body of elder lore, forming the basis for a whole new generation of fictive Egyptopithicenes such as Richard L. Tierney and Ann K. Schwader, whose cycle of verse "Ech-Pi-El's Ægypt" first appeared in David Barker's fanzine *Ye Olde Lemurian* #9, 1993. Ms. Schwader recalls that

> Getting them written proved to be rather more difficult than I'd thought. Y'see, HPL didn't really write all that much about Egypt—though his atmospherics were wonderful when he did. ... All are more or less Mythos Egyptian (only slightly for "Dream-Gates," alas), though I did take some liberties. I don't think HPL ever noticed what color Anubis was in some of the tomb-art! ... [M]ost of the gods are rather pale outside of their animal heads, but Anubis is coal-black all over. This got my sick mind thinking, & "Lord of the Land" resulted. (This really was one of Anubis' titles—"The Land" being the graveyard or necropolis, of course.)

Ech-Pi-El's Ægypt: Lovecraftian Poems

by Ann K. Schwader

Ech-Pi-El's Ægypt

Necropolis since Khepren's days,
Saracen gilt on a godlost maze
Twisted to mimic black wizards' ways ...

Silent tread of the Sphinx's Beast
Down galleries where ghoul-things feast
On well spiced meats of the elder East ...

Pyramid midnights when ka-wings fly
On a murmured curse through moondark skies,
& magics live which cannot die ...

Hieroglyphs graven in ageless stone
Quarried at last for a Pharaoh's throne
Where once They ruled ...

                                    & ruled alone.

The Elder Lords

(after HPL's "The Nameless City")

Alhazred dreamed them, at the last:
Their city old as Sarnath's doom,
Half-buried by an age of sand
Like bleached bones in a broken tomb;
Their walls so weirdly wrought & low,
Misshapen by geometry
Not of this world, nor any place
A mind less mad than his might see.

Theirs was no death-cult, though they raised
Strange altars to some nameless rite
In temples carved for crawling things
Who finally did not love the light;
But fled to paradise below,
Where hairless apes might never find
The last enigma of their lives.
Immortal, yes—& proud, & blind.

Their shadows stain the chill night wind
Whose grit erodes each bas-relief
They shaped as blazon to the years.
Their wraith-claws scrabble endless grief
Across the very sands they ruled,
Yet certain turnings of the Nile
Still bear their living eidolon ...
Sebek, the sacred crocodile.

The Tomb of Nephren-Ka
(Inspired by Robert Bloch's "Fane of the Black Pharaoh")

Coiled under Cairo's ageless heart it waits
For seven thousand years to cycle past
Until Earth shudders at the Blind Apes' gates
Burst open to unleash cursed truth at last,
The aimless flailings of such Destiny
As no sane mind should ever crave to see.

Dread Nephren-Ka dared more at Egypt's height:
Usurper-prince of sorcerers & priests,
He fled the common blessing of Ra's light
To wrest strange wisdom from the long-deceased.
Anubis howled aloud ... but Sebek smiled
Reptilian relish at the land defiled.

One god alone this darkest Pharaoh served,
Displacing all the Nile's great pantheon
With temples to that Mighty Messenger
Whose shadow fouled the stars in ages gone—
Nyarlathotep spread his daemon-fame
From Memphis to Irem in blood & shame.

Prophetic prowess was the poisoned boon
This Messenger bestowed ... at hideous cost.
Thrice-glutted jackals bayed a bitter moon
In Nephren-Ka's bleak empire of the lost
Till desperation festered into war,
& temple steps ran black with wizards' gore.

They razed his name from every monument,
Effaced it from Thoth's roster of the dead,
Yet still that shadowed Messenger had sent
Some solace to his hell-cult & its head:
A secret palace-tomb torn deep in stone
Where Nephren-Ka might claim his promised throne.

One hundred priests went willing to his blade
Before his last ambition came to be.
Death-fevered shower of immortal shades,
He filled the very walls with prophecy;
Mad truths inscribed in flawless black & white
From Egypt's birth until her final night.

Coiled under Cairo's ageless heart it waits,
Yet no man living claims its hidden lore;
Those heedless souls who seek the Blind Apes' gates
Soon hold their heathen peace forever more ...
Fresh stains beneath these walls recall the price
Of Nephren-Ka's last horrid sacrifice.

Lord of the Land

Before Osiris rose to life-in-death,
One jackal shadow slunk around such tombs
As sorcerers command: strange-patterned rooms
Wherein the echoes of each final breath
Still whisper visions to eternal night.
Anubis heard—& hearing, laughed aloud
At fatal ignorance in those too proud
To host the humble grave-worm's final blight.

No simple jackal, he; but Night made flesh
Of senseless shadows & fear-maddened dreams.
The Thousand-Named, yet never what he seems;
Dread Messenger of chaos & despair:
Nyarlathotep, whom no life can bear.

Dream-Gates

Outside the harmless dark of wholesome sleep,
Grim wonders wait on mortals to destroy;
That Beast whose bloodthirst blemished Egypt's joy
In its young wisdom ... secrets night-gaunts keep
Beneath their black-veined wings ... what Hali hides
Amid its noisome waves ... all these and more
Inhabit lightless lands beyond the door
Called Dreaming, & command their kin besides.

Those luckless ones who trouble nightmare's gates
Return not always untouched, nor alone.
From ebon heights where elder Things have flown,
They plummet earthward to a madman's fate
Of private torment to their dying days;
Learning too late *each dream-gate swings both ways*.

ABOUT ROBERT M. PRICE

ROBERT M. PRICE has edited *Crypt of Cthulhu* for fourteen years. His essays on Lovecraft have appeared in *Lovecraft Studies*, *The Lovecrafter*, *Cerebretron*, *Dagon*, *Étude Lovecraftienne*, *Mater Tenebrarum*, and in *An Epicure in the Terrible* and *Twentieth Century Literary Criticism*. His horror fiction has appeared in *Nyctalops*, *Eldritch Tales*, *Etchings & Odysseys*, *Grue*, *Footsteps*, *Deathrealm*, *Weirdbook*, *Fantasy Book*, *Vollmond*, and elsewhere. He has edited *Tales of the Lovecraft Mythos* and *The New Lovecraft Circle* for Fedogan & Bremer, as well as *The Horror of It All* and *Black Forbidden Things* for Starmont House. His books include *H. P. Lovecraft and the Cthulhu Mythos* (Borgo Press) and *Lin Carter: A Look behind His Imaginary Worlds* (Starmont). By day he is a theologian, New Testament scholar, editor of *The Journal of Higher Criticism*, and pastor of the Church of the Holy Grail.

RECENT TITLES IN CALL OF CTHULHU® FICTION

THE HASTUR CYCLE
Second Revised Edition

The stories in this book represent the evolving trajectory of such notions as Hastur, the King in Yellow, Carcosa, the Yellow Sign, Yuggoth, and the Lake of Hali. A succession of writers from Ambrose Bierce to Ramsey Campbell and Karl Edward Wagner have explored and embellished these concepts so that the sum of the tales has become an evocative tapestry of hypnotic dread and terror, a mythology distinct from yet overlapping the Cthulhu Mythos. Here for the first time is a comprehensive collection of all the relevant tales. Selected and introduced by Robert M. Price.

5 3/8" x 8 3/8", 320 pages, $10.95. Stock #6020; ISBN 1-56882-094-1. Available from bookstores and game stores, or by mail from Chaosium, Inc.

THE XOTHIC LEGEND CYCLE

The late Lin Carter was a prolific writer and anthologist of horror and fantasy with over eighty titles to his credit. His tales of Mythos horror are loving tributes to H. P. Lovecraft's "revision" tales and to August Derleth's stories of Hastur and the *R'lyeh Text*. This is the first collection of Carter's Mythos tales; it includes his intended novel, *The Terror Out of Time*. Most of the stories in this collection have been unavailable for some time. Selected and introduced by Robert M. Price.

5 3/8" x 8 3/8", 288 pages, $10.95. Stock #6013; ISBN 1-56882-078-X. Available from bookstores and game stores, or by mail from Chaosium, Inc.

THE NECRONOMICON

Although skeptics claim that the *Necronomicon* is a fantastic tome created by H. P. Lovecraft, true seekers into the esoteric mysteries of the world know the truth: The *Necronomicon* is a blasphemous tome of forbidden knowledge written by the mad Arab, Abdul Alhazred. Even today, after attempts over the centuries to destroy any and all copies in any language, some few copies still exist, secreted away. Within this book you will find stories about the *Necronomicon*, different versions of the *Necronomicon*, and two essays on the blasphemous tome. Now you too may learn the true lore of Abdul Alhazred. Selected and introduced by Robert M. Price.

5 3/8" x 8 3/8", 320 pages, $10.95. Stock #6012; ISBN 1-56882-070-4. Available from bookstores and game stores, or by mail from Chaosium, Inc.

THE CTHULHU CYCLE

Millions of years ago, when the stars were right, Cthulhu ruled from his black house in R'lyeh. When the stars changed, R'lyeh sank beneath the waves, and Cthulhu was cast into a deathless sleep, eternally dreaming. He has used his dreams to communicate with his believers, from prehistoric times through to the present day. Cthulhu has been, is, and always will be. Now the stars may once more be right, and Cthulhu may rise from his millennial sleep and reassert his rightful rulership of the Earth. The thirteen stories in this book trace Cthulhu and his influence through the centuries. General introduction and individual story prefaces by Robert M. Price.

5 3/8" x 8 3/8", 288 pages, $10.95. Stock #6011; ISBN 1-56882-038-0. Available from bookstores and game stores, or by mail from Chaosium, Inc.

THE DISCIPLES OF CTHULHU
Second Revised Edition

The disciples of Cthulhu are a varied lot. In Mythos stories they are obsessive, loners, dangerous, seeking not to convert others so much as to use them. But writers of the stories are also Cthulhu's disciples, and they are the proselytizers, bringing new members to the fold. Published in 1976, the first edition of *The Disciples of Cthulhu* was the first professional, all-original Cthulhu Mythos anthology. One of the stories, "The Tugging" by Ramsey Campbell, was nominated for a Science Fiction Writers of America Nebula Award, perhaps the only Cthulhu Mythos story that has received such recognition. This second edition of *Disciples* presents nine stories of Mythos horror, seven from the original edition and two new stories. Selected by Edward P. Berglund.

5 3/8" x 8 3/8", 272 pages, $10.95. Stock #6010; ISBN 1-56882-054-2. Available from bookstores and game stores, or by mail from Chaosium, Inc.

THE DUNWICH CYCLE

In the Dunwiches of the world the old ways linger. Safely distant from bustling cities, ignorant of science, ignored by civilization, dull enough never to excite others, poor enough never to provoke envy, these are safe harbors for superstition and seemingly meaningless custom. Sometimes they shelter truths that have seeped invisibly across the centuries. The people are unlearned but not unknowing of things once great and horrible, of times when the rivers ran red and dark shudderings ruled the air. Here are nine stories set where horror begins, each story prefaced and with a general introduction by Robert M. Price.

5 3/8" x 8 3/8", 288 pages, $10.95. Stock #6009; ISBN 1-56882-047-7. Available from bookstores and game stores, or by mail from Chaosium, Inc.

MADE IN GOATSWOOD

Ramsey Campbell is acknowledged by many to be the greatest living writer of the horror tale in the English language. He is known to Mythos fans for the ancient and fearful portion of England's Severn Valley he evoked in narratives such as "The Moon Lens." This book contains eighteen all-new stories set in that part of the Valley, including a new story by Campbell himself, his first Severn Valley tale in decades. This volume was published in conjunction with a trip by Campbell to the United States. Stories selected by Scott David Aniolowski.

5 3/8" x 8 3/8", 288 pages, $10.95. Stock #6008; ISBN 1-56882-046-1. Available from bookstores and game stores, or by mail from Chaosium, Inc.

THE BOOK OF IOD

Henry Kuttner (1914-1958) was a friend of young Robert Bloch and a promising writer in his own right. He also became one of the Lovecraft Circle, submitting plot ideas and draft manuscripts to Lovecraft. He had an important impact on the development of the Cthulhu Mythos, especially with his contribution of a mystical tome, the *Book of Iod*. This collection of stories comprises all of Kuttner's Mythos tales (including one cowritten with Bloch) and a story by Lin Carter about the infamous *Book of Iod*. Introduction and commentary by Robert M. Price.

5 1/2" x 8 1/2", 224 pages, $10.95. Stock #6007; ISBN 1-56882-045-3. Available from bookstores and game stores, or by mail from Chaosium, Inc.

THE AZATHOTH CYCLE

At the heart of the universe the mad god Azathoth pulses like a cancer. As with the physical universe it created, no purely reasoned argument, no subtle scientific proof, no brilliant artistry, no human love affects the unyielding will of Azathoth. As an entity it is of transcendent power and unthinking immortal sway. It can sometimes be avoided but never challenged. Here are fourteen tales concerning Azathoth by authors as diverse as Ramsey Campbell, Lin Carter, John Glasby, and Thomas Ligotti. The macabre poet Edward Pickman Derby contributes his immortal "Azathoth", the title piece of his single printed volume. Introduction, exegesical essay, and notes by Robert M. Price.

5 1/2" x 8 1/2", 256 pages, $10.95. Stock #6006; ISBN 1-56882-040-2. Available from bookstores and game stores, or by mail from Chaosium, Inc.